DISTILLED DUPLICITY

BY LOUISE FURLEY

Distilled Duplicity

ISBN- 978-1-7357712-0-5 (Paperback)
ISBN- 978-1-7349807-9-0 (eBook)

Cover design by Pixel Mischief Design

ALSO BY LOUISE FURLEY

Solitar

Halo Valley

Isle of Orainn

Anastasia

The Kissing Number

The Poser

Wrath of Wolf

Devil's Prince

Devil's Seed

Distilled Duplicity

Chapter One

Zhilov Adranokov's eyes narrowed in contempt at his youngest son as the twelve-year-old came in the door. "Naithon Rámon, in the sacred breath of *Dio*, you let your brothers beat you again? When are you going to stand up for yourself?"

One of Naithon's eyes had swollen almost completely shut, a gash split his lip, and a gouge near his cheek was deep enough it will scar him for life, compliments of his brother Misolav.

Yet, clearly he had fought back against his older brothers, his knuckles were lacerated and bleeding. A young boy with three against one, he had given as good as he got.

Without responding to his father's belittling, Naithon started across the grand room stripping off his torn bloody jersey. The material had covered massive dark bruising rapidly spreading over his thin torso.

Not a wisp of a feminine touch appeared in the décor of the house. Verona Adranokov, the matriarch of the family had no say in decorating Zhilov's ancient, ancestral mansion.

Just as dark and gloomy as it had been in the medieval era, high ceilings overlooked heavy, dark furniture comprised of masculine leather with gold studding.

Brown bricked fireplaces lent only warmth, not cozy comfort. Vintage burgundy drapes held back with gold tassels let in muted light through lead-paned, mullioned windows.

Gilded photographs of ancestors progressed above the burgundy carpeted stairs. An edge of fear in their whispering, guests claimed ghastly sightings of a phantom Dracula disappearing down sinister, shadowed hallways.

Following his son, in a base Romanian dialect, Zhilov groused, "It is your fault, Naithon. If your mama hadn't died while bearing you, I could have kept her and you set up in the townhouse in the city, housed you apart from this family, my wife and your half-brothers. They beat you because they're jealous that I loved your mother more than theirs."

Naithon took a sharp turn to avoid him, but Zhilov stayed on his heels still going at him. "I've never hidden the fact that I loved your mother, my mistress, more than I cared for their mother, my legal wife. The crappy matter of it, boy, is that you have her beautiful face, her flaxen hair, and those strangely contrasting, black eyes. On her they were intoxicating and mysterious, on you, hell, they're just spooky weird. You're a constant reminder of my loss, I can hardly bear to look at you."

Shaking his fists, Zhilov continued railing at his son. "Why did my beloved Iyla have to leave me? You took her from me in your selfish birth, boy, every single day I wish you had died instead of her."

Naithon halted so abruptly Zhilov gasped and took a step back. Annoyed that his young son could so easily unnerve him, he waved at the boy demanding, "Go, get the fuck out of my sight, your presence sickens me."

Wiping the dark green football jersey across his bloodied nose, Naithon didn't cower when his father got back in his face.

Zhilov sneered at the jersey. "I told you, boy, you are not playing football. You will work the business. When I grow the company big enough, I'll bring it to America. You will put school and your useless dreams of playing football aside, and when you become good enough, I will make you a leading exec."

"What," the youngster snorted, rolled the jersey in a ball, and clenched it in his fist. The shiner already dark purple, his young voice sardonic, he sneered, "You call being a conman, a thug, a murdering gangster an executive? You want me to drop out of school to sell fraudulent credit card protection, collect protection payments from the neighborhood shops? *Bah*," he spat.

Zhilov swept the tails of his suitcoat apart and tucked his hands in his trouser pockets. Bending over to tower above his son, he snarled at him, "*Ja*. You will do as I say starting tomorrow. I will

2

train you to be the best fucking knee breaker in the business. You will be in charge of collecting from the gamblers. You get good enough you can manage the hotels and clubs I plan on opening in the States."

His son merely blinked at him with his good eye, which raised Zhilov's ire. He snapped, "You hear me, boy?"

At Naithon's stony expression and refusal to eagerly acquiesce to his father's demands, Zhilov's face pulsed red in fury. Shoulders bunching, mirroring his son he clenched his fists, "Go, get the fuck outta my sight before I scar up the rest of that pretty face."

The boy stood firm, lifted his bruised jaw, not cringing from his huge angry father.

Wearing a designer suit with silver tie, ebony hair slicked straight back, Zhilov appeared more the elite businessman than the lowlife criminal gangster that he was.

Father and son glared at each other, neither backing down.

But then Zhilov was the first to lower his eyes. When he looked up, Naithon was gone.

Chapter Two

Three Years Later

America

Smoke of all kinds, cigar, cigarette, weed, filled the back room of the restaurant. At 15, Naithon was the youngest of the five men playing poker, but he was one of the biggest, brawniest, toughest males there. European cigar crunched in the corner of his mouth, he hunched over his cards.

He'd barely started shaving, voice still deepening, but to do the enforcement job his father had thrust on him, he spent every second of his free time lifting steel at the gym or running the hills, boxing or fighting MMA. Every second that is when he didn't have a girl under him. Even now, young women in tiny outfits strutted the room.

The young males were part of a terrorizing gang headed by Zhilov Adranokov that made a lot of money, and also made a lot of grown men quiver in fright at the mere thought of them. However, sleazy females knew where the big bucks hung out.

Mercedes Mardelini perched on Naithon's knee. Plucking at a button on his shirt, she stroked his chest to get his attention, he ignored her. Below the rolled up sleeves, she raked long blue nails down his rocky forearms. Concentrating on his game, he absently swatted at her hand.

Pouting, she whined, "Come on, Nait, you've been playing for hours, I wanna go down by the wharf. You've only been in the country a short time, there're places I can show you. I can drive, I have a license, I-"

He may be only fifteen but that didn't stop Naithon Adranokov from doing anything he pleased. Drive, gamble, drink, smoke, fuck. Having a stepmother who despised the sight of him, and surrounded by strippers and whores since birth, Naithon had little respect for women.

Right now, he resented the girl throwing his age in his face because she was six years older than him. That she was legal to drive. Her skirt microscopic, the front of her tight blouse cut so low she might as well not be wearing it, Naithon put his broad hand on the bare top of her bosom, and shoved her. She tumbled off his lap and landed on her ass with a squeal.

"Shit, Nait, quit foolin' around, you holdin' or you gonna call?" The young man across the table grumped at him.

Grunting Romanian curses, Naithon threw money down on the pile, at that moment his cell buzzed in his pocket.

Sitting at his feet, Mercedes griped and whined for his attention.

"C'mere honey," another man leaned over and dragged her off the floor and sat her on his lap. His hands slid underneath her blouse and skimmed up to fondle her breasts. "I'll take care of ya, babe."

Glowering at Naithon, Mercedes snuggled into the man.

Nait grunted into his phone, shoved it in his jean's pocket. Scraping his winnings off the table, he stood up, folded the wad together and stuffed it in another pocket. Stabbing his cigar out in the ashtray, speaking in English but his accent was so thick it distorted his words, he muttered, "Gotta go, Vlad's in trouble."

"Wait, bro," one of the young men grabbed his own money and got up. "You need back up."

A second male copied them, said, "Yeah, my ride's out front."

Without a word to rest of the group, the three young men left the room, trod through the darkened restaurant and out the front door. They climbed into Yashin Varushkin's BMW SUV and peeled down the street.

"Where we going?" Blok Basnakev asked from the back.

"Got a call from Vlademir, one of our warehouses is being burgled," Naithon replied from the front seat. "Half of what he said was unintelligible and he was slurring. Didn't sound like drunk slurring, sounded like broken teeth slurring."

The car raced across town until they left the bright Louisiana city lights and tore out of the commerce area to the docks. Focused on what kind of trouble might lie ahead, the men were unmindful of the air cooling in the pitch black night.

Well past midnight, stars twinkled through hazy clouds. Like Vegas rising from the obscure desert, in the far distance from where they'd come, only a thin line of glimmering lights identified the bustling city of Chaleur they'd left behind.

Yashin slowed the car, turned off the headlights, the black SUV purred down the deserted street. Rustic warehouses, half with broken out windows crept like crusty roaches along the seawall.

Yashin parked in the shadows, the men hopped out. Salt from the ocean drifted in mingling with the musty, dank, wooden smell of the docks.

His voice low, Blok asked, "Which one, Nait, your old man has three down here."

Naithon's voice quiet, he murmured, "Vlad said it was the Krouston at the end. You guys check out the other two, I'll hit the Krouston." The trio took off in different directions.

Naithon wished he'd changed his shirt, white with thin blue stripes, that and his yellow hair would catch what meager light there was. *Shoulda grabbed a hat.* At least his pants and boots were black, his tanned skin would blend in the shadows.

He paused near the warehouse and listened. Not a sound but the ocean slapping the seawall, there wasn't a car in sight. Forklifts and other work trucks scattered the entire lot, but no personal vehicles. Then he saw Vlad's Mustang.

With practiced stealth, he stayed silently in the shadows creeping along the back of the warehouse, careful to not scrape his boots on the asphalt or crunch over the broken fragments. Cautiously making his way around the building, he kept on until he reached a window. Most of the windows were intact in the warehouse. The window was over his head.

Trained to scale any type of structure, the wood and brick building wouldn't slow him down. In seconds he'd scrambled up enough he could grip the jutting sill, pull himself up and peek in.

"Aw, fuck," he ground a string of Romanian curses through grit teeth. The window was caked with grime but he could make out his friend Vlad, one of his father's staff, an enforcer like Nait, prone on the floor.

Dropping silently to the ground, Nait hustled quietly around the building, he didn't want to barge in the front door in case the thieves were still there, but he didn't know what shape Vlad was in either. There was a side door they used to take out the trash, Nait found it quickly. It was locked. That wouldn't stop him. Tugging a tool out of his boot, he quickly picked the lock.

Stuffing the pick back in his boot, he slowly turned the knob, cautiously opened the door and peered inside. It was dark. He could just make out Vlad's body. One of the few parking lot lamps outside that didn't have a broken globe dispersed stingy light through the grainy glass, barely illuminating him. It was dim, but Nait could make out blood on Vlad's head and pooled on the floor around him.

Urged to help his friend, Naithon pushed through the door and took a step inside. He paused, didn't hear a thing, no movement. Taking a breath, he moved deeper inside trying to adjust his vision to the darkness-

Wham-

Pain exploded in the back of his head, dropping him to his knees with a grunt. Before he hit the ground, bodies jumped on him. Whacked half unconscious from the blow, Naithon fought back, but the four bruisers had the advantage, and they wailed on him. They punched and kicked him until he could do nothing but curl into a ball to protect his head and gut.

"Ha, you puny pussy, filthy gypsy," a male voice taunted over him accompanied by a vicious kick to his already broken ribs. "Your old man's business is infringing on our turf. Take this as a fucking warning, bitch, we see your pretty face again on our turf and you're dead. Finito," he kicked him in the head.

"Actually," aiming a kick to his kidney, the thug grinned with sadistic glee, "we'll just save ourselves the time and trouble and eliminate you now. We can use the other fucker we took down to send our message if he's still alive." He caught Naithon in the temple with his steel-toed boot.

Clinging to consciousness, through eyes swelling closed, Naithon recognized his attacker. Choking on blood clogging his throat, he spat, "Fuck off, Duce Delducci, go play in your rum farm." Coughing up blood, his voice weak, he tried to cover his head from another bone-breaking kick from Duce.

Infuriated at Naithon's bravado, Duce barked, "Fucking shut him up boys." The last thing Naithon saw was Duce and his brothers Piero and Janero, and another asshole grinning like marauding jackals down at him as they railed brutal kicks to his punished body.

****

Zhilov blamed the ambush on Naithon. When he visited him the only one time while Naithon rehabilitated in the hospital, he ranted and raved that Nait was so stupid to fall for the trick that brought him to the warehouse.

Duce Delducci and his men had caught Vlad, beat him almost to death, stabbed him until he was so delirious he wasn't even aware they were making him call Naithon to set him up for an ambush.

8

Nait was the youngest member of the mob so they had gone after him.

If Blok and Yashin hadn't found him and chased the butchers off, Zhilov would be at his son's funeral instead of his hospital room, and Vlad would have bled out.

Imprints of Duce Delducci's ring with his family's crest on it were embedded in Naithon's face. Duce's initials on the side of the ring were easily identified. Of course the police were never called, the Adranokovs and the Delduccis handled their own business.

Zhilov didn't want war with the Delduccis so Naithon and Vlad's murderous beatings were never avenged.

Berating and swearing some more at his deceased mistress' son, infuriated at the teen for making him look foolish, weak, Zhilov coldly ordered, "Don't come back home, boy. Find somewhere else to hang your hat. I don't need incompetent losers working for me." He never returned the months Nait suffered his healing in the hospital of broken bones and internal injuries. While his son recuperated, Zhilov wiped out his bank account.

Finally on the mend, against doctor's orders, Naithon had had enough of the hospital. He was bored out of his mind. After signing himself out, he changed into clothes one of his friends had brought him, black chinos, shirt and boots. Clasping his gold watch on his wrist, he pocketed his wallet and beat a hasty retreat before any of the nurses or doctors could nag him into staying longer.

When he exited the hospital with a slight limp and an arm still in a sling, Naithon was shocked to see the Lincoln Town Car and the chauffer waiting outside the front entrance of the hospital.

His friends were working; he'd planned to catch a taxi to his friend Mazonn's place. Maz got him a new phone since Duce smashed his other one, and also gave him a key to his apartment yesterday. He'd joked that he wanted his locks to still be virgins when he returned home, not poked by Nait's tool, that is, his picklock.

His joke brought the first hint of smile to Naithon's harsh face since the night of the ambush. Not that he'd ever quite smiled before, but for once his jaw unclenched, and to his friends that was as close to a smile that he ever came.

Nait stood on the sidewalk with his phone out ready to dial a taxi when the chauffeur left his guard post by the car and approached him. "Mr. Adranokov," he dipped his head in deference to Nait. "Your father sent me to retrieve you."

A dark blond brow rose over a cool onyx eye, Nait asked, "Retrieve me to where?" He was vaguely amused that the man who had to be twenty years older than his own fifteen years called him mister.

A window in the back of the Town car rolled down, Naithon's brother, Misolav stuck his head out. His sadistic mouth curving in a mocking grin, Misolav called out, "Come on, get in. We have orders to bring you home."

Both blond brows arched. "Whose orders?"

Misolav's head dipped back, he said with sarcasm, "The old man's, who do you think?"

Naithon was as fair-haired and sharp faced as his mother. He had her high cheekbones and fuller lips. If not for the severity and strength of masculinity in his looks, he would be as pretty as she had been. His three brothers carried their father's dark looks and heavier features.

Zhilov's wife, Verona, stayed in her own apartments to the farther south wing of the mansion. He married her to coup her family's lands, and after having the deeds transferred into his name, he wisely made her sign a pre-nup. Tall and angular, she could have been mistaken for a relative with her thicker features and dark hair, eyes, skin.

Nait's older brothers had teased him relentlessly about his pretty face that was cursed with the demon eyes. Well, it wasn't quite so pretty now, he bore scars from fights with his brothers, brawls on the streets, working as an enforcer, and the ambush had toughened up his already masculine features.

Duce Delducci's boot had cut a deep gouge near a cheekbone. Someday, Naithon was going to pay Duce back for the attack.

Naithon responded to his brother, "The old man banished me, Mislo, didn't you get the memo?" The brothers spoke in Romanian, their mother tongue. The chauffeur studied his nails; he had a hard enough time with English.

"*Ja*, well, he's had three months to think about how much his mistress, dear Iyla would have cried over his exiling you."

At Naithon's silence, Misolav coaxed, "Come on. You have no job, no home, no money, Elena is preparing your favorite, *cartofi cu carne de porc*, stew of pork and potatoes. Papa wants you back in the business. He has so few he can trust." He waited while Naithon pondered his choices.

Mislo was right. The only work he'd be able to get at his young age and lack of education would be with a gang. Life in gangs was notoriously mean and short. Perhaps he could learn everything about his father's enterprises then when he had a cushion of cash, go out on his own.

Why not use his father? Zhilov stole from him, and cared nothing for him but as a body to do his bidding. Now it was his turn.

Chapter Three

Named after her grandmother Kiri Rose, Kiritina, meaning little Kiri skipped home from the school bus stop. Ringlets of cherry wood, the color as if distilled in oak barrels until it was a dark and rich reddish brown, flapped against her back.

Actually, she was only graduating kindergarten, but her class had been given their new room assignments for first grade starting in the fall. When school started, she'd be a big girl then, so she was practicing walking to and from the bus stop.

Dancing with joyful anticipation, she hummed her favorite song from an animated film, it wasn't until she was almost upon it that she saw it. Even then, her brain didn't resister what her eyes beheld.

Slowing as she reached the front door to the three-story residence, beyond the white columns on either side of the portico, she could see... Kiritina inched closer, squinting. Her stomach lurched, it must be a toy.

Creeping closer, she slapped a palm over her mouth, green eyes wide over her hand. Then, *oh no, no*, her lunch gorged up her throat, her hand fell to her chest. Eyes popping, her mouth opened and closed and opened but the scream was caught in her throat.

Her new puppy, Muffin, was lanced down the middle, the flaps of his furry body splayed open, and he was nailed to the front door, his bloody entrails oozing out. His little head lolled unnaturally to the side, tiny pink tongue dangling.

The scream climbed up her throat and broke loose and hurtled into piercing shrieks of despair bounding throughout the neighborhood.

The front door opened, and her brother Duce poked his head out. Saw her horror, twisted his neck to take in the decoration on the door, and grinned. "Hey, Kiri, baby button, Piero dissected your first dog so I called dibs on this one."

Admiring his work, he smiled broadly at her, pleased with himself. "Whattya think?"

The screams dried up but her lips still flapped open and closed trying to force words out. Face as stark and white as a winter night, "W- why? Why? Why would you-" she couldn't finish.

Stepping out onto the portico, his brows daggered down in a scowl. Duce crossed his arms. He was in his early twenties, the oldest of the Delducci brood. "I told you, little girl, what I want." His nasty gaze lowered to between her thighs.

"But I- don't, under, Duce, I..."

He took a few steps off to the side of the porch. Wrapping an arm around a white column, he swung around it, and smirked down at her.

Averting her eyes from the destroyed dog, Kiri started up the steps to the landing.

Grinning at her distress, Duce said, "Yeah, you know what I want. I told you before. You let me stick it in you and I'll leave your pups and stupid dolls alone? Okay? I'm gonna get you eventually, chile. Pa says he's gonna preserve your virginity, he plans on selling you in marriage to gain more land when you are legal age." He laughed at the confused look on her face.

"You'll understand some day, baby button, but I'm getting my action off you first. They'll never know I got me some; all bitches lose their hymens from bicycle accidents, tampons, shit like that. I'm bored of the other bitches around, and I'm tired of boinkin' our homely sister Melonie, she's only ten and already getting a pudgy belly and a butt on her. Butt ugly, get it?" he laughed like he thought he was hilarious.

His dirty gaze slimed up and down Kiri's tiny body. With a lewd smirk he said, "On the other hand, you're gonna grow up curvy and gorgeous like our slutty ma,"

Recalling their mother had run off with another man leaving her family behind, sobered him. "Really," he snorted bitterly, "how do they expect you to grow up normal when your own whoring mother ditches you? Come on now, you'll keep your mouth shut about what I'm gonna do to you-" he reached for her.

With a squeal of fright she dodged his hand and ran into the house.

Scurrying across the foyer and to the stairs, she didn't look back; she could hear his thudding boots coming after her. Kiri fled to her bedroom, rushed inside then slammed and locked the door. Leaning her back against it, she panted out of breath, her pulse racing in terror.

A loud bang bashed the door jolting her body forward and shocking her heart.

"You open this door you little bitch!" Duce pounded on the door until the wood bent and splinters fragmented around the hinges.

Her brain buzzing with fright, Kiri couldn't think what to do! There was nowhere to hide, she was on the second floor, she couldn't go out the window. In a panic, she whirled around the room looking for a weapon, even as she searched she knew it would be futile. Duce was huge and fifteen years older than her, she hadn't a chance against him.

The ringing of the doorbell clanged through the house, the pounding ceased. She heard Duce muttering through the door. His footsteps moved away and she heard him thudding down the stairs. When she heard him open the front door, Kiri snuck out and hid at the top of the stairs. She peered around the corner.

Two young men stood in the doorway. One of them glanced up at her, Kiri snatched her head back to hide behind the wall.

"I'd just a'soon kill you where you stand you bleedin' bastard," one of the young men had a weird guttural accent. A blue knit hat covered his head, blonde curls turned up under the bottom. Both males wore dark sunglasses.

Duce chuckled. "Yeah, sure, no doubt, gypsy boy. But you need our corridor to move your guns. So pay the fuck up and get the hell out."

"Nice holiday decorations," the other man commented, nodding towards the dog nailed to the door. Both visitors didn't look more than teenagers, but they were big, both had muscles on top of muscles, lean hips. The bulge under their jackets told Kiri, who had been around her mobster family long enough to learn, were guns.

Snorting a smirk, Duce took a leather bag the man handed to him. "Yeah, cool, huh? My baby sister will learn to give me what I want, won't she?"

Kiri couldn't see their eyes, but she could see the brows rise on both young men, and the blond tilted his head facing up to where she hid. She tugged her head back again.

"You nailed her bloody dog to your fucking front door? You're one sick bastard, Delducci."

Duce laughed. "This coming from the infamous Crack Adranokov. Crack as in no neck too thick for you to break, eh, Naithon?"

The other man glanced at the dog then around the inside as far as he could see, he asked, "Why would you kill your sister's dog? What'd she do to you?"

The side of Duce's mouth curved in a wicked smile. "It's more like what she's gonna do *for* me. Young, tender meat, gentlemen."

Both men stared at him. The man with dark hair asked, "Are you saying like in fucking?"

Duce crossed his arms, nodded. Lifting his amoral smile higher, he confessed, "Gonna get me some before our old man sells her. He can't do that 'til she's legal age, so I got me some years I can play with her. Gonna enjoy all the changes to her body as she grows up, you get my drift?"

The head of the man in the knit hat swiveled up to Kiri. She thought she was out of sight but a mahogany ringlet curled out a bit from the wall. "You talking about banging your...baby...sister? She's not even what, four?"

Laughing, Duce set his hands on his hips, shrugged one shoulder. "Chick's a chick whatever age. She'll be the freshest, the tenderest, juiciest lamb you ever gonna get, boys. You gypsy scum want a taste of her you'll have to come by later, after I've had my fill, bring cash."

A limo pulled up to the house. The driveway was wide enough for three cars to sit side-by-side. The door opened, the chauffer climbed out, opened the back passenger door, and Ignacio Delducci stepped out. The elder Delducci frowned at the two males on his porch.

Neither teen said another word. They turned and strode across the porch, their boots clumped down the steps. Making their way to their car, they didn't pause, greet, or even look in Ignacio's direction.

Now that her father was home, a buffer between Kiri and her brother, she hurried down the stairs. Her black patent leathers slapping the tile of the foyer, skirt flouncing around her thin legs, she ran to her father. When she went to throw her arms around his waist, Ignacio turned sideways to avoid her hug.

"Papa," she pouted, "you home. I- I need ta talk ta you."

"Kiri," Duce warned as he closed the door.

She didn't acknowledge his threat. Either way, if she kept her mouth shut or told on him, she'd have trouble. "Papa, please…"

Ignacio's gaze lit on his eldest son's guilty face then transferred to his youngest child's pale, frightened countenance. Her big green eyes read like a trashy novel. "Ah," he sighed, unbuttoning his suit coat. "It's time for boarding school for you, girl. Your mother's aunt in Northern Italy will find me a secure, girls only institution, far away from any males or city trouble."

"What?" Duce blurted, glaring at Kiri he moved towards his father. "What the hell, Pa?"

Black brows with a few grey hairs slivered in them lowered over bored eyes that settled with jaundiced cynicism on his son. "I can't sell a well-used daughter. She'll bring me a lotta good land. I can't have you getting her pregnant when she hits puberty. No," his eyes flicked to Kiri who stood frozen, eyes blinking in confusion, he

16

said, "she'll stay locked in her room until I can get her on a plane, I'll have the only key."

Brother and sister burst out with words of protest speaking over each other, but Ignacio turned his back on them muttering, "I need a drink."

Chapter Four

Seventeen Years Later

Two large, burly men entered the room hauling a man between them. The man's head hung, sweat dripped from his hair, blood oozed down his face. His feet scraped the floor as they half-carried him inside.

"Here, Boss," one of the men said. "We caught him red-handed. He was drinkin' and sellin' cases of the vodka on the black market. He denied, denied, denied." They dumped the man on the floor.

"Yeah," the second male chuckled, "he drank tons of the stolen shit himself, and gave it away to his friends and family practically faster than he could sell it."

Naithon Adranokov sat, his fingers twined in his lap, thumbs tapping. Seventeen vicious, harsh years passed since that last payoff to Duce Delducci. Those violent years carved Naithon like a savage hammer and chisel into the brutal, callous man he was now at 32.

He still had dreams of torturing then butchering Duce, then wiping out the rest of his entire family. At the end of the dream, it would turn into a nightmare as flashbacks of the ambush and vicious beating Duce and his brothers had given him, then a pair of four-year-old green eyes taunted along with them as he blacked out.

Life had only gotten worse after the near death thrashing. Nait blinked out the memories and looked down at the sniveling man sprawled on his office floor.

The bleeding man hunched over, supporting his body on a forearm. He struggled to lift his head to Naithon. Face a mangled pulp, tears gushed, he spat out a tooth. Swallowing blood, he blubbered, "Gaw, please, Boss, I didn't do nuthin', I didn't mean to, I didn't do it."

At Naithon's stoic expression, sniffing, the man slobbered, "Please, please, I'll pay it back, I'll pay double, please, Boss, gimmie a second chance!" Crying frantically, his body shuddering with terror, he begged for mercy.

His expression wooden, Naithon said calmly, "You knew the consequences of stealing from me, Arvin. I let you screw the strippers, and treat your friends to the casino, and you stole my bloody vodka. Come over here." He pointed to the floor by his chair.

Arvin cried harder, "No, please, no, Boss, I'm sorry, I'll never do it again! Please," he sobbed, "have mercy."

Face sharp and rough and as merciless as corroded tank, Naithon held his finger pointed to the floor. The bottom of the afghan draped over his legs just barely covered his feet, a corner touched the polished wooden flooring. He waited patiently while Arvin Polaki looked around the room, knowing it would be the last time he saw it.

Naithon's office was darker themed than his home. His mansion had cream-colored carpets, sturdy masculine furniture made of chocolate brown leather. Not the arcane furnishings of his father's ancient manor in Romania, Naithon's taste ran to modern. He preferred huge windows that let in strong light, and favored cultured ivory and gold marble, and plush cushions. To offset all the dark inside Naithon, his decorator had surrounded him with lighter furnishings.

He wanted sofas and chairs strong enough to hold his men as they lounged without fearing a chair leg would break, or a seat crash in. The only black in his home was the gold-veined, onyx fireplace that matched his eyes. Just the black matched, not the gold, there was nothing bright or sunny in his eyes.

Currently they were in Naithon's office. Tan leather chairs, built-in bookshelves of oak, dark yellow birch tables with glass tops, some paintings of Romania decorated the champagne walls. The floor was wood planked to make it easier for him to maneuver. Naithon stared blankly at Arvin sitting on his butt sniveling.

Gulping his resignation, Arvin wiped at his tears, and crawled so he was within arm's reach. Climbing weakly to his trembling knees, he lifted his head. His last words were, "I'm sorry, sir, for stealing from you." Naithon leaned over and with one hand, gripped Arvin's throat.

As he strangled the man, his fingers digging in like a vice, Naithon said calmly, "If it had only been the second time I caught you, warned you, I would have made it quick, broke your neck like I normally do, it would have been painless and over in a second. But, you got caught again and again and again, you were warned dozens of times and yet continued on. So," he squeezed.

Arvin's eyes bugged out, he choked, gagged, but didn't fight back. He knew better. Naithon would get angry, and then really hurt him before killing him. So, Arvin remained still, except for the choking and gasping, until he made no more sounds and his body hung like a boneless cat in Naithon's grip.

Slowly, one by one, Naithon opened his fingers and Arvin slumped to the floor. "Get him out of here," he ordered.

The two men came forward and lifted Arvin, and dragged him out the way they'd hauled him in.

"So," a voice drawled from the doorway. In the same guttural accent as Naithon's, his best friend, Mazonn Diavolo commented, "Already tough as a bull, wheeling everywhere has made your arms even more powerful and your hands freakishly strong, Nait. I guess it was a good idea after all, your decision not to have an electric one."

Mazonn was the negative copy of Naithon. Both good looking men, even with harsh expressions and scars on their tough faces. Naithon had fair hair and ebony eyes, Mazonn's hair was black and he had light blue eyes that often twinkled in amusement. Nothing ever twinkled in Naithon's eyes.

Naithon pushed the aluminum hand rims and steered the wheelchair over to the bar. The wheels rumbled over the hardwood. Three coats of polyurethane painted over the resin ensured the planks were always glossy and gleaming. A low shelf had been added to the bar for his accommodation. He chose a bottle of his own Desăvârșit Vodcă, in English, Perfect Vodka.

Pouring the clear liquid into a rock glass, although it had only a faint scent, he sniffed it anyway. The familiar, slightly pungent perfume filled him with bitter memories. A grievous reminder of the wretched years when he went from destitution to prison; from prison to the devastating plunge into a wheelchair, and then on to building his own empire.

The casino and strip joints and various other enterprises brought in the money he used to build his dream, a vodka distillery dynasty. There, he could design, fuse his old country's harsh roots, with the modern, lustrous, wealthy American. Create something of his own like painting a picture or birthing a baby.

"Nait." Mazonn had come up behind him, grasped a bottle of bourbon and poured three fingers in a glass. Taking a healthy sip, he said, "Misolav is here."

Naithon's hand paused, the glass an inch from his mouth. Taking a long drink, he said nothing. Setting the glass between his thighs, he pushed the wheelchair, the wheels clunkering back across the wood. Stopping at an end table, he set his drink down and pulled a pack of Sobranie Black Russian cigars from his pocket.

Maz stood silently, patiently, while Naithon flicked his lighter and toked a few times on the end of the cigarillo then retrieved his drink. "Nait…" Maz watched his friend's skin darken, head lower, staring at the drink he held in his lap. Maz said, "He wouldn't be here if it wasn't important."

An ugly snort, Naithon spouted fiercely, "Not important? You mean like my legs?" Shaking his head, he took a heavy swallow. "First he stole my girl, then he fucking broke my goddamned back. But," he said, shaking his head again with a mirthless laugh, "I'm sure there's something much more *important* than being paralyzed and cuckold." He drained his glass then sat while Maz grabbed up the bottle of vodka and brought it over, and refilled Naithon's drink.

"Hmm," Maz murmured noncommittally.

Exhaling harshly, Naithon grumbled, "Fine, go get my brother."

"Okay. Teodor's downstairs, I'll bring him up too. You'll have our enduring support, Nait. We're your true family now, your brothers by choice. Your disloyal blood brothers are just your father's spent sperm." He clapped Naithon on the shoulder and ambled from the room leaving Naithon alone with his ravaged thoughts, memories flowing of when his body had shattered.

"Hey, Naithon, baby." The blonde female didn't wait for permission to enter because Silver Dae Foxx, not her real name of course, never marched to another's beating drum. She sauntered in, skirt barely covering her large bottom. The fuchsia wrap-around blouse did little to contain her enormous breasts. Either way she leaned, a tit threatened to tumble out.

Heavy makeup painted her face, lips dark red, thick liner swooped over brown eyes. Strong perfume overpowered the faint smell of the cigar.

Naithon put the cigar out, set the glass next to the ashtray and moved his chair to a window. The office building and his home crawled with his soldiers as well as strippers from his clubs, and groupie girls that wanted to live on the wild, dangerous side. The chair didn't faze the women, they followed him around like felines to cream. Silver Dae claimed dominance over the others for his attentions.

Ignoring her, he stared blankly out the glass. Autumn was in full bloom, turning the green leaves to flaming colors. Under trees the grass was sprinkled with dried leaves like crinkled red and orange dandruff. When the wind gusted, the leaves wisped and rolled like tossed confetti.

The city of Chaleur, Louisiana stretched out below him, steel and glass hodge-podged with old timey shacks. Muffled roars of engines and blaring horns made their way up to his floor.

Used to his perpetual smoldering rage and broodiness, Silver sashayed to him. Leaning over Naithon from behind, she draped her arms around his neck, crossing her wrists over his broad chest, platinum locks brushed the sides of his face. He gave no reaction to her touching him.

"Baby," Silver's voice against his ear a tad husky from cigarettes, "you have amazingly strict discipline. Even in that chair you dress every day in a pristine suit and tie. Where'd you get that habit? From your dad?"

Naithon sat immobile entrenched in his dark thoughts, letting her pet him, his mind was immersed in his tormented past.

Pushing his tie aside, she slipped her fingers inside his shirt between buttons and stroked his chest. "Naity," she cooed. "Such fair hair on top and such dense dark hair on your chest. So sexy."

Forcing her fingers in further to caress the matting of hair, she sighed. "The tattoos on your back, your arms, here," she brushed a fingertip up and across his collarbone. "Are these from the gangs or prison?"

Flashes of images of being initiated into the first gang struck him. A male had to be pounded by the others, almost to the extent Duce Delducci and his brothers had done to him, to the very edge of death. And he had to submit to the gang tattoos to be accepted, amongst other heinously evil things he had to do to prove his loyalty.

He blinked to vanish the images, but new ones arrived. The gangs were nothing compared to prison. Held down again and again, restrained while other inmates whipped him, carved tats on him, and sank the occasional shank into his ribs. *Ja*, he carried his life in colors on his body.

At his continued ignoring her, Silver came around the front of him and tried to slip onto his lap. Shoving her away, he growled gruffly, "You know I don't like bitches on my lap unless you're taking my dick. Don't want that right now."

She let his ire roll off her back. "Come on, lover, I know what you can do in and out of that chair, on a bed. Maybe you want me to service you? My pleasure. I'll get right on it, sugar."

Licking her lips, Silver lowered to her knees in front of him. Lifting the pedals under his feet, moving both aside, she pushed his legs apart to wriggle between them then positioned the plaid afghan down to his knees. Tugging on his belt, she cooed, "We know this ain't broke, huh, sugar?"

Shoulder-length blonde curls bounced around her shoulders as she bent over him. Her murmurs muffled from her head bending over his lap, "Yeah, how you manage such feral sex with paralyzed legs I can never figure, but," she shrugged with a smile, "I'll take it."

Silver frowned up at him. "But you need to drop it down a notch, honey, no more hospital visits for me, okay? You know you really hurt Veronica bad that time you were with her. You need to leash the ferociousness of that rage a bit. I mean, not that we're complaining, and, sure, Veronica being the true masochist that she is, asks for it super violent," she ran a spread hand over his male package before unbuckling his belt.

"Nice, brother," Misolav snarked in Romanian as he entered the office, his wife, Fiereza on his arm.

Never hesitating, Silver unbuttoned Naithon's trousers as if they didn't have an audience and grasped his zipper. Naithon considered letting her suck him off in front of everyone, but he really wasn't in the mood, he put his palm on her head and pushed her aside.

She whined in a curse, but climbed to her feet. Smirking at the other occupants, she strolled to the nearest chair and ungracefully plunked on it.

Fiereza stared down her nose at Silver with a blatant sneer.

Silver sniffed, fluffed her fluffy blonde hair and returned the same disdainful look.

"To what do I owe this...non-pleasure?" Naithon asked in Romanian as he fixed his pants and buckled his belt. He swung the chair around to face his guests.

"Hey, it's rude to speak in a language not everyone knows," Silver pouted. Crossing her legs, her skirt rose up her thighs to an almost indecent height, she draped an arm languorously over the chair arm, her fingers dangled. The wrap blouse exposed more than it covered, part of an areole showed, she shifted slightly and the nipple peeked out.

In an impeccable Gucci suit, Louboutin stilettoes that she made every effort for the red soles to be seen, Fiereza sneered at Silver's cheap hussy outfit. Arrow straight, sleek scarlet hair swished across her back, long bangs hair-sprayed to the side looked as shellacked as the varnished floor. Fiereza's attention moved to Naithon's lap, a penciled scarlet brow arched.

He stared back at her unblinking. Copious lashes thick and unnatural as her hair flapped over Fiereza's golden eyes, a challenge?

Remembering her coming to his bed one night after Fiereza and Misolav had married, she had told Naithon even paralyzed he was ten times the lover Misolav was. He fucked her to spite his brother. Fast, violent, he came, didn't wait for her, then, with contemptuous disgust, he tossed the frustrated harlot out of his room. Discarded her as fast as he had the condom.

Although she begged, he hadn't let her near him since. He'd fallen for her sultry tricks when he was young, now she repulsed him. He didn't find her narrow-hipped body any more attractive than one of the tall shedding trees outside.

His brother Misolav, as husky as their father with the same coloring of dark hair, brown eyes, thickening features, had moved from his wife to cross over to the bar. "Whad'ya want, babe?" he asked over his shoulder to his wife.

"Make mine bourbon rocks, thanks, honey," Mazonn said cheerfully entering the room. "And for you?" he grinned at Teodor Ivchenko who was right behind him.

Mazonn and Teodor were longtime friends of Naithon's from the old country. They had all met while in prison when they were in their teens and considered themselves true brothers. Each would give his life for the other.

The three friends resembled each other in that they were all tall, broad shouldered, and handsome in a scary, brutally tough way. They could frighten a person to a heart attack with one ruthless look.

Maz winked a blue eye impudently, a ridicule to Fiereza, and grinned at Naithon. Naithon's face was rugged and cold, the hard, black cinder eyes blank.

"All these years and you never learned manners," Fiereza chided Maz with a snooty air. Turning from Maz to Misolav, "I'll have wine, Misolav," she told her husband, "you know that," her words held a hint of condescension.

Over by the bar, Misolav sighed. Reaching for the cooler door that held the wines he asked, "What kind, babe?"

Naithon uttered in a bored tone, "Veuve Clicquot Brut."

Misolav stiffened. Fiereza smiled widely, purred, "Ah, you remembered." She turned her golden brown eyes to Naithon, lips rouged a deep red curved in a sexy kitten smile. Her gazed flicked to Silver then to Naithon's groin. "Showing the hooker that you aren't completely broken? Perhaps I married the wrong brother."

At her husband's harsh gasp, and Naithon's cold blank blink, she shrugged. "Just kidding. Relax, Misolav, it was a joke."

Teodor muttered, "*Ja*, as soon as you realized Misolav, not Naithon, was the heir apparent, you closed your slutty legs to Nait and spread your ass cheeks wide for Mislo."

"Shut your filthy mouth, you bastard." Misolav shoved the tip of the corkscrew into the wine bottle with irritation.

Used to Naithon's friends disparaging her for her trampy ways, swaying lean hips, Fiereza sauntered over to where her husband was making the drinks. She set a manicured hand on his shoulder, he stiffened under it. She whispered in his ear, most of it was inaudible, but the word 'cripple' was clear.

Standing near Naithon, Mazonn flushed dark red, shoulders rigid, fists clenched, he started across the room to where the couple whispered, barking, "Your fault, you bastard, Mislo, it's your fault he-" Naithon shot out a hand, stopping him.

Steaming, Maz glanced at Teodor who looked just as grim, then he let out an angry breath. The two friends moved to flank Naithon as if protecting him.

Naithon started in Romanian, then at Silver's glare switched to English. The years in America hadn't softened his behavior or thick accent. "What do you want, Misolav? Why are you here?"

Everyone waited while Mislo passed out drinks. He refilled Naithon's glass without asking, took a healthy swig of his own drink and replenished it, then took another huge gulp. "Ah," he groaned, "that's good. Of course you always have top shelf, Nait."

"Mislo," Naithon growled. Mazonn and Teodor edged towards Misolav.

"Okay, fine. We've had trouble with the Delduccis."

Naithon shrugged wide shoulders. "So what? That's nothing new."

"Yeah, but Brother-"

"*Don't call me Brother!*" Naithon barked so furiously the women jumped.

Guilt scribbled across his thick face, Mislo said, "You need to forgive, Brother. We are family, blood, it was an accident-"

"Accident?" Instead of rising, Naithon's voice lowered, deepened with darkness. His fingers coiled around the wheel rims and tightened, his knuckles turned white.

Trying to soothe the ruffling feathers, Fiereza tutted, "Come on boys, it's water under the bridge, let's-" at the seething, dangerous look on Naithon's face, she broke off and drank her wine.

Naithon growled, "Just spit out your garbage, Misolav, and get the hell out of here while *you* can still walk."

Mazonn and Teodor with matching fuming expressions crept closer to Misolav as a double threat.

Gulping hard, Misolav sucked down his drink and set the empty glass on the bar. He faced his brother. "They're trying to take over our territory, Nait. The Delducci family has become brazen and fearless. We tried to meet with them but Ignacio, the old man blew us off."

Settling his bulky shoulders back in his chair, Naithon drew big fingers through the thick blond hair that curled on the ends, and bumped a shoulder. "So? What's it to me? Da took everything I had, every dollar I'd saved, every business I opened and owned.

"He forged papers to rob me blind then kicked me out on the street when I was a teenager. Left me with nothing. The gang I had to join to make a living got caught, and I got thrown into prison and then had to start all over at 22. Two years later you steal my girl, cripple me. Get the fuck out of my house." He swung his wheelchair away from his brother.

"No, wait." Mislo held his hands out, palms up. "Just because you and Fiereza were lovers when you were a teenager, you couldn't expect her to wait for you while you were in prison."

Naithon swung the chair back, his face a reviling mask of hatred he spouted, "You forget, *Brother*, we were together when I got out. For months, until you fucked her."

"Get over it, Nait," Mislo said in sneering exasperation, "you were an infant, she needed a man-"

"Get the fuck out." Eyes narrowed to slits, Naithon spun his chair and wheeled across the room, away from his brother.

Misolav stepped towards him then halted when Maz and Teo blocked his way. His hands back up, Mislo said hurriedly, "Listen, our old man is sick. Delducci's taking too much, we're gonna lose our shirts."

"So what," Naithon grunted. "Means nothing to me. Let that bitch Verona take care of him, she certainly was never a mother to me."

"Don't you talk about my mother like that!" Now angry, Mislo rolled his hands into fists.

Maz and Teo, faces like rocks moved to stand a blockade between Mislo and Naithon.

Silver Dae took that heated moment to slide out of the room. Fiereza merely sipped her wine and watched the action.

Calming down, Misolav said with careful pleading, "The cousins. Think about the innocent cousins, Naithon, the babies, Verona's nephews, there'll be no roof over their heads, you want that for them?"

Scowling, Naithon rumbled coldly, "No one ever gave a damn about me. What do I care?"

"Da might have kicked you out, Nait, but it's still your heritage. You want the Delduccis to take over what is the Adranokovs'? You want Delduccis living on our land? In our house? Rubbing it in our-your face?"

Brows low over angry hooded eyes, Naithon stared at the plaid afghan on his lap. Squinting one eye, he looked up at his brother. "When did they get so big? Last time I saw them I was…ah, 24. That girl, the baby sister was home on holiday."

He thought back to that day. They'd attended a meeting at the Delduccis' with another gang, the Riveaux Knights. A fourth faction, a motorcycle gang, the Foes of God, was trying to take over everyone's territory. They'd come muscling in with AK-47's and kamikaze attitudes.

Practically native Cajuns from the beginning of time, early on, the Riveaux Knights had fought the Adranokovs and the Delduccis, but realizing all sides were losing too much, they made a pact. Each stayed to their own territory, no more battles amongst the three gangs.

But when the Foes of God decided their shit up north Mississippi wasn't good enough or big enough, they made the error of coming to Chaleur and trying to take over. It'd been months of hell, heavy losses on all sides. But, the three original mobs, the Adranokovs, the Delduccis, and the Riveaux Knights conquered the gang.

It had been a brutal bloody battle. What was left of the limping Foes of God turned tail and skedaddled back to whence they came and peace carried on again.

Naithon remembered the meeting after the smoke cleared. They were in the Delducci mansion, Ignacio Delducci had a banquet served. Women hanging all over Naithon, drunk and sloppy he had looked up and caught a glimpse of the little girl he'd seen years ago. Duce's baby sister.

The child Duce had been titillating them with his plans to deflower. He'd nailed her pup to the front door. What had he said? Old man Ignacio had plans to sell the girl when she became of age, but Duce had plans of his own.

A rare guilt had tugged at Naithon's gut that day. He'd seen her, a beautiful child, a terrified child, and he was going to leave her there knowing her future, her brother's plans to rape her. Repeatedly, for years. Duce tortured and killed a tiny puppy, *Dio* knows what hell he'd rain on her.

For once, the guilt bit him and he was pulling his cell out to call the uniforms, the police. None of them ever had dealings with the cops unless it was the corrupt ones they owned. His phone in his hand, Naithon was just about to dial when Ignacio had pulled up. The way he glowered at everyone, Naithon thought the girl was safe, and he left. He'd always wondered. Had Duce torn her up? Destroyed that innocent gentleness out of those amazing green eyes?

Still, she was a hated Delducci, she was one of them. She was what, maybe three, a year before her brothers had almost beaten him to death, and then around four the day Duce threatened her rape. Still, she was one of them and deserved his undying hatred and vengeance.

At the time of the banquet she was close to twelve, he was going on twenty-four. It was before his old man ripped everything from him again and tossed him destitute out on the street for the second time.

After Misolav stole his girl, Fiereza, and after the horror of prison that had changed his life for the worse, again…he shook his head. But it was before he broke his back. He remembered the girl though. At her young age she had the promise of becoming a great beauty, there was still the gentleness, and pure innocence glowing in those great green eyes. Her father had sent her abroad, thank *Dio*, it saved her, for a while anyway, kept Duce from between her child's legs.

Naithon recalled there was another unremarkable sister, Melonie. Plain as mud and tubby, Melonie made no secret of her crush on Naithon. He kept a wide berth between them, rudely brushing her off, she never got the hint. Talk about octopus hands.

He'd tried to talk to Kiri at the banquet, don't know why, she was just a kid, yet he was drawn to her. But she stuck that little chin up in the air and scurried off.

He only saw her briefly during the years after that. He'd tried to approach her, speak to her, but she shrugged him off like yesterday's newspaper-wrapped fish. Which was fine. After the vicious, almost deadly beating her brothers had dealt him when he was a young teen, he'd sworn vengeance on the entire family.

Besides, shortly after the banquet he was sentenced to a wheelchair, and Ignacio had hidden her away somewhere only bringing her home for the holidays.

Heaving a sigh, Naithon said, "Fine. What do you want from me?"

A smile creased his brother's face. His features so much heavier and darker than Naithon's it was hard to see any resemblance between the brothers. They had different mothers.

When Naithon had been being beaten and assaulted in prison, images of his own wretched family and the Delduccis had courted him. The visions tried to make him seek revenge the minute he was released. But, he had stepped back, biding his time. Maybe the time had come?

Refilling his wife's wineglass, Misolav said, "We're gonna have a meet."

Chapter Five

Before the meeting could be held, Kiritina Delducci was called home from her school in Italy. Her brother had been murdered. Murdered. Duce was dead.

She couldn't wrap her mind around it. He'd been so full of arrogant, bullying, wicked life. Torturing and killing dogs, and stomping on people until they moved out of the way or were crushed out of existence under his malignant heel.

It had been close, but she had gotten away from his clutches. A few visits on the holidays when she was home he had tried to break into her room, but Ignacio finally put a guard at her door. Her virgin price would bring big bucks.

She'd had only a brief time to enjoy her independence at college. Ignacio thought she was taking business courses so until she married, she could help run their rum distillery, Maestá d'oro, Majesty's Gold.

Their latest liquor brand was labeled Maestá Primeo, Majesty's Prize. If he knew she was taking photography, graphics and creative art design, he'd have pulled her right out and brought her straight home.

Ignacio had already arranged a marriage deal brokered with Rueford Montoblanco. Another mobster who owned a city north of Chaleur. Rueford had claimed her the first time he set eyes on her, she'd been eleven or so, and he'd wanted her then. He was thirty-five at the time. She was almost twenty now, he was forty-four, and chomping at the bit to have her.

Kiri was trapped. Ignacio threatened the lives of innocent people, and to crush his thumb harder over her, he said he'd accuse her of stealing from him and have her thrown in jail if she didn't acquiesce to his demands she wed Rueford.

Rueford was a barrel-chested, husky man with crinkly red hair and lewd blue eyes that never left her body whenever he was around her. She'd had to be quick to hide when he tried to corner her during the few holiday visits she had come home.

An unsmiling butler opened the door, the chauffer left to park the car. A wreath crossed with a wide black ribbon covered the door, the drapes were drawn, the inside sorrowful, dark, depressing. Kiri carried her suitcase up to her room.

After freshening up, she traipsed down the wide, curving staircase, her shoes clopped lightly on the sapphire carpet. The mansion was done in mostly shades of blue and yellow. As she moved through the hallways, the colors of the rooms darkened, the furniture became more substantial, masculine.

She found her father and brothers in the den. Her mother had left the family a long time ago. She'd gotten a boyfriend and never looked back, leaving her young daughter in the talons of lawless, sick men, along with an older sister, Melonie, who despised Kiri.

Thankfully, her father had sent Kiri away, to an all-female boarding school tucked securely deep in the mountainous Alps of Northern Italy.

Currently, she was interning with a scene photography company. Kiri had a knack, a gift if you will, for creating faux food, or a scene such as furniture in a room, and photographing it so it jumped vibrantly off the page, or the TV, for the ad for the restaurant or house.

She was building up a following, last thing she wanted was to leave Italy and come back home, to…here. Dread weighed heavy on her heart.

Sucking in a long, deep breath, she exhaled slowly. Smoothing the full patterned skirt that landed above her knees, she straightened her shoulders, lifted her head and stiffened her spine.

The dark cherry brown hair was doubly French-braided down her head, then threaded together in a long double-braid that fishtailed into two long pieces. It was a slick, sophisticated style for the simple, shy girl. She stroked her fingers down the braid, a calming gesture, the loose ends fluttered at her hip as she graciously entered the room.

Her two brothers, Piero and Janero, looked up at her entrance. They reclined on easy chairs with cocktails in their hands.

Her father, Ignacio skulked in a corner, one hand stuffed in a trouser pocket, the other clenched a drink. He didn't turn from the window he was staring out. Ignacio's hair was still full yet thinning on top. His nose slightly bulbous, chin not as severe as she remembered it.

Piero resembled his father with dark hair and eyes, but Janero had the burnished cherry brown hair like hers, he kept it short and it waved naturally. They also shared the same green eyes.

Ignacio, Piero, Duce and Melonie had midnight hair and shadowed eyes. Ruthless savagery resided in all four of the Delducci males. Kiri was never anything other than a sexual toy or a dollar sign to them. Melonie was mostly ignored.

Taking another deep breath, Kiri splayed a hand over her flat stomach hoping she could still the quaking inside. "Papa," she said quietly, moving further inside the room. Her father didn't glance in her direction.

"Hey, ya, Kirs," Janero, the youngest of the three brothers rolled off his chair and loped over to her. He reached one arm around her and pulled her in for a hug. His cologne was piquant and overpowering. She pushed gently from his embrace. Smiling, Janero said, "What can I get you to drink, little sis?"

"Ah, uh, just a cola, please." Her eyes on her father, she saw the bleak despondency sloping his shoulders. He seemed as unaware of her as he was of his glasses sliding down his nose. "Where's, uh, Melonie?"

Janero answered on his way to get her soda, "She's upstairs planning the...funeral." His eyes darted to his father who hadn't moved a muscle. "Staying busy is her way of coping, with...it. She's handling his...death, uh, better than the rest of us." Janero brought Kiri's drink to her.

Piero nodded a grim greeting, his face black with wrath. Slamming his hand on the chair arm, he shouted, "It was the Adranokovs, goddammit!"

Kiri's heart clenched at his vehemence, she stepped back. "How do you, uh, how, I mean, what happened? How did Duce...pass?"

"Pass?" Piero leaped from his chair and stomped to her. It was all she could do to hold her ground. "He didn't *pass*," he snarled with sarcastic fury. "He was motherfucking murdered you dumb bitch!"

"Geesh, Piero, she didn't do anything, don't yell at her." Janero smiled somewhat kindly at Kiri, he explained, "He was set up."

"Yeah," Piero grated with fury. "He received a message from someone identifying themselves as one of the Adranokovs' crew. The message said he wanted to meet with Duce and some other businessmen regarding some new weapons pipeline. Set a place and time to meet. When they reached the meet they were ambushed. The bastards killed them all." His fists clenched, jaw grit so hard Kiri could hear his teeth grinding.

"Of course the Adranokovs denied any involvement in it," Janero said. "But, hell, we know what thugs and crooks they are."

"Yeah, and pa says we have to wait until we're stronger in number before we can retaliate against those smarmy gypsies," his tone indicated what Piero thought about waiting.

"Oh, um..." Kiri had no idea what to say. Setting her untouched soda on a table, she stammered, "Um, so, did they...shoot him, or-"

"Or?" Ignacio screeched from his corner. He grabbed up a sheaf of papers off the desk and stalked over to her. "Here, look you bloodthirsty, nosey little bitch," and he grabbed a fistful of her braid and shoved the papers in her face.

Rubbing them over her face as she fought to get away, he roared, "Wood chipper, honey, yeah, they stuffed your brother down a fucking wood chipper! Nothing left of him except blood and his...ring. The ring we all wear." He held up his hand for her to see the ring she was well familiar with.

He ran out of steam, stood back, threw the photos in Kiri's face and stomped back to his corner, grabbed his drink and slugged it down in one gulp.

She was stunned, shocked, sickened. Tears in her eyes, she stared down at the photographs scattered at her feet. One showed the wood chipper, another the DNA tests, another focused on a streak of blood on the inside of the chute.

Wiping at the tears, she stared at the other photos, there were several close ups of Duce's bloody ring lying garbled on the ground where the chipper had spat it out. The family crest clear as a bell.

Piero threw himself back in his chair with a huffed growl, sprawled out in festering rage and grief. Janero made himself another drink and sucked it down.

Lowering to her knees, Kiri gathered up the pictures, then getting to her feet, keeping her eyes averted from the grisly images, she set them on the desk and moved slowly, carefully to the door. Her father's harsh voice stopped her.

"You're done with school, missy. No more playing for you. Tomorrow you start work at the distillery. The tasting room needs polish, you can start renovating it so it attracts decent folks instead of the bar scum we've been getting. And you will help Melonie serve."

"But, I-"

His face darkened red, eyes narrowed with rage, spittle flew out with his words, he barked each word short and hard, "You will start work tomorrow at the distillery. We all need to absorb...Duce's tasks." His shoulders slumped.

As he turned his back on her, he decreed, "You will design and work at the distillery while planning your wedding to Rueford Montoblanco. Enough of your stalling, delaying. You will marry him by the end of next spring. If I have to have you taken somewhere and forced to do it, keep you locked up until it's a done deal, I will."

His back was turned completely to her, shutting off any protests she would make.

Chapter Six

Months later, Kiri was still adjusting to the work her father had foisted upon her when Piero came storming into the Molten Gold Rum Tasting Room. There were only a few customers at the tables, but seeing the fury on his face, she hustled over to get him out before he exploded.

She had enjoyed decorating the tasting room and creating the flyers and ads for it. She came up with the idea to infuse the various rums with slivers of gold and silver, amethyst crystals, turquoise and diamond chips. The chips imbue each individual brand of rum with a different slight coloration and sparkle, making Maestá d'oro Rum unique.

Kiri had set up crystals and flowers, cedar and smoked oak chips in various designs and photographed them. Their ads popped right off the magazine pages, she'd made the rum appear alluring, vivacious and alive. Customers thronged to the new tasting room.

Business had jumped dramatically since she'd taken over. The large round room was comfy with a white-bricked fireplace that was alight with orange flames. Tables were covered with cheerful blue, and a few sunflower decorated tablecloths, along with soft golden lighting.

Old cask barrels sprung with bright flowers, even the displays of the rum bottles were colorful and pretty, the counter that stretched the back of the room welcoming and pleasant.

Kiri had strewn rose petals and lilacs here and there, their soft fragrance refreshing and relaxing. Customers came more for the inviting ambiance than the rum, and the view out the back was spectacular.

People found Kiri shy but engaging, honest and creative. They enjoyed talking with her. Although she wore as conservative and loose clothing as possible, kept her hair pinned up, men came to watch her pour the rum into the tiny glasses and mix in different chasers.

Customers left Melonie's section as soon as Kiri came in and set up, they flocked to her part of the counter or tables. That did not help the ongoing jealousy and blistering hate Melonie held against her sister since the little bundle of attention-stealing joy erupted into her life. She had resented Duce's polluted incestualized interest constantly on their baby sister, and not on her.

Kiri hurried over to her steaming brother.

"Piero, what's wrong? Here, come into this alcove." She glanced at Melonie who was serving a customer.

Melonie shrugged, she was used to all her brothers' explosive, sometimes not even provoked tempers. An imagined slight would set them off and heads would roll. Literally. Duce had been proficient with machetes, and like a hit of ecstasy, he got a buzzing high using them on people that angered him.

Kiri clasped Piero's arm and rustled him gently into the alcove where they couldn't be overheard.

"Huh," he huffed, arms bowed, nostrils flaring like a bull, fists clenched, his usual stance. "It's those fucking Adranokovs, Kirs."

Keeping her voice low and calm, Kiri uttered quietly, "Hush, now, Piero, the customers, your language." She glanced out at the room. A matronly woman with pinned up grey hair and a flowered dress was glaring at them.

"Yeah, yeah, whatever," he growled and huffed.

Sighing with weary patience, Kiri asked, "What have they done now?" Skirmishes had broken out after Duce's death. One of the Adranokovs' crew had been ambushed and murdered. His body was found in an alley with a knife pinning a note to his chest. The note claimed retaliation for Duce's death.

The Delduccis swore up and down and sideways they'd had nothing to do with it. Ignacio Delduccis had told them to back off. With Naithon's assistance, the Adranokovs had grown too big and too powerful, the Delduccis had no chance to survive a potential war.

"Donnie, our third cousin was found today." He took a breath, arched his neck and glared at the ceiling, then closed his eyes. Lowering his head, his voice gripped tight, he said, "That's the last of them, Kirs. There's only you, Janero, Melonie, me and Pa left of the Delducci clan. The others were gunned down last week."

Fear hitched her breath, she swallowed around it. "But, why? Why the killings?"

Piero angrily shrugged his shoulders humped in despair. "Who the hell knows? They think we're taking out their people. Misolav Adranokov was grazed by a bullet yesterday. Another inch and he'd have no left eye." Kiri shuddered with the picture her brother drew.

"They claim a note was left on his car proclaiming we did it for revenge. Hell, Kirs, they're wiping us out. Even the workers are afraid. If something isn't done soon, we're history." A heavy sigh rolled down his big chest, chin lowered, he stuck his hands in his pockets and stared at the ground.

One more thing to worry about, Kiri thought desperately. Her wedding to Rueford loomed on the horizon, he'd been coming around every other day now. Nudging her into corners with his barrel chest, putting his beefy hands all over her, playing grab-ass. A shiver of grossness rippled through her. Her future husband repulsed her.

So far she had balked at choosing a wedding gown or wearing Rueford's ring, but Ignacio had hired a planner to make all the decisions and choices. If only she could get out of the arranged marriage. But, her sigh drooped her shoulders, saddened her eyes. There would be no rescue for her. Ignacio was callous enough to make good on his threats.

"What are we going to do?" Fear stuttering her voice, Kiri clutched her fingers together, twisting them roughly in her agitation.

"Ah, I dunno." Piero let his gaze fall on her. He seldom looked directly at her as if she was too insignificant to give his attention to. Growing up, every time he got close enough to touch her, big bad brother Duce would knock him upside the head.

Duce was possessive of his baby sister, 'Incest is best only with the eldest' he always chimed.

Piero went on, "Pa's worrying himself sick. He's lost weight, his hands tremble all the time now. He's scared, Kirs, we all are."

Her lips bunched. Again, there was nothing constructive or comforting she could say.

"Ah, well." Piero clapped her shoulder once. "Pa just sent me by to warn you to keep on your toes, watch your back. He's put guards up all over the plant and the house, but," he raked a hand through his unruly dark hair. "Those Adranokovs are wily, sneaky, mean motherfuckers. Filthy gypsies. They wanna get us, they will, ya know?"

Appalled and distressed over his foul language in the tasting room that she had struggled and sweated over making elegant and refined yet soft and pretty and comfortable, she bit her tongue to keep from rebuking him.

She had plans on redoing the patio out back and having light lunches available, make it family friendly. Parents would not want to bring their children to an establishment where the owners were blustering and cursing all the time.

A chill prickled up her spine at his words of warning though. They all could be in danger. Everyone knew how deadly the Adranokov men were. She'd heard horrendous stories about the youngest one, Naithon. Youngest but the most lethal. She glanced anxiously around, what if a customer was there to assassinate them-no, surely not in broad daylight.

"Anyway, I gotta go, got a delivery on some, uh, sugarcane-" he broke off, shifty gaze sliding around the room. There were undercover cops and spies everywhere; he shut his mouth before he spilled their illegal activities. "Pa's called for a meeting on Friday with the Adranokovs hoping he can put an end to this trouble."

Glancing slyly slit eyes up at her once more, he said, "Watch your back," and then strode out of the room.

Kiri let out the breath she'd held since first catching sight of him coming in.

Smiling weakly at customers who waved and called out greetings to her, she made her way over to the windows that spread the length of the room showcasing the view out back. Lush, softly rolling hills of green satin spreading to a backdrop of autumn's vivid colors, a feast of nature's bounty spanned as far as the eye could see.

She was even thinking of adding more enticements like horseback riding as the land was so beautiful. Autumn this year had seemed to go on forever but was now starting to wane.

She'd had gardens put in, rosebushes fought the fall coolness, and trees still littered their crimson and orange leaves. Sloping up a gentle hill they'd started a vineyard. A crochet of green and purple vines wavered in even lines up the hill.

It had been Kiri's idea to branch out to start their own winery. They had even held a wedding in the rose garden with promises of more to come.

Chapter Seven

The week passed slowly, Kiri had spent her time at the tasting room, working on her displays and ads, and ducking Rueford. The tasting room was currently empty, it was Monday and they sometimes closed on Mondays as business tended to be slow then.

The meeting between the Delduccis and the Adranokovs was pushed from Friday to Monday. Kiri hadn't planned on being present.

She stayed in her room at the house, and locked her door. Pushed a chair under the knob as an added precaution. Now that Duce wasn't around lurking by her door, Piero, and sometimes Rueford prowled the halls near her room.

Before returning home she had set up the tasting room ready to receive the men for the meeting. Males only. Both families were sexist and old fashioned. The only female present would be Melonie, and that was because she would be serving the dessert rum.

Melonie Delducci glanced around the room. She made an excuse to be there every time the Adranokovs and the Delduccis met. Even though he was in a wheelchair, she harbored a crush on Naithon Adranokov. Melonie's brown eyes grew all glassy and dreamy whenever the Apollo god was there.

Normally she wasn't partial to blonds, but his pretty face and hair were offset by harsh masculinity that sharpened the would-be pretty features, and scars that also roughed up the prettiness, along with the perpetually fierce grit to his strong jaw.

Melonie had heard the rumors of his escapades in and out of bed. The paralysis and wheelchair did not slow him down. He was one of the most feared men in Louisiana, and according to the women, one of the most cruel and punishing, and breathlessly superlative, lovers.

But, he was very particular whom he bedded. The ones he did bang complained he never learned their names, didn't look at their faces while he screwed them, and was cold and rough, right on the edge of damaging violence. But the ride was wild and not to be missed. Somehow, even though paralyzed, they said he could maneuver his hips on his knees, and he was quite creative.

There was some story about how he'd hang a woman with a chain from the ceiling, bind her hands so she was helpless, her legs pulled up, spread, and tied wide open, and he had a specially made swinging chair so he could-

"Ooh," an erotic shiver raced goosebumps up her arms, Melonie clamped her thighs together. She had thrown herself at Naithon time and time again, but he rebuffed her. She knew she wasn't his type. He seemed to prefer tall, bawdy blondes with big fake tits.

She ran her hands down her plump sides and sighed. Maybe she should die her brown locks, get a boob job. She looked down at her drooping chest. Maybe just get a lift. Her pudginess helped fill out what little she had.

One of Naithon's brothers had told her she was a troll compared to the women Naithon dated. Well, not dated, he was a confirmed bachelor, he had sex, he didn't date. He also did not have sleepovers. He didn't even bring the women to his bed, he either went to theirs or used a playroom designed to accommodate his handicap.

Melonie gossiped relentlessly about Naithon, she knew his house, no, they called it a compound, had a serious amount of rooms where many of his soldiers resided. Naithon's brother, Vitalik, Melonie's nose wrinkled in resentment, had said even her shy, closed off, matronly dressed little sister Kiri shone like a bright star next to Melonie's round, brown, dull stump of a body.

Piqued at the recalled insult, Melonie picked up a bottle of rum on display and hurled it at the wall. The glass crashed and splintered, tinkled to the floor. Amber liquid streamed down the wall. "Great," she groused, "now I have to clean that up. Kiri should be here to do that, she's the one that does the servant work."

Sighing, she grabbed a rag to clean the wall and a broom and dustpan. Knowing she had no chance with Naithon, she turned her horny thoughts to his brothers. They'd do in a pinch.

Sweeping up the glass, she pictured his brothers, all older than Naithon. Vitalik was second oldest, then Novikav, and Misolav was eldest. Misolav was married to that shrew, Fiereza. Melonie had heard that didn't matter, he still got around.

They were all good looking men, but none held the restrained brutality that hovered around Naithon like a rampant haze of fury, he seemed to barely keep it under control. Apparently he didn't always keep a leash on it though, she'd heard he could be quite cruelly lethal and pitiless when riled. Still, she'd chance one night with that Apollo!

Even his friends were hot, Melonie thought as she wiped down the wall. Yashin, Mazonn, Teodor, Vlad, Blok, they'd all come from the old country, Romania. She would do any of them in a heartbeat.

"Oh!" Melonie grinned. She could hear the approaching ruckus of cannonading engines heralding the men's arrival. Hurrying to the window, she peered out.

Top-of-the-line vehicles were pulling into the curved drive. Doors slammed and male voices rumbled as they approached the distillery, pinpricks of excitement, and lust needled her pudgy body as they grew near.

The door thrust open and Melonie's father, Ignacio Delducci swaggered in, Piero and Janero came in next, then dozens of men trooped in behind them. The only female, a smug Fiereza Adranokov sauntered through the door, her hand clinging to her husband Misolav's arm. She wore a skin-tight bandage dress in pale yellow that molded over her curves. What she had of them, that was.

Melonie's eyes narrowed at Fiereza's chest, not even a B-cup she judged. Her hips were narrow, almost boyish. Melonie could not see what Misolav, or Naithon for that matter saw in the tramp. The whole world knew Naithon had once been enamored of her, of course Fiereza was seven or so years older than him. He had been young, a teenager, but she had gone all out gangbusters on him pouring on the charm, and constant sex, she had hooked him before he could blink.

According the servants that heard the ensuing fight, Naithon had planned on asking Fiereza to marry him when he caught her and his brother in bed, well, in the parlor, on all fours screwing their brains out.

He'd disappeared for a long time after that. Misolav and Fiereza married, and Naithon came back a cripple. There had been rumors that somehow Misolav caused the accident, whatever it was, that broke Naithon's back. But, no one was talking. Naithon built up his businesses apart from his father and brothers', he seldom saw them if he could avoid it. He'd built his distillery in the country, in the rural town of Marécage.

Marécage means swamp, but it was no where's near a swamp. It was spacious bountiful land with winding roads that were dappled by shade trees. The serpentine roads curled through a countryside of green fields laced with wildflowers. It was an enjoyable Sunday drive to get to the distillery.

Melonie craned her neck to look for- there he was. Encircled by his men, Naithon rolled his own wheelchair inside. Her pulse raced and bumped. Damn he was hot in an aggressive warrior yet damaged but still strapping kind of way. Naithon wore his requisite suit and tie, plaid afghan over his lap. Blond hair cut shorter on the sides and longer on top.

He removed his shades and exposed those demon's eyes. They flicked to her, then wandered the room as the men settled in. Only a brief glance from him and she felt tingles spark in her lady parts.

The majority of the men wore suits, a few of the enforcers just tailored shirts and black slacks, weapons glaringly visible in shoulder holsters. Some sat on chairs, others leaned against the counter or perched on stools. All of Naithon's men remained standing.

Piero and Janero, Melonie's brothers, headed straight for the food. Earlier, Kiri had set up a brunch style buffet.

Piero lifted an aluminum lid, steam poured out, he inhaled, smiled. "Yeah, Kiri always makes my favorite corned beef and cabbage. Go on, Janero." He motioned to the next heating plate. "I bet she made your lasagna stuffed with meatballs and sausage the way you like it." The brothers grabbed plates and started opening all the warming containers.

Frowning at his sons' discourteous manners, Ignacio announced, "Ah, please, gentlemen, help yourselves. My daughter Kiritina is an exquisite cook."

Rueford Montoblanco strolled in, smiling. "What are you saying about my betrothed?"

Ignacio shrugged. "You know what a stupendous cook she is. Soon you will enjoy all of her…attributes, eh?" The men chuckled obscenely together.

Off to the side, Naithon lifted a brow at their banter. His expression indicated that the picture of the stocky, lecherous, redheaded much older man humping the young, delicate, innocent girl struck him as grotesque.

Rueford moved to the full bar Kiri had set up. Along with the help-yourself bar, she'd stashed bottles of beer in big bowls of crushed ice in the center of the tables. The meeting was private, they didn't want servers overhearing their conversations.

"Come on, Nait." Mazonn nudged his arm. "Smells incredible, let's see what this chickie can rustle up."

Naithon's friends, Mazonn and Yashin flanked him as he rolled to the buffet. Teodor and Vlad stayed back, their eyes constantly roaming the room for any danger to their boss and friend. Outside, more men patrolled under Blok's direction. Naithon's familial blood brothers blew him off and hurried ahead of him to the food, but his friends stayed with him, guarding him.

Ignacio had his own crew armed and on alert. There had been too many killings on both sides for either man to let their guard down.

47

Ignacio waited until Naithon settled at a table then strolled over. Peering at him through round glasses, he said, "Well, young man, you look like you're doing fine. Where's your father, Zhilov? This is about *his* business, no one has attacked your vodka distillery or your other enterprises have they?"

Chewing on a succulent barbecued rib, Naithon swallowed then replied, "He's in Romania. He grew...concerned," *scared, old and ill, too weak to fight*, "about the murders. He's checking on his businesses there. My brothers asked me to assist in ending this...war?" A half empty beer pooled a wet spot near his plate. Since his brother Misolav sought his help, Naithon had brought in more men to buff up their territory, watch over the businesses.

"Oh, no, no," Ignacio chuckled nervously. "Let's not say war, let's say, uh, misunderstanding?"

"Huh," Mazonn grunted, stuffing a cheesy noodle in his mouth. "A half a dozen of our men slaughtered is hardly a misunderstanding."

Scowling to hide his fear, adjusting his glasses with a scrunch of his nose, Ignacio countered, "We have lost more men than you. Our kin have been butchered, left in pieces in cruddy alleys, the- the wood chipper. You-"

"We are not responsible, Delducci," Naithon said flatly, showing his disrespect by calling the elder man by his last name, "for any of the deaths of your people. We have told you that ad nauseam."

Ignacio huffed a grunt. "Get real, Adranokov, our men aren't killing our own people, or yours, dammit."

"And neither are ours," Naithon replied. He slathered butter on a bun and shoved it in his mouth whole.

"Listen, you can't-" Ignacio backed off. Sweat dampened the back of his shirt, red flushed his flaccid face. He took a deep breath, exhaled slowly. "We have a new rum, you must try it. Melonie," he gestured to his daughter who hung on the fringes, peeved that not one man looked over at her.

She sighed in annoyance and trudged over to the bar area and to the tray her sister Kiri had prepared.

The silver tray held several bottles of different kinds of rum. Kiri had placed stacks of shot glasses at each table. As the men chowed, they held up a glass for Melonie to serve them the rum.

Another laborious sigh, damn, Melonie hated being the servant. That was Kiri's job. The little witch should be here doing the slave work. Not that she'd lifted a finger to help Kiri with all the cooking and preparation.

Melonie served her father last. He raised his glass and toasted, "To peace between our factions, let us call a truce."

All of his men raised their glasses and saluted in agreement voicing, "To a truce." They downed their shots then grabbed bottles for refills. Ignacio noticed Naithon's brothers saluted, but Naithon and his friends did not.

Naithon nudged his elbow in Mazonn's side. Mazonn set his fork down. "Ignacio," he called out, "we desire to thank the cook. Please present her so we can do so."

Rueford grinned, Melonie scowled, Ignacio shrugged. Again, ignoring the second slight, this one coming from Naithon's second in command in calling him by his first name, an insult as Mazonn was half Ignacio's age, he said, "Of course. Janero, call your sister to come over. Have Jeffries drive her." His pleasant smile didn't disguise the churning of his stomach.

Concerned about the outcome of the meeting, he tossed his rum back and poured another. A short smile tipped his nervous lips up hearing the men vocally admiring the prettiness of the rum bottles from the crystals and gold Kiri had the distilleries infuse into them.

Off to the side of the room, Janero frowned at his cell.

Kiri argued with him. "No, I don't want to go there. There is no reason for me to," she protested.

"Pa orders it, Kirs. What're ya gonna do? Pa's afraid to disrespect the crippled gypsy bastard, he has to honor Adranokov's request. It'll only be a minute. They thank you, you smile, and leave. That's it."

Chapter Eight

Everyone looked to the doorway when Kiri appeared in it. Her gaze shyly roved the room not making eye contact with any of the occupants, except her sister. Melonie's hateful scowl at her could scorch sand.

The girls had never been close, besides Melonie's insane jealousy of her little sister, Kiri had been away to boarding school most of their lives. On the good side, it had kept Kiri out of her dangerous, perverted brother Duce's clutches, but also kept her shielded from her hostile sister.

Ignacio waved her over. "Come, my flower, the gentlemen would like to proffer their appreciation for such a lavish, and delicious spread."

Hating to be the center of attention, she didn't move. Ignacio's brows lowered, he lifted his chin, an order.

Folding her hands demurely in front of her, with her head down, Kiri walked slowly to where her father stood. Her heart dropped. Her future intended, Rueford Montoblanco was positioned beside him, his rapacious piggy eyes drinking her in.

Why he was so interested in her, she couldn't fathom. She had dressed in her plainest clothes, a flowered skirt that touched her knees, a plain, not in the least sexy, white button-down blouse, small heels, her hair in a tight bun.

"Ah, my beautiful fiancée," Rueford enthused; going right to her and set a heavy arm around her shoulders and squeezed, hard. Hard enough she winced.

She stood as a statue while the males in the room plied her with compliments for her cooking. Her sister and Fiereza Adranokov didn't bother hiding their glowers of loathing.

Rueford grabbed Kiri's hand, jerked it up. Blue eyes suddenly angry, he asked with ire, "Where is my ring? You took it off again? Didn't I tell you I would beat your ass if I caught you again without it?"

Kiri tugged her hand from his grasp. "I was cooking and washing dishes, Rueford, did you want it to go down the drain?"

Somewhat mollified, he blustered, "See to it you have it on whenever you leave your house. I insist everyone knows you are claimed." Bending his head, he spoke harshly in her ear, "You don't want to defy me, honey, you will pay for it."

"Okay," Ignacio announced, "please continue enjoying yourselves, gentlemen. My girls will be serving my new dessert rum. It's called 'Maestá's Dolci Fine Pizzico di Caffè', Kiri named it."

Sitting beside Naithon, Mazonn smiled warmly at Kiri, but her eyes were downcast, she didn't see him, he asked her, "Sounds elegant, what is it in English?"

Naithon didn't speak, just stared blankly at Rueford Montoblanco. Rueford didn't dare look back at him, he tried to ignore the demon-eyed glare icing through him but his body twitched under the perusal.

Janero answered for his sister, "It means 'Majesty's sweet endings with a hint of coffee.' The rum has just the faintest trace of coffee flavor. It was all Kiri's idea. She decided on sweet endings as a double entendre, it is an after dinner dessert wine, and also the hope of this…issue being settled between us. She suggested the coffee flavor because she likes adding unique twists to things."

"Very clever," Mazonn praised, trying to catch Kiri's eye, but she kept her head down.

"Please enjoy," Ignacio declared with nervous courtesy.

After everyone settled down again, Ignacio instructed his daughters to keep their glasses full. He had to tell Rueford two times to release Kiri before he grudgingly let her go.

Rueford whispered loud enough for everyone in the vicinity to hear, "I will get with you later, my pet, we will have an assignation. No more avoiding me." He sounded more threatening than lover-like.

As she turned, the aggressive pat on her behind with his huge meaty fist was not gentle, neither was the disrespectful squeeze, she swung around, a furious retort on her tongue. He grinned, he liked it when she was angry or scared, it fed the pathological sadism in him. Provoking her was his new pastime. He wanted her to exhibit her anger and then he'd have his first excuse to punish her. Show her who was boss.

Clenching her fists, Kiri spun and stalked off to do her duty.

The group shuffled and shifted, chatted and drank. Some went back for seconds and thirds. Only crumbs were left on the pie and cake trays. A man leaned against a wall shoveling the last of the au gratin potatoes into his mouth.

Ignacio pulled out a chair at Naithon's table and wearily lowered his thinning heft onto it. Tugging his glasses off, he dragged a linen napkin over his eyes and shoved the glasses back on. Even though it was not Naithon's own business, it was his father's, and regardless of the tales of his monstrous ruthlessness, to Ignacio, Naithon appeared relatively helpless in that wheelchair. Yet, clearly Naithon Adranokov was the man in charge. He was the one to deal with.

It stung Ignacio to have to do business with a man half his age, and a cripple at that, but he had no choice. The father, Zhilov Adranokov was a vicious violent man, the word was, his youngest son was even more so. But Zhilov was out of the country, and apparently instead of one of his older brothers running the show, Naithon was the crown prince of their industry.

"So," Ignacio took a breath to calm his nerves, ease the shake from his voice. "What do you say about a truce, eh, young man?"

Under low-lidded eyes that frosted over at Ignacio calling him a young man, the tone indicating as if he was still in diapers, Naithon scanned the room, his dark gaze stopped at Kiri.

Kiri felt his creepy eyes stroke tangibly, invasively up and down her body, she was unable to suppress the shiver of fright it brought. He had watched her exchange with Rueford with an unreadable face and those deeply hooded eyes. No expression, just a vein beating at one temple, and his jaw working. Did he want to hurt her too? Near the far side by the entrance, she set the rum bottle on the bar counter with trembling fingers.

Calm down, she told herself, she was in a roomful of men, with her father and brothers, the disturbing thug couldn't hurt her. She had noticed the angles in the man's hard face grow sharper, lids lowered further hiding his thoughts when Rueford had smacked her butt. All horrid men, Adranokov probably was thinking she, as a woman, had deserved the humiliating insult.

These mobster males believed women were property and to be treated as errant children, and of course as sex objects. Great. She couldn't wait to be alone with Rueford. He would probably lock her in an iron maiden when he wasn't home, and knock her around when he was.

Naithon answered Ignacio, his heavy accent all the more chilling at the guttural sound of it. "What I want, right now, while I ponder this truce, is that girl," he nodded to Kiri and said, "on my lap."

The room hushed, all eating and talking halted. The group looked to Naithon, then to Kiri, to Ignacio, back to Naithon. Naithon sat calmly with a bland expression, as if bored with it all.

Standing in the middle of the room, Rueford bristled, his ruddy cheeks reddened.

Kiri's face flushed at Adranokov's offensive request. He must be just trying to stir her father up, surely he doesn't really mean it.

Awkwardly getting to his feet, Ignacio spurted, "Ah, I- did I hear you correctly? You want my daughter-"

"You heard me. Now. Right now or this meeting is over," Naithon's quiet, deep voice whipped through the room.

53

Moving to where Rueford stood, "Hmm," Ignacio grunted, scratched his head, then his chest, then shrugged. "Well, I guess if that's what you want..." Disregarding the look of disbelief and horror on his daughter's face, he said coolly, "You heard the man, Kiritina, get over there." When she didn't move, he barked, "Now!"

Next to him, Rueford started to speak, Ignacio slashed his hand down telling him to shut up. Still Rueford protested, "She's *my* girl, he can't-" Ignacio sharply shushed him.

Kiri stood frozen on unsteady legs, no way was she crossing that room and sitting on that gangster's lap. He was only joking around to humiliate her father.

Naithon put his hands on the wheel rims. "I guess we're out of here."

"No, wait," Ignacio said quickly. "Janero, Piero," he jutted his chin at them. The brothers started, then, they trod over to their sister, each gripped an arm.

She gasped. "No, stop, what are you doing? I'm not going near that- that monster!"

Naithon's brow quirked as if amused at being called a monster. He tightened his fingers on the wheel rims.

Seeing he was really going to leave, Ignacio snapped, "Piero!"

The brothers tugged Kiri, she had to walk with them or she'd fall and be ignominiously dragged. "No, wait, listen-" she cried.

"Shh," Piero whispered in her ear. "Pacify the crippled bastard. He can't hurt you. He's just doing this to claim dominance over the meeting. It'll only be for a minute. Worst he does is feel you up a little. Just let him give your tits a squeeze or two and he'll be satisfied."

In her other ear, Janero murmured, "Don't worry, they say he hates when chicks try to sit on his lap, won't last a second." They pulled her across the room stopping in front of Naithon.

His eyes were so hooded she could barely discern them. God, he was going to maul her in front of all those men. Suddenly, Kiri found it hard to breathe, her lungs constricted, stomach tensed and flipped over. She tried to resist them, but her brothers forced her onto Naithon's lap.

As soon as her thighs landed on the plaid afghan, Naithon swung a surprisingly hard, strong arm around her, preventing her from getting back up. Terrified to look at the gangster, her body rigid, Kiri sat half-sideways and pushed at his arm and chest to break from his hold. He easily restrained her from moving off his lap.

Lowering her head without looking at him she murmured, "Please don't do this. He's already humiliated by losing the battle. Please, just call your truce, and let me go."

His arm tightened, hard, but not enough to crush the breath out of her. Her left arm pressed against his chest, she gripped the strong arm that held her with her right hand trying to pry if off her. Still pushing at him, she squirmed on his lap, he squeezed her to stop her wriggling. In seconds she realized why. The man was hardening under her thighs.

Kiri gasped in abhorrence and fought frantically to get off him, his arm only held her tighter. She stopped squirming, but it didn't seem to make a difference. The lump under her grew longer, harder. She could feel his nose push into her hair, she thought with revulsion, *oh my gosh, he's sniffing me like a hunting animal*!

The room broke out in uneasy conversation. Ignacio didn't know what to do. His daughter was sitting, cheeks bright red with embarrassment, on his enemy's lap. This last insult almost too much too bear, Ignacio slung off his glasses and daubed the napkin over his sweating face.

Adranokov's stony expression didn't change an iota. He just wrapped his right arm around Kiri's waist caging her, and splayed his large left hand possessively over her stomach. She tugged at his hand but it was like trying to open a locked safe.

Beside Ignacio, Rueford huffed and puffed, but he was not stupid enough to harangue Naithon Adranokov. The man could kill with one damned hand without getting out of that chair, for crying out loud. Rueford had to stand there like the rest of them and take the sneering disrespectful show of power. His blustery face so mottled with crimson in his anger, it matched his hair.

That's all it was, Ignacio sighed, a damned show of power. Little punk, thug. Convict. A true bastard in every sense of the word, his mother had been an unwed whore, his father's concubine. He turned his head from Naithon with a twinge of fear. He'd heard that Romanians were spooky gypsies with voodoo powers, if the fucker could read his mind, he's a dead man.

People got up and shuffled around the room, getting more to eat, drink, the atmosphere was uncomfortable as hell with Delducci and Adranokov in a face-off, and both Melonie and Fiereza shooting daggers of hate at Kiri.

Kiri's face was red as a beet in her mortification. The only one that seemed at ease in the entire room was Naithon. His thumb stroking Kiri's belly, he sat casually staring at Ignacio, making him speak first.

"Uh, well, then," Ignacio cleared his throat. "Let's talk about the truce. What can I do to stop your people from killing my people, razing my businesses?" He stared levelly at Naithon looking for a sign, a tell, that he was the least bit nervous, awkward. Nothing. The man was a steel rock. Zero expression, sable eyes blank of anything, everything. No light, compassion, mercy. Nothing. A killer's eyes.

He waited for Naithon to reply, and damn the man, he sat silent, his gaze steady on Ignacio. All the attention in the room was on Naithon with Kiri trapped on his lap. When she saw lust flare in many eyes as the males were mentally putting themselves in Naithon's place, Kiri resumed struggling, her face blushing with degradation and fear of what would come next.

She could feel the horrible gangster's strong arm wrapped around her, feel his heart beating against her arm. Feel his big hand spread over her stomach in a boasting show of possession. The scent of faint aftershave and soap still lingered, he must have showered right before coming.

Everything about the man was fully and totally masculine, from his broad, muscular upper body, strong jaw, eerie eyes, faint dark shadow on his lower face a contrast to his light hair, even his unused thighs felt firm and hard beneath her, as well as the thick erection that pressed into her bottom. Apparently power turned him on. She wailed silently to herself, *would this day never end?*

"Adranokov? What do you want?" Ignacio prompted him, it was too uncomfortable waiting for his response.

Naithon replied, "We have told you we are not responsible for the murders. But if you insist," a humorless, unpleasant smile curved his lips with the familiar cruel bent. He lifted the arm that held Kiri, and he stroked his huge palm over her shoulder and down her slender arm, drawing a shiver from her. She held her breath, waiting for him to forcefully grope her.

"I want this girl," he stated, and proceeded to pluck the pins from her hair until the mahogany ringlets tumbled down, covering her like a shiny curly shawl. He tossed the pins carelessly to the floor.

The room braked into sudden silence again.

"Excuse me?" Ignacio's brows arched to his hairline. Rueford's nostrils flared, his breath rushed out hard.

Naithon's men shifted closer to him. Kiri froze. The man was just taunting her father, this will be over soon, soon.

"I said," Naithon repeated calmly, "I will take this girl. She will come with me now."

One of Kiri's pins could be heard dropped in the aghast room. Melonie and Fiereza's mouths fell open. Piero and Janero's brows furrowed in confusion, was the man joking? Naithon's crew remained impassive.

Ignacio cleared his throat again. "I uh, I mean, what uh, do you mean? You want to take her for the night?" His lips pushed out in consideration, he shrugged with an arched brow. "I suppose that would be okay." Kiri's heart stopped.

"What!" Rueford shrieked. "You gotta be fucking kidding me, man, no way is she going with that gypsy piece of-"

"Not just a night. I plan to keep her," Naithon announced matter-of-factly. "She is my price for the truce."

Puzzled, Ignacio asked, "Whatt'ya mean, like collateral?"

Eyes bounced around the room, gasps and muttering prevailed. "Ignacio, man, *please*," Rueford begged, freckles spotting his round, tomato blotched face.

Ignacio said, "For what, Adranokov? A couple of days? A week? I guess we could let her go for a week if that's what you want."

"Ignacio!" Rueford bellowed.

Ignacio made a calming motion with his palms. "So he fucks her a couple of times and gives her back to you. So what?"

Rueford screeched, "But she's mine!"

"Uh, yeah. Listen Adranokov, that one is engaged. Why don't you take my other daughter? Keep her as long as you want."

Melonie's eyes popped, a grin lit her plain face. "Yes! Yes! I'll go, I'll go with you! I'll be your collateral!" She pushed through the crowd of stunned men.

"No. I'll have this one. We're leaving, now." Naithon lifted his jaw to signal Mazonn. Maz grinned at him, drew his weapon and started to move to keep the others away so Naithon could leave unheeded.

Everyone spoke at once. Melonie kept coming, Fiereza dug her nails in her husband's arm. Apparently, she was furious that although she'd jilted Naithon and married his brother, Misolav, she was upset he'd choose another woman right in front of her. He should have asked for her!

She didn't care that her husband was Naithon's brother, and that she wasn't a Delducci, ergo she couldn't be considered collateral. He still should have chosen her! Maybe he was just trying to make her jealous, of course, that's it.

In the commotion, while he was distracted, Kiri pushed herself off Naithon's lap and ran for the door, she was out and gone in a flash.

"Piero, go get your sister, bring her back," Ignacio ordered. He kept a hand clamped on Rueford's arm holding him from going after her.

"No, I'll get my property." Naithon calmly pushed the afghan aside and stood up.

Again the room was instantly silent.

"What the hell?" his brother Misolav muttered.

"You can walk?" his brother Novikav gasped.

58

"Since when?" his brother Vitalik squawked.

Naithon ignored them all and strode out the door, going after his prize.

Mazonn grinned with Yashin, he said to Misolav, "Took him almost two years to heal, get on his feet again. You didn't do a perfect job of it, Mislo." Mazonn's voice dropped dangerous and vengeful, "You didn't paralyze him. He's stayed in the chair to keep everyone off balance, underestimating him."

He chuckled. "The cops never look at him for our crimes, I mean really," he glanced at his friends who laughed with him. "Who would accuse a cripple of scaling a building or making a hit? Joke's on all of you."

Fiereza was stunned. "You mean he's- he can walk? All this time?"

His features degrading into a hateful sneer, Mazonn said, "What do you care, Fiereza you whore, you tossed him aside like yesterday's garbage when you learned Misolav would inherit the business, the money. Fuck you."

He waved his arm. "Yashin, Vlad, let's get the cars." He ordered three of their other men to prevent anyone else from leaving. Guns drawn, no one else in the room moved.

Chapter Nine

Outside, her heart in her throat, Kiri ran as fast as she could. She didn't have a car, her father kept her dependent on him, kept her isolated. Without her consent he appropriated her identification, and took over her bank account as soon as she'd landed in America.

She'd been driven to the distillery today. She couldn't go to the police for help; daughters of mobsters did not do that. With no money, no ID, and threats of imprisonment and beatings, she was trapped. There was nowhere for her to go, no one to help her.

But she was damned if she was going from the frying pan into the fire!

Frantically, she raced down the drive heading for the street. She thought she heard the tasting room door slam shut, she ran faster, rushing across the grass, no way was she going anywhere with that monst- "Oof!"

An arm flung around her waist, slinging her off her feet and around, and he dropped them both to the ground. Naithon took the brunt of the fall then rolled over forcing her on her back, and flattened her with his weight. A smirk lifted the side of his harsh mouth at her shocked eyes.

"You- you- you can walk? How?" At first she lay stunned, then realizing he was on top of her, she struggled to get out from beneath him shrieking, "Get off of me! Let me up!"

Naithon scoffed coolly in her dismayed face. "I can do a lot of things, little lamb to slaughter, that you are going to learn quite quickly." He maneuvered his hips between hers, intentionally settling his still burgeoning erection on her pelvis.

Bracing on his forearms, blond tufts flopped over one eye as he smirked down at her. Deliberately, he rubbed his chest on her breasts, humped her sex, grinning more broadly at the shock and terror that radiated from her rounded green eyes.

Her hits at his chest were useless; he didn't even flinch at them. She cried, "You're insane! Get off me, I am not going anywhere with you! Someone is sure to have called the police by now." Struggling under his weight, she heaved, "You should leave, run while you can, before they come and get you."

That brought a barked laugh from him. "Honey, you forget who's up in that building. There is not a soul in there that would call the uniforms."

"M- Melonie, my sister, my brothers, they'd call-"

He laughed again at her naiveté. "Your dear sister would rather watch you get hung from the gallows than help you. Your brothers know better than to thwart your father," the sarcastic mirth left his hard face, eyes narrowed with menace, he said coldly, "or me." He rolled off her and leaped to his feet then bent and grasped her arm pulling her up.

She wobbled unsteadily, he kept his fingers wrapped around her arm. "Come along, little lamb to slaughter, isn't that what they say?" He tugged her back up the drive.

She dug her heels in the tar. "No! I refuse to go with you, you can't make me!"

With a laugh, he paused, bent, and swung her over his shoulder. She landed with an 'oomph,' he placed one hand under her knees, the other splayed across her butt.

Screaming, kicking, hitting at his back, Kiri fought to get free.

After a few steps, he smacked his palm hard on her bottom. "Settle down, girl, I do not want to have to thrash that fine ass of yours, but I will if you keep fighting me." His boots thudded up the driveway, she kept hitting and kicking him, he swatted her again, several times, each one harder than the last. Still she struggled.

He growled with a stinging smack, "You want me to lift that skirt and yank those panties down and wail on your naked behind for all the world to see? Just test me, lamb," he hissed, "just test me."

He was crude and menacing, Kiri believed he would carry out his threat, she forced herself to hang limply over his shoulder.

When they reached his vehicle, she could hear more male chuckling and realized his friends were there waiting for him. They spoke in their own language, she couldn't understand what they were saying. But judging by the tone of their laugher it was ribald. Of course, he had forced her onto his lap, and she was now hanging over his caveman's shoulder like fresh kill, a chauvinist joke to him and his barbaric friends. Kiri cringed with mortification.

She heard a car door open, and Naithon let her slide to her feet. Breathless, she pushed at him and turned to run. "Uh huh," he remonstrated. The door was open on the right back passenger side. Grabbing her arms, he forced her into the limo.

As he climbed in after her, she caught a glimpse of his friends grinning foolishly at them. Naithon gave her a shove to move over for him. When she did and he slid inside, a man in a black uniform shut the door. She felt the limo rock as he climbed in front, the driver's car door slammed shut and the engine roared to life.

At least the other males weren't coming with them. Imagining gang rape about froze her mind with horror. Kiri didn't dare look at Naithon. He terrified her. Huge and aggressively strong, foreign and relentlessly angry. Her brothers had told her how ruthless, how bone chillingly vicious he was. Even while in the wheelchair he killed men by either breaking their necks, or garroting them with one hand.

Her gaze lowered to his hands, her stomach clinched. He had huge hands. Everything on him was big, including his manhood that he had shoved at her like a rutting beast when he'd had her pinned to the ground. Fearful of what he was going to do to her next, she quickly looked away and tucked herself as tightly into the corner as she could, facing the side window.

When they had travelled in silence for some time, she dared a peek at him. He had a computer on his lap, the keys clicked away under his broad fingers. He was calmly working while she sat there in abject terror. What a hideous beast.

He'd taken her as a mean joke, to provoke her father and now he could care less about her. But, she would take that as a blessing. Surely he'd let her go soon.

An hour passed and Kiri was strung taut with nerves. Finally she took the chance and asked in a small voice, "Why have you taken me? What do you plan to do to me?" She watched his fingers pause.

Then, he powered the computer down, closed the lid with a click and set it on the floor, and turned to her. Maybe he was just going to keep her locked in a room for a couple of days to make his point of superiority to her father then send her home.

Odd onyx eyes gleamed at her under those perpetually hooded lids. She felt like the duck swimming by the gator. He didn't move, but his weird demon's eyes trailed all over her as if she was nude. She felt her skin tingle with fright, her pulse raced. She curled into the corner of the left side of the limo seat from him as far away as she could get. He was clear at the opposite end of the long bench seat.

His voice cool, low, he asked in a quiet, coarse accent, "You want to know what I want to do to you?"

Kiri held her breath, no, she didn't want to know. Green eyes wide, mouth firmed with fright, she shook her head.

"Ah." His smile more profane than pleasant. "But you asked. So I will tell you. No," the smile turned licentious, "I will show you. I want this," he lunged across the seat at her.

"No!" she shrieked and held her hands up to stop him. As he came at her, she grabbed for the door handle and frantically tried to jerk it up, open it, she was going to jump out. It was locked. She wrenched at the secured lock but couldn't engage it.

"You stupid girl," Naithon snarled from halfway across the long seat. "The car is going at least 60 miles an hour, you would never survive the fall. What the hell is the matter with you?"

"It would be better than being here with you!" Kiri shrieked as he stalked to her, she thrust her hands out to stop him.

His body leaning into hers, Naithon brushed her hands aside and clamped his palms under her ribs. He lowered his head; his gaze dropped to the plush lips then rose back up to her frightened greens.

He growled, gaze flickering up and down her body, over her face. "I did not come today for the truce talk, little lamb," he said, "I came for you." His fingers were hard, like steel, he gripped her waist then shoved his hands up and grabbed her breasts.

Pressed hard into the corner, Kiri screamed and hit his arms, pushed at him. He groped her breasts, kneading them hard, roughly over her blouse, she whimpered at his ferocity.

He muttered thickly, "Wanted this, all of it, since that day at the fucking banquet. You were too young then, still a child, and then Ignacio spirited you away. But I couldn't get those green eyes out of my damned mind. Over the years every fucking time I saw you I couldn't get near you, you ran from me."

Her struggles were in vain, he was too strong, too big. His lips a breath from her mouth, he murmured, "And here you are, all grown up. And exquisitely perfect. I want to possess every damned part of you, outside...and in." His left hand released a breast and he moved it up, shoving his fingers into the back of her hair. He moved his other hand to grip her chin.

He yanked on her hair, forcing her head back, her mouth opened in protest, and he slapped his mouth over it. His kiss was forceful, brutal, just like him. He slanted his head and ate at her with a raging fever of hunger and desire. The rumbling sounds deep in his chest, an animal devouring its catch.

Kiri screamed into his mouth. Why wasn't the chauffer helping her? Of course the little door between the front and the back was closed. He wouldn't help her even if he did hear her cries for help.

His grip on her hair and jaw was so tight it hurt. His mouth tore at hers, he tasted, sucked, shoved his tongue down her throat and tasted her innocence and it enflamed him more. Gripping her harder, Naithon climbed on Kiri, he released her chin and shoved his hand up her skirt. He grabbed the top of her panties, wrapped his fist in them and started to tear them off.

"Sir," a tinny voice came through the intercom. "We're about there."

He didn't want to stop, he couldn't stop, he won't stop. Blood rushed in Naithon's head, he couldn't hear, couldn't think, he had to have her, now, right now. He'd waited the years, her father had freely handed her over, she was his, he can take her now. Ignoring her futile flailing and pushing at him, his mouth still consuming hers, he pulled her panties.

"Sir, we're heading up the drive," the tinny voice informed.

"Fuck," Naithon muttered curses in English and Romanian. It was the toughest thing he'd ever had to do, except for learn to walk again, but he slowly, gingerly removed his hands from Kiri's body.

Shifting off her, he tugged on his shirtsleeves to straighten his cuffs. Panting slightly, his eyes glassy and dazed never moved from her as he fixed his tie, his shirt, and pulled at his slacks to rearrange himself. Smoothed his hair with both palms.

Kiri was plastered against the corner of the seat and the door. Bosom heaving, her breaths fast and shallow, her arms rigid, hands planted on the back seat cushion. Those eyes that had done him in the first second he'd seen her at her father's banquet, now bulged in terrified hysteria at him. He grunted, clearly she didn't share his lust for her. Didn't matter, he had enough for both of them.

Naithon's gaze rolled down the front of her. If they hadn't arrived, he'd be inside her right now, pounding away, at his property. His. Snorting his contempt, fool Ignacio Delducci. He was keeping her for a night, *ja*, every night for the rest of their lives. She was his now, he owned her. Collateral, her nasty sister had called it.

Whatever, he was never giving her back so that redheaded fuck could destroy her. It had taken an enormous effort to keep himself from going at the stocky man and breaking his arms before cutting off his dick for touching Kiri so intimately. She had always been Naithon's, it had only been a matter of time.

Her chest still rapidly rising and falling with frantic breaths, she watched him stare at her, his dark eyes inscrutable. She couldn't read them, probably was a good thing. When his gaze stroked over her again, pausing on her breasts, then lower, she gasped and fixed her blouse. He'd pulled it out in his frenzied attack, she smoothed her skirt back down. She covered her mouth with her hand, he'd been tearing at her panties like a demented ravenous wolf.

The limo came to a stop, the engine shut off. The chauffer's footsteps on asphalt came along the back of the car, he opened the door then stood aside for them to exit. He held a hand to Kiri to help her out. She glared at it, then with Naithon pressing at her back, she set her trembling palm in it and allowed him to assist her to her shaking feet. The chauffer leaned in to speak to Naithon, and she ran.

There were woods, she headed towards them. Pedaling her feet as fast as they'd go, she raced to the cover of the trees. She could hide, she could-

His arm circled her waist and he lifted her in the air.

"No!" she screamed and thrashed at him. Naithon swung her around so her back was against his chest, wrapped his arm under her breasts and over her arms holding them down, he clamped a hand over her mouth to stifle her screams. He held her so tightly against his torso she couldn't move her head to shake his hand off.

"Okay, little girl, we aren't going on like this." He jerked her hard to still her struggles. In her ear he said harshly, "I own you now, little lamb, you are my property and you will not run from me again, you will not fight me, you will do what I say without argument. Is that clear?"

She held still for a second, then wrenched her body and tried to kick him. His arm squeezed across her so tightly, his hand pressed hard against her mouth, he crushed the breath out of her.

He shook her. "Enough. I said stop. Do you wish to incur my wrath, darlin'? You won't have ever seen anything like me, a junkyard dog with my rage unchained. I promise you won't enjoy it." He lowered his hand from her mouth to cup her chin, held the back of her head against his chest.

"Wh- what," she stuttered, angry and afraid, "are you going to punch me?"

His chuckle stirred the hair at her ear. "Don't be ridiculous. One hit from me and you'd be dead before you hit the ground, little delicate lamb. No. The way to handle wayward, disobedient females is to blister their asses until they can't sit for a month of Sundays. I have no problem disciplining my woman."

"You're- you're," she huffed, "I am not your woman! You have no right to take me from my home, assault me, spank me! You release me right now!"

"Calm down, my small cattle, I've told you, I own you now and you will do as I say."

She paused, blinked, frowned. "You mean chattel, not cattle, you idiot!"

"Oh, tomato, tomahto, whatever, now, you settle yourself down or over my knee you'll go," he shook her again. "Kiritina Delducci," his voice hardened, "trust me, I would not hesitate to bare your ass and wail on it until you surrender to my will."

Kiri hadn't eaten since the day before, she'd been in a constant turmoil about Rueford claiming her. Her brothers and cousins were being picked off one by one. Now this behemoth gangster threatening her. He molested her, her mind started spinning, he was squeezing her too hard, shaking her, her body fell limp.

"Ah, finally, you capitulate, you will submit to my commands." He went to set her on her feet, but her knees buckled. "What the hell-" he scooped her up in his arms. Her head lolled on his shoulder. "Hey," he shook her, she moaned indicating she wasn't unconscious.

"What are you playing at now, woman? I am tired of this game." He let her slide down his body to her toes, but she was still limp. "Kiritina?" Concern edged into his hard voice. Was she faking, going to make a run for it again, or was she ill? His fingers wrapped around her tiny waist to help steady her.

Kiri clutched his arms to hold herself up. "I'm okay," she murmured, her eyes closed. "Just tired, so tired, I cooked all night and day, scared, hungry. I…don't want to be here, with you. I want to go home."

Relieved for a second that she was just light-headed, not ill, his lips pushed out in irritation. "Well, lamb, you are here with me, and you are not going home. Ever. Your home is with me now. Cooperate with me, give me what I want and your life will be easy and pleasant, I will buy you anything your heart desires."

Still clutching his arms, her neck arched tipping her head back so she could look blearily up at him. "What…do you want from me?" Her long wavy hair brushed over his hands, felt like corn silk feathering his rough skin.

Naithon lowered his head, almost touched their lips, he breathed into her mouth, "I showed you in the car what I want. You. Me. Sex. Together. I plan to marry you to keep you from leaving me."

Auburn lashes flew up. "What? You're not serious! Are you schizophrenic? You're a nutcase!" Her little fingers dug into his arms. He smiled down at them.

"Why?" she yelled. "You can have any woman you want! Piero told me you have strippers hanging all over you constantly. Melonie, she was more than willing to go with you. You don't want me, you want to punish, what? My father? Humiliate him? Hah," she snorted. "You saw him hand me over to you without a missed beat. He doesn't care one whit about me. He plans to marry me off to Rueford Montoblanco."

"*Ja*, that prick with the red hair. No wonder he was all bent out of shape when I claimed you." His weird eyes narrowed at her. "Hell, he's got to be double your age, you can read sadistic letch all over his ugly mug. I heard he's into heavy S and M, the kind where he gets off on seriously torturing and injuring his, and I understand, nonconsensual submissives. Hands bound behind their backs, he restrains them naked against cages, pulls their tits through the bars and binds them so tight they engorge to the point of rupture, clamps their nipples until they bleed. What was your da thinking?"

Kiri cringed, sickened at his words, then sighed wearily and was unaware she laid her head on his chest. He was acutely aware of it.

She said, "I don't know what that S stuff is, but, Rueford owns prime land my father thinks he can get from him with our union."

"Hmm, I can understand that. But what does Montoblanco get out of-" he bit the words off. "Oh duh, he gets you." Naithon could understand that too, he'd set up a false meeting so he could get his hands on her himself. His lip twisted in disgust. "He's old enough to be your father. The prick's a twisted pig. You see, you will be better off with me. Now you will eagerly do as I say."

"I will not. I will fight you every inch of the way until you tire of me and let me go," her words were full of fire, but her voice was weak, small shoulders sagged, her knees wobbled.

"Uh huh, sure my little lamb for slaughter. Your da wants to put you on a silver platter for men to," he tipped his head down to look at her and growled, "devour." One side of his mouth curled up. "Hmm, *ja*, I want lamb chops on my plate for dinner."

She didn't get his innuendo, she was fatigued, her head was lowered still on his chest, he stared at the top of her head. The waning sunlight made her hair look like it had just been polished to brilliant cherry brown.

"Okay, let's go." He bent his knees and lifted her in his arms.

He carried her across the vast grounds, she'd run farther than she'd thought. When he reached the enormous house, like a castle, a fortified compound, he slowed, then stopped. A soldier opened one of the double front doors. The door was huge, heavy looking, Kiri doubted she could push it open herself.

Naithon said, "Here we are, Kiritina, home. There are always people milling about. My soldiers, friends, guards, and as your sister mentioned, women. My men need to let off steam, I allow the females to 'hang out' as you Americans call it. They are going to stare at you. Do you want me to set you on your feet so you can walk through the house with dignity and pride? Or shall I carry you?"

She had no desire to see the criminals and fallen women that littered his home. Kiri gripped a handful of his shirt. His chuckle hummed against her breast. "Carry you is what it is then."

He traipsed up the steps, his boots thumping on brick.

"Sir, shall I have one of the spare guest rooms made up?" A man was asking about her. *Lord, help me*, she prayed.

"No," Naithon responded, "I'm taking her to my suite."

She stiffened in his arms. "No, please," she whispered.

"Hush," he said. "You will go where I put you."

Then she could hear voices murmuring. As he stepped across the threshold, the murmurings grew louder, some sounded curious, others astounded. Kiri twisted in his arms and buried her face in his shoulder. His chuckle rumbled amused at her childlike behavior. "Just because you can't see them, lamb, doesn't mean they can't see you."

Voices surrounded her as he strode through the people that seemed to be gathering around them. Thank goodness she'd worn a long enough skirt to cover her bum.

"He can fucking walk!" Boisterous confounded voices rolled over each other in loud dismay.

"What the hell, who is he carrying?" A male voice asked.

"Hoy shit," a female shouted, "you can walk!" Then she grated angrily, "Yeah, who is she? Naithon, why are you carrying her?" Her voice grew fainter as he continued moving, she shouted, "Where are you going with her? You're not taking that bitch to your room!" Her voice thinned strident and then louder as she trampled after them. "You never let a woman into your room! Naithon! Wait, I'm coming too!"

Kiri burrowed her face into Naithon's thick shoulder. It sounded like the woman was gearing up for a fight, oh dear, what does that mean for her?

Naithon rumbled, "Blok, get Silver out of here. Have Elena bring up some food." He quipped, "Tell her no lamb chops."

Continuous shocked voices exclaiming stunned surprise at their backs, Kiri bumped in his arms as he carried her up steps. "No, let me down, let me go!" she cried, now frantically looking around. The higher up she went in the house the harder it would be for her to escape.

Chapter Ten

His grip under her knees and back only grew tighter, holding her in place. How had this happened? Kiri's brain screamed in captive frustration. One minute she was happy at school, was interning at jobs she loved, the next she's being carried up the stairs in the arms of some mobster freak who planned to do who knew what to her and she would be helpless to stop him.

Inexperienced to the max, Kiri still chided herself, she knew what he planned to do to her. He'd told her, sex. Forced sexual assault, because she will never submit to him, never.

Naithon Adranokov had the worst reputation in Louisiana for just pure brutality with zero mercy or forgiveness. His barbaric actions were practically legend. Clearly he took whatever the hell he wanted regardless of what anyone else thought.

The carpet under his feet was cream colored, even in her grinding fright she wondered how he kept it clean with all those people around. He was rich and powerful; he probably had armies of servants cleaning ceaselessly.

They travelled up four flights. A steel door at the end of a foyer blocked the entrance at the top. Juggling Kiri, he put his thumb to a pad on the door and it slid into the wall like a pocket door. As they passed through, it clanked closed behind them.

On the other side of the steel door, he turned to the right, Kiri saw to the left was a long corridor with many doors. The hall he traipsed down was long, too. That steel door in the foyer slammed any thought of her easily escaping right out of her mind.

He wasn't even breathing heavily as he carried her effortlessly. He was so strong, she wondered how he'd fooled so many people for so long that he was paralyzed. Including his family. She chanced a glance at him, and cringed. His hard features were coldly impervious, flinty cruelty threatened in those scary eyes.

At the end of the hall, he used his thumb again on a security pad and the door swung open, he trod inside. Her heart hammered against her ribs, she hadn't realized she was clutching his shirt again, her fingers tightened.

He walked through a sitting room made up of tans and browns and blues, heavy furniture but comfortable looking. An entertainment system covered a wall, fireplace another, a bar another.

Sofa and several easy chairs faced each other in a semi-circle. Big, sturdy, dark maple coffee table in the middle matched smaller tables in the room.

He trod down one of the several halls she saw, and then stepped inside a bedroom. He'd said he was taking her to his room. Why would he want to keep her there, in his personal space? Why not another room, a closet, the basement, where he could take her out when he wanted to play with her and put her back when he was done?

The lush ivory rug muffled his footsteps. The bedroom was huge, enormous bed near a balcony that could be seen beyond the glass doors. Dresser and other furnishings spit-polished and gleaming dark wood. Naithon carried her to the bed and set her down on it. Kiri immediately scooted to the side away from him and jumped up.

His dark blond brows lowered, lids slid down his eyes giving the stare he aimed at her disturbingly like that gorilla in the zoo that stood waiting, watching for a mistake, a minor lapse in security, and he would get you.

The probing look smoothed into inscrutable blankness as he tugged at the knot on his tie, got it loose, pulled the end down and off, and tossed it on top of a dresser.

Next went the suitcoat, he dropped that over the back of a settee by a window. When his fingers went to the buttons on his shirt, her eyes on his every move, Kiri started stepping backwards. A bell chimed.

Naithon left her for a moment then returned with a tray. He set the tray on a table. When he turned his attention to her, Kiri backed away, towards the door. The brows lowered again in irritation. "We are not playing any games, here, Kiri. I told you, you will do as I say. Stop moving away from me."

Her lashes fluttered rapidly with her panicked breaths, she turned and fled out the door and down the hall. She didn't make it to the end of the hall, he grabbed her hair. Twisting it around his fist he pulled her head, forcing her to look up at him.

Glaring stoically at her, he said coldly, "Last time you do that, lamb, run from me." Releasing her hair, he slid his hand under her hair and grasped the back of her neck, directing her back to the bedroom. By the time they returned, her body was in a full-out shake-down.

Pushing her to the bed, he let her go and said, "I have to speak with my men. There's food there for you." His gaze slid up and down her form, turning the shaking to a fierce shiver. He tromped to the walk-in closet.

Came back in a second with a long sleeved, button-down white shirt. "I didn't think to arrange for your clothes. I could borrow something from one of the girls, but," a shoulder bumped, "I don't know how you feel about thongs and nipple tassels." His lip twitched at the pink that flooded her face.

His eyes still on her, he laid the shirt on the bed. "I'll be gone a few minutes. You can shower in the bathroom," he nodded his head towards an open door. "When you're done, you will put on that shirt. I want nothing on you but that shirt. No bra, no panties, nothing. Do you understand?"

73

Kiri stood with trembling knees, glanced at the shirt then back to him and blinked anxiously.

Naithon dragged a finger over one eyelid and sighed. "Okay. I get that you're scared. But, Kiritina, you see, there is nothing you can do stop me from having you. No one will be coming to your rescue. You will find that you will be far better off here with me than with that redheaded swine. Just resign yourself to the task of pleasing me and everything will go easy for you."

She blinked more, then, "Pleasing you? You are totally irrational! What you are doing is wrong. Kidnapping me, holding me against my will, any...thing...uh, you plan on doing to me...it's wrong. Don't you see?"

His lip curled up on one side. "*Ja,* I do. But I don't care." His expression sobered, eyes narrowed. "Little girl, I'd been kicked around as a child, spent years on the street with a no conscience murderous gang, then endured years of prison savagery.

"Twice my old man took everything from me, leaving me with nothing. My brother stole my girlfriend and then made me a cripple. I had to build everything I have from scratch. In prison, a cellmate told me when I got out to contact this man that owned a whiskey distillery and he'd give me a job."

Kiri empathized, but still, he was going to cold-bloodedly assault her.

"It was back breaking work, he used me like a dog, beat me like a goddamned mule. I was on parole, I couldn't leave the job." He went on, "But I learned enough, and did some...below the law work shall we say, until I'd built up my own business again. No one ever gave me a damned thing, they just took and took. So," his hands tucked in his pockets, he shrugged, "now I take." Those devious gorilla eyes had turned to blank, deadly shark eyes.

Her arms crossed over her front, she wrapped her hands halfway around to her back as a full-body shiver rattled her. Involuntarily she took a step back.

"See that, that shit is what you are gonna stop." He prowled a foot to her, scowled with his whole face. "You will not run from me, or move away from me. You heard my men address me?" She blinked confused, then nodded. "And what do they call me?" He waited, she shuddered, he moved closer.

"Uh, B- Boss."

His boots planted akimbo, he unbuckled his belt, slid it out of the loops, her eyes stayed on it until he tossed it on a chair. "Do you know why they call me Boss?"

She shook her head. Terror was creeping back up her spine. Flight or fight was smacking her in the head, but she knew she dare not run. There was nowhere to go. He'd catch her in two strides like he'd just done. His chamber door was locked, as was the steel door that led to the stairs.

Shark eyes narrowed to mean slits, he told her flatly, "Because I am the boss. You know what that means, lamb?" When she didn't speak he barked, "Answer me!"

Kiri jumped, wrapped her arms more tightly around her body shivering with fright. "I, uh, not sure…"

The edge of his mouth quirked. "That means, I give the orders, and everyone follows them. You know what happens when people do not do as I command?"

Silently, she bit her lips and shook her head.

"Bad things, Kiritina, very bad things. I'm sure your brothers have shared with you some of my…punishments?"

She nodded, pulled her lips in and gnawed on them to still their trembling.

"So…" Crossing his arms he mirrored her. Although he was obviously angry, he was ten times calmer than Kiri. The shark eyes glittered at her from under slit lids. "That means," his deep, thickly accented voice hardened, "you do as I say. Or else…"

He watched the emotions ripple across her face. Fear, resistance, anger, fear. "Now that we've had this little talk, and I seldom repeat myself, I am going downstairs for a brief meeting. You are gonna eat," he indicated the tray on the desk, "clean up, use my toothbrush," his mouth twitched at her wrinkled nose at the order.

"You put that shirt on." He motioned with his head to the shirt he'd set on the bed. "No bra, no underwear, and you be in that bed," he lifted his chin to the bed, "when I return. If you don't do as I say, I will do it for you. Trust me, you will not like it. I'm doing you a favor, girl, just for tonight, allowing you to wear something in bed."

What an odd experience, he thought, first time he ever had to order a female to disrobe and get in bed. Usually they were tearing off their clothes, and his and climbing on him like monkeys after his banana.

Holding herself, Kiri's eye flit to the bed, the red blanched out of her face, her gaze lowered to stare at the shirt. *He's out of his mind-* When he spoke again, her eyes leapt up to his. It felt like he could hear her thoughts, read her mind, *oh*, another shiver rippled through her, and he saw that too.

"That belt," he jutted his chin to his discarded belt and said, "will be put to use on your ass if I come back and you aren't in that shirt, in that bed. We clear?"

She nodded miserably.

Naithon glared at her, her eyes stayed staring at the floor. He waited a minute, she didn't move. Without another word, he turned on his arrogant heel and the door to his chamber closed, then the lock clicked.

Chapter Eleven

Naithon went in search of Mazonn. Unfortunately that meant traipsing through the main floor to get to the back den his friends liked to relax in, play cards, billiards, drink.

His long legs strode quickly but he wasn't fast enough, Silver Dae Foxx darted out of a doorway. She'd been gossiping with a few other girls, exotic dancers they liked to be called. Naithon had other names for them.

"Naity, there you are!" Silver scurried to him, threw her arms around his neck. "Lord, what a shock we had seeing you *walking*, and then you were *carrying* that creature!" One hand moved to flatten on his upper chest. "We were so *stunned*! Blok filled us in since Mazonn said the cat was out of the bag. You are so clever, my baby boy." She reached up to comb her fingers through his hair.

Naithon caught her wrist and pushed her away and kept walking. He'd made an error in judgment fucking her. One day he had been home annoyed and tense. Normally he didn't do the talent in the house, but it was a nasty rainy day and he needed to relieve the tension and she was the first bitch to pass him.

The week continued long and rainy so he'd done her more than once. Now, the whore felt he was hers. She was showing up at his office in the city. He'd screwed a few other girls to get her off his back, but she still clung to him like frost on a glacier.

"Sugar," she pouted and hurried after him. Silver dashed around to walk beside him, her legs working extra hard to keep up with his. "Anyway, we were so surprised, and happy, we need to celebrate!"

He ignored her as he kept walking, she took fast steps to keep up. "Honey, sex was out of this world when you were paralyzed, it's gonna be dynamite now! Come, let's go to your room, we'll see how different it is," she grabbed his arm.

Naithon yanked it away and kept moving. Silver was almost jogging now. "Wait!" She hopped in front of him with her hands up to stop him. He did or he'd trip over her. "Honey," she wooed, "your bedroom. Now that you're banging other bitches there we can-"

"I am only going to say this once, Silver, so listen carefully." Shark eyes slit to such cold enmity Silver shut her mouth. He gripped her shoulders, crushingly hard, her face pinched in pain. His voice so chilled the words came out frozen, he said, "We will not be fucking ever again, Silver. I will not be with anyone except that girl I brought upstairs."

"But, but who is she? If you want it that way," Silver's shoulder lifted in a coy pose and an incendiary smile, "I can join you. Does she dig chick action? She like whips? Nipple pumps? We can bring in all the girls you want, Naithon, you have the stamina of a stallion. We can-"

He shook her so hard her head snapped. "I said," his words clipped and cold, "I am done with all of you, any of you. I only fucked a few of you, I can't even remember which ones. Doesn't matter, we are done. Now, get out of my way." He released her with a little shove and started walking again. The past few years he'd only been biding his time banging other females while he waited for the opportunity to get his hands on Kiri.

"No, but wait, Naity, come on, what's so special about her? I can do whatever it is that she does that turns you on so much! Just tell me her action, let me watch, I'll learn!"

His strides grew longer and faster.

Huffing to keep up, Silver cried, "Who is she? Who the hell is she? Naithon!" She screeched after him but he reached the den, strode inside and slammed the door in her face, locked it. The door muffled her shrieks but they continued on, along with her fists pounding on the door.

Taking a deep breath, he rolled his eyes at a chuckle. Turning around, he saw Mazonn lounging in a big chair, feet up on a hassock, a drink on the table beside him, European cigarillo clamped between his teeth.

"Sounds like Miss Silver Dae is having a bad day." Mazonn chuckled again, blue eyes mischievous. Silver's rants and pounding carried on.

Naithon snorted and moved to the bar to pour himself a drink. Once done, he carried it to a chair and plunked down. "She'll get tired in a minute and go away."

"What bug flew up her ass?" Mazonn asked, dragging on his cigar without taking it out of his mouth.

Naithon tipped a long drink down his throat then set the glass on an end table and lit his own thin cigar. A few tokes, watching the smoke spiral from his mouth, he shrugged. "I told her whatever unremarkable shit we were doing before is done now."

Mazonn squinted through the smoky haze in front of his face. "What does that mean?"

The screams and pounding diminished then ceased after one last bang, which sounded like a kick. Sitting back, Naithon set an ankle over a knee, sucked in a drag. "Fucking. I told her I was done fucking her and whatever bitches I did or didn't do before. I stayed away from most of them that hang here anyway, they get too clingy."

Pondering his words, Mazonn asked, "Why? You have more pussy dropped in your lap than there are stars in the sky. Why would you turn it away? Everyone else here has been through each bitch at least a hundred times around, and all the other strippers at the clubs that you turn your nose up at."

Naithon's lips twisted in revulsion. "Why would I want to stick my quill in every inkwell that every other male here and more has?" He shook his head, sipped his vodka. "I have what I want. Took a while to get it, but I got it and I have less than zero desire to shove my dick in any other cunt."

79

Brows arching, Mazonn's lips pushed out. "By 'it', you mean the girl, Ignacio's daughter? I thought you took her just to screw with him. You aren't seriously thinking about…banging her? I mean, you forced her to come here bro, she was clearly petrified when you tossed her in the limo."

Lids lowering, Naithon glanced briefly at his friend. "I told you why I was taking her. You were all well aware of my intentions. Why are you surprised I have her in my bed?"

Mazonn studied his friend. Naithon had told his men, his friends, that he was going to take Ignacio's daughter, by any means. The meeting was his opportunity. He had made a plan on how to take her easily, without harm or gunfire, and Ignacio had fallen right into his hands, as had his daughter.

Naithon hadn't gone into depth about his attraction for the girl with his friends, he hadn't needed to, it flamed out of his eyes every single time at the sight of her, but he hadn't given them details. Just that he wanted her.

Mazonn asked, "Ah, so, what does the girl think about all this? She didn't look too happy being on your lap or stuffed into the car. If I recall, she ran from you."

One shoulder bumped with indifference. "She isn't. So what. I took her for my wants, not for hers."

"Hmm." Mazonn drank carefully, took a slow drag, sucked in the smoke, blew it out. "Is she willing to have sex with you? She didn't look the type to bed hop with just any dude that asks her."

"She isn't. And no one is asking her."

Mazonn's head tilted back in misgiving, blue eyes narrowed. "You planning on taking her against her will?"

Naithon's shoulder bumped again, he didn't respond.

Mazonn set his drink down, laid the cigar in an ashtray and stood up. He wore grey trousers and a black sweater, he stuck his hands in his pockets and looked with serious intent at his friend. "Ah, Nait, bro, they call that rape."

Staring at his cigar in his hand, Naithon didn't reply.

"You never have done that before…"

"Didn't need to. Never had one I wanted bad enough to force if she declined. Never been declined."

"Apparently there's a first time for everything. Did you ask her if she wanted to fuck you?"

"Hmm," smoke trailed out of Naithon's nose and mouth. "She has made herself quite clear, no, she does not."

Maz waited, when Naithon didn't continue, he said, "Well then?"

Naithon shrugged again.

"Nait, are you seriously considering forcing yourself on this girl? The word is Ignacio claims he's kept her a virgin, man."

"Even better."

"She's gotta be terrified out of her mind, Nait. You really plan on taking her when she is unwilling?"

Naithon silently sipped his drink, tapped the cigar ash on the ashtray beside him on an end table.

Thinking carefully, Mazonn said quietly, "Listen," he moved nearer to stand in front of Naithon. "You want this girl long term?"

Naithon looked up at him through a lock of fallen hair. "*Ja.*"

Both brows rose in surprise then lowered. "Like in forever?"

"*Ja.*"

"Whoa, shit, I didn't..." Mazonn forked long fingers through his hair. "I knew you had the hots for her, I never thought...you mean like forever forever?"

Naithon's lip twitched. "*Ja.* Forever and ever. I will marry her. She will carry my babes."

Mazonn looked at him like he'd grown three heads. "Whoa, I feel like I just fell back a few centuries, like into barbarian times. This ain't like you, bro. Why do you want to marry her? Why not just do her and send her home? Ignacio won't squawk that you fucked her, even if she didn't want it, he knew what would happen once he allowed you to take her."

"Can't explain it, Mazonn. Second I saw her I knew I wanted to be looking at that face for the rest of my life. The thought of another male's hands on her," a scowl darkened his face, his fist clenched the glass.

He told him, "If I'd been able to get at her sooner, I would have already taken her. But Ignacio had her stashed away somewhere in Italy. I've only seen her briefly and infrequently, yet each time I have only grown more captivated with her."

"She was too young before for you to snatch her, Nait. And now she's an adult and she doesn't want you."

"Don't care." Naithon raised his head, the corner of his mouth lifted. "She will be mine for life, bro. It may take some time, but she will eventually get used to it and settle down." His snort mocking, "And, Ignacio didn't *allow* me to take her, I just let him think he was."

Mazonn's dark brows drew together. "Didn't Delducci say she was engaged? You're stealing her from her fiancé?"

"Her da was forcing her to marry that fat ugly pig with the red hair. I don't give two shits about his claim on her. Fuck him."

Mazonn considered his words, then said, "Why all the trouble with this one? It'd be easier to choose a woman already familiar, comfortable with a man's ways. A broad tough enough to handle this life, one able to deal with your roughness. You're hardly the gentlemanly flowers and candy, regular Joe kinda guy, ya know? Plenty of bitches we know would love to hitch their wagon to your star."

Naithon's lips pursed in distaste. "I do not care for the...modern woman that throws herself at every man, bold, brazen, promiscuous, I prefer to do my own choosing. You will find it amusing, my friend, the cutthroat that I am, but...I want a...lady. Kiri is my perfect lady."

That brought a surprised grunt from his friend and a raised brow.

"*Ja*, surprised myself too. Considering my upbringing you would think I wouldn't want to be in the same room with a real lady. They are so...dainty. Not sure how to treat one. Anyway, I do not like it when females chase me. I want to do the...hunting and chasing, the conquering. Kiritina Delducci is my catch, my choice, my...captured prey."

"Hell, bro, she's not a fucking rabbit. She's a girl, not something to be hunted and captured, kept caged and fucked as you desire."

Ignoring him, Naithon went on, "I will conquer her, Maz. I don't care how old-fashioned it is, I am the older, experienced male, I will teach her, that's the old way, that's the way it should be done. She is young and untried, it is my job to guide her, discipline her when needed."

"Wow. Kinda chauvinistic and macho, but, uh. Okay, well." Mazonn's brain trying to work out his friend's intentions, he blinked, then said, "Nait, would you rather she opened her arms and legs freely to you with real desire?"

"Sure, of course."

"Bro, if you rape the girl, she will hate you for life. She will never like you, forgive you, or trust you."

"I didn't take her to be friends with the bitch, Maz. Don't care if she doesn't like me, she doesn't need to trust me, just do as I say. She can resist me all she wants, it'll still be the same in the end."

Staring thoughtfully at Naithon, Mazonn, said, "That broad is a sweet, gentle, gorgeous young babe. If it were me, I'd want her hands on me as eagerly as I want them on her. You feel me? You rape her once, every time after will be the same. You will have to fight her every time, hurt her over and over. She will never give you her sweet self. She will turn to other men to help her." He stopped talking, went and sat back down. Settling back in his chair, he set an ankle over a knee and picked up his drink.

Anger flashed across his fierce face, Naithon snapped, "She will never be with another man. I will kill anyone that goes near her." His temper starting to build, then, Naithon's eyes went blank as he thought about what Mazonn was saying. He pictured a terrified, crying, fighting, closed up Kiri as he held her down and pushed between her legs, forcing his way into her dry channel.

Then, he imagined a different picture of her face with a pretty smile, arms open welcoming him, eyes hazed with passion for him, lips ready for his kisses. He imagined telling her he wants a blowjob and she smiles and eagerly hops to it. If he rapes her, huh, he'd rather see her smiling up at him with his dick in her mouth than angry and gagging. He said confidently, "She will learn to like fucking with me."

"Uh huh. So, what are you gonna do if she says no?"

"She will do what I tell her."

"Hmm. You gonna keep her locked up 24/7? 'Cause a girl kept prisoner and sexually assaulted is gonna try to escape."

A rueful grunt, he admitted, "Already tried. Couple of times, and tried to jump out of the moving car."

Mazonn's brows hit his hairline. "No kidding? Feisty."

Naithon nodded grimly. "*Ja*, and reckless when scared."

"Means she'll do something stupid, get herself hurt."

"I know. Plan on keeping her secured now that I have her here. Delducci's going to want her back, and that fat red-haired pig her da engaged her to will come for her. Whoever is hitting our people may try for her. Especially if they know she is a weakness for me. If they can't kill her they'll snatch her to use her to manipulate me. She's staying under lock and key. She is going nowhere."

"Well, you-"

Naithon stamped his cigar out, emptied his drink, set the glass down with a thunk and stood up. "I told her to be undressed and in my bed by time I get back, or I would whip her behind with my belt until it blistered."

"Geez, Nait-"

"Gotta go." He traipsed out not seeing his friend shaking his head.

Chapter Twelve

He strode with his head down, hoping Silver didn't come after him. He was already pissed off from his conversation with Maz, he wouldn't treat Silver gently if she bugged him now. He took the stairs two steps at a time, all four flights.

The steel door swooshed open and closed behind him. Moving quickly down the hall, he frowned, muttered, "That little girl better have done what I told her. She thinks I'm bluffing she won't be sitting for a week."

He visualized her naked butt lying over his lap and spanking her. Once she'd learned her lesson, he would stretch her thighs apart and feel if she was the kind of woman that got wet when spanked, a little light pain mixed with pleasure can produce amazing orgasms.

A raging hard-on pressed at his pants as he reached his chambers. Printing his thumb on the secure pad, the door unlocked with a click. He closed it behind him. The place was dead quiet. She couldn't have gone anywhere the suite was as secure as Fort Knox.

Before he'd gone to the meeting at the rum house, knowing he was bringing her back with him, he'd removed anything that could be used as a weapon against him, even the steak knives in the kitchenette. But the thought of that tiny dainty thing harming him was a joke.

His boots tramped down the hall to the bedroom. Holding his breath, he stepped inside. The room was dark, she hadn't turned a light on. Naithon moved to the bed, he could see her small form curled up as far to one side as she could get without falling off the edge. The blanket and sheet were up over half her head. Well, she got in the bed. Time to see if she followed all his orders.

Naithon slipped into the bathroom and cleaned up. His toothbrush was wet, she'd used it. Probably figured since he'd had his tongue halfway down her throat what was the difference. He'd have one of his staff purchase her own things for her tomorrow.

He pictured girly shampoo and soap, makeup and whatever else women used lining his shelves. The thought should have given him the willies. It did not. He'd anticipated for so long having her, he couldn't wait to see her things in his space. Things he bought her, not her things from the Delducci home.

Changing into a t-shirt and pajama bottoms, he turned out the light in the bathroom and reentered the bedroom padding in his bare feet. He wanted his naked skin on her naked skin, but he allowed her one tiny concession, at least for tonight, his shirt to protect her chaste modesty, and his body swathed as well.

Seeing the covered plate on the tray sitting on the desk, he went over and lifted the lid. An irritated frown tugged his mouth down. She hadn't taken a bite. He knew she was hungry. He hadn't taken his eyes off her since she'd entered the tasting room. Her sister ate like the cow that she was, but Kiri had not stopped serving the men to eat. She had told him earlier when she was limp in his arms that she was tired and hungry…and scared. Maybe too scared to eat.

Well, that doesn't mean she won't do as he instructs her. She's small enough as it is, she really can't afford to lose any more weight. Clearly the time she's been home with that perverse family of hers has taken its toll on her health. At least the glass of milk was empty.

Sighing, Naithon stepped away from the desk and to the bed. Lifting the sheet off Kiri, he smiled. She was wearing his shirt, legs and feet were bare and she was curled up tight in a fetal position. Like that was gonna stop him from touching her.

Naithon slid onto the bed and reached for her. Looping his arm around her waist he pulled her to him. She didn't wake, her breathing stayed soft and steady. He ran his palm down her back, and was pissed. She hadn't removed her bra. Damn, he was going to have his hands full with this stubborn female. Sliding his hand up the back of her shirt, his shirt actually, he unclasped her bra and slid it through one rolled up sleeve then the other.

Tossing the offending lingerie to the floor, he stroked his palm down her back to her ass, and now he was really mad. Panties. He could feel the silkiness of the material. He curled the top and bottom in his fist and wrenched them. The silk tore and he ripped them off her body, the ruined underwear landed on the floor. And, now she woke. He felt her turn rigid in his hands.

Before she could react, Naithon moved Kiri to lie on her back. Bracing on one forearm next to her, he slid his leg between hers, locking her in place.

"M- Mr. Adranokov, what, I mean," she blinked the sleep from her eyes. She was disoriented. He watched her lashes flutter, those beautiful large green eyes still drowsy bounced from him hovering over her, to around the room.

At first she was confused, didn't know where she was, how she got there. Then she blinked and blinked, swallowed. When her small hands came up between them and pushed at his chest he knew she recalled the events of the day. "Get- get off of me, I need to go home," she ordered and pushed harder at his chest, as if she could move him if he didn't want to be moved.

His voice husky with need that was building in his lower extremities, Naithon growled, "You don't give the orders in my bed, woman. Let's get that straight right now." He observed the panic flare in her eyes as she realized she was truly trapped. He lowered some of his weight on her forcing her hands to move off his chest.

"O- okay, then," she stammered, her hands now pushing at his shoulders. "Let me up and you won't have to concern yourself how I act or what I say. You've had your day with me, I'm going home now. You have no claim on me, my virginity will be for my husband."

He could feel his body seethe with jealous rage, her thinking he would send her home to marry that deviant redheaded blimp. He would kill that fucker before he'd let Montoblanco put his hands on her, his dick in her. Kiri has a lot to learn about Naithon, how he takes what he wants, keeps what he wants. She is his now, she is never going home, she needs to get that through that beautiful thick head of hers.

Naithon allowed a slight tug to his lip. "I think I was pretty direct, lamb, about our situation. If you have any confusion of my plans," his gaze rolling over her figure showed his intentions crystal clear.

"I will reiterate what I told you in the car and earlier here if you'd like. But," his gaze stroked over her body again, he said, "I'm pretty sure you can figure out that you are in my bed, lying under me, dressed in my shirt, sans underwear," his brows drew down at the reminder of her disobeying his orders. Seeing the color leave her face, she remembered his threat if she didn't do as he had ordered. "That you don't need me to clarify, eh? Your virginity is mine, Kiritina, mine."

She blinked hard, her hand moved to her hip and the color flooded her cheeks when she realized he'd removed her underwear. The embarrassment and fear pebbled her nipples, he could feel them harden against his chest, and that made him shift his own throbbing member. He could tell the second she realized his erection was thick against her thigh. The color in her face deepened, her breaths rushed.

Shoving at his shoulders as hard as she could she demanded, "Get off of me right now!"

His deep chuckle and non-movement was his answer. "I want to see what I purchased." Naithon leaned back, fingered the bottom of her shirt.

"No! Stop, I am not a-a purchase, you can't force me to-to-" she shouted, started struggling so frantically with elevating terror, Naithon feared she was going to injure herself.

"All right, lamb, calm the fuck down." Naithon grasped her wrists and staked them to the mattress, moved his leg to hold hers down. Nonetheless, her body thrashed and humped and twisted under him, her cries stifled as he pressed his body more tightly on her.

"Kiri, calm down. Listen, just…" he took a breath, let it slide out. His fingers squeezed her wrists, he tried to hold them carefully or he'd break the fragile things, but she fought so hard. Maybe he should just spread her legs and thrust inside, get it over with. She'd be okay with it once her fear of how it would feel would be gone.

Mazonn's words came back to him, she'd hate him if he forced her. His lips pulled in, he didn't care, he'd take what he wanted. But, he'd likely hurt her, a lot. She's small and unused, she'd be bone dry from her fright, and he's a big man. No matter how carefully he did it, he'd hurt her. Well, that's what KY and shit is for.

He never cared about the female's part in sex before, it never entered his mind if he pleased them, only about getting what he wanted. Even so, he did pleasure some of them just because he felt like it. Most of them wanted the rough ride he gave them. But this girl, he looked down at her big, wide terrified eyes, tears rolling over her plump cheeks.

She had no chance of getting away from him yet she still fought like a wild thing. "Leave me alone!" Her chest heaved with panicked breaths and her fighting him, voice tight with fear she cried, "Don't touch me, let me go!"

Growing exasperated with this untenable situation, inevitably he was going to take her, why is she making such a fuss? Naithon said quietly, "Kiri, calm yourself. Listen, for tonight, a deal. You let me kiss you without giving me a hassle and I won't…force myself inside you."

His words and cool voice, and because she knew she had no hope of getting away from him, Kiri sniffed, endeavored to stop fighting him. Her limbs rigid, she peered up at him with suspicion. "That's all? Just a kiss?"

His dark eyes tapered in annoyance at her denying him, he was even angrier that he was allowing her to. "What the hell is the big deal, Kiritina? Sex is natural between people."

"*Uh,*" she grunted, furiously shoving her hips up at him hard, a last effort to buck him off her, and then was sorry she did. His iron hard, thick rod pressed hungrily back at her, expressing how badly he craved her. "Between consenting adults, Mister, this is absolutely not consensual."

Her words made him sound like that vile pig she was engaged to. But Naithon wouldn't torture or seriously hurt Kiri. "You are wearing my patience, girl," his warning growled, eyes thinned crossly at her. Kiri turned her head to face away from him.

With anger tingeing his low, accented voice he said, "Obviously I can do whatever I want. I've offered you a compromise," *what the hell, since when was that word part of his vocabulary*? "Now, look at me. Kiri," his voice deepened in steeping irritation when she didn't.

"I won't say it again," he threatened flatly. He was being lenient with her but that would only go so far. Slowly she positioned her head back facing him, and raised her eyes up to his.

Naithon released a wrist to capture the side of her face and hold her still for his mouth to seize hers. He licked her lips then bit at them. The kiss he'd taken from her in the car had unbelievably blazed through him like a struck fuse of a dynamite stick, lighting up and sizzling every atom in his body.

He hadn't stopped thinking about it for a second. Even while conversing with others he still tasted her on his tongue, his lips, and he couldn't wait to do it again. He had almost convinced himself it had been a fluke, but no, he wasn't even inside her mouth and his body burned.

"Open your mouth," he breathed against her lips. He licked at them, sucked the upper then the lower, they remained stubbornly closed. "Do as I say, little lamb or I will rescind our compromise."

Naithon was perplexed that he wanted to kiss her so badly, he seldom kissed other women, to him it was more intimate than sticking his dick in her. He pressed against the side of her mouth with his thumb, she reluctantly parted her lips and he dove in like plunging from a high wire.

The more voraciously he kissed her, ate at her mouth, the more she squirmed. Naithon clutched both sides of her head, slanted his head and drove deeper, a diabetic on a sugar rush. Kiri was soft and so tasty if he could literally eat her he would. If she knew what her squirming was doing to him she'd lay still as a board.

Those lush tits pressing into his chest, rubbing, smearing across his pecs, her rounded hips writhing against his in her distress. In her innocence she didn't realize they were basically dry humping. Nothing but his thin pajama bottoms separating them, she wore no panties, he could be inside of her in a flash.

Needing to catch his breath, and cool a degree or he would shoot off like a rocket, he licked across her mouth and panted into her neck. Still she squirmed, he sucked her neck hard enough to make her whimper, then he leaned back to take her in. Breathless herself, Kiri gasped and pushed at him.

A smile drifted across his face, she was so inexperienced she wasn't even aware how his kisses had affected her. Her cheeks were flushed, eyes half closed, the green glimmering in decadence from under the thickened lids. She licked her lips and he about went over the edge.

Feeling the way that she looked, dazed, over the top aroused, he grasped at the top button on her shirt. Clumsy in his haste and searing lust, his big fingers moved awkwardly opening the buttons. Then she realized what he was doing and grabbed his wrists.

"Stop! What do you think you are doing?"

He blinked eyes swimming in turbulent arousal, and kept at the buttons. Accent so thick she could barely understand him, he muttered with a rasp, "I want to see what is mine," and he tugged open another button.

"Wait! No, wait, you said kiss, you said only a kiss! You said you wouldn't force me, you wouldn't have sex with me!"

"Darlin'," eyes gleaming in lusting fever, his mouth lifted in a lopsided grin. "I said I wouldn't fuck you, I didn't say anything about looking at you, touching you. That is all part of kissing." He spread apart the halves of the blouse he'd gotten open almost to her navel, and leered down at his prize. Her chubby breasts were well more than his big handfuls.

"See, your pretty tits want my attention, see how your nipples are hard for me?" Naithon dropped his head and sucked a pebbled nipple into his mouth.

"No!" Kiri shrieked and hit at him. "You promised me you wouldn't!" She resumed her struggles, fighting him off.

It was hard for him to enjoy what he was doing with her little fists pounding at him. "Dammit, Kiri," he groaned. Lifting his head, he tried to drink in his fill of his gorgeous collateral, but she punched at him. That only made her breasts jiggle and fan the heat of his desire to touch her. Holding both her wrists above her head, he slipped his hand in her shirt and went to clutch a breast, she shrieked, wrenched a hand loose and hit him in the head.

Laughing, it was kind of funny. The most feared man in the state, and beyond, and the tiny chit was hitting him, trying to fight him off her. He could have his pick of a million women, they were always throwing themselves at him. Sometimes they just dropped to their knees, exposed their tits to him then proceeded to undo his pants. Without a word, well, they simpered and such, but total strangers, just did their bloody best to please him. Because they wanted more. Sometimes he gave it, sometimes not.

It was ironic really, the only woman he had ever wanted with his entire body and soul, and she couldn't bear his touch. But she would. She would learn to want him, do as he ordered. But she was almost in hysterics now. Naithon grasped her wrists, "All right, stop, little lamb, no more."

He let her go and her fingers gripped the sides of the shirt and she yanked them closed covering her breasts from his sight. Hell, he hadn't even gotten a good look at them. Again, the thought crossed his mind of just stripping her, splitting those young legs apart and slamming inside. It would be easier if he bound her, then he could look and feel his full without her interfering.

As if seeing the bold, burning lust in his eyes and reading his mind, she whispered, "Please," her voice wobbled, huge eyes filled with tears. "Please don't."

His sigh laborious, Naithon shifted to lie down on his side. Speaking quietly, he said, "Okay pigeon, calm yourself. Lie on your side, face that way," he motioned for her to turn her back to him. "Go on, I won't hurt you."

Buttoning her shirt, lips bunched, Kiri scrutinized him with suspicion through low lashes, he appeared sincere. Huh, that attribute would never be used to describe him. Yet, he wasn't touching her when clearly he could do as he pleased to her. She rolled on her side, pulled her knees up.

"Okay," he shuffled a bit, then curled his arm around her and pulled her to his chest. She jumped and tried to move away from him, he tightened his arm. "Hush little lamb, I promise I won't attack you tonight, I'm just going to hold you."

Naithon bent his knees to settle under the curve of her legs. Trying to keep his erection from touching her and freaking her out all over again, his nose in her hair, he contentedly inhaled her fresh scent. She smelled irresistibly amazing, like no other woman, there must be some truth to those pheromones the scientist spouted.

It took a long time for her breathing to slow again, for the rigidity to leave her body. When it did, he moved his hand under the front of her shirt and cupped a breast. *Ja*, like pillows of silk, she felt like home. He was lowered to copping feels while his captive slumbered, yet, for the first time in his life he felt good, felt right with the world. Finally, he had her in his house, in his bed. Then, although his dick was hard as cement, he fell asleep.

Chapter Thirteen

The dawn's light peeking in around the curtains woke him. At first Naithon was confused, a woman was curled up in his arms, he never allowed a female in his room, much less to actually sleep with him. Then, he inhaled, ah, and relaxed. It was his little collateral.

During the night they had moved around, he was now flat on his back and she was curled up on him, her top half on his chest, arm flung across his stomach, a leg tangled in his. Her naked sex pressed on his hip; his hand clasped a bare butt cheek. Okay, this was the way he wanted to wake up every day for the rest of his life.

Squeezing the round, firm cheek, Naithon stroked a hand up her side to palm the side of her breast. She snuggled into his embrace. Nice. It was time he saw what he had stolen from Rueford Montoblanco.

Carefully, he rolled her onto her back, started on the buttons again, the shirt almost all the way open he impatiently pushed it up fully exposing Kiri's top half to his complete viewing pleasure.

The sheet still covered her lower body, he'd examine that next. He'd been semi-hard from waking up with her in his arms, her lying on him. Now, he was like granite. Granite that wanted inside that little girl. *Ja, right the fuck now.*

Studying the sight laid out beside him, Naithon moved to his knees to get a better look. Delicious fat breasts, perfectly round, perfectly tipped with gumdrop nubs. His hand started to move to feel them when his gaze lowered. He moved the sheet down. "Ah, fuck, little beauty," he moaned. So young, so painfully gorgeous. Slender legs joined at the sweetest pussy he'd ever seen. He leaned towards her and cupped her mound.

And she turned rigid, eyes shot open, with a squeal she jerked away from him. Kiri managed in one movement to land on her hands and knees a foot away from him, the shirt fell down over her hips.

"What do you think you are doing!" she shrieked so loud it hurt his ears. The sight of her took away the pain though. The shirt was mostly open, those hot breasts dangled like fresh fruit, nipples hard from the cool air. Bad thing was the shirt bottom covered her lower parts.

He said, "Listen, sweetheart," and pushed some pillows against the headboard and shifted to half lie on them, one arm bent under his head. "You were the one that was lying on top of me, not the other way around. I kept my word, you on the other hand," he wriggled an eyebrow at her open blouse. "Well, I guess I'm the one that's not safe, eh?" He almost burst out laughing at the appalled look on her face.

Kiri lowered her head and saw her shirt wide open exposing her breasts to him. Red flamed up her face, she snatched the shirt closed. "I most certainly was not lying on- on you. You are a degenerate, a- a depraved monster! Stop laughing at me!"

He couldn't help it. Damn she was hot. Hair all bedroom mussed, cheeks red with mortification, lips still puffy from his aggressive kisses last night. Bosom heaving, she could have tumbled right out of a romance novel. And, he wanted her so badly his body ached. But, not yet, he couldn't take her yet. Blink an eyelash at her and she'd be all screaming and fighting again.

Besides, he had a meeting he needed to get to and he was already running late. He'd take the time later to tame his wild lamb. Teach her, show her who was the boss, and how to please him.

Naithon rolled off the bed to his feet. She made a small defensive sound, he turned around. Kiri looked like a sensuous tiger, on her hands and knees, tousled hair fluffing around and over one eye. If only he had time right now to play with her, start some lessons on how she would behave with him. Alas, he sighed. "I am taking a shower. I will be out for a meeting. I will have a servant bring you clothes and retrieve you for breakfast."

Unmoving, she eyed him with suspicion.

The corner of his mouth nicked up. "Unless you'd rather be naked, I'm up for that. Or," his lids levered down like that hunting crocodile, "you may join me in the shower if you'd like." He almost laughed out loud at her mouth opening astounded then flatten in repulsion. *Hmm, she'd better adjust that attitude, and soon.* "I'll leave the door open if you change your mind."

As he expected, he showered and shaved alone. Naithon exited the bathroom with a towel around his waist. First thing he noticed was the bed was empty, his ears and senses automatically fine-tuned. He could feel her presence, hear her rapid breaths behind the door. He kept moving towards the bed, letting her play out her plan. Quick pads of bare feet rushed at him.

Kiri ran up behind him and held a knife to the front of his throat. Stupid him, leaving it out on the table. He'd put his other weapons in the lockbox under the bed. How unexpected of his brave little lamb. She had to stand on tiptoes to reach around and up, she was more likely to hurt herself than him.

"O- okay, now, Mr. Adranokov, you- you are going to go to the front and unlock the door and then the steel one. I'm go- going to stay behind you, if you try anything, I'll have to- to hurt you," her voice shook and raced with apprehension. He was too tall and too broad shouldered, she couldn't hold the pose. Lowering to her the soles of her feet she moved the knife to prod his back.

A flash, and Kiri found herself lying on her back on the bed and Naithon straddling her. He held her hand and was forcing her to hold the knife at her own neck! "No! How did you- Mr. Adranokov, please-"

"Please what, my pet?" He leaned over her, his wet hair flopped in his eyes. He held the knife firmly against her skin. "You were going to kill me, my sweet lamb. Maybe you're not so sweet, eh?"

"No! No, I wasn't going to harm you, I just wanted to leave." Big frightened eyes batted at him, she lay not moving a muscle, only her chest rose and fell with her terror.

A hint of a smile, the attacker was more frightened than the victim. He tossed the knife onto the dresser with a clatter of metal on wood, and lowered his body closer to her. Still on his knees, he straddled her but didn't touch her.

"Let this be a lesson for you, lamb. I lived with a vicious gang and survived hellish prison. There are very few that can take me on, and tiny delicate females are certainly not in that league." The towel stretched across his thighs, a blush colored her cheeks. Well, he was a man, it wasn't like he was used to sitting in a skirt.

"Please, Mr. Adranokov, I'm sorry. I won't do it again."

"*Ja*, you are correct. You will not do something so foolish again. You could have been seriously hurt. You pull a weapon on a man you better be sure you are in complete control of it, the man, and the situation. Or they will do to you what I just did, only they may carry through with the deed. We on the same page here?"

Kiri nodded silently. Her gaze traveled the length of his bare chest, over the rocky pecs covered with surprisingly dark hair. Tattoos ran down his arms and part of his neck to his back. Her lips pulled in, they were not pretty tattoos. He watched her studying his body.

"You can touch anything you want, my curious pigeon." A grin threatened at her appalled gasp.

She jerked her gaze away and turned her head. She lay with her arms up, hands by her head in surrender. His attention was drawn to her still heaving bosom. Her shirt was bunched up, his neck heated at the awareness he was naked under the towel. His naked male parts were almost touching her naked female parts. He needed to go.

Naithon hopped off the bed and stalked to his dresser. Pulled out underwear and let the towel drop. There was that gasp again, a chuckle tickled his throat. His lamb was so inexperienced the sight of a naked male butt shocked and embarrassed her. He should punish her for the knife attack. But, if it was him, he would have done the same thing. Only with success. His opponent would be bloodying the floor right now.

When he was dressed, tie knotted, hair combed, he swung around. A sound escaped her throat, she'd been watching him, and he caught her at it. Instantly red flowed up her neck to blossom on her face. She turned her head from him, scowling at his chuckle.

He trod to the door, put his hand on the knob. "Okay, as I said, I'll be out an hour or so. Someone will bring you clothes and take you to breakfast then bring you back up here."

Her lips pushed out in a pout. "Must I stay locked in here, Mr. Adranokov? Can't I at least explore your home?"

A frown of irritation tugged his brows down. "Kiri," he said coldly. "I have had my hands on your body, my tongue down your throat, you slept half naked in my bed, in my arms. We will be consummating our…relationship soon. I do not want to hear you call me by my surname."

"Hmm," her murmur slight, she shifted up on her knees in the bed. Sitting back on her heels, her head tilted at him demurely, with a just a sliver of mocking, she said, "Okay, *Boss*."

The frown deepened. "Do not get smart with me, Kiri, it won't bode you well." Satisfaction firmed his mouth at the look of fear that pushed away her snotty expression. "You will remain secured in this room. The servant will bring you back up after breakfast."

"But-"

"Kiri," he sighed. "There are dangerous men roaming this building that will think you are there to do their bidding. And they won't ask for permission or stop like I have. There are unknown people killing men in my crew and also your father's. There is no way of knowing if they plan to dispose of you too. With all that, since my taking of you was so…let's say dramatic, word will get out fast that you mean something to me. They may try to abduct you as a way to control me. And," his lip quirked, "let's not forget your boyfriend, that redheaded asshole will come looking to take you back."

"Oh, no, I don't think Rueford would go to any trouble to come and get me."

His smirk humorless, Naithon informed her, "Yes he would. If someone stole you from me, trust me, I would be stepping over their mangled bodies to carry you back home."

Ignoring the disbelieving shake of her head, he opened the door. "So, to answer your question, no, you cannot explore anything beyond this suite. You want a tour I will take you when I return. From now on, you won't leave this room, or this house without me."

She scrambled off the bed to her feet. "But surely the grounds are secure-"

"Kiri," his sigh short of irritated. "Nothing is secure enough to ensure your safety. Now, you will do as I say. Make sure to eat breakfast, you didn't touch the food last night. I will have a report on what you eat when I return."

She kept a dozen feet between them, her arms outstretched to the side. "You can't really mean to keep me a prisoner in your chambers trying to control what I do, what I eat." Her head tilted back, she gazed up at him perplexed. "I don't understand this, any of it. Why? What happens if I just walk out the front door?"

Eyes squinting, his voice roughened, "First, I have instructed you to stay here, do not attempt to leave. However, even if you try, you can't get out of this suite much less the front door." Frustration edged his words, "You do not want to see what happens if you disobey me. I've already let you get away with too much. I brought you here to please me, not to argue about you leaving." At her angry, shocked expression, he stepped out and shut the door.

Kiri fumed, groused out loud, "How dare he treat me like I'm his prized puppy? Keeping me locked up, ordering me around like he was my father." She hurried to the window and peered out, looked down. A chauffer held a door open to a limo. There were several in the drive.

It was quite some time before she saw Naithon moving from the house to the car. His blond hair shone in the morning light. He wore a trench coat that went to his ankles. The chauffeur nodded respectfully as Naithon slid into the back and the man shut his door. In seconds the car whisked away.

A knock at the door had Kiri scurrying out of the bedroom and down the hall to the front room. This was her chance to get out. The door opened before she got across the room. A woman slipped inside carrying clothes.

"Ms. Delducci," she said, bowing her head politely. "Mr. Adranokov asked me to bring you some items to wear. He gave me a description of your, uh," her speculative eyes traced over Kiri's body, "size and height. I searched around, asked the girls to loan something…suitable. I must say," she smiled, reviewing Kiri's form again.

"There are not many that have your…attributes. You are small, dainty, but, oh Miss, curves like mad. As delicately gorgeous as a butterfly, no wonder the Sir is so enamored with you." A grin turned her thin mouth up she added, "And no wonder Miss Silver is in such a snit."

"Uh, Mrs…um, I am not, I mean he and I we're not, I mean…oh," she groaned consternated. Clasping her hands together in prayer she said urgently, "He took me from my home. He kidnapped me, and he plans on assaulting me. You have to help me! Call the police!"

The woman's face paled. "Oh dear. Mr. Adranokov does take what he wants. However, if I assisted you in leaving, well," she shook her head with a serious flattening of her lips. "He might not hurt me, I am a woman and there aren't really rumors of him ever seriously harming a female, other than the ones who ask for it specifically. But…well, he is an angry hard man purported to have been born without kindness or mercy. I don't really know for sure if he would use his fists on me, or worse."

Shaking her head, she said, "Ah, that's neither here nor there, dear. We all do as he commands. Why don't you try these on?" Nervously the woman moved to Kiri and held out the clothes.

With a resigned sigh, Kiri accepted the bundle. That gangster had everyone cowed for crying out loud. Honestly, the man was such a barbaric heathen. "Okay." Ever polite, she smiled and introduced herself, "I'm Kiri, what's your name?"

The smile was returned. The woman looked to be in her late forties, dark hair was up in a twist, a polyester uniform of black top and skirt covered her plump body, sturdy shoes encased her feet. Her legs were almost straight up and down with little shape to them like fence posts. She had a kind smile on her rather plain face. "I'm Francy Mouldare."

"It's nice to meet you, Mrs. Mouldare. These are odd circumstances," Kiri said shyly.

"Please, Miss, call me Francy."

"And you call me Kiri."

A frown pulled a line between her brows, she vehemently shook her head. "Oh no, Miss, the Master would be not pleased if I didn't speak strictly respectfully to you."

Looking confused, Kiri asked, "Does he have that rule with everyone?" After all, the man is clearly a barbarian.

This brought a laugh, which softened her plain face. "No, certainly not. Only people that are very important to him, and honey," she grinned conspiratorially at Kiri, "the Master has made it very clear that you are important to him. He has extra guards to protect you, and he has sternly admonished me to direct you to breakfast. He was quite adamant that I make sure you eat. I can't say he has ever ordered that before!"

Thinking that over, Francy expressed surprise. "Actually, Miss, he has never shown any interest in guarding, feeding, clothing or otherwise with a woman. Certainly he has never brought a whor- uh, woman to his suite." Her finger tipped to her chin she regarded Kiri. "Yes, you are certainly important to him."

Kiri gave in, for now. Really, she had little choice in the matter. After showering and dressing she followed Francy out of the door and downstairs.

On the first floor, breakfast was set up buffet style along one wall of a handsome dining room. Pale peach wallpaper with silver etchings, gleaming hutch and highboy, long buffet counter, and a table that could seat well over two dozen people easily strode down the center of the large room. The room was empty. There were a few dirty plates showing someone had eaten, but the most of the settings were untouched.

"Please, fill your plate and have a seat anywhere, Miss Kiritina." Francy nodded to the table. "Shall I bring you coffee? Tea? Juice and milk are there on the sideboard to help yourself."

"But where are the others?"

Francy chuckled while gently taking Kiri's arm and guiding her to the beginning of the covered heating pans. "Honey, except for the crew that have gone to work, the rest here are lazy slagabouts. The women won't be up and about for hours. They stay up late, um, entertaining the men."

"Entertaining?"

Francy picked up a plate, opened a lid and stuck a serving spoon in the heaping steaming grits. She poured a large spoonful on the plate and handed it to Kiri, then nodded to the next heating dish. "Um," a slight pink tinged the older woman's thin cheeks. She had to speak carefully. Mr. Adranokov had been quite explicit that his new...guest was quite an ingénue and was to be treated with kid gloves. "Well, the men are...how do you say..."

"Gangsters?"

Francy coughed out a choke, wiped at an eye. "Well, sort of. Anyway, they get tense sometimes, all that brute testosterone, aggression and such, and well, they get to brawling. So Mr. Adranokov lets the girls come in and, well, help them relieve their stress."

"Are they the men's girlfriends or wives?" Kiri placed a sausage on her plate and a piece of toast, added a dollop of gravy to the grits.

Francy coughed again. "Um, no, Miss. Most of them work at Mr. Adranokov's clubs."

"Clubs?" Kiri turned to go to the table but Francy lifted a lid, scooped up some scrambled eggs and plopped them on her plate.

At Kiri's frown, Francy said, "Please, Miss. He will ask me what you had. If you don't eat a sufficient, well-balanced amount, he will be angry with me. He is a very perceptive man, he will know if I lie."

"Okay, this is so absurd, but I don't want to cause you trouble." Kiri sighed, and let Francy add fruit to her plate, then she firmly turned and set the dish on the table and pulled out a chair. "You were saying? About his clubs?"

"Well, Miss," Francy started uncomfortably, "they call them Gentlemen's Clubs. Can I get you coffee? Tea?" Her voice rose thinly.

Kiri sat down and buttered the toast. "You mean like strip clubs."

Francy choked and nodded.

Smearing raspberry jam on the toast she asked, "How many does he have?"

"Oh, I'm not really sure, three or four?"

"Wow. So, do they entertain Mr. Adranokov too?"

"Um, I don't think so anymore since you are here. He already had words with Silver."

"Silver?"

Francy's face reddened, she'd already said too much. "Um, she's a dancer, she kind of tries to claim the Master as hers. But, I think now that you are here, uh...I need to go, I'll bring you coffee," and she darted out of the room.

Chapter Fourteen

Naithon's mind had wandered the entire meeting. Several times Blok had nudged him in the side when Naithon didn't respond to a question.

He was at the Riveaux Knights' clubhouse. He didn't think he and his crew were in any danger, the motorcycle gang knew if they did anything untoward with Naithon that his faction would come down pitilessly hard and wipe every one of them off the face of the earth.

The clubhouse made up of stucco, brick, steel and wood was designed to withstand most artillery assaults. The outside was dirty and grey, barbed wire encircled the cement wall that surrounded the perimeter, and heavily armed members patrolled. They were trained to shoot first ask questions later.

Still, Naithon's faction was bigger, stronger, smarter, and even more ruthless. No one who valued their life was stupid enough to screw with him.

Currently, Naithon was ensconced in the meeting room where the club held their church. Church was their term for meeting. The place was as secure as a fortress, but if Naithon and his men wanted at them, nothing would stop them.

Naithon looked up to see Rory 'Roar' O'Landon regarding him thoughtfully with a mild smile. In his early thirties, Roar was fairly young to be President of an MC, but the last president didn't survive the battle with the Foes of God.

Thankfully, unlike some of the others, Roar liked to shower. His long hair tied back in a ponytail hung cleanly down his broad back. Armed to the teeth, as was Naithon and every other male there, Roar wore a black t-shirt under his cut, and ancient blue jeans.

"Mmm," Naithon made a vague sound, apparently Roar had asked him a question.

A small laugh rolled out of the president. His accent was an odd mix of country, redneck and Cajun. "Ah, so the rumors are true."

At Naithon's lifted brow, Roar grinned. "They said you had grabbed up Ignacio Delducci's beautiful young, *engaged* daughter as surety to keep the peace, and dat you are quite smitten wid her and refuse to return her. Only half of your mind has been on this meetin', the other must be on what's between the girl's legs, hmm?"

Snickers rippled around the table. The grin widening, Roar went on, "Swiped the bitch right out from under the noses of Montoblanco, Delducci, and every other red blooded man dat had designs on her."

His face blank, Naithon said coolly, "You had a question, O'Landon?"

Roar laughed. "Okay, big man's not gonna spill. Fine. To answer your original question, no, you know it's not my crew takin' out yours and Delducci's people. It took too long for the three of us to make a fuckin' treaty, ain't gonna break dat now. Tings are goin' too smooth, we're all makin' bucks hand over fist, not gonna mess wid dat."

Naithon's lips pressed, he hadn't thought they were involved but he had to cover all bases. He was only here now as a courtesy, he had his soldiers snooping around to see if the Knights had any spokes in the assassinating wheel. "All right. What about those fuckers the Foes? You think they're trying to cause a war between my family and the Delduccis?"

The president shrugged a rugged shoulder. "Nah. Dere weren't enough of ta bastards left to rob an ol' lady much less try to git involved wid ya'll again." Folding his hands on the old scratched up table, Roar leaned in. "What do you tink is goin' on? I hear dey took out four from your side, and six countin' dat prick Duce Delducci on his side. Good riddance to shit, I say about Duce. What could they want? You tink Ignacio Delducci is doin' it to maybe clean out your folks and is killin' his own people to take away the suspicion?"

Naithon sat back on the hard wooden chair, dragged on his cigar, slowly exhaled the smoke. "No. His own boy was killed. I saw him at the funeral, it broke him down." He'd also seen Kiri there in black, veil covering that gorgeous face. He hadn't been able to get near to her there, either. Ignacio had her surrounded by his men and a bunch of freaking nuns. "Can't figure it, O'Landon. Someone wants something and they're killing to achieve it."

Naithon stood up signaling the end of the meeting. Vlad on one side and Blok on his other got up as well. Roar and his men stayed seated.

As they departed, Roar called out with a mock in his voice, "Don't you go and forgit to send dat little lady back home to her fat, old, fee-ahn-say, Adranokov!" Male laughter ushered them out the door.

All the way back to the mansion, Naithon could think of nothing except Kiri and how soon he could get her to not fight him while he took her. He was happy that she was a virgin, that no man but he would ever be inside her, but on the other hand it was giving him blue balls to give her a bit of space. If she was more experienced she might not be so afraid, so resistant to him.

When he first snatched her, his only thought was to bang her and keep her. Her feelings didn't figure into the equation. However, after Maz's speech, he decided he wouldn't pounce on her, not force her, but he wasn't going to be able to be around her, have her sleeping in his bed much longer without doing her. And he was going to be around her, and she would be sleeping in his bed, so it has to be soon.

Once inside the mansion, he pulled out his phone to call Mazonn. He needed to debrief with the rest of his men before he went to see Kiri.

He texted Mazonn and was passing the grand room where most the occupants hung out drinking beer, playing cards, necking, when he stopped dead. Kiri wasn't upstairs in his room like he'd ordered; she was sitting across the room on one of the sofas. She was tucked in a corner, Mazonn sat next to her and Yashin perched on the arm of the couch on the other side of her. The three of them were laughing like old friends.

As Naithon pulled out his phone and glanced at the message that beeped, Mazonn leaned over and whispered something in Kiri's ear and she giggled.

She wore jeans and a skintight red shirt, and even from where he stood he could see she was braless. Every other man in the room was blatantly gawking at her. Of course they were, her round, firm, plump breasts were bobbing and jiggling with her movements. The blouse was like red cling wrap.

Naithon saw blinding, raging scarlet. He stormed over to them, grabbed Kiri's arm and jerked her to her feet before anyone even knew he was there. She stumbled in surprise and he gripped her arm. "You little fucking whore. You won't give it to me but you'll spread your legs for all the other men?"

"Nait-" Mazonn started.

But he was already stalking to the elevator with Kiri in tow. He normally didn't bother with it, he liked the added exercise of hitting the stairs. But now, he was so enraged he was going to move fast and she wasn't going to be able to keep up with him.

He pushed her into the elevator. As the door closed he saw astonished expressions on his cheating *ex*-friends' faces. Naithon was so angry he kept a space between him and Kiri. There was no doubt he was infuriated, smoke about came out of his ears. The air seethed around his grit, scowling face.

Pressed against the wall as far as she could get from him, timidly, Kiri spoke quietly, nervously, "Um, Mr. um Boss, is something wrong? Did something happen?"

The look he gave her could laser a hole through steel. The elevator pinged and the door opened. Without a word he opened the steel door then grasped her arm and dragged her down the hall to his room. She tried protesting, digging her feet into the carpet, he was blowing his top and she was afraid to be in the vicinity when he exploded.

Opening his door, he shoved her inside so hard she stumbled again, catching herself on a chair to keep from falling. "Mister-"

He stomped over to her and got in her face, wrath burned out of his eyes into hers, his fists clenched, shoulders bowed. Accent thick and outraged, he bellowed, "You fucking call me mister or boss again, so help me *Dio* I will beat that ass of yours black and blue!"

Kiri tried to move back, but he was on her. Grabbing her, he shoved her to the floor, forcing her on all fours.

She cried out, "No, wait, please-"

"Done waiting," he muttered, lowering himself down behind her. He put a hand on her back forcing her down on her forearms, face almost on the floor, ass in the air. Rounding his body over her back, he reached under her and seized her breasts painfully.

Kiri screamed and tried to fight him, he pressed his chest on her back holding her immobile. "Wear shit like this for men to see your tits," he kneaded and squeezed so hard, so crudely, she cried out.

He ranted on, "Spread your legs for any man that walks by," he reached for the button on her jeans. "A whore like Fiereza, I'm gonna fuck you like my brother took her."

"No! Wait," she screamed again, "I didn't, I didn't, please-"

"Tried to be nice, give you time to get used to me, relax, fuck Mazonn telling me that shit. He wanted you for himself, the bastard." He shoved his erection into her bottom and rubbed it abrasively back and forth and pressing angrily so hard, if he hadn't wrapped an arm around her waist to hold her he would have smashed her into the floor. He ripped at the button on her jeans, it flew off across the carpet. "Taking that cunt, then I'm taking that ass."

"Mister-"

That did it. Naithon lifted her and flung her on her back. He pushed the shirt up exposing her breasts then pulled the zipper on her jeans down. She kicked at him, punched at his arms, it was like a flea hitting a bull. She couldn't stop him from shoving his hand down inside her pants and palming her sex.

His phone buzzed in his pocket, again and again and again. He ignored it and gripped Kiri's mound cruelly hard, she cried in pain.

"Taking you now, bitch, you won't be fucking any other men but me," he growled. Grabbing the tops of her jeans, he tugged them. His phone buzzed again, then there was pounding at the door. He would have ignored that too but Mazonn was shouting his name.

"Fuck," cursing, Naithon stood up, looked down at Kiri. Tears streamed down her face, she tried to cover her bare breasts with her small hands, her jeans splayed open revealing tiny pink panties with a lace trim.

"Don't you fucking move," he commanded, pointing at her, "not an inch." Storming to the door, he wrenched it open. Mazonn's fist was raised in mid-knock.

"What the hell, Maz, you banging my woman? What the hell-"

"No you dumb ass. Sam Guerrero was-"

Ready to slug his best friend, Naithon stormed, "What does he have to do with you and Yashin and your hands all over my girl? What the hell-"

"Shut up, you jerk for a second, cripes."

Taken aback, Naithon cursed a string of words in Romanian, "Maz-"

"I said shut up."

Naithon shut his mouth.

"Okay, geesh." Mazonn wiped a sheen of sweat off his forehead. "The girl, Kiri, she had finished breakfast and was sitting in that alcove near the dining room waiting for the servant to take her back upstairs when Sam Guerrero found her. Yash and I heard her screams. Of course here, screams from females are generally screams of pleasure."

"Maz," Naithon grunted. Then he frowned, "Why was she screaming? What-"

"*Ja*, shut up. Guerrero had her smashed up against the wall groping her all over, she was fighting like mad. He...slapped her." Mazonn's rage at what he had viewed rang in his fierce voice, brows lanced straight down.

Naithon's face darkened to black, brows so low his eyes disappeared.

"We saw from down the hall. Shit, Nait, by the time we got to her he had his fist raised; he was about to slam it into her face. Told her he'd knock her out and take her to his room where she could scream all she wanted."

So angry, Naithon almost gagged on his fury. "Where is he?"

"We stopped him, bro. He didn't hit her again, but she was so in shock at the brutality of his attack she was shaking and crying and, hell, it was horrible. Blok and Vlad took Guerrero to the cellar, I brought Kiri to the grand room so I could sit her down and calm her, get her something to drink. What you saw was totally innocent and I am fucking pissed you would think I would try to fuck your girl."

"*Ja*, yeah, deep down I didn't. But, she won't let me touch her and there she was dressed like a hooker and laughing with you guys." He had been boggled with jealousy. She never even smiled at him much less laughed.

"Uh huh. I was trying to calm her. I told her about Blok stepping into that open well that time, you remember? He was all muck and scum by time we got him up, and fit to be tied."

Naithon almost smiled at the memory, then his face set, jaw worked. "What kind of condition is Guerrero in?"

A big grin curved Mazonn's handsome face. "Yeah, we roughed him up pretty good. Even if she was one of the strippers, he still deserves to die for striking a female. But, we left him for you. I knew you'd want to do it yourself."

"*Ja*," Naithon nodded cursorily. "Keep him on ice, I will deal with him later. Right now, I…" He saw Mazonn's concern when he peered inside the room and could see Kiri curled up in a ball on the floor weeping.

"Aw fuck, Nait, what the hell did you do? That girl doesn't deserve-"

"I know. I lost my mind. I'm all right now. Seeing her in those clothes, you guys hanging on her…"

"The maid brought her the clothes, she had no choice in it, Nait. I'm thinking they loaned her the shirt and jeans, panties maybe but nothing to hold her tits in."

Nation considered this, it was his fault. He'd taken her clothes, her bra and panties since she'd defied him and wore them to bed when he'd told her not to. Hell, he didn't know some bitch would give her a tight, thin shirt to wear and no bra. At least she had on underwear. "I didn't hurt her, Maz," *but he might have if Mazonn hadn't stopped him.* "I need to go to her, thanks for watching out for my property."

"Nait, really, she's a woman, not a chair for fuck's sake," Mazonn remonstrated him.

"*Ja*, I know she's a woman, that's the problem. Later." Naithon stepped back and shut the door. He had expected trouble from the outside, didn't think he'd have trouble inside as well. With his violent rep, his men were afraid to argue with him much less attack his woman. Of course he'd never had a woman before. Guerrero will be a lesson to the other males, what happens if anyone touches Kiri.

When he trod over to where she still lay curled in a ball, he heard her whimper at his approach and it pinched his gut. He knelt beside her and she shrank from him with another whimper.

So much for getting her used to him so she'd let him fuck her without fighting him. Now she was terrified of him again. She had pulled her shirt down and fixed her jeans, except for the button he'd torn off. He set his hand on her shoulder. "Listen, Kiri, I-"

She shifted to get his hand off her. Okay, this wasn't going to be easy. Ignoring her whimpers and struggles to get away, he slipped his arms under her and picked her up. He carried her to the couch and sat down with her on his lap.

Kiri kept her head down, what would he do to her next? Her arms crossed over her chest, she lifted her knees in protection.

Naithon kept his arms around her, just holding her. Her entire body shivered in his arms. "Listen, ah, Kiri…" what could he say? I was so jealous and angry with you I was going to fuck you into the ground then paddle your ass so you'd never even think of another man?

Gently, he put his fingers under her chin lifting it so he could see her face. His gut quelled at the red mark Guerrero's slap had made. A spanking was one thing, striking a woman in the face was not going to be tolerated in his home.

She wriggled to make him let go but he netted his thick fingers around the side of her face, his thumb under her jaw. "I…might have overreacted a bit-"

Mouth open in gall, she cried, "Overreacted a bit! You called me a whore in front of other people, dragged me up here like I was a recalcitrant convict then viciously groped me, hurt me, humiliated me. You were going to savagely rape me."

"I…" seeing the shamed tears gathering in her eyes, he felt shame himself. Other girls would have appreciated his rough handling, but she was so young, tender, he had been too rough with her. He had barely been able to contain his rage. If Mazonn hadn't interceded, he would have done worse.

Using his thumb he brushed at an escaping tear. "Kiri, I'm…sorry." Those words he had never spoken in his life before, what was this woman doing to him? Turning him into a pussy, for shit's sake. But, he was wrong and he had treated her abominably. It would have been okay if she'd been one of the dancers here, they choose to have sex freely and didn't care how mean, cruel, or sadistic you were to them.

But not this girl, his girl. He'd taken her, she was his. It was his job to protect her, and he'd been the one she needed protecting from. Point for Maz, he bearded the lion, told him to shut up then told him off, and protected her from Guerrero the attacking soldier.

Swallowing his pride he started again, holding her so he could look her in the eye, he was no coward. "Kiri, I treated you badly and I apologize for my brutish behavior towards you." He waited, she only sniffed and lowered her eyes. "Kiri, I said I was sorry, say something." He surely could not recall ever using that word before in his life. To anyone.

Silence, then she hitched a breath, her lips bunched, tears garbling her voice she said, "Brutish and heathen. You were a brute and an unconscionable wild boar." She wiped at a running tear with the back of her hand.

She was calling him a feral pig basically, and, if the shoe fits, well... Feeling a smile tugging at his mouth, he nodded stoically. "Yes, I was. Can we move past this now, put it behind us?"

She regarded him quizzically. "Move past that you are a mean bully to where? Just wait until the next time you get upset and violently assault me?" Kiri shook her head, he still held her chin albeit gently. "I just don't understand, I am your prisoner, what is it you want from me?"

Groaning his sigh, his fingers stroking her soft skin he said, "I promise to curb my savage tendencies, Kiri, around you. I made a mistake, jumped to conclusions. This is an unusual situation for me as well as you. I've never, ah," he paused. His stomach just clenched in pain at her tears. "Well, I've never grabbed a woman and held her against her will before. My...emotions," he chuckled, "there you go, something I never even thought I had- anyway, they go wacky with you. I need to assimilate these weird feelings I have about you."

Their eyes joined, roaming each other, both confused.

Then Kiri said, "It's easy enough to resolve, just let me go."

A scowl grit his teeth and narrowed his eyes. All this *feelings* talk and crap was too much. He was done with it. "I have told you, Kiri, you are staying with me. Permanently." When she opened her mouth to retort he set two fingers over it shushing her. "Hush, pigeon, there is no discussion about it. You will come around eventually and accept your position."

"My position?" she huffed. "As your prisoner? As your sex slave? You expect me to- to accept that and- and be happy?" She squirmed to get off his lap, he tightened his arm and wrapped the other one around her.

Growling his irritation, he said, "You don't have to be happy, Kiri, you are here for my pleasure."

Her affronted gasp ballooned her chest drawing his attention to it. His pupils dilated like crazy, growing huge under suddenly heavy lids. There was no mistaking his mounting lust.

113

"Uh, Mr. Adranokov, please let me down now. We don't need to converse any more. I'm good, thank you for your apology," she gave a wriggle but he didn't let loose.

Glowering at her, Naithon said, "For the record, you will never leave this room again without a bra. If there is none here for you to wear then you won't leave the room. I won't have you parading around showing every asshole here your tits. Do you understand me?"

"It wasn't my fault. I did as you commanded, *Boss*. I donned the clothes brought to me, went down to breakfast, escorted as you ordered. Then, contrary to your earlier words that you were keeping me locked up to keep me safe, if that man sexually assaulting me against the wall and hitting me was keeping me safe, well, huh," she snorted her indignation.

Casually he responded, "I said you will not be anywhere without me. If you had stayed locked in the room you would not have been attacked."

"But," she spurted furiously, "it was your orders, Mr. Adranokov- hey!" He suddenly lifted her, turned her, and laid her face down, her belly over his thighs. "What do you think you are do-ow!" His hand came down hard smacking her butt.

"I have told you not to call me by my surname. You did it on purpose to rile me. Well, it worked." *Whack whack whack*- he railed more smacks on her wriggling butt.

"No, stop it!" she squealed and moved her hand over her bottom to protect it.

"Uh huh, not doing that." He grabbed her wrist, bent her elbow and held her forearm against her lower back while he paddled her.

"You can't do this to me!" she cried, her voice rasping with roiling tears in her throat.

"Apparently I can." *Whack*- "I told you I am the boss. Everyone obeys me, including you." He gave her a few more spanks then lifted her to sit back on his lap, when she did she winced. Her face was red and blotched with tears. "Now, do you want to have further discussion on who is the boss, and who will do as the boss says?" His accent thickened in his gruff anger.

Her face was angry and humiliated; she scowled at the couch cushion.

He gripped her jaw, lifted her head to look at him. "You will look at me when I talk to you. You will answer me when I ask you a question. Do you need more spanks to loosen that tongue? *Ja?*" He knew he spoke to her and was treating her like a child, but in comparison to him she was.

She blinked the tears away, shook her head.

"Out loud, pigeon, you answer me out loud. Now."

Her sigh beleaguered, she wiped at her eyes. "Yes. You are the boss."

"You will do as I say, repeat it."

Rolling her eyes with another heavy loud sigh, resentment in her voice she said, "I will do as you say."

"That attitude, rolling your eyes, the heavy sighs, makes my hand itch to meet with your ass again." He stared at her, she glared at him.

"Can I ask you a question?"

"Of course," he said with a sharp nod.

"I understand the lamb thing, you think my dad put me on a silver platter to be figuratively sacrificed, slaughtered by Rueford, and you. Why do you call me pigeon?"

His eyes dropped to her chest. The red shirt clung to her curves like second skin. A grin started to form. "Because your tits remind me of plump, round pigeons that strut the rooftops."

"Oh! You are a despicable pig!" she snapped and pushed to get off his lap, this time he let her. His chuckles trailed after she left the room.

That night he made her wear his shirt as before. When they settled into the bed, he hooked her belly and pulled her against him. Her body went into instant rigid mode. "Just sleeping, little lamb, I promise."

After a while she settled and relaxed in his embrace. She was warm and soft in his arms, he sniffed her hair and then he relaxed. He had bashed a hole with a sledgehammer today into any budding trust she might have gained of him. He'd treated her disrespectfully,

115

and she was alarmed at how enraged he became, how he could have hurt her. A dog, he was just a filthy junkyard dog. Always had been, but it had never bothered him before.

It hadn't been a good day. He had accused his best friend of stealing his girl, and he had treated her badly. Naithon regretted that. But not the spanking. She needed to obey him for her own good, her own safety.

When she acknowledges that he is in charge, she will submit to his orders. Everything is for her protection. He was trying to build a relationship with her and she was blocking it by calling him Mister. That wall is going down. Cuddling her, he sighed content with the moment, he was starting to really enjoy when she was sweetly curled in his arms, all tender and gentle femininity.

This night he only held her, he didn't fondle her as she slept. She'd had enough abuse for the day.

Chapter Fifteen

Every day was like the last for Kiri. Naithon would leave the bed while she still slept. When she woke, she felt strangely…alone. Ridiculous. He was manipulating her into…what? Missing him in bed? "Ugh." Shaking her head she did as she had been doing, showered and dressed in clothes Francy told her Naithon had purchased for her.

Apparently he had told one of the servants her dimensions and what he preferred she wear. But, he had told her that when she was downstairs what he'd really prefer she wore was a big sack, when in his suite, nothing.

Fortunately, the woman who bought the clothes had lightened up a bit on the jeans and blouses and purchased Kiri's size, not three sizes larger as Naithon had instructed. This time she got bras and panties. There were dresses too, and heels, in his closet. For her. She didn't understand. He acted like they were a couple. The man was insane. She was his prisoner, nothing more.

When she asked him why he'd bought her dresses and put them in his closet, he had responded sarcastically, "What? We should leave them packed in boxes?" He also had toiletries for her put in his medicine cabinet and on the shelves. A hairbrush, makeup, blow-dryer, he had brought in a pretty white and pink vanity with scrolling around the frame of the mirror, and a matching chair.

None of it made any sense to her. Surely when the whole war thing was over he'd send her home. She didn't believe for one second that he really planned on keeping her for the rest of their lives. But why buy her so many new clothes? Perhaps he thought when she left the other women could have them.

Kiri had said if he insisted on keeping her for now, just have someone go to her house and get her own things, but he had ignored her comment. A knock at the door sounded, she couldn't open the locked door so she had to wait for the person on the other side to open it.

The door opened slowly, a head peered around the corner, Mazonn grinned at her, blue eyes twinkling. "Okay to come in?"

She was always amazed how kind and courteous he was to her, for a gangster. He had rescued her from that animal that had attacked her downstairs, and he had stopped Naithon from hurting her. He had brushed off when she tried to thank him. Since the assault, Naithon ensured only his close friends escort her downstairs for meals when he was out on business.

When they brought her to dine, she figured they deliberately did it when it was off main hours to eat. If there was anyone else present, sometimes the women lingered, whoever was escorting her kept her at a distance from the others, and sat between her and them discouraging any contact. Of course that only encouraged more curious gawking.

Mazonn told her she was kept apart from others because first off, Naithon didn't want her to know more about him and his businesses, she already had enough reason to fear and dislike him. The other was he was afraid she'd make a friend who might help her to escape from him. So, except for his close friends, she was kept isolated. It sucked.

Naithon was gone most days from dawn to dusk on business. She was asleep when he came to bed and when he left in the morning. For the love of God she couldn't figure out why he kept her. He'd cuddled her but hadn't molested her again. Since he appeared to have lost his sexual interest in her, his agenda must just be to harass her father.

Today the building was mostly empty. The men were out, another of their crew had been murdered and Naithon ordered most of the girls stay away for a few days while they investigated.

Mazonn walked her downstairs and sat with her to keep her company while she ate. A man entered the room, his eyes shifted from Maz to Kiri. Speaking to Maz he stared at Kiri, "Ah, John got whacked."

"John Kendall?"

The man nodded. "Yeah. Over on 31st, shot coming out of a bar last night. Boss called and said for me to stay with the girl," he nodded at Kiri, "and for you to go check the Kendall scene out."

"Hmm." Mazonn frowned at the man. "You sure he said that?" He glanced at Kiri, she was finishing up her eggs. Naithon was a dictator when it came to ensuring Kiri ate. She had curves, but she was still on the thin side.

"Yeah I'm sure," the man sniped. "I ain't stupid you know."

The twist to Mazonn's lips told he felt otherwise. He got up, muttered, "Okay," and motioned for the man to step to the side, out of Kiri's earshot. When the man leaned in to hear what he had to say, Mazonn suddenly gripped his collar and twisted his fist in it and pulled him up on his toes bringing them nose-to-nose.

"Hey what the-"

"Shut up, Dan," Mazonn ordered. The man's lips clamped. "You keep an eye on her. Right after she finishes she gets taken straight upstairs, no detours. No one goes near her. You do not go into the suite, you do not touch her, anywhere, anyhow. You do and Nait will gut you and drop you like a dead skunk in a hole. You hear me?"

Dan nodded. "Yeah, yeah, I know."

Mazonn twisted his fist making his hold tighter, cutting off Dan's air; he glared hard in his face, making the man aware that his life span would be short if anything happened to Kiri. When he opened his fist, Dan staggered backwards into a wall.

Mazonn went back to Kiri. "Kiri, honey, I have to go out. Dan here will stay with you until you're done and take you back upstairs."

119

She set her fork down. "Maz, if he's with me, uh, protecting me, can't I stay down here? It's lonely and boring up there all day by myself."

Maz shook his head. "No. You know his orders." He smiled at her sad sigh. "I know honey, but when we settle who is taking out ours and your family's people, things should lighten up. I'll see you later, you behave now, right?"

Rolling her eyes, she exhaled her exasperation. "Of course, what trouble could I get into locked in a room?"

"Okay." He squinted a warning at Dan then took off.

Kiri sipped her tea very, very slowly. Sitting in a chair, Dan pushed back on the rear two legs and propped himself against the wall. Staring blankly into space he started yawning…and yawning. Finally, his head lolled back and he started snoring. She got up quietly, carefully, and slipped from the room.

Breathing a hunk of relieved air, she wandered around the first floor. She didn't come across a soul, Thank God. They would have snitched on her and sent her back upstairs.

She passed a grand room, then the kitchens which she didn't go near in case a cook was in there, she checked out a salon, a den, gym, dozens and dozens of rooms scattered the huge mansion. With the four floors and several wings, Naithon could, and did, house an army in the compound. If she heard voices she avoided that room and moved on.

She made her way to the front door and peeked out the window. She saw the boots of a guard standing in front of it. Every door she checked she found the same thing. Frustrated, she wasn't getting out through a door.

Creeping into room after room, she started checking the windows. "Yes!" Back in the library, she peered out the window and not a guard was in sight. It was tough to get the lock open and the window up.

Kiri climbed out the window and dashed across the lawn. She ran and ran for what seemed like forever until she reached the 14-foot high fence surrounding the back lawns. Her heart plummeted, how was she going to get out? She raced along the fence, praying it wasn't electrified then she came across a part that looked like it could open.

A thick steel beam lay across handles securing them. If she could get the beam off, the gate could be pushed apart and she could slip through.

****

Naithon was at one of his businesses when his phone buzzed. Swiping it on, he answered, "*Ja?*"

"Ah, sir," the voice sounded edgy.

"What, Johannssen, cough it up, I'm busy."

"Yes sir. Well, that girl, the new one that stays in your room?"

Naithon's heart started racing. "What about her?"

"Um, well, it seems she managed to climb out a window, and, well, she's running across the back area. What do you want us to do? Do you want us to apprehend her?"

That little... "No. Keep her in your sights on camera, and tell the stable kid to bring out my steed, I only need the bridle." She would be in the woods by the time he got there.

He wasn't far from home, he sped the entire way. By the time he parked by the stables, his horse was ready and outside the barn waiting. Naithon tossed off a terse, "Thanks," and slapped the horse's flank. The stallion took off and Naithon grabbed the reins and jumped up throwing his leg over, mounting the already racing steed.

Galloping across the lumpy grass, Naithon placed an earpiece in his ear to follow the guard's tracking Kiri's location. "Huh," he grunted, he didn't feel so bad now for the waling he'd given her on her fine little ass. The grunt turned into a frown. Of course that could be why she fled. However, she'd only earned herself another beating.

Maybe he should use his belt this time to make it sink in she was never to leave him. Her being outside the protection of the mansion was damned unacceptable. He was so pissed his gut churned acid.

She had gone quite a way by the time he'd driven home and saddled up. She was at the far west perimeter gate. The only gate other than the front one. They used it to travel the woods and also to run the horses.

Way up ahead he could see Kiri struggling to lift the steel bar off the handles. Looked like she had been working at it for some time. She managed to push one side up and jumped back as the end slammed into the ground just narrowly missing her foot. She quickly pushed the gate open and slipped through it.

Naithon could feel his blood boiling, he was almost as mad as he was when he thought she was fucking his friends. He needed to tether his temper before he got to her. Man and steed roared over the grass, the hooves pounding faster then slowed as they reached the gate. They just managed to slide through, and trampled the tall grass chasing after her.

Kiri heard the sound of thunder. She turned, eyes widened like green saucers at the sight of Naithon coming at her on a horse. With an 'eek' she spun around and ran as fast as she could. The pounding hooves galloped up behind her, then beside her, and leaning way down, Naithon's long arm snaked out, hooked her under her arms and hauled her up and dumped her in front of him on the horse.

His arm dropped down under her breasts and he slammed her against his torso so hard the breath snapped out of her lungs. He held her tightly as he turned the horse to head back to the gate. Her long curls fluttered from the wind at their movement, the tresses tickled his chin.

"Mister, uh, sir," she gasped, "I can't breathe, please."

He didn't want to, but he loosened his hold on her. The horse trotted at a slower pace, causing their bodies to jostle up and down. Kiri's breasts bobbed on his arm,

Naithon felt the sudden constriction in his pants, it got worse when her bottom rubbed against his dick. He'd ordered the horse ready without a saddle, he didn't want to try fit the two of them on the saddle. Without the saddle, Naithon directed the horse with the reins, his knees and his heels.

When they passed through the gate, Naithon dismounted from the steed landing lithely on the ground. Holding the reins, he moved to the gate and shut it. What had taken her several minutes to wrestle the steel beam off the handles, took him a second to lift the end up off the ground with one hand, and drop it back down.

He turned back to the horse and scowled his ire up at Kiri. His heart clenched. She sat tall and proud, her beautiful mane tossing in the wind, blouse ruffling, and she looked petrified. But the brave little thing was trying to hide it. She shrank from him when he mounted the horse and dragged her body back against his.

He tapped his earpiece and said, "Johannssen, I want a lock on that gate, and you can turn the electricity back on."

Her breath hitched. "Electricity?"

"Huh," he grunted and fished a coin out of his pocket. Tugging on the reins to turn the horse, he tossed the coin at the fence, the coin sizzled and sparked when it hit the metal. Naithon heard and felt her shuddered gulp.

"How, I mean," she stuttered, "when I touched it, it wasn't electrified."

As livid as he was, Naithon huddled her gently against his chest. "When you opened the window a silent alarm went off announcing the breech. There are cameras everywhere on the grounds, and in the woods. You were spotted immediately. A guard called me to advise the situation. He shut the electricity down as soon as you neared the fence."

Kiri tried to keep her body from touching his, which was impossible in the tight grip that he held her, but at the thought that she could have been electrocuted, the air left her lungs and she sank into him. She didn't see his satisfied smile.

Hooves clumping the hard packed ground, the pair riding the horse was quiet on the way back to the barn until they were almost there. Then, Naithon asked softly, "Why did you run? Because of the spanking?"

"Hmm," she murmured with a brief nod. The top of her head brushed under his chin. He lowered his head and pushed his nose into her hair, then indiscernibly kissed the top of her head. "Yes," she replied, "and I was bored out of my mind."

His body hitched, he growled, "You put yourself in danger because you were bored? Girl, you have a television, computer, music, movies, books, everything you could need is in my suite. What more could you want?"

She made an irritated sound and twisted her body to look back and up at him. He appeared so confident riding the huge steed, easily controlling it. Which he did as he controlled everything.

He was a powerful, arrogant, dangerous man that grabbed the world with his teeth and tore asunder any part and anyone that didn't please or obey him. Another shudder rolled down her spine. Judging by the blackness of his intimidating eyes, the grit of his jaw and the furious way he gazed down at her, currently she wasn't obeying or pleasing him.

Kiri sighed and settled back in his iron embrace. He hugged her to him and stuck his nose back in her hair. "I am used to working or being in school. I had an intern position I loved, and even designing and working at the Molten Gold Tasting Room at my father's distillery was fun. I don't want to sit around like a lump and watch TV all day."

"Hmm." He pondered her words. "What about you know, your nails and stuff. The other women are always painting them and whatnot, reading magazines, doing each other's hair. You want some magazines? Maybe get your hair done?"

She snorted out a laugh. "Please. Even more boring. No," she said seriously, "I want to work. I want to create, I want to…" she trailed off.

He snapped, angry again, "You want to go home. I know. Well, you can forget it. I've told you, you are not leaving here. So stop-"

"No, Mr. Adranokov, I don't necessarily want to go home. My father is a tyrant, my brothers try to molest me whenever they're near." His arm tightened like a vice around her ribs. She said breathily, "Please, you're hurting me."

124

He lightened his grip, slightly. "Then there's Rueford. If I go home I will be forced to marry him. But if I could be on my own, I could paint, set scenes like I did and photograph them. Maybe have a little studio of my own," her sigh filled with longing.

"What do you mean set scenes?"

"Oh, I create like fake food then put it together attractively then photograph it. I have this I guess you'd call it a skill, I can make the food look realistic but then not exactly. Kind of when you paint a landscape or something and it looks as real as a photograph, but also...not, it's...more. Like it's alive and breathing, more dramatic.

"It's so exciting, my work seems to draw passionate interest. Magazines and restaurants and things like that use them in their ads. I did a commercial one time for a restaurant; they even let me design the whole scene. It was great fun!"

Naithon was quiet, then he asked, "You take the pictures with your phone?"

Her laugh held resentment. "No. My father took my phone from me as soon as I came home. You darn mobsters, you all want to control me."

She scowled, then her tone lightened, she said with a small smile, "No, I have a special camera. Very expensive. My father allowed me a pittance while I was in school to pay for snacks and incendiaries. I saved forever for it. A Kastali Special Z. Came with all the lenses I needed for lighting and blurring, tinting, you know, all the things you do to make something look different, fascinating, tempting."

"Perhaps I can have someone retrieve the camera from your home."

Sadness in her voice, she said bitterly, "No, my father destroyed it. Said I had dreams of grandeur. He told me Rueford would not be allowing me to work once we were wed, that he would keep me pregnant with his heirs, and he said my little *hobby* was a waste of good money. He ignored the fact that I actually *made* money at it."

She twisted to look up at him, eyes filled with unhappiness. "You see why I ran from you? You men, you dictate my life like I'm a puppet slave to only do what you say, do what you want. But, I am a free, human being, adult, it is wrong to try to clip my wings, keep me locked in a cage. Force me to have sex."

When her head lowered, Naithon tightened his arm around her. Speaking with stony authority, he said coldly, "It is the life you were born into, Kiritina. You can't run from it, if it wasn't me, or your father, or that fat prick, some other made man would take you, do the same. In our world, males have the right to take, control, and discipline our women."

She swung around, glared at him, cheeks pink with pique she declared, "Then I won't live in your world, I will be my own boss."

A small rueful chuckle, he said, "You have no choice, lamb. As I said, you were born into this life. If you went to the police they would send you home, they would not get involved with mobsters' family issues. You can run all you want, but one of us is going to snap you up and lock you away, it's your curse for being so beautiful, so sexy, so," he hugged her close, kissed the top of her head, "so damned sweet. It will be good with me, Kiri, I will treat you well, haven't I so far?"

"Huh," her snort ugly. "Oh yes, I've always wanted to be held prisoner, forced to sleep with a stranger wearing pretty much nothing, get molested, always under the threat of sexual assault by you and your...soldiers. I loved the way you humiliated me by calling me a whore in front of those people.

"Oh, don't let me forget the spanking, the discipline. Sure you've treated me well," sneering scornfully, "I've always wanted to be treated as a child and abused. Forced to live trapped inside a box unable to do the work I love or go where I wish." With an angry huff of frustration she crossed her arms over his arm that held her.

Anger was also in his voice as he replied, "I can be a lot worse, Kiri, a lot. I have been so indulgent with you that my friends call me a pussy, they tell me you wear the pants in this relationship. Fuck with me and see how fucking tolerant I can be." His arm tightened uncomfortably. She wiggled to loosen it, he ignored her struggles.

"We are not in a relationship," she muttered.

At that, one arm around her, his hand holding the reins, he lifted his other hand and curled it around the front of her throat. He didn't squeeze, just held it there. Kiri took it as a threat, she'd gone too far.

They were silent the rest of the way. Naithon led the horse up to the main house and Mazonn rushed out.

"Jeezus, girl, you scared the life out of us!" He hurried over to them. Naithon wrapped his hands around her waist, and lifted her then lowered her so Mazonn could grasp her and gently set her on her feet.

"*Ja*, well, dumb ass," Naithon rebuked his friend. "You should have checked with me before leaving. You should have known I would never leave her in Dan's care. He got the message wrong. You were to stay with her, he was to go to the crime scene. I was busy, on three lines at once, I called him to have him tell you what happened, then go to the murder site, and he got it fouled up. What was worse, he allowed Kiri to run off into danger. I want him in my study in twenty. And get your hands off her."

Mazonn still had his palms on Kiri's waist, he laughed as he moved them. He was teasing his friend, lately pushing his buttons was easy, and entertaining. "*Ja*, you big jealous asshole. Listen," his tone dropped. "Dan is just stupid. He didn't mean to do anything wrong. You don't need to-"

"I will take care of things the way I want to. You take Kiri upstairs." He snapped the reins and gave the horse a light kick. The horse turned around and headed to the stables.

"Ah," Mazonn sighed, his hand on Kiri's back. "Man's got a mountain of a temper." He led her back inside.

"He isn't going to…kill that man is he, Maz?" She stopped and faced him. "Tell him it was my fault, Maz. It was. I deliberately stalled while eating until the poor guy got so bored he nodded off. You have to tell him, I," she paused, took a deep breath. "I will take his punishment."

Mazonn laughed out a choke. "*Ja*, I don't think so. Dan's punishment would be a bit too much for you to handle, honey."

"But it was my fault! Is he going to…kill him? He mustn't, Maz, you have to stop him!"

"Okay, calm down little one." Mazonn started her walking again to the elevator. "He won't kill him, but he will make sure the man gets things straight the next time, *ja*?" His fingertips on her lower back, he said gently, "And, you must consider the repercussions for other people from your actions."

In the elevator, he said, "Kiri, you are safe and coddled here, you need to ease up."

Kiri jabbed the fourth floor button hard. "I am a prisoner, Maz, there is no ease about that."

Chapter Sixteen

A day later, Naithon was up and gone before dawn. But he returned to take Kiri downstairs for breakfast. It was late enough there were a dozen women and a few men sitting at the table eating. They called out greetings to Naithon, which he mostly ignored, the women glowered at Kiri as he pulled out a chair for her.

"Tell me what you want, lamb, I will get it for you," he told her. Both of their tempers still stirred, but they didn't revisit the conversation they had while on the horse. It only pissed Naithon off, her running from him and still wanting nothing to do with him, and Kiri brooded sullenly on her situation.

Once he'd gotten both their plates full, he sat down beside her.

When they were halfway done, Kiri was sipping her orange juice and watched over the rim as a tall blonde woman pulled out the chair next to Naithon and sat down. She set her hand on his forearm. Today he wasn't wearing his normal suit. His block of shoulders filled out a button-down black shirt with the sleeves rolled up, and he wore black jeans, black boots.

"Naity, sugarbear, you haven't been around in a while. I've missed you," the woman purred, stroking her nails up and down his arm.

"Silver," he grunted and shifted his arm but she just moved with it. Her fingers traced up to his bicep and crept across to slide a finger between buttons to touch his chest.

"Honey," the purr oozed huskily, "you need to come back to my bed," she leaned over so her huge breasts could rub on his arm. "We had so much fun," she glanced over at Kiri, appearing to check her out. Her nose wrinkled like she'd seen something nasty, and leaned more heavily, proprietarily on Naithon.

Kiri's eyes rounded watching the woman slide her body all over Naithon.

His shoulders hunched, his head down, he forked up a piece of sausage and tossed it in his mouth. He glanced over at Kiri and saw her wide eyes watching Silver paw him. He shrugged Silver off and turned so half his back was to her. "Take off, Silver, I told you how it is now."

His rebuff did not deter her. "Sugarbear," her coo deep and husky. "You know you want what I have between my legs. You know you like my big tits, and I can take it as rough as you dish it. My lips know how to work that big cock, that tramp, that puny child can't give you what I can-"

Kiri shoved her plate aside, hopped up and hastened out of the room.

"Goddammit, Silver, I told you to knock it the fuck off," Naithon threw a bunch of filthy Romanian oaths at her and shoved his chair back so hard it fell over with a clatter when he stood up. He left the room to find Kiri.

She was running down the hall towards the salon area, he chased after her. Caught her in seconds and grasped her arm to stop her. "Kiri, wait-"

Kiri yanked her arm to break his grip, he held on. "Let go of me. Your lover wants to- to do whatever it is that she can do so special for you."

His face darkened, Naithon loomed over her, more than a foot taller, 150 pounds heavier. His shoulders blocked her view of the hall. He gripped both her arms and squeezed them. "Stop it, Kiri. I am not with Silver, I told you-"

"Yeah, sure. You said you wanted me, and also apparently every other woman in the vicinity! Let go of me!" She twisted to get away, he pinched her arms and shook her, snapping her to still her.

Secretly, Naithon loved her little display of jealousy. He knew she wasn't aware she was jealous, but the angry spark in her greens, the mulish set to her lips, her chin stuck out, damn she was hot. "Okay, just calm down now. If I want to fuck the entire building I will, it isn't any of your business."

At her gasp, he sighed, weary of having to keep repeating himself. "But, Kiri, I do not lie. I don't have to. I meant it when I said I want only you, I have zero desire to even look at another woman much less touch her. I chased after you, I am not back in the dining room sitting with Silver. Now, come with me, I have something to show you."

Ignoring her protests, he grasped her hand and took her to the stairs and they trod up to the second floor.

Naithon led her down a hall with her expelling huffs of annoyance and tugging her arm to make him let go the whole way until he stopped at the last door. Opening it, he pulled her inside, and watched with delight as her eyes popped, mouth fell open in awe.

The room was bright, well-lit because it was a corner room and garnered full windows on two sides. The view was of the pastures, the horses were out chowing on grass. Butterflies flit around them like colored winks. But it was the inside of the room that Kiri was marveling at. She took a wary step further inside, her mouth dropping open further.

There were several tables, on them lined up were fancy boxes containing tubes of paint, paint brushes, tools, tubs, drawing tablets, colored pencils, cases of materials he had found out she needed to create her faux food, and more. Easels stood with blank canvasses ready for her to create her dreams.

Eyes rounded in wonder she wandered around, looked at everything, gently touched everything. Then she saw the camera. It was like the one her father destroyed but a newer model. She frowned, then turned to look at him, her brow furrowed in confusion. "I...don't understand, Naithon?"

She would not know how his heart fluttered when she finally said his name. He told her, "It is for you. I figured if you weren't bored you wouldn't run from me. This is your studio. You can work to your heart's content. There," he indicated a computer on a flat drawing desk, "you can take orders via online and scan your designs by email."

Kiri stood blinking, she turned a small circle. "I…I don't understand," she repeated.

Sighing at her uncertainty, Naithon wound his fingers around her upper arm and turned her to face him. "Little lamb, I want you to be happy here. If you want to, you can help me design a tasting room for my vodka. It would be more like tasting the vodka in mixed drinks than just tasting the vodka. Currently, I produce five different kinds of liquor. I have a mixologist that is working with me creating unique cocktail recipes to blend with the vodka."

He waited, she just stared up at him, her lips still parted in surprise and bewilderment. "Kiri, I saw what you did for your father's tasting room. You have talent, excellent taste in design and colors. You have a magical way of creating a space that is pleasant and interesting to all kinds of people, men, women, even kids. The outdoor patio you started is inviting and exciting. I want you to do the same for me. That is," he paused, "if you want to."

"Mr. Adranokov, I don't know what to say."

There she went again. How the hell was he supposed to fuck a girl that called him by his surname? Frowning at her regressing, he said, "You can say, '*Naithon*, thank you. I appreciate my gifts and look forward to working with you.' " Squeezing her arms, he threatened, "I would hate to christen your new studio with a spanking for calling me by my surname, eh?"

Kiri grinned. "Okay, Boss." She laughed gaily at his annoyed frown. "Thank you, Naithon, I can't believe you did all this for me! When did you do it?"

Hiding his thrill at her fey laughter that for the first time was directed at him, he tucked the tips of his fingers in his front jean's pockets, shrugged as if it was nothing. "I have an acquaintance who is an artist. I called him, told him what I wanted. He had his assistant contact the proper shop and set up the overnight delivery."

"But, Naithon, it's so much money, I can't-"

He held a hand up to stop her. "Don't. Don't say you can't accept it. I owe you something for taking you from your home and your livelihood. Just accept it and enjoy it. *Ja?*"

She strolled to the camera and touched it tenderly with just a finger. "Naithon, I don't know how to thank you."

His voice was right behind her, low, deep, growly, "How about a kiss?"

She froze, then sidestepped him and headed for the door.

"Shit," he swore and went after her. Quickly he stood in front of the door, blocking her exit. "Okay, okay, I'm sorry," *did he just say that for the second time in his life?* "I'm not trying to buy your affections."

Kiri crossed her arms and angled a foot out in front of her. "You're not?"

Stiffening, he muttered, "*Ja*, well maybe. I just want to kiss you, Kiri, is that too much to ask? I haven't grabbed you and forced you like I want to do. Just a kiss, it's not that big of a deal, one kiss, Kiri. Not for the studio, just…because."

"The thing with you, is that you don't stop at just a kiss."

Lips pulling in he had to agree. "That's true. But I swear, right now, I will stop at a kiss. Or kisses. Okay?" Damn, was this him, Naithon Rámon Adranokov, big rough tough, ex-con lethal bossman begging, whining instead of just taking? *Ja*, she'd made a pussy out of him. If his friends saw this…and for only a lousy kiss. Yet he waited for her response.

She glanced around the room, everywhere but at him. Then she centered her attention on Naithon. A tall, muscular, ill-tempered, dangerous man. His fair hair combed straight back, dark eyes glimmering white-hot heat at her. Already his jaw was dark with stubble. His head level, he stood, likely impatiently, staring down at her under those secretive hooded lids.

He muttered, "I swear, you owe me nothing for the studio. You don't have to kiss me, I just would like it."

He was handsome even with the scars, he would have been almost pretty without them. Except his features were male tough.

She couldn't believe he was asking her for a kiss when he could easily shove her to the floor and do whatever he pleased to her.

"Kiri," he said softly, "stop thinking. Just do it."

"You promise only a kiss?"

"*Ja*, kiss*es*."

"Naithon…"

"Okay, okay, one damned kiss. Come here, already," he commanded, his arms out.

She hesitated, then took a shy small step to him and looked up.

"Ah," he rattled off a bunch of Romanian words and slipped his hand under her hair to grasp her nape and pulled her to him, that hand slid down to her lower back while his other hand moved to cradle her face. He bent to her slowly, giving her the opportunity to stop him, he held his breath that she wouldn't. She didn't, and he lightly kissed her lips, then licked them, nibbled both.

When Kiri responded slightly, Naithon let out the held breath, slanted his head and attacked her mouth like a pirate plundering a ship. Both of his hands moved to encircle her head, he murmured against her lips, "Open your mouth, baby, let me in." He pushed at her lips with his and hers parted just enough he sank his tongue inside, and the pillaging began in hot and heavy earnest.

He squeezed her soft skin with his fingers, growled into her mouth, groaned when her little tongue responded to his licks and sucking. Naithon foraged every part of her mouth inside and out with the frenzy of a warrior battling a combatant he hungered to conquer. His fiery mayhem elicited a moan, then a hum that sifted through her throat to his mouth and he thought he'd come right then and there.

Stretching to her toes, Kiri wrapped her hands around his neck and kissed him back hot and sweet. A turmoil of sensations, blazing arousal burned through his body. Naithon slurred his mouth over hers, gobbling, nipping to her jaw, he bit her skin, then groaned while dragging his mouth, his teeth down her neck where he latched on and sucked until she whimpered.

Mumbling, "Fuck, baby," against her throat, he licked down to the top of her breast. With a rumbled groan, he bent and lifted her, carried her to a settee he'd had brought in and placed by a window so she could sit and look out. Naithon laid Kiri down so fast and climbed right on her before she could let out a squeal of protest.

Brain frying on bedazzled lust, his mind shut down, he was all primitive animal shoving his face down her cleavage, grinding his chin, his mouth into her plush skin. With beastly growls he chewed and sucked the swells of her breasts, then pushed her blouse up to feel every inch of her exquisite skin. But, she was shrieking and hitting him, shouting at him to stop.

Naithon shook his head, blinking dazed eyes, his mouth wet, he looked down at her, mumbled, "What's wrong, baby?" Their chests panted in unison, he'd pushed her blouse up above her bra, he looked down and licked his lips. Lowering his head, his mouth open to suck a plump breast, Kiri pushed at his head and yelled, "Stop! Naithon, you promised, stop!"

Her shrieks pierced the hazy film of scorching lust that fogged his brain, he leaned back. Seeing her distress, he sighed, and sat up, pulling her up with him. She tried to scoot away from him but he snagged her arm.

Heaving rapid heavy breaths, his big chest billowed in and out as he caught his breath. Damp blond hair flopped over his eyes. "All right, I'll stop, Kiri. *Meu Dio*, I can't help what you do to me. You blast every thought out of my head and make me a beast that wants to devour you. If I could climb inside your mouth, sweet pigeon, I would."

She couldn't help herself, Kiri giggled at the image he presented. Her giggles brought a rare smile to his hard face. Leaning into her, he went to slide his hand back around her nape and pull her in, his head already slanting, lips parting to resume kissing. Kiri set a hand on his chest and pushed admonishing, "Naithon, you promised."

A groaned sigh, "*Ja, ja*, okay, okay." He stroked his hands from her shoulders down her arms to clasp her hands briefly. Shifting off the settee, he lurched to his feet, forked shaking fingers through his hair. "The only way I can keep my hands off you, pigeon, is to get away from you. At least until I calm down," he looked down at his pants. The thick bulge there outlined how inflamed with desire he was.

With a little frown, Kiri scolded, "I don't think you should call me that, Naithon. It's sexist."

He threw his head back with a loud laugh. "No doubt. It's not my fault your tits are so round and full and perfect."

Rolling her eyes she said, "And that crudity. There are other words to describe parts of anatomy, you know."

Brows arched, he said with a tease, "But tits is easier to say than breasts. Breasts sounds prissy." He laughed again as the color rose in her cheeks.

"How about you don't talk about my, um," pink darkened to red, "body parts at all. Like a gentleman."

Naithon surprised himself as another loud laugh burst out. "*Ja,* yeah, I never claimed to be a gentlemen, my sweet. Besides, I get such pleasure from calling you that, your face turns a gorgeous shade of pink. It's endearing and intoxicating." He bent and kissed the top of her head then stepped back.

"I will go now or you will be naked and under me in two seconds." Laughing again at her embarrassed expression, he started for the door. "Pigeon, uh, lamb, you can lock this door from the inside. Do not answer it if someone knocks. If I send anyone to you, I will call and tell you," he nodded to a phone on a wall. "That will hook to my phone. When you are tired of working, playing, whatever you intend to do with all this stuff, call me, I'm the number 1 on the pad, and I will come get you. Okay?"

Standing up, Kiri gazed around with wide eyes, where oh where to start? "Okay," she said absently, her head already buzzing with ideas.

Naithon started back to give her a kiss goodbye, then thought better of it, he opened the door.

"Naithon?"

He hesitated. "*Ja,* baby lamb?"

She said shyly, "Thank you. Thank you so much for doing this for me."

Another rare smile, he replied, "I am hoping that if you are content, you will not try to run away again."

Her lips bunched. "Naithon, everyone desires freedom." She was crazy, he was holding her captive and she was thanking him! But, she had her very own studio, even if it was under Naithon's lock and key.

The smile gone, replaced by a serious firming of his lips. "We've discussed this. You are the daughter of an infamous mobster, Kiri, for as long as you live, you will never have pure freedom again. There will always be people that will come after you to get to him or your brothers. And, men with power will always desire you, and they will always take you, with or without your consent. In your situation, as unfair as it is, the law will never be on your side."

Sniffing back a sadness, she said with irritation, "I was safe in Italy, no one ever bothered me there."

"That's because no one knew about you. Now they do." Except he'd known about her, and had waited and plotted how to get his hands on her.

"I would be safe if I moved back to Italy."

The frown turned into a scowl. "You will never go to Italy unless I am going there." He left her before they got engaged in another argument. He locked the door before pulling it closed behind him.

It grew late, Naithon checked his watch. He had brought Kiri dinner because she claimed she didn't want to stop working to eat. But, now, hell, it had long grown dark. He marched upstairs, unlocked and pushed the door open. One small lamp was on by the table near the window. Kiri was sitting at the table, but her head was down resting on arms folded on the table.

"Kiri?" he spoke softly not wanting to startle her. She didn't move. He trod quietly over to her, bent over. Her eyes were closed, lips slightly parted. She was sound asleep.

Smiling, Naithon looked around. There were materials and concoctions in bowls. She'd sketched a scene she must be planning to design on a drawing pad; she still held a pencil in one hand. Beside the pad lay a page that had been detached.

Removing the pencil from her hand he set it down and looked at the page. A smile like he'd never had before filled his face. She had drawn him. Sitting astride his stallion, the horse's front hooves scraping at the air, she had drawn Naithon dressed as a warrior, his face fierce, a sword raised as if he was launching into battle.

"Damn but you are so sweet, I knew you would add light to my dark soul," he muttered, slipping the picture in his pocket. Leaning over, he slid his hands under her. She sighed when he lifted her in his arms. Naithon carried her to the door and out to the stairs, and up to his, no, their room. When he used his thumb to unlock the chamber door, Kiri stirred.

With a tiny yawn, she slid one arm up around his neck and half asleep mumbled, "Thank you Naithon, thank you for the studio. No one has ever done anything so nice for me."

Other women wanted diamonds and shoes, this one is happy with an art studio.

"Anything you want, lamb, is yours," he said softly, kissing the top of her head he brought her to bed.

Chapter Seventeen

Two weeks passed. Naithon brought Kiri to his distillery complex and showed her the room he wanted to turn into a tasting room. The entire distillery complex was sleekly designed yet maintained a rustic quality that fit right into the enchanting countryside.

The tasting room was attached to the main structure by a glass-enclosed walkway, but it also had an outside entrance at the back. It was a large, round building with a lengthy view of the back grounds and forests that were now almost completely bereft of the autumn leaves.

"Oh Naithon, it's charming," she exclaimed. Spinning around, she examined every corner, niche, window, the bar area. It was only the most basic structure of raw exposed wood, a blank canvas for Kiri to spin her creative magic. Goose bumps of excitement tickled her arms.

"What is it that you're looking for?" she asked, as she studied the area, her brain already cooking with ideas. "I mean, like what kind of theme do you want? Modern, country, aristocratic, old world renaissance, masculine, family, ritzy, exotic, cozy?"

He came to stand by her. "Hadn't thought about it. It had never entered my mind until I saw how you did your da's place. You made it so, I don't know, interesting and welcoming. Enchanting actually. Makes you want to sit a while and soak in the…friendly comfort, enjoy the attractiveness of the place, I guess? Comforting, yet visually stimulating. Made me start thinking about having something like it here."

"Oh," she pretended to be offended. Crossed her arms and stuck her foot out like she does when she's piqued. "You only abducted me so I could create this room for you."

Laughing, Naithon scooped an arm around her and pulled her in. Smoothing strands of hair from her cheek, he kissed the tip of her nose. "*Ja*, sure, I stole you to design my place. That's why I can't keep my hands, or mind, off of you, pigeon." He bent to give her a real kiss and she swiveled out of his arms.

"No, Naithon, you kiss me and one thing will lead to another, you know."

Sighing, "*Ja*, I know. The another is where I want to get to." The more time he spent with her the more he wanted her willingly in his bed. He wanted it, but he was rapidly running out of patience and living with blue balls that he had to take care of himself.

He could have any number of women eager to help him with his problem, but as he told Kiri and Maz, he had zip interest in fucking anyone but Kiri. The thought of having another woman's hands on his body made his insides shrivel.

"Okay, be serious now, tell me what you want, and not me, the room."

He chuckled, thinking how clever and cute she was. "You got me pegged, lamb." Glancing around, he shrugged. "I don't know design. A comfortable chair and bed is all I ever cared about. I hired a decorator to do the mansion here in Marécage, and my office in Chaleur. Told her nothing frou-frou or girly, just sturdy furniture for my crew. You come up with something, you're the talent."

Nodding thoughtfully, she surveyed the area again. "Okay. I would want to stay with the theme of the rest of the plant and offices. Sleek, modern, yet keep the rustic appeal of being out in the country. The best of both worlds, chicly urbane and rural picturesque."

Finger to chin, she strolled in a small circle, taking in the high arched ceilings, wide windows in the back, tucked away clandestine alcoves. "I'm thinking I'd like to make it…intriguing."

Peering around, smiling abstractedly as she imagined the room completed, then a pleased smile lifted her pretty lips. "I have an idea. Because your vodka is crystal clear, I think it would sparkle luxuriously displayed on shelves of black velvet."

Tongue poking out the side of her mouth as she continued looking at the room, eyes squinting and revolving as she pictured concepts. Her ruminating thoughts murmured out loud, "I'd like to do like I did with my dad's Maestá d'oro. I put gold, silver, turquoise and diamond chips in the different bottles, making each differently hued amber rum sparkle with a hint of wealthy color."

He watched as ideas flickered across her face. "Would you do the same with my vodka? That does sound intriguing."

Kiri strolled over to the unfinished bar, tapped her finger on the raw wood. "Sort of, but different. Your liquor is clear, I'm thinking of adding crystals like amethyst, smoky topaz, rose quartz, aquamarine and others. Against the clear liquid, they will be slightly blurry, but each will have a unique glittering coloration. Set on the black velvet with lights above, maybe colored lights to match the individual crystals, I think it would make your vodka come alive with fire, radiance."

Naithon was speechless. He had always thought she was smart and talented, but shit, the girl was a bloody genius. "Wow, babygirl, you got it going on. That sounds fantastic."

Nodding, she walked around in thought. "With the variety of colored crystals, each mixer you add will continue to alter the look and unique appeal of the drink. You and your mixologist can sit around and come up with exotic names for the cocktails."

He chuckled at the idea, but tilted his head at the thought, it was a good idea.

She went on, "I think I'd like to make this room dusky and mysterious, have your pourers be young, attractive men and women in sexy, yet classy outfits. Not pasties and thongs!" she said quickly and turned to see him grinning at her.

She'd never seen him grin before. It was...nice. Took the edge off his normal hostile nature. "I'm thinking black tie kind of, in a way but not exactly, for both the males and females, a sophisticated

Playboy kind of appeal, again classy, not plain like Hooters. And yet simple so guests don't feel uncomfortable or overwhelmed.

"Customers won't want to come out to a daytime tasting if they feel they have to dress to the nines to fit in. So, keep it sophisticated, sexy, simple." She thought a minute. "Yes, I want serene aplomb."

Rubbing his hands together, he smiled. "I'm liking it, lamb, can't wait to get started."

"Yes, softly steamy and romantic, think red roses and black velvet. We can switch it up when seasons change, maybe sapphire and diamonds, this would be for adults only. Outside, in the summer on the deck, you can bring in cooling food like salads, sandwiches, sodas, or, maybe a changing theme for fall like spicier enchiladas and carnitas, tortillas and salsa for snacking.

"Make them thirsty for drinks. The next season do Italian food with purple heather and so on. People will want to come back just to see what's different.

"You can make a patio like I started at Dad's and cater to families. I mean, adults buy the vodka, but if you pull in the children you'll get more foot traffic. I even started to add horseback riding, we could think of things people would enjoy doing here like that. Maybe croquet or badminton on the lawn. Sophisticated, simple, family."

"Uh huh," he nodded, picturing it all. Proud gaze on his girl, he smiled with enthusiasm. "Will you photograph it so I can put ads in magazines, *ja*?"

Her grin went from ear to ear. "I would love to!"

****

A few weeks passed, the tasting room was well on its way to completion, and Kiri worked in her studio every day. The only time she saw Naithon was at dinner, or when he briefly took her by to see the progress of the tasting room. He made sure he broke from business every evening to eat dinner with her.

As usual, she was asleep when he came in and when he left in the morning. Sometimes she woke in her clothes in the bed and realized he had carried her from her studio and tucked her in.

Staring out the window of her studio, she watched red cardinals swooping after each other, and a fat-breasted robin hopping in the grass. She realized she was actually missing Naithon. He was broody and crude, violent when someone did something really egregious, he cursed and said vulgar words that brought pink to her cheeks.

But he was gentle with her, had his hands all over her, but not sexually whenever he was near. He stroked her arm, her back, her thigh, hugged her. When any people were around he did it more blatantly, advertising his claim, warning the others off.

His subtlety was working; she was growing used to him, and enjoying his touch. What frightened her was she was thinking about wanting more, and, she hadn't thought about trying to escape since that day he brought her back on the horse. She didn't want a repeat spanking, but it really was more than that.

He praised her work, and his eyes, she sighed. Smoldering onyx whenever he looked at her. She knew the time would come when he would push her again for the sex, but he was giving her time to adapt to him and her situation. He was basically courting her.

Whenever she talked about going home, he brushed her words away. He didn't tell her anymore that he was keeping her, he just showed her. He bought her more clothes, pieces of jewelry, art supplies.

Part of her understood the truth in what he said. That due to her heritage they would never let her live free, totally alone. She would never be safe in the world without protection. Naithon gave her everything she could possibly desire, her cage was gilded, her warden was dating her, and she was under a thumb. A handsome, sexy, sometimes charming thumb, but nevertheless, it held her down. Well, in.

Mazonn had told her Naithon had done a complete 360 in his behavior towards her, he treated her different than he did anyone else, especially women. He wasn't a nice person, a patient person;

he was rough and callous, yet to her, he was tender and patient. He'd made it clear he believed she was worth the wait, the patience and work involved in wooing her.

She begged him to stop buying her things, not that he did. And, she'd found he had a sharp wit, was dryly funny, and he loved to make her laugh. Yes, she missed him. He had done it, he had wormed his way in. Instead of bulldozing over her, forcing her, he did it like a stealthy war; he had snuck in and won. She still wanted her freedom, but she wanted Naithon too.

Watching another robin hop in and the two fighting over a worm, Kiri realized she didn't think Naithon had slept in bed with her for the past several nights. His pillow wasn't smushed, and his side of the bed stayed unwrinkled.

Was he tired of waiting for her and was getting his needs met with another woman? That Silver girl perhaps? A shaft of pain stabbed her belly at the image of Naithon on top of Silver, his mouth on her big bare breasts-

"Would he?" That disturbed her. Setting the paintbrush in a glass to soak, she removed her apron, dropped it on a counter and went to the phone on the wall. She'd only called him previously a few times, he'd always come to her right away. But now, the phone rang and rang, and he didn't pick up. He had entered Mazonn's, Blok's and Yashin's numbers as well. She dialed Mazonn.

He answered on the second ring. "Kiri, what's up?"

"Maz, I just realized, I mean, I haven't seen Naithon in days, and he isn't answering his phone, is everything okay? Is he away on business? He didn't mention it to me." Naithon kept his business from her, but when he traveled for brief amounts of time he always told her where, when and how long he was going to be away.

There was a pregnant pause, then Mazonn said, "I'll be right there."

By the time she put her shoes on and combed her hair, he was in the doorway looking grim. Her heart clenched. "Maz, is he all right?"

"Ah, *ja*, sort of."

"Sort of? What does that mean?" Maz was making her anxious with his vague words. "He isn't- has he been arrested? He isn't hurt is he?"

Mazonn stepped inside, hesitated, then strode over and sat on a chair and gestured for her to sit on the sofa.

"You're scaring me, Maz," her voice caught as she sat down.

He dragged a hand through his dark hair, the twinkle in his eye was absent today. "He...he's okay, really, Kiri. It's just," at her anxious eyes, fingers twisting themselves in her lap, he sucked in a deep breath, let it out.

"All right. It's like this. Naithon has had a...hard life. His da yanked him out of school at a very young age and put him to work. Very violent work. When Naithon had made a good bundle of dough, his da took everything he'd earned and kicked him out to the streets." Folding his hands together, Maz leaned forward with his elbows on his knees.

Kiri could see the torment that Naithon had gone through imprinted in Maz's poignant blue eyes. "What a horrible thing for a father to do to his child."

Nodding, Maz raked his hair off his forehead and sat back. "*Ja*, bastard of a man. With no money and nowhere to live, Naithon ended up in one of the most vicious gangs in the United States. The horrendous things they'd made him do, he had no choice, you do what they say or they kill you.

The deeds, still, they plague his mind. Once they caught a prospect, that's a guy trying to become a full member of a gang, he was stealing from the gang and snitching to the Feds."

Maz glanced at her to see how she was receiving the information. Would she hate Naithon even more? But, he decided, she needed to understand Naithon's world, see why he was the way he was. "Ah, so, they staked the guy to the floor, hammered steel pegs through his hands and ankles. They, uh, made Nait cut pieces off him, slowly, one at a time. Fingers, toes, and so on until he confessed everything and gave names of other men involved with the Feds."

Wiping his palm across his sweating forehead, Mazonn took a breath. "Honey, there are some things you never forget, can't scrub out of your mind."

Drumming his fingers on the edge of the chair arms he studied Kiri to see if she was sympathetic or judgmental of the things Naithon had been forced to do. Pity and concern laced the green of her eyes, mouth turned down in sorrow.

He went on. "At one point, one of the gang members made a mistake and they all ended up in prison. Nait was sent to an adult prison at seventeen. For five years he endured worse in prison than in the gang. They did things to him, made him do unspeakable things to others. It...well, now, once in a while the heavy, hideous memories break through his protective wall and cloud him and he...shuts down I guess you call it. Goes into a deep, dark depression, a tortured black fugue. We've tried, but none of us have ever been able to pull him out of it."

"What does he do when he shuts down?"

Mazonn sat back, crossed his legs. "Ah, well, he disappears. Goes somewhere isolated and dark, and he drinks. A lot."

"For how long?"

"Until it passes, a few days, sometimes longer."

"Where is he now?"

Mazonn didn't answer her, he looked away.

"Maz, I know you know, tell me where he is. Is he with...women?"

Vehemently shaking his head he said quickly with a frown, "No, no. He has too big a thing for you. No, he was gone, but he couldn't stay far from you. He's in the macabre gardens now."

"The macabre gardens?"

"*Ja*, at the end of the long corridor in the east wing, past all the rooms there are gardens in an enclosed courtyard, like a greenhouse. We call them macabre because they are dark, gloomy, no one goes there. I don't know why he keeps them going. Has UV lights for the plants, and someone tends them. Sometimes it's him."

"Take me there." She got up and went to the door.

"Kiri-"

"Take me there, now."

Shaking his head, he reluctantly followed her to the door and opened it. "Listen, Kiri-"

She stepped past him out to the hall. "Take me to him."

Closing the door, Mazonn let out a heavy sigh and walked with her to the stairs. Down to the first floor, they walked, and walked, the mansion, or compound, was enormous more twists and turns, hallways and rooms than a castle.

At last, he slowed. Stopped outside a large wooden door. "Kiri," he stood in front of the door. "He doesn't like to be bothered when he's like this. He's come to blows before when we've tried to intervene. I don't think you should-"

"Open the door and step out of the way, Maz. Please."

Mazonn arched his neck and stared at the ceiling with a groan. Exhaling hard, he said to her, "I'll be out here. Any trouble, scream and I will come. Okay?"

"Yes. Open the door."

Silently he opened it and watched her disappear into the dark. Then he sucked in a deep breath and closed the door almost but not quite all the way.

Kiri could smell the damp soil, the delicate scent of flowers, but it was dark. She stood to let her eyes adjust to the light. She almost called out his name, but assumed he wouldn't answer or he'd tell her to go, so she moved slowly through the gloom.

Although there was the soft fragrance of flowers, the place was horribly dismal. So dark the flowers and plants all looked different shades and depths of black. The UV lights weren't on. A shred of light gashing in through a skylight up high cast glum shadows, only made it gloomier.

Kiri picked her way carefully through the spooky garden, ferns and leaves brushed her jeans, tiny gnarly branches grabbed at her hair and sleeves as she passed by them. Hearing a slight sound, she paused and listened. A bottle clanked on a hard surface. She followed the sound and found him. She moved up silently behind him.

Naithon's jaw showed he hadn't shaved in days, his black shirt and jeans were dusty. The shirt partially unbuttoned, he sat slumped on a wooden bench. His spine against the back of the bench, his neck was arched, his head hung back, eyes closed. His fingers wrapped loosely around the neck of a bottle of his vodka. The base of the bottle was on the bench. He looked like hell.

"Go away," he growled, his voice sore, thick and rusty from days of drinking.

Ignoring his order, Kiri moved slowly, not wanting to anger him with a sudden approach.

He didn't move, eyes stayed closed, he growled again, accent slurred and thick as mud, "Get the fuck outta here, don't want you here." He lifted the bottle and chugged, there was only about an eighth of vodka left in it. Dropping his limp arm, the bottle clunked on the bench.

As if he hadn't spoken, she trod around the bench and stood in front of him.

Slurring into inaudible, he snarled, "I said fucking go away. I fucking mean it."

Without a word, Kiri lowered to her knees, then sat on the cool floor and laid her head on his thigh. He twitched, jerking her head, but didn't push her away.

They sat, for a long time, neither speaking. Then, she felt his hand on her head. Her eyes opened, but she didn't move.

After a few minutes, he brushed his hand over her hair once, then again. They sat, for an hour, and he stroked her hair, played with it, let curls coil around his fingers then let them slide like silk ribbons out of his hand.

"Baby," he said hoarsely, and patted the seat of the bench beside him. Her legs were stiff, she climbed up and sat next to him. Naithon rolled an arm around her shoulders and pulled her to his chest, he laid his head on top of hers. He should have smelled bad, but he didn't, he smelled like him, virile, masculine.

"I came up behind you, your eyes were closed, how did you know I was here?" she asked him quietly.

"Ah, baby, I am so attuned to you I can feel, smell you when you are near. That's why I brought my bender back here. I needed to be close to you. Maz watched out for you while I…"

Again, they sat for a while. Then he spoke, "You save me, lamb. You save me from myself more every day." He lifted his head, lowered it to look at her. "You have pulled me out of the darkness, just your sweet presence, saved me today. Thank you." He sounded drained.

Kiri gently touched his face, caressed the rough whiskers. He leaned into her palm.

"Still," he said, "it eats inside me like rot, I can't get away from it. You should go. I never should have taken you, I'm no good for you. But," he kissed her palm, "I can't give you up, I'm sorry." A light chuckle rumbled in his chest. "Only three times in my life have I used that word, and they've all been with you."

She tilted her head, eyes half-mast, smiled up at him.

"Baby," he murmured, cupped her chin and kissed her. Then let her go, like she always says, he won't stop at one kiss. He was filthy, drunk, had no business touching her with his dirty hands, cruel mouth, rotted mind. "You need to go, Kiri, back upstairs to our room," he sighed.

"Okay," she said cheerfully standing up. She grasped his hand. "You're coming with me. I have something we need to do." Tugging his hand, she tried to pull him up.

"No, baby, you shouldn't be near me right now. I'm…fetid."

"Naithon," she said quietly. "I never ask you for anything, ever. Do I?"

His lips pursed, he shook his head. "No. You know I would give you anything you asked, except, to leave me."

Her smile slanted up at one corner. "Right. So, I'm asking you to come with me now, do something with me."

A brow wobbled quizzically. "What do you want to do?"

"You'll see. Come on." She tugged his hand.

Chapter Eighteen

He'd been sitting for a long time; it took a minute for him to shuffle to his feet. He looked down at the vodka bottle sitting on the bench, and slipped his fingers to twine with hers, leaving it there. "Okay. I need to shower," he frowned, scratching under his chin at the scruff.

"No, trust me, you're better off the way you are, come on." She pulled him with her through the gloom and into the light.

He squinted and covered his eyes with his arm. He didn't see Mazonn sitting on the floor on the other side of the door, phone in his hand, with his surprised gaze on the pair.

"Give me the key to the upstairs and our room," she said to Maz with her hand out. The key could bypass the security of his thumbprint.

His brows arched, he fished it out and dropped it in her palm.

She grinned at his perplexity and tugged Naithon away down the corridor.

When they reached the grand room, Kiri gave Naithon a little push so he flopped down on a chair.

Wait here, I'll be right back." She ran off to the stairs.

Mumbling, "Aye aye, Captain," he saluted, missing his forehead. His hand fell heavily to the arm of the chair. Looking down he saw his shirt was unbuttoned, revealing the darker hair on his chest. Muttering drunkenly, "Can't look the heathen my pigeon

150

calls me," with unsteady hands he buttoned it leaving the top two undone.

Five minutes and Kiri returned carrying a case. "Okay, I'm ready." She motioned to the door.

At the front door, she said, "Naithon, we need a car."

"K," he staggered, righted himself. "I got my Viper in the garage. I'll get it."

"Uh, nope. We need a driver. I don't have an American license and you are in no condition to drive. Call a driver."

"Geesh you're bossy today." He grinned crookedly and slurred, "Kinda like it." Patting his pockets, he muttered, "Don't know where my phone is."

"Excuse me," Kiri said to a guard that was watching them, suppressing his grin. This was a lighter side of Naithon never seen before. "Can you get us a driver, please?"

"Right away, ma'am," he pulled out his cell and dialed. Hanging up, he rushed in front of them. Taking her case from her, he said, "Let me get that door, Miss. It's really heavy."

Naithon scowled at him. "I can get the door for my girl, Shawn."

"Yessir," Shawn grinned, holding the door open.

"Come on, tipsy." Kiri pushed Naithon out the door as he glowered at Shawn.

"It's too bright out here," Naithon complained, covering his eyes.

"After being in the dark for the better part of the week I would think so."

His chuckle more of a slur, "Sarcasm becomes you, my sweet," he lurched to kiss her but she ducked her head and he almost toppled. "But then," he grinned wickedly, slurring, "everything becomes you, pigeon, 'cause you're as sweet and beautiful on the inside as you are on the outside. Maybe someday I can experience the inside," brows wiggled, smirking his innuendo.

His mouth curved downward, he sighed morosely, "What would I do without you, pigeon? You can't ever leave me."

"We decided you weren't going to call me that anymore, Naithon," she reproached him. "It's sexist."

He leered drunkenly at her chest. "I don't mind. Those plump babies are calling me to crush them in my hands," he tottered towards her with his hands out. Eyes rolling, Kiri moved out of his way, he was too unbalanced to easily follow her dodge. The car pulled up. The chauffeur exited and hurried around to open a rear passenger door, and the guard stowed her case in the front.

Naithon swooped his hand indicating for her to get in first. She did and slid over to make room for him. He mostly fell inside and shuffled over, squishing her against the side.

The chauffeur poked his head in, asked. "Where to, sir?"

Naithon shrugged with his palms turned up. "Gotta ask the lady, she's really bossy today."

Pursing his lips to hide his grin, the chauffeur looked at Kiri with a questioning brow raised.

"To the distillery."

"The distillery?" Naithon frowned with a negative shake, blond hair flung over one dark eye. "We are not goin' to your da's. It's too dangerous for you there." He slurred, "An' I'm not lettin' that red-haired fucker get near you. He'll try to take you away from me."

"No, silly, to your distillery," she said with a smile and nod to the driver. He winked at her and closed the door.

Only thirty minutes later, and a short snooze for Naithon, the limo stopped in front of the distillery. It was Sunday so the place was deserted. Perfect. No one needed to see Naithon in his condition. He'd drowned himself in liquor for days and wallowed in horrifying, dreadful memories.

Still, he didn't look disgusting to her, he looked roughed up. Black clothes wrinkled, Blond hair mussed, bleak eyes heavy and unfocused, the scruff made him appear a little more on the sinister side, but she didn't fear him. Not anymore.

Kiri hoped if she got him doing some kind of action he would sober up with less of a headache and feeling so bad. Because she wasn't letting him near a drop of alcohol. They were going to the tasting room, it was still being renovated so there wasn't any liquor

152

in there yet. She asked the driver to stop at a drive-through to get some coffee for Naithon.

Smoothly coming to a halt when they reached the distillery, the driver parked and hurried around to open the limo's door. He stood to the side as the couple climbed out. The driver held out her case. "Miss, the guard said this was yours."

"Got it." Naithon snatched the case from the driver. "Now what?" he burbled to Kiri, slurping his coffee.

"Hmm, do you have the keys on you, Naithon?"

"Dunno." Setting the coffee on a ledge, he clumsily patted his pockets. "Don't think so. Drinkin', so can't have keys when I'm drinkin'."

One side of her mouth pulled in. "Oh. I didn't think about the key to get into the distillery. We'll have to go back."

"No worries." Naithon stumbled to the entrance. "It's a combo pad."

Kiri followed him; the driver slipped into the car and opened a newspaper. Folding the paper, he took out a pencil and started on the crossword puzzle.

Naithon tried three times, but he couldn't push the right combination of numbers. His thick fingers moved too clumsily over the buttons, hitting two or three at once.

Sighing with amusement, Kiri said, "Tell me the numbers, Naithon."

He put a finger to his lips. "Shh, it's a secret, don't tell anyone."

Rolling her eyes for the third time that day, Kiri said with a dry grin, "Sure, who am I going to tell?"

Rattling off the combination, he said with a lopsided smirk, "*Dio*, more sarcasm. You are so cute when you try to speak mean. But," he leaned in to kiss her, "you are too sweet to be mean. Gimmie soma dat sugar, pigeon."

Kiri pushed the buttons, grabbed his coffee cup and stepped quickly through the door out of his reach.

When they were inside the lobby, Kiri took hold of Naithon's wrist and pulled him through the complex then through the glass-enclosed walkway leading to the structure containing the tasting

153

room. It was still being worked on, but the carpenters had almost finished the room. The walls were freshly painted a week ago. The room still retained a hint of the pungent paint smell.

Naithon's brow wrinkled in puzzlement. "Why are we here, pigeon?"

"Naithon," she said with a frown.

"Sorry. Why are we here, lamb?" He grinned at the face she made at him.

Slapping the coffee cup into his hand, she reproved the recalcitrant man, "Really, lamb to slaughter isn't any better. You can set the case on that table, please," Kiri pointed to a nearby table.

"Ookey doke," he complied, plodded to the table and thumped the case down.

Kiri shook her head with a smile. This playful Naithon was fun. And endearing. She went over and lifted the lid on the case. Naithon peered over her shoulder and looked puzzled. "Paints? Why did you bring paints?" Inside the case were extra-large tubes of paint.

"Well," she said removing tubes and brushes, "I had an idea for this place." Glancing over, she smiled at seeing several buckets of paint the painters had left stacked near the door.

"K." Naithon watched her set some things on the table. He was up for any of her suggestions, as far as he was concerned she was a freakin' Michelangelo. A girly one. Trying to be discrete, he clumsily scanned her curves, smiled with a not so subtle nod, oh *ja*, all girl.

Ignoring his wolfish leering at her, she said, "Yeah, remember I said romantic and mysterious for this tasting room?"

He nodded wobbly, agreeable. Finishing the last of the coffee he set the cup on the bar counter and combed his hair with his fingers. His eyes were growing clearer, stance steadier, he was sobering up. A miracle considering how much booze he'd put away.

She took out a pencil and gestured to a wall. "I thought about some paintings and pictures of Hawaii I've seen. There were some that were twilight darkish, yet iridescent. A mountainside barely discernable in the indigo nightfall, halfway down is a shack partially covered with palm trees and thick dark foliage."

She moved to the wall and pretended to trace a picture. "A mural, Naithon. The mountain on the right side, deep mossy green and botanic, shadowed and bold and mysteriously curving down as it slants to the ocean, and the dark violet sky and glittering stars on the left. Silver moon partly shrouded with wispy bands of clouds. Just a hint of inundating ocean below."

Naithon stared at the wall, following her gestures, the flowing descriptions of her imagery.

"High up in the background, the barest slash of a blueish waterfall disappearing into the dark side of the mountain. Stars in the midnight sky twinkling along with moonlit glistened points on the mountain and the waterfall." She raised the pencil high for the waterfall then dotted all the way down it then the mountain where she imagined sparkles sprinkling areas from the silvery moonlight, all the way to the slightest glittering ripples of the ultramarine sea.

"See, semi-dark, everything almost invisible, but a smidge of red color from a flower, a bit of lighter green on parts of the mountain, trace of grey and beige in the shack, faint blue and white of the waterfall in the distance, and the slightest pinpricks of iridescent sparkles throughout." She turned to him. "What do you think?"

Naithon stood mutely staring at the wall.

"Naithon? With the black velvet shelves, your luminescent colored vodka from the crystals and lights, I think the mural will pull it all together. A lot of greenery in the corners of the room. Make people feel like they are there, in the scene, at the mysterious mountain. Later in the evenings you can dim the lights, all the sparkles will light up, get a fire flaming in the fireplace, it'll be totally romantic, atmospheric. Well?"

He stared, unmoving.

"Naithon?" she said louder.

He blinked, shook his head, turned to smile at her. "You are fuckin' amazin' my beautiful lamb, amazin'. When can you start?"

"Well," she drew a line on the wall. "I'm going to draw the picture, you and I will paint it."

"Huh?" His lips pushed out in confusion. "Me? I can't paint."

155

"Sure you can. I'll help you. You will love it, watch." Kiri went to the table and squeezed out some green paint on a board, dashed a brush in it, traipsed over to him and put the brush in his hand. She wrapped her hand around his, as best she could it was so big, and pulled him to the wall. She raised his hand, set the brush on the wall, and pulled his hand down leaving a streak of green on the white wall. She stood back. "See?"

He stood unmoving, blinking at the green streak. Then he turned and grinned at her, "Show me more, lamb."

An hour later, Naithon went out to speak with the driver. He told him to go to the mansion and ask Mazonn to get his phone, he'd left it in the suite.

"Of course, sir," the driver acknowledged, lowering his head in a slight bow. "Anything else, sir?"

"*Ja.* Have Mazonn get me a clean pair of jeans, shirt, boxers, socks, a toothbrush. I can shower here in the men's lockers. I want you to go to Gariellos and tell Marty the owner to pack up a really nice dinner for two."

The driver bowed again. "Wine, sir?"

A full bodied red would be appealing and romantic. Candles too. But, Naithon sighed, next time. He wanted to show Kiri he didn't need to drink alcohol, only when he slid into those devouring black funks. He had to drink to drown the demons that threatened to pull him under and bury him for good. "No. Ice tea. Oh, and candles and a blanket. That's it."

Covering his smile, the driver nodded and left. Naithon stopped in the kitchen, grabbed some salt, rubbed it on his teeth, gargled with it, spat it out. He washed his hands and face then went back to painting. He loved it. Talk about cathartic. Damn his girl was smart. Best thing he had ever done was kidnap her. Brushing aside the twinge of guilt in taking her, he hurried back to the tasting room.

After deciding to start with one of the walls that was painted black, Kiri let him choose the colors he wanted to put down. And he eagerly got right to it.

As he laid his paint over the wall, Kiri went over his work blending and pulling things together, making areas sharper, deepened dimension with contrasting lighter shades. She outlined the shack and the waterfall, the trees and flowers. It was going to take a few sessions to complete it, which was fine with both of them.

They chatted comfortably while they worked, stopping briefly when the driver returned. He gave Naithon the clothes and his cell, and put the dinner in the fridge in the employees' break room. Naithon told the driver he could go home, he'd call him when they were ready to leave.

Back to work, eventually their light chatter grew more in depth, serious, as they asked the real personal questions. She told him about her early life, having to dodge Duce, he and Piero killing her pets for fun.

Melonie had played endless malicious tricks on her like cutting limbs off her dolls. Once when Kiri was very little, Melonie told her she could be like Supergirl, and Kiri could use mind-control to control the vicious guard dogs down the street. If Janero hadn't been near to stop Kiri, Melonie would have pushed her inside the fence to play with the pit bulls. Kiri would have been torn to bits.

Then, Ignacio shipped her off to an isolated, highly secured female boarding school. Her father wanted to keep her as chaste as possible for whatever arranged marriage he could broker for the most land or money.

Naithon nodded as she spoke, he gripped the paintbrush on the verge of snapping it in two in his escalating rage. That bastard, some father. He was as bad as Naithon's old man. But Naithon could fend for himself, Kiri was a defenseless little girl. Ignacio should have protected her from her sadistic siblings. Her sister Melonie was as bad as his own brother, Misolav.

She told him Rueford had come in with the highest bid for her, and her father had a wedding planner already on the job. Naithon didn't ask her questions about Rueford, he would lose it for sure and go storming off to take the old pig down. Undoubtedly the bastard had been grabby with her, something that would send Naithon off like an attack missile if he thought about it. He would take care of Montoblanco later, right now he wanted to stay in the moment.

"Naithon?"

"*Ja?*" He slashed a bold angry stroke of jungle green.

"Tell me about you. Mazonn told me your dad stole from you and threw you out on the streets. He said you hung with a gang and went to prison."

Face scowling like he'd bit a sour lemon he growled, "Mazonn has a big mouth. He has no business telling you that shit. You have a low enough opinion of me."

Kiri feathered almost imperceptible lighter green over his dark mountain adding depth. Standing back, she regarded their work. "You are holding me captive, Naithon, I think I have the right to know a little bit about you, what formed you into the man you are today."

Making a sound of irritation, he jabbed his brush into black paint, slapped it on some green and mixed them making the green darker. "Hell and Satan and my brothers along with my da took serrated icicles and stabbed and scraped and gouged me into who I am, little innocent pigeon. They created me, ice cold and broken. The gang and prison only sharpened and twisted the corrosion that they created."

Her sympathetic exhale expressed she comprehended his plight. She could tell him all day long that he wasn't broken, just damaged, he could be repaired, but she knew he'd never listen to her, accept that he could be fixed.

His bleak, miserable, brutal life was ingrained from his birth, and punctuated throughout his motherless childhood, violent teens, and continued to his ruthless adulthood. So she asked instead, "What happened with your mom?" She'd heard his mother had died young.

Naithon swiped his paint on the wall until the brush was dry. Setting the brush down on the table, he picked up a rag and wiped his hands. Rubbing hard at a black smudge on the back of his hand, he peered over at Kiri. She was watching him, her expression sad. With an aggravated grunt, he said, "I don't want your pity Kiri, or your repulsion of me to plunge to even lower depths."

She picked up a sponge and dabbed at the wall giving the paint texture and blending colors. "I want to know you, Naithon. If you have any hopes of building anything…between us, I need that."

"Damn women," he muttered under his breath. Men don't care how you were made, they just deal with who a man is. "Fine," he snapped, then let out a harsh breath. "My mother was my da's mistress. She died bearing me. My da hated me for killing her, and for looking like her, and my older half-brothers hated me because Da loved my mother more than theirs. The three of them beat on me every day of my life."

Ignoring her big sympathetic eyes he went on. "Their mother, my stepmother Verona, never looked at or spoke a word to me. Ever. I did not exist, she looked right through me. Being invisible was worse than if she cursed me or beat me. It meant I was nothing, I didn't exist."

He kept his eyes on the rag he scrubbed over his fingers. He didn't want to see her pity. Kiri had a huge soft heart, and she would feel sorry for the rejected boy that he'd been.

She stayed silent waiting for him to continue.

He took a deep breath, let it out slowly. "Okay," he said, his voice void of any emotion, feeling. "So, my da made me drop out of school when I was twelve and start in his business. I rode along with other enforcers and learned the art of knee breaking. A couple of years and I'd put away a nest egg. Learned to gamble, had to have older guys place my bets as I was underage. I also ran a few…businesses under the table."

He said quickly, "Those you don't need to know about." He grinned slightly at her disapproving pursed lips. It was better than her pity.

"So, when my da found out how rich I was getting, he forged papers with corrupt bankers, stole my money and kicked me out. With nowhere to go, sleeping in store doorways freezing my ass off, eating out of dumpsters, and fending off perverts sucked. I joined a gang. I won't go into detail about that or prison, so don't ask." His face tightened and paled at the recollections that threatened to flood him again like some kind of PTSD triggers.

Kiri replied quietly, "Okay."

He glanced at her, she was facing the wall holding the sponge in her hand. His heart warmed, she was deliberately not staring at him so she wouldn't see the harrowing feelings the memories dredged up, and he couldn't see her disgust and shame for the life he's led. "I suppose you want to know about the wheelchair?"

She nodded and sponged the wall with a few dabs.

His drawn inhale was rough, then expelled like he was spitting out a bad memory. "You probably heard about me, and my brother Misolav's wife, Fiereza. This town gossips like parrots at a tea party."

"Just that you were involved at one time."

"*Ja*. When I was young, for some crazy reason Fiereza thought I would inherit the wealth of my da's business when he passed, so she set her sights on me and proceeded to reel me in. Of course I didn't know it at the time, I was young, dumb and horny. She used sex, sometimes sick and dangerous sex, to keep me tied to her. I don't know why she thought I would inherit, I'm the youngest of four boys."

"Maybe because you were clearly the smartest, the most effective of your brothers?"

A nice smile lifted the dour set to his mouth. "Thanks for that, baby. I don't know why she thought it. Anyway, the slut that she is, she slept with our attorney and discovered that not me, but Misolav as the eldest would inherit. I was basically considered a bastard child as my mother was not wed to my da. So," his chest swelled then thinned, "I came home one day and found Misolav and Fiereza going at it like dogs. Literally. Like rutting Rottweilers. He was banging her from behind on all fours, and not in her pussy if you know what I mean. Grossed me out for weeks."

A perplexed divot dug between her eyes. "Not really," she said naively. Her head cocked as she then grasped his meaning. "That was what you were going to do to me that day you thought I was sleeping with your friends?"

Naithon's head hung, he nodded. "Not my proudest moment. Thinking you were with Maz put me back to that time of seeing

Misolav fucking my girl. But," he looked over at her, "it was different with you. Fiereza is sort of slim all the way around, on the edge of bony. When Mislo was slamming into her, her small tits flapped back and forth like insipid flags. The minute I wrapped my body over yours, I smelled your scent, your freshness, your body is lush, baby. Your tits are full and perfect, ass a perfect round peach."

With an air of self-consciousness, she said, "Hmm, Fiereza is a beautiful girl," her tone indicated his description of Kiri was way exaggerated.

His head twitched towards her, was that jealousy? Cool.

"You hurt me that day, Naithon."

Ears ringed red with shame, he looked down at his boots. "I was furious with you, but I wanted you anyway. I grabbed your tits so roughly because they made me remember Fiereza's scraggy body and how sordid she had looked getting rammed up her ass by my brother. I don't know, maybe I felt I was punishing you for her.

"Or entranced at how different you are. How different you smell, feel. Your scent is fresh, sweet, your perfect body is rocking lush as shit. Fiereza's natural scent is always blocked by heavy perfume, her figure is scrawny, like a boy's almost." He chuckled, "Like they say, if you were a rose, she would be a cactus."

Now that she understood about what Fiereza and Misolav were actually doing, Kiri cringed, then commented, "But you loved her at one time."

Shoulder bumped with a disputing snort. "I was in lust with her at that time. Normal for a teenaged boy. She was easy pussy and taught me some..." he glanced quickly at her then away, "kinky, some real heavy violent stuff. For the life of me I don't know what the hell I saw in her way back then, she's disgusting.

"Thank *Dio* I dodged that bullet. She and Misolav deserve each other. They make each other miserable, and both cheat like there's a swinging door to the bedroom. Now, you," he set the rag down and moved over to her.

Naithon took the sponge from her and set it down, took her hand. "I adore everything about you, your hot little bod, your smart brain, insane talent, that brave, sweet heart of yours. Everything. I would never seriously hurt you. I would have stopped that day, Kiri, but, *ja*, I might have harmed you somewhat before I did by handling you too roughly."

He stroked a hand through the back of her hair to clasp her head. Clutching her hair, he pulled it back until her face tilted up to his.

"You were going to force me when you first brought me to your home, Naithon, you told me. You would have hurt me then."

Silence permeated, then, he released her hair and grasped her hand. "I hadn't thought it through at first. I was so blinded with desire for you, I just wanted you anyway I could get you. In my world women have very little say, the men rule, you know that. The way I grew up, women are possessions, objects, their feelings and desires don't...matter, to the kind of man I am. We just take what we want."

"But," he rubbed the back of his neck with an embarrassed grin, "the day I brought you home, Mazonn and I had a little talk. He made me aware of how much I would seriously injure you by forcing myself inside your virgin body. He told me if I raped you that you would never forgive me, we would have no chance of a real relationship, which once I had you in my home I realized that was what I truly wanted. He said if I wanted you willing more than not, that I needed to go slow with you."

His words sifted through her brain. A line crunched between her brows, she asked, "How long would we have a relationship? A week, a month, before you tire of me and desire those women that can give you that, uh...kinky sex you want? Would you expect me to stay around while you...slept with them? Or, I'm silly, of course you would push me out the door." Her self-disparaging laugh told she was growing upset.

Rankled that she continued to doubt his complete and utter devotion to her, Naithon bent to Kiri, whispered against her lips soft as a butterfly to a flower, "I would never cheat on you, my lamb. Never. Because you are the only woman I ever want to be with for the rest of my life, our lives. I've never felt this way before, like I want to protect you, cherish you, make you happy. I can't imagine my life without you in it. Not seeing this little face every day, hell," a shiver rippled goose bumps up his arms.

Not wanting her to feel under attack, he cupped the back of her head and his kiss was slow and gentle, softly exploring. Needing her to believe him, he kept his hands off her sexual parts and kept his erection turned away from her.

It was a cherishing kiss, and Kiri felt that, and she responded. Naithon's heart did a high-five, *finally*. He didn't rush, or push her, just cradled her head with his hands and swallowed his grin when her hands stroked up his chest to latch behind his neck. Not wanting to, but he broke off the kiss before things got too steamy. Letting go of her, he stepped back.

The green in Kiri's eyes shimmered blurry. Surprising Naithon how quickly and deeply she responded, dazed, she just stood, lids heavy, lips parted as if waiting for his to return. She blinked confounded up at him as if asking why did he stop?

Grinning, *ja*, he was finally breaking through. "Baby," he said in a low voice. "Mazonn sent me a fresh change of clothes. You were right about me not changing before coming here," he grinned down at his paint-splattered clothes.

"I'm gonna shower in the locker room then we can eat. It's cool outside, but I think warm enough for us to sit on the patio and watch the stars. If the night is clear, we're high enough up on the hill we can see the blinking city lights. Okay with you, pigeon?"

That brought her out of her stupor. Mahogany brows drew down her tone chastised, "Naithon."

His laugh teasing. "Can't help it, baby." His gaze drifted down to her chest. "That's what they look like- hey!" he barked when a towel hit his shoulder. Kiri swatted him, only made him laugh more. She swung it again, he grabbed it, and used it to pull her close, and kissed the tip of her nose.

"You wanna play with the big boys, honey, you need to watch yourself. I can take this towel and tie those pretty hands of yours behind your back and have my way with you." At the alarm that struck her face, he smiled and said, "In fun. I would only restrain

163

you with your permission. I swear." His fingers crossed behind his back.

One brow lowered in mistrust, her hands landed on her hips. "Uh huh, one of those kinky things you referred to, no doubt. What about when you think it's okay to punish me?"

"Ah, well, then, I guess you'd better behave yourself so we don't have to find out, eh?" The grin slid into a leer.

He looked so boyish, relaxed, playful, she almost smiled at his joking. But she didn't, because that would encourage him to feel he had the right to spank her when he felt she had disobeyed him, or displeased him. "Go shower, Naithon. I'll clean the brushes and put the stuff up."

"Ah, there's my bossy little pigeon." Grinning, he leaned over and gave her another light kiss on the tip of her nose then took off.

Chapter Nineteen

Naithon hurried through his shower, he'd finally gotten Kiri to respond to his kisses and he didn't want to lose the mood. Rubbing his face, he frowned at the mirror in the locker room. The driver had thrown in deodorant and a toothbrush and paste, but Naithon forgot to ask him to bring a razor.

He planned on more kissing and her skin was so delicate. And tasty, he licked his lips. For sure he was hungry and not for dinner. He wanted Kiri to be his dinner. But, you feed a lady like her first, then jump her.

Not like the bitches he was used to. Fuck 'em and go chow with your boys. A smile warmed his face, his Kiri was a lady, his lady, and she deserved to be treated like a queen. He was pretty sure he was growing on her.

He'd been so careful to not touch her sexually, and to eat dinner with her every night the past weeks, court her properly. That way she'd think of them as a couple, a family someday, not as kidnapper and captive, horndog and victim.

Even if he let her go and tried to date her normally, Ignacio would hide her away so fast, and she would be in danger from whoever was assassinating their people. Not to mention that red-haired paunchy dick that had tried to lay claim on her before Naithon had snatched her out of his pudgy hands.

Not that he actually kidnapped her, Ignacio handed her right over to him with his blessing. Then again, it wasn't with *her* consent to go with him, or to stay with him.

In the beginning, he only knew he wanted her. Desperately, obsessively. Naithon hadn't cared what she wanted, but that had changed. Now he would do anything to make her happy, give her anything to see her smile at him. Stay with him willingly.

Those green eyes had always haunted him, but the weird thing was how the second he saw her for the first time when she was out of childhood, he'd known he'd want her forever. That feeling had only intensified once he brought her home to the point he couldn't imagine his life without his little pigeon.

That made his smile widen. She got so blushing pink when he called her that. Even if she was mad, she was hot no matter what her mood, so he said things to see her blush in embarrassment, or glower at him in anger, his prudish, prim, lamb.

Stuffing his comb in his back pocket, he checked the small gun tucked in a holster at his lower back, then bent and checked the weapons he kept in his boots. He'd love to make love to her here, but they'd be vulnerable to attack. It'd have to wait until they were safe in the mansion.

Smiling at his reflection, he thought, *ja*, she is ready. He could tell. If anything, he knew when a woman was aroused. With others it was immediate, with Kiri he'd have to move in small steps or she'd shut down.

While she continued cleaning up the tasting room, Naithon removed the dinner he'd put in the oven to warm before he went into the shower. The plant was full functioning with a commercial kitchen, laundry service.

Tucking the blanket under his arm, he carried their dinner, and the basket that held candles and their iced tea. Also, how could he forget, he could smell the rich chocolate of the cake. Plates and cutlery were in the basket.

He set everything up outside on a patio table, and lit the candles. Standing back and surveying his work, he mumbled, "Who'da thought Naithon Adranokov would have turned into a romantic, domesticized gangster?"

It wasn't long when Kiri strolled on uncertain feet outside. Her eyes flicked from the food to the glasses, the candles, to the blanket he laid on a lawn chair, then to him. As usual, he felt the instant throb in his pants, his heart raced at the sight of her. He was going to show her what it was like to be his.

Only a few puffs of dark clouds humped like round grey sheep blotched the black dome of night over them, not enough to hide the stars or veil the glittering lights from the city in the distance. The air was cool but not yet uncomfortably so. Later in the night it would get chilly. Naithon pulled out a chair for her to sit, then joined her. He set the food out in the serving dishes.

Kiri inhaled and closed her eyes. "Oh my goodness, Naithon, it smells delicious. What is it?"

"Well," he started, spooning some golden potatoes on her plate then his. "We have beef bourguignon, gratin dauphinoise, roasted root vegetables and a melty goat cheese salad with hazelnuts." Handing her a basket of warm bread, he waited until she took one then he set one on his plate.

"I have to say, Naithon," Kiri commented, watching him scoop some of the beef loaded with carrots, pearl onions and mushrooms on her plate, "I'm impressed that you knew what all this was called."

His lips pushed out. "Because I dropped out of school at such a young age?"

Buttering a roll, Kiri set the breadknife down, her brow puckered. "Of course not. Clearly you managed to gather an education along the way. You are well spoken," she said quickly with mild admonishment, "when you want to be. You dress tastefully to the nines," her admiring smile swept over his length.

Even in casual clothes he wore top label. The sweater was cream cashmere, boots worn yet expensive, his black jeans were well worn as well, fitting perfectly on his lean hips and tight butt that she *did not* look at.

"I meant men don't usually seem to be too preoccupied with fancy dishes like these and what they're called. The few times I've eaten out with my father and brothers they just grunted and pointed."

Stabbing a hunk of salad, Naithon slid it in his mouth, chewed then swallowed it down with a sip of tea. "There's sugar and lemon for your tea," he gestured to the condiments on the table. "Gariellos is one of my favorite restaurants, I haunt it quite frequently. Conduct a lot of business over drinks and meals."

Munching a hazelnut, Kiri asked with casual indifference, "You take your dates, your girlfriends there?"

A hard laugh almost tossed his beef. Wiping his mouth with a napkin, he said with humor, "Baby, I don't do dinner, or dates, or girlfriends. All that is fuck more trouble than it's worth. The only thing I get from women is sex, the rest of my time I spend with my crew or friends."

They ate silently, Kiri brooded. Then she set her fork down, lips pursed in a slight moue. "I see. So, once we have sex, per your plans, then you will send me back home?"

Naithon wiped his mouth again, folded his napkin and set it beside his plate. He reached to her and took her hand, thumb caressing the top of it. Dark eyes like smoldering cinders, he smiled, his rough accent thickened with emotion he said, "Kiri, I don't know how else to say it, I've told you a dozen times. I took you deliberately to keep you. I told you I plan on marrying you. I want children with you. I do not, will not," his voice lowered in unequivocal fervor, "want any other woman, ever again. The only thing I'm waiting on is for you to get on board with my train."

He waved at the table laden with food and candles. "Trust me, I have never done this before, Kiri. When things settle down, I'll take you to Gariellos, and other places. I can show you the world, lamb, I want to do that. I want to experience things with you. I never have before with a woman. You're the only woman I've ever wanted to spend time with, talk with." He squeezed her hand. "I want you as my friend as well as my lover."

Kiri stared into his ebony orbs only partially visible under hooded lids, and shivered at the intensity he was trying, but not

168

succeeding, to hide. Tugging her hand from his, she grabbed her tea, sucked hard on the straw, then stirred the liquid rapidly with the straw, the ice bounced and rattled in the glass.

Seeing her sudden nervousness he said, "Talk to me, baby," his deep voice low, hushed.

Slanting her head she gazed at him, studied his harsh face, the roughness of his features and the scars made it so incredibly masculine. "Your mother must of have been gorgeous."

"Huh?"

"If you weren't so brutally manly you would be beautiful."

Face screwed up in repugnance, he said, "I've heard that all my life. Men do not want to be called pretty, honey." Sitting back in his chair, he said, "You didn't respond to what I said about us and children."

Long cherry brown lashes fluttered, fanning her blushing rounded cheeks. Keeping her eyes lowered, Kiri picked up her fork and fiddled with it. "Naithon-"

"Please look at me, Kiri, when you are talking to me, stop hiding yourself," his voice skated on demanding.

She raised her eyes, gazed levelly at him. "You abducted me, you are keeping me against my will. I've said before, that's not normal, it's wrong. People go to jail for that."

Pushing his empty plate away, he twined his fingers, set his hands on the table. "Not too worried about that, lamb. We in the...organizations do not have others arrested. We settle things ourselves. Trust me, the police do not get involved with our issues. I told you, if you went to them, they would only cart you right back home."

"But, my father, he's going to want me back, I'm a meal ticket to him. And Rueford he will be-"

"*Ja, ja*, Ignacio has burned up our phone lines with demands of your return. And, Montoblanco has been to the compound every other fucking day declaring his claim on you."

Shock shot her lashes straight up. "What? I didn't know this, why haven't you told me?"

He merely shrugged, lavished butter on a piece of roll and stuffed it in his mouth.

Brows daggering down in ire, Kiri said angrily, "I have a right to know these things. They are about me! I refuse to be treated as an object!"

"You are to be protected, I don't want you unnecessarily worried. One reason why I don't want you running around outside without me because if that red-haired fucker finds a way in, which he can't, but if he could get past the gates, he would filch you right up and be gone with you in a blink. I need to ensure your safety."

"Naithon," she uttered, appalled, stating for the thousandth time, "I am not a child, and you will not treat me as one. You think we're going to have any kind of relationship when you are a dictatorial bully? I refuse to-"

He leaned forward towards her with a grin. "So, that means we do have a relationship?"

"Huh? What?" Shaking her head with an eye roll she said, "We are talking about how you want to control me. Keep me locked up, keep things like this from me because I'm just a weak female, I won't have it!"

"Damn, baby, but you are hot when you're pissed." Leaning on an elbow, he ogled her.

Clenching her fist on the table, she growled, "Ooh, you are such a chauvinist."

One brow arched with a mocking half-grin. "Never denied it, darlin'. Raised by, and hung around with male street thugs, the females that chased after us were as tough as us and just as crass. My stepmother looked right through me like I didn't exist, her hatred of me glowed bright though. I didn't have the best role models for broads. You are like night and day compared to them. To me, you are like fragile crystal that needs to be kept behind a curio cabinet glass door so no one can get their filthy fingerprints on it or break it."

"How did you break your back?"

Now he was the one taken aback, a dark scowl instantly shut his face down. "I don't talk about it."

Kiri raised her chin haughtily and crossed her arms. "You know everything about me, my early life was no bed of roses. Certainly nowhere near the hell you lived. But, if you don't tell me things when I ask about them, then we have no hope of anything evolving between us."

The scowl gone, replaced by a smile. "At least you are admitting there is something between us, that you want it too."

Another eye roll with a huff. "I did not say that, answer my question."

Lips pushed out, eyes darkened, he picked up a butter knife and absently poked the table with it. "Ah, if you must know…"

"I must."

"Fine. Since you insist." Sucking in a deep breath, he exhaled slowly, set the knife down. "I had been summoned to my father's house. My da confronted me with the accusation that I had been embezzling funds from his companies. It was when I'd started making my way after prison and we were doing some work together. He called me into his home office, sat behind his big black cherry desk toking on a fat cigar, and had the fucking gall to accuse me," he stabbed his thumb into his chest with emphasis, shouted, "of robbing him, when he'd done that to me twice!"

Keeping her voice composed, she said quietly, "I'm glad he's out of the country, I would hate to have to meet him after the abominable, despicable way he has treated you."

Her calm, compassionate demeanor settled Naithon down a bit. "*Ja*, no worries, I would never let the treacherous bastard get within ten miles of you. Anyway, I told my da that it wasn't me that was stealing from him, it was Misolav. He didn't believe me of course. He called him in, there was a big fracas of shouting words between them. Of course, Mislo denied it all.

"I'm no snitch, I knew about the stealing all along and kept my nose out of it. But, when I'm accused, the gloves are off. I didn't need to be subjected to their shit, I'd already said my piece, so I left. I was outside, lighting a smoke, when…" his eyes closed at the grievous memory.

She waited, giving him time to come to grips with the horrific event.

Slow, deep breaths, he opened his eyes but stared blankly into the night, as if seeing the incident all over again. "Fiereza followed me out. I wanted nothing to do with her. She begged me to go around back and talk with her. I still had things to do at the house so I thought, what the hell, and we went to the back of the mansion. It was almost winter, trees were bare, and the pool had been drained.

"She…started hitting on me, rubbing her tits on my chest, trying to kiss me, paw my nuts, she just sickened me, I pushed her off. She said being with Mislo had been a terrible mistake and she was so sorry and she wanted me back.

"Said some nasty things about their sex life and the lack of… strength and…robust…adventure on Mislo's part. He was apparently quite dull under the sheets.

"Don't wanna brag baby," he winked at Kiri, the only bright moment in his countenance. "She said I was much bigger than my brother, which of course I knew, we grew up together. I will show you later, I know now you'll be curious to see it." His grin lightened the mood. For a second.

Stating, "Naithon," she just shook her head with an amused smile and reddening cheeks.

Tenderness, a rare cadence in his voice, he said with a delighted grin, "I forget what an innocent you are. I can't wait teach you…everything," his eyes dipped to her mouth. Then remembering their conversation, his expression sobered, a mask of blankness fell over his face.

His voice an accented monotone, he went on, "*Ja*. So, she begged for me to take her back, kept throwing herself at me, mauling me and shit. I was trying to get away from her when, of course, Mislo comes out and catches us. He went ballistic. Said I lied to Da about the theft to get him in trouble and now I was trying to steal his girl. Huh, that's a laugh. He cheated with her first. As it turned out, that had been a damned blessing, got her hooks outta me." He made a face of disgust.

"Anyway, he came at me, we fought, I easily took him down. Only made him madder. He grabbed a baseball bat and started swinging it at my head. I was backing up to gain leverage so I could grab it out of his hands, and, well, took a step back and there was nothing there, down I went into the empty pool."

He pinched the bridge of his nose between his eyes, mumbled bitterly, "He fucking knew I was going to fall and didn't try to stop it."

Folding his fingers together, he set his hands on the table and stared down at them rather than see more of her pity. "I..." his eyes twitched back and forth as he viewed the scene from long ago.

Untwining his fingers he rubbed his thighs with his palms as if remembering how it had felt. "I couldn't move my legs, couldn't feel them. It was...terrifying. I don't remember much afterwards, I had a concussion and between that and the agonizing pain I blacked out.

"Took me almost two years to recover and learn to walk all over again. Let's say excruciating is an understatement. I had to run my enterprises from a goddamned wheelchair. The chair made me look weak, so I had to be doubly violent and ruthless to hold my own. Anyway, you know the rest, basically." Staring at his hands, he blinked the memory away. Looking up at her, he asked desolately, "Okay? Are you satisfied?"

"Oh, Naithon, I'm sorry. It was a horrible thing to happen to you. I wasn't trying to make you live through that awful night again. I just...want to get to know you."

Mouth turned down, eyes wretched, he said miserably, "But you did, you did make me recall it, and, well, I think I need to find a bottle of vodka, I can't take the memories."

He looked so forlorn, depressed. Kiri pushed her chair back, got up and leaned over him, hugged his head. "I am so, so, sorry Naithon. You don't need to drink, we can talk it out- eek!"

He twisted, lifted her off the ground at the same time shoved his chair back and deposited her on his lap. Big, shit-eating grin spread across his face. "I know how you can help me feel better," he wriggled his brows.

She playfully slapped his shoulder, scolding, "Oh, Naithon, you were pretending, you tricked me."

"*Ja*, babe, and it worked, you are so gullible, it's too damned sweet." He gripped the back of her neck, slanted his head, and zoomed in on her for a long, heady, breathless kiss. While their lips were still attached, he stood up with her in his arms, trod over to one of the wide lawn chairs and laid her down on it.

Grabbing the blanket, he sat down on the edge of her chair facing her, the back of the chair was angled up. Their eyes connected, he shuffled up the seat, leaned in to her, lowered his head, and didn't close his eyes until he brought their lips together.

Soft, plush, met firm, full. Naithon set a palm on the back of the lawn chair, the other caught around the side of Kiri's face, his thumb on her throat, he felt her pulse speed up, felt her nervous yet excited swallow. When she didn't resist him, maneuvering to lie on his left side, his left arm rolled under her neck, his right hand still cupping her face, he kissed the living hell out of her.

Kiri, now an eager participant, and student, copied what he did to her with his tongue and mouth. Naithon slipped his palm from her face, stroking down her neck, collar bone, skimmed lightly over her breast and came to a halt just below it and stayed there. She didn't protest, but pulled her head back to take a trembly breath.

Moving his hand back up to caress the side of her face, he whispered in a husky baritone, "Hey, you okay?"

Smiling so innocently, she nodded shyly, words came out breathy, "Yeah. Just, needed to catch my breath."

"Okay. Tell me when you're ready for more," he murmured with a hint of grin. "I could spend hours and hours just kissing you." Freeing strands of her hair stuck to her lashes, Naithon brushed them back and stared in heated wonder at the woman in his arms, there of her own free will, at last.

Kiri's eyes misting with desire darkened the wide green moons, her tongue travelled around her lips, his gaze followed it. Clearing his throat, he murmured huskily, "You ready yet?"

Her nod came with the shy smile.

"Ah, good." He captured her mouth again, his palm made the trail back down her face, neck, this time it stopped on her breast and he closed his hand over it. The only sounds in the night were a roosting dove cooing in a far tree and their heavy panting, wet noises from lusty kissing, and ardent moans.

Moving his body to cover more of Kiri, Naithon moaned into her mouth, "Kiri, baby," and halfway sat up, pulled the blanket up to cover them just to the thighs. The air was crisp but not yet cold. His fingers went to the buttons on her pale yellow blouse while his heated gaze burned into her intoxicating eyes. "You are so beautiful, Kiri, so fucking beautiful."

The blush rolling up her cheeks brought his soft smile to wicked. The buttons were tiny in his thick fingers, he looked down at his task.

All the buttons undone, Naithon pushed the sides of her blouse apart and drank in the sight of her luxurious body. The girl was made for sin. His sin. Only his. She was eating better now that the strain of being under Ignacio's thumb had lifted, filling out those spectacular curves even more. Still slender, she was womanly rounded, and he was so hard his dick ached. With the way she gazed up at him in the dark with those large, luminous emeralds had him fearing he was going to explode all over the patio.

He trickled his fingertips across the top swell of her breasts, down her cleavage, then he stroked the full flesh of her breast. Kiri's back arched to his palm with a keening gasp that slid to an imploring whimper, it was so hot, supercharging Naithon into a burning, all encompassing, ravaging hunger for her.

He pulled the cups of the lacy bra down exposing her nipples. Lightly, he dusted his fingers over one nipple then the other and grinned at the goose bumps that rose on her arms, and the pebbling of her nipples, a shiver shook her breasts.

Bending his head, he webbed his big fingers under a plump globe, squeezing it up and sucked the nipple into his mouth. Kiri's chest rose with a small cry of what he hoped was pleasure. Kneading both breasts, he pinched, twisted and tugged one nipple while

175

sucking and biting the other, and he thought she was going to arch right off the chair.

She was gorgeous in her maturing innocence, a soft wanton warmth brushed in her eyes, lids lowered leaving only a bit of green sparkle showing. Her lips bowed up, she moaned his name, "*Naithon.*"

For so long he'd wanted to hear his name moaned on her lips, right now he could die a happy man. If he didn't come soon he *would* die of the agony bursting in his swollen shaft that wanted at her. It was time for her to become familiar with his body. Next lesson.

He caught one of her hands and tugged it down, lacing her palm over his jeans to cup his bulging manhood. Rubbing her hand up and down the hard length of it, he made her fingers squeeze the heaviness that she was causing.

"Naithon?" she sounded unsure, apprehensive.

"No worries, baby, I'm not gonna do anything here." No, he had to keep his head, couldn't allow anyone to sneak up on them. Besides, he didn't want her to find the gun at his back. Her da and brothers were mobsters, they all carried, all the time. He didn't want to have anything remind her that he was a gangster too.

Squeezing her hand harder over his erection, he moved her palm up the thick length, and down, and groaned. The best thing was, she wasn't balking. Encouraged, Naithon moved his hand off hers, and was thrilled when she kept her palm clenched over his throbbing shaft.

He unbuckled his belt, undid the button on his jeans, and watched her watching what he was doing. Her curiosity excited the fever in him, raising his desire to such a high peak it was going to take a long time coming down from it.

Lowering the zipper, he pushed his jeans and underwear down just enough to pull his manhood out. His fist encircled it, and he pumped it up, squeezed the head, then stroked it down. The intent look on her face as she watched him almost made him laugh. But he felt too goddamned good to jolt the moment. Her wonder and naïveté were a million times more engaging than the other women he'd been with.

He lifted her hand and wrapped it around his erection and moved it up and down. Only a few strokes, then he let go, and she kept going. "It's kind of soft on top, but under is really hard, like iron, Naithon," she murmured, raptly studying his penis.

"Yeah," he croaked, "hard," he could barely conjure a thought. Naithon was drowning in her aroused eyes while her soft little hand caressed his member, the shaft pulsing with the torment of holding himself back from jumping on her and taking her.

Her tongue poked out the side of her lush mouth mesmerized as she watched her hand move up to the tip, then she squeezed like he had done, and he grunted. The only other penis she had really seen in person was Duce's when she was a child. He had enjoyed exposing it to her and telling her what he was going to do to her with it. "Are all men this big, Naithon?" her voice interested yet edged with concern. She was a small woman.

Chuckling at her ingenuous curiosity, he told her, "I'm kinda on the big side." At her eyes rounding in unease, not wanting her to be afraid of him all over again, he said with a heated smile, "Women are designed to adapt, my little lamb, you will be able to take all of me."

Her hand stroked down then back up, Naithon growled roughly, "Baby, you turn me on more than anything ever," he rambled almost incoherently, "more than my first time at twelve with the housekeeper when I was just a pup." He groaned, "Sorry," then grumbled when her hand stalled. "I didn't mean to say that, to bring another woman into our bed so to speak. I never thought of her exactly as a woman, just the housekeeper that initiated me."

A shade of anger crept in her voice, she murmured fiercely, "You were too young, she should have been arrested. Did you tell your father?"

A chuckle eased out of his rasp, "Honey, he's the one who sent her to me. Come, don't stop," he cuddled her breasts with both hands, bent and nipped a budded nipple.

With a sultry sigh, Kiri kissed then licked his forehead while he nibbled on her breasts; her hand grew more confident and stronger as she stroked his manhood. Naithon buried his face between her full breasts, roughly kneading and suckling them in a building frenzy of hunger, but then his strength was too hard.

She whimpered and unconsciously squeezed his dick. Naithon gasped and grabbed her wrist, pulled it away from his throbbing member. His breath hissed damned hard and fast, one more squeeze like that and he would come in her hand. Not the way he wanted to introduce her to love making.

She looked quizzically up at him. "Did I hurt you? Did I do something wrong, Naithon?"

Laughing, he painfully tucked himself back in and did his pants up. "No, baby, but I don't want to come like that, and we need to go, or I'm gonna fuck you in this chair. And, that ain't gonna happen." He bent, kissed each breast, then pulled the bra cups up and closed her blouse. "You need to button it, lamb, my fingers are too big and too shaking to do it."

Watching her, he thought, that was the first time he'd ever necked or petted, whatever it's called. Since jumping right in with the housekeeper, he never had to start from first base with girls, women. Didn't need to and never cared to.

But with his lamb, he smiled at her awkwardly buttoning her blouse with shaking fingers, hell; they were sort of learning intimacy together. She was certainly all and so much more than he had thought before taking her. It was almost like he had been saving parts of himself…for her.

After demolishing the cake, they packed everything up, the paints, the food, and were waiting out front as the limo pulled up. The ride home found Kiri nestled against Naithon, his arm around her, they held hands and dreamy smiles. The driver grinned in the rearview before closing the door between the compartments.

It was late when they arrived home, but his friends were up and waiting for them. Naithon had to endure Mazonn, Yashin and Vlad grinning like donkeys at him when he came in with her wrapped in his arms.

Ignoring their teasing chuckles, he took her upstairs. She was almost asleep when he herded her into the bathroom to change and get ready for bed. For the first time since he took her, Naithon slid into bed content and feeling positive about what was happening with them. Stockholm shit aside, didn't matter, whatever it was, it was working. Sure he was seducing her into wanting him, but now she did, and that's all that mattered.

She was asleep by the time he climbed in. Coiling his arm around her, like every night, he pulled her back against his chest. His legs curling under hers, he slipped his hand under her shirt and possessively grasped her chubby breast in his greedy palm, and quickly dozed off.

Chapter Twenty

Naithon stopped by the next day from work to lunch with Kiri. When he had left before dawn that morning, her head was buried in a pillow. He'd placed a soft kiss somewhere in her mass of hair and headed to work.

She was at the dining table already when he returned, Mazonn beside her. Lunch was generally a buffet. A dozen or so other people were seated eating and talking.

Naithon noticed a man standing between Kiri and Mazonn. Maz must have had some concern regarding this because his arm was laid across the back of her chair like a cage around her.

Feelings of possessive jealousy rolled over Naithon again like they had the other day, tightening his gut, he choked them down, Maz was his best friend, he would never poach. But the asshole standing there, what was his game?

Approaching the table, Naithon observed the man bending down to Kiri speaking only to her. Mazonn's jaw worked and he appeared to be about to stand up and back the guy off, when Kiri saw Naithon. Her face lit up with a natural happy smile that reached her gorgeous eyes, and his heart crimped with joy and tenderness.

A broad smile eased the tightness in his belly, she was genuinely happy to see him. How could he have ever thought he could have a life with her and not enjoy, desire, *need*, her affection?

Mazonn hadn't seen him come in and was getting to his feet. The other man who was a relatively new employee, snarled belligerently at Maz. Apparently he was about to get a lesson in hitting on the boss' woman. But it was Naithon who was going to give it, Kiri was his.

By the time he reached the table, Kiri's smile had dimmed at the darkness in Naithon's fierce face. Mazonn placed his hard, hulking body between Kiri and the man. Neither male saw Naithon approach, until Kiri murmured, "Naithon."

Maz turned to see Naithon, and Naithon knew he'd been right in his assumption. Maz was furious, face rigid, jaw still working. He may have a mischievous side and twinkling blue eyes, but he was as quick and lethal a killer as Naithon. They had grown up in the gang and then prison together, watching each other's backs.

"Maz," the quiet calm in his voice belied the fury snaking through Naithon's body about to unleash. There was something disturbing going on concerning his Kiri and he will do anything to protect her. Anything.

The man gave Naithon a sneering pugnacious glare. "What the fuck, Adranokov, is wrong with your man here? The bitches are here for us to bang. I want this one, and this prick is trying to run me off." Thirty-something, he was big with the requisite tough appearance. Neat braids scrolled tightly down his head, tattoos ravaged much of his dark skin and a few painted along with a deep scar beneath one chocolate brown, glaring eye.

Naithon tramped around the table coming to a stop near the men.

Mazonn grinned, then moved to the other side of Kiri. Discreetly, he clasped her arm and pulled her gently to her feet.

Voice cool and even, Naithon said to the man, "That's Mr. Adranokov to you. Did Mazonn tell you she was the boss' woman?"

The man's dark eyes shifted from Mazonn's grin to Naithon's harsh expression, his mouth tightened in slight apprehension. Still with bravado, he said, "So what? You share like everyone else. Silver's upstairs fucking Antonio and Eugene right now."

Rage bubbled in Naithon's voice that lowered in imminent threat. "Don't give a fuck about Silver. She is not my woman, her," he snapped his head towards Kiri, "she is my woman. No one touches my fucking woman, Andre. They do, they die."

Seeing the menace in Naithon's coal black eyes, Andre balked, cleared his throat. "Uh, well, you expect a man to come to you and ask to plow her? Well, I'm asking. I'll bring her right back to you when I'm done with her."

Kiri gasped. Grin expanding, Maz wound his fingers around Kiri's upper arm and said cheerfully, "Time to go, honey." He pulled her away from Naithon and Andre, and towards the exit of the dining area.

"Wait, Maz," Kiri craned her neck to look back at Naithon, "aren't we going to wait for Naithon?"

"Nope," Maz said, drawing Kiri down the hall to the grand room. "He'll come in a minute, there's something he has to do first."

"No, but wait, Maz, I don't understand, what's going on? Why do we have to leave?" She tried to pull back, make him stop, but the man towered over her, if he wanted her to walk, she'd walk, he towed her along.

"Hush, now," he told her as they reached the grand room. "We're gonna sit down and wait here."

Puzzled, Kiri made a move to return to the dining area, when Mazonn's friendly face hardened, eyes tapered exhibiting a cold command, he stood in front of her. She could go nowhere but to sit in the chair he had steered her to. "But Maz-"

"It's men stuff, Kiri, Naithon doesn't want you exposed to that shit."

"But why not?"

Maz looked heavenward, muttered, "God save me from falling into this female snare that has caught my friend." He smiled wryly at her, "Kiri, that man was hitting on you. I told him to buzz off, he didn't go. I told him you were Nait's and Nait ain't gonna share, he didn't budge. Everyone here knows you are off limits.

"Even if you weren't Nait's, the jerk still shouldn't have approached you because clearly you were there with me. He didn't know I was there for your protection, still, trying to take you away to fuck when I'm sitting there and I had said no was disrespectful to me. And, ah, Nait's gonna give him a lesson in respect."

Eyes wide as she comprehended that Naithon was going to fight with the man she cried, "Oh, Maz, what if he hurts Naithon? You have to help him!"

The laugh burst from Maz, he wiped an eye with mirth regarding her frightened face. "Honey, no one in this land can best Naithon Adranokov. He learned to fight on the streets with the worst of the worst, and he's strong as an ox, fast as a jungle cat, ain't nothing to worry about."

Ten minutes passed while Kiri sat anxiously chewing on a nail. On a chair next to her, Maz sprawled comfortably, hands folded loosely in his lap, eyes almost closed as if he were drifting off to sleep with nary a worry in the world.

Kiri was about to get up and go back to the dining room when Naithon appeared through the archway. He carried a box and came right over to them.

Setting the box down on a table, without touching her, he leaned over and kissed Kiri, long, lingering, too long, Mazonn grumbled, reminding them of his presence. "You bring us sustenance, bro?"

Naithon broke the kiss, then gave her another quick peck and moved the table so they could eat at it. He pulled out sandwiches, macaroni salad, pickles, chips and sodas.

Groaning, "Mmm," Maz licked his chops, said, "I'm starving," and snatched up a sandwich and took a huge bite making Kiri giggle.

"Nice, Maz, how 'bout some manners?" Naithon chided, handing a sandwich on a plate to Kiri.

Speaking through the food in his mouth, Maz countered, "This coming from 'Mr. Let's Pound Their Faces In Before Asking Questions'."

Biting his sandwich almost in half, food stuffed in one cheek, Naithon retorted, "We don't tussle when there are ladies present."

Mazonn opened a soda and handed it to Kiri. "Speaking of tussles, you have a conversation with Andre?"

"Hmm," Naithon mumbled, side-eyed Kiri then frowned at Mazonn.

"It's okay," Maz assured him. "She knows you were going to give him a beating. You washed your hands but should have changed your sweater," he nodded at the blood stain on Naithon's sweater.

Naithon looked down and swore, "Damn, gonna be hell for Laundry to get that stain out."

Her fingers covering her mouth, Kiri said softly, "Oh, Naithon."

Scowling at Maz, Naithon growled, "You know better than to talk about that shit around her."

Ignoring his friend's ire, Maz grinned. "It was adorable, Nait. She was worried Andre was going to beat you up. She asked me to go save you."

Cocking his head to send Kiri a look of disbelief, Naithon shook his head. "Let's not talk about it anymore. Andre says he will be more respectful from now on, and he said he wouldn't dream of attempting to fuck his boss' woman again," and he tossed some chips in his mouth.

"Before or after he gets out of the hospital?"

Naithon shot him a look that said 'shut up.' Washing the chips down with soda he muttered, "When he gets out of the basement, no hospital for pricks that fuck with my shit."

"You calling Kiri, shit?"

Kiri's head went back and forth between the men like watching ping pong.

When she wasn't looking at him, Naithon gave his friend the finger, and rolled his eyes heavenward at Mazonn's smirk.

Biting the end of a pickle, Kiri asked, "Who's Silver?"

The men shared a look. Maz grinned.

Irritation and a speck of worry reddened the tips of Naithon's ears. Damn. He'd hoped by keeping her away from the people at the mansion she wouldn't know he had fucked a few of the women there. That information could in no way benefit their budding relationship.

Picking up the container of macaroni salad, Naithon said blandly, "No one important." He plopped a spoonful on Kiri's plate, added some to his own plate and handed the container to Maz with a frown of warning.

His grin as big and troublemaking as always, Maz took the container and spooned a heaping pile of noodles on his plate.

Before she could inquire further about Silver, Naithon quickly started talking about the upcoming football game. He and Maz chattered about the game while Kiri pondered who Silver was and why Naithon didn't want to talk about her. She remembered Francy had mentioned Silver too and never answered Kiri as to who she was.

As they were finishing, Naithon's cell rang. He answered it, and his mouth tensed. Muttering, "*Ja*," he put the phone back.

"Nait?" Maz watched the dread in Naithon's gaze swerve to Kiri. Her brows rose in question.

"Baby," he put a hand on her thigh, "your da…"

Panic gushed, she gripped his sleeve. "What? What's happened to my father? Is he…" She didn't dare say it.

Naithon stood up and pulled her to her feet. "No, but he's in bad shape. He's at Holy Cross, he's been poisoned."

"Why is he at the public hospital and not with his own physician?" Mazonn asked, tossing the remnants of their lunch into the box.

"He was in a restaurant when he keeled, one of the servers panicked and called an ambulance. Come, Kiri, I'll take you upstairs and I will go see about his condition."

She tugged her arm from his grasp, head shaking she declared, "No, I'm going to the hospital."

Brows lowered, his jaw rigid, Naithon replied, "No you are not. You are staying here. It won't be safe for you there. Now, come with me." He reached for her hand but she yanked it out of his reach.

"Naithon, if you don't take me to the hospital, I swear I will never talk to you again, and you will never touch me again."

Angry eyes narrowed, he warned, "Don't threaten me, Kiri, you know you can't stop me from doing what I want." They glared at each other.

Kiri crossed her arms. "You want to force me to kiss you, to not respond to your caresses? Not feel my hands, my mouth…on…*your*…body?"

Mazonn's gulp was audible. Grin lopsided, he said, "I'll go get the car ready and a crew to go with us," and split, fast.

"Kiri-"

"I mean it, Naithon. Did you like what we did yesterday?" His head nodded like a puppy wanting its favorite toy. "Do you want more of that between us? My touching you, and wanting, enjoying your hands on my body?" She stared at him, until he broke.

"Oh, fuck, Kiri," the air blew out of his lungs in resignation. A month ago he wouldn't have blinked at her threats. She was there for his pleasure whether she wanted it or not. Now, when he'd discovered how sweet, how agonizingly amazing it was when she responded to his hands on her, his kisses, and *Dio*, her hand on his dick. He was not giving that up. He'd just have to be extra bloody careful to ensure her safety.

"Get a jacket, one for me too," he said with an aggravated sigh, handing her the keys to the security doors and their room.

On her toes, she kissed his cheek, whispered, "Thank you, Naithon," and then rushed to the stairs.

Pulling his phone from his pocket, he grimaced. He could not believe that hard, violent criminals cowered in fear of him, and delicate, dainty Kiri Delducci bravely stood up in his face, even though she was still afraid of him.

Mouth twitching, his head shook in begrudging mirth, he muttered, "That little girl has teeny, tiny, lady balls. Damn, that's hot."

Chapter Twenty-One

They drove in a caravan, the Lincoln with bulletproof glass was dead center; Naithon was taking no chances of an ambush. Last thing he wanted was to take Kiri out of his house, and to the damned hospital with its hundreds of people and numerous exits.

He'd called his IT guy, well, hacker, for a schematic of the hospital when they got in the car so he'd know where all the exits were.

Naithon closed the car door in Kiri's pouting face. She wasn't getting out until he secured the place. She was anxious and impatient to see her father, but she was lucky Naithon allowed her to be there at all, so she was going to cool her heels in the car until he was satisfied the hospital was secured. The whole incident could have been created just to draw her out of his house.

He saw her make a frustrated and annoyed face when she tried to open the door and it was locked. She would not be able to unlock it. Only Naithon, the driver, and his head capos had key remotes that locked and unlocked all the doors.

His cell phone buzzed, swiping it on, he said, "*Ja.*"

"Boss, it's Ken Kenav, your cane-fields manager."

"I know, Ken, caller ID. What's up?"

"First, let me say it's all under control-"

"What is? What-"

"Boss, the north field near the forest was on fire. We put most of it out before the firetrucks arrived. I was up to my ears in smoke is why I didn't call you right away-"

Naithon cut him off again with a terse, "How much damage?"

"Listen, Boss, not much, not even a quarter of an acre. The thing is, there was a body-"

Naithon shouted, "What the fuck? Who? A field hand-"

"Geez, Boss, let me spit it out."

"Go," Naithon ordered impatiently.

"Not a field hand, Boss, it was Piero Delducci."

Dead silence. Was this a joke? "Repeat that?"

Kenav huffed. "Yeah, imagine our shock at finding the body. Cops were there. He was burnt to a crisp, Boss, nasty sight, terrible God-awful smell burning flesh-"

"Ken, what the hell happened? Why was Delducci even there in my fucking sugarcane fields?" He could picture Kenav shrug as he replied, "Dunno why he was there, no clue. He was baked, but a cop checked him out, said he found a bullet hole in his head. 9mm."

Cripe, great. "Anything else?"

"No, sir. Forensic people all over the place, we were moved off, told to stay away. Chief Ivchenko said after he spoke with the Delduccis, and his men questioned the field hands here, he'll call you."

Smoothing a palm over his hair, Naithon said, "Keep me abreast if you hear or know anything." He hung up without waiting for the foreman's reply.

Wait until Kiri finds out that her brother Piero's body had been found torched in one of Naithon's fields. What the hell had he been thinking bringing her here? She was undoubtedly in dire danger.

"Ha," he snorted, he knew why she was there. Kiri was a stubborn little thing, if she said she would never speak to him again, or touch him, or let him touch her without a fight, she meant it. He was way too far gone for her to let that happen. He wasn't about to tell her about Piero now though, she had enough on her mind to worry about.

Sighing frustrated, *ja*, he was pussy whipped, and he hadn't even had her pussy yet. Only *Dio* knows what will be left of his infatuated brain when he finally gets her in bed. And not to sleep. Shaking off his lust for Kiri, Naithon stomped from the Lincoln as his men spilled out of their cars, and he started barking orders.

"Vlad," he told his friend, "you take squad A and go straight up to the 4th floor where Delducci is. Check out exits, hallways, storage closests, the works." Without a word, Vlad strode over to his group of men and told them their job.

Naithon did the same with Teodor. "Teo, you're squad B, you put your men on every floor, I want soldiers on the roof. Check every stairwell and elevator." Teodor took off to do as instructed.

"Yash," he called his friend over. "Spread your squad C all over the first floor, I want a man at every door, and I want the garage and basements searched." A sharp nod and Yash hurried to do as Naithon bid.

Last, he called Blok to his side. "Your soldiers cover the outside exits. I want men posted on the perimeter grounds and parking lots and driveways. Check the cars, the trees and surrounding buildings for snipers."

"You got it, Nait." Blok jogged to his waiting men. Naithon watched his men spread out, some surrounding the building and grounds, the others went inside the hospital. He tapped the earpiece and said, "Capos, check in when you are at your posts."

Moving to a van they'd set up for surveillance, Naithon poked his head in.

"Cosmin," he jutted his chin at a man with deep coffee-colored skin and dreads in a ponytail. All of the team wore black pants and button down long sleeved shirts to at least try to blend in with the hospital population.

"Sir," Cosmin acknowledged him.

"Everything, everyone, eyes on everything."

"Yes, sir." Cosmin nodded sharply. His eyes were already glued to a computer screen. The rest of the men in the van were equally absorbed with identical equipment.

Naithon glanced around the inside of the van, checking that all the apparatus was up and running, the men were intently engrossed with their tasks. "Okay, anything, any little thing, Cosmin, even if it seems innocuous but draws your attention, you tell me. Got it?"

Another sharp nod, his eyes on the screen, he replied, "Yes, sir."

Naithon left the van and joined Mazonn's crew that was waiting for him. He didn't look towards the Lincoln, Kiri would be beside herself having to sit there helplessly and wait while he organized everything. She gives him any shit and he'll take her straight back home, threat of withholding her body from him or not.

He had a bad feeling and in his years on the street he had learned to pay attention to the chill that ran up his spine. He needed to get this the hell over and get her home. He wouldn't breathe easy again until she was back locked in his suite.

It took about twenty-five minutes before every squad captain called in that they were in position, and confirmed the hospital was as secure as they could get it.

"As soon as we're rolling, Maz, your men stay with Kiri and me. I want a fucking steel wall around her, got it? I want eyes on you too, watching your own back. We all can be targets."

"Of course, Nait," Maz assured him. "Tony is getting that small vest for her to wear. Should have a hat there too for her head." Mazonn's words stabbed porcupine quills in his gut, Naithon picturing Kiri on the ground with a bullet hole in her head. Fuck, he never should have brought her.

He glanced at the Lincoln. Her pale face was pressed to the glass watching him. Ignacio was a rotten bastard that allowed her to be abused and then tried to sell his own daughter, but that doesn't make his child dread his demise any less. He was still her father.

Gruffing a long exhale, Naithon trod to the car and took the small vest from Tony the driver. Unlocking the door, he pushed her down the seat and climbed in the car next to her.

"Naithon, aren't we going-"

"In a minute. Lift your arms." He waited while although puzzled, she did as he said. He slipped the vest around her and started taping the Velcro across the front.

190

"What's this?" she asked as he pressed the tape closing the vest.

"It's a bullet proof vest, Kevlar." Taping the last binding, he tugged it down her hips.

"Oh, Naithon, I don't need-"

He suddenly gripped her jaw. His agitation and concern made him hold her more roughly than he ever had. "You wear it, you do exactly as I tell you. You will not leave my side, you will not go into the ladies room. Any protests or divergence from my orders and we're out of here. You understand me?" He gave her jaw a commanding shake. At her blink and wince, he realized he was hurting her and loosened his grip.

"Answer me, Kiri."

Lips bunched, she mumbled, "Yes, Boss."

"You get smart with me-"

"I know, we go straight home," she mimicked his threat that he had expounded again and again the entire ride to the hospital.

A tug at the corner of his lip, a miniscule leer lifted the lip and clouded his eyes, "I'm thinking when we get home that someone needs a little refresher course in proper behavior."

She tried to pull from his grip, back away, but he held her with steel fingers and the leering grin. "Naithon, please…"

Lifting her chin up, he lowered his head and kissed her quickly. "Okay, let's go."

He opened the door. Tony stood with a helmet much like a hard hat but smaller and covered with black material. Naithon took the hat and plopped it on her head. At her protest, he tugged the strap under her chin and buckled it. She gave up protesting his safeguarding procedures, and let him buckle the strap without further comment.

He got out of the car first, then held out his hand for her to take. She slipped a small cold hand into his and he drew her out of the Lincoln. As soon as she was out, a dozen men encircled them. They stood so close, it was suffocating.

"Naithon, really, all of this isn't necessary, there has to be fifty men here." It was embarrassing to be hustled down the walk like she was a princess or a celebrity or something.

More like a hundred men. His arm tight around her shoulders, he tucked her against his side, pulled her head to his chest, "Hush," he growled.

When they reached one of the smaller entrances, Naithon's men were standing guard outside the door and inside it. Naithon didn't draw a deep breath until she was safely inside. They'd have to do it all over again when they left. This was it, he was never letting her out of the mansion again, he won't have a nerve left by time they get home.

With a crowd of men around them, they were propelled down a hall and to the elevators. Teo had already cleared them with hospital security. The elevator doors pinged open and a man came hurrying over to get on. Mazonn blocked him. "Take the next car," he told him in a cold voice.

"Hey," the man blurted, "you can't commandeer the goddamned elevator!" He tried to push through. Two of Mazonn's team flanked him and moved him twenty feet away. The man sputtered and cursed and struggled, threatened to call the cops, to no avail.

Naithon hurried Kiri into the elevator, as many men that could fit joined them, the others would take the next car. There were guards posted at the stairwells and elevators on every floor.

Squashed against the back of the elevator, Kiri could hardly breathe with all the testosterone in the car. Especially from the one roiling in it, aggressive waves rolled off the man in front of her. Naithon's back pressed against her, smashing her to the wall, she couldn't see a thing around his massive body.

The door hit the 4th floor, the top floor, and the men fanned out first, then Naithon. When he was satisfied it was clear, he held his hand to Kiri. Seeing the helmet in her hand and the vest undone, he gave her a ferocious frown of displeasure. "Goddammit, Kiri-"

Kiri stepped from the elevator. "We're inside, Naithon, there are no snipers lurking from the ceilings." She started walking.

Looking to the heavens for help in dealing with his tiny intractable dynamo, Naithon rushed after her.

Throwing his arm around her, he growled in her ear. "That's one, Kiri, one disregarding my orders, another one and-"

"I know, I know," she sighed, "we go home."

He halted and brought her abruptly in front of him, his hands gripping her upper arms. Face a mask of fury, he said in a quiet shout, "Kiri, your brother Duce is dead, your father is seriously ill," he had to bite his tongue when he started to say, "and your brother Piero is dead."

Rotating his shoulders to ease the strain, he said more calmly, "Your family, my people, are all in danger. If you don't do as I say, you will never step out of my house again. I mean it."

She blinked in anger and distress at him and saw that he was as serious as a heart attack. He would keep her locked in her ivory tower for...however long it took him to tire of her, she supposed. "Okay." She huffed silently.

He glared at her for a second, aware his men were likely grinning at their lethal mobster boss being jerked around by a tiny female. He was notoriously misogynistic; treated women purely as sex objects, the mobs were reputably sexist, and here he had an army to surround and protect one petite girl.

Dragging a hand through his hair, he raked his fingers in ire. Nothing he could do about it. He'd fallen like a rocket ship from the sky slamming into the earth for this female, he was wrapped around her finger and he knew it. "All right, let's go."

The group moved towards the large, semi-circle counter of the nurses' station.

Their shoes stomped on blue and white flooring to the curved counter tiled in beige, the wall behind it pale blue. Some of the nurses wore blue smocks, others green. The counter was about four feet high, closing off the station behind it.

Naithon had prepped Maz to do the talking. He didn't want to get distracted from the environment surrounding them. Mazonn's men blended with Vlad's men that were already there.

Maz approached the desk, spoke for a minute, then returned to where Naithon waited. Maz pointed to an open, wide doorway. "She says that's the waiting area. I told her we'd be waiting out here. She said a nurse had been out there earlier stating he was waiting for Kiri Delducci, and said he would be back in a second to bring her in when she arrives."

Naithon nodded. His arm around Kiri, he hugged her against him, his eyes never stopped moving around the area. He studied every door, every nurse, everyone in their vicinity.

Only a minute went by and a male nurse appeared from an automatic door, it whooshed open and then closed behind him. He came right to them. Dark brown eyes widened when they set on Kiri, he smiled broadly with his hand out. "Miss Delducci, I am Haziq Jaleel. I will take you in to see your father. You will be happy to know he has the best of care."

In his late twenties, Haziq had taupe skin, thick black hair that waved around his head, dark eyes that never left Kiri, and full lips tipped up in a friendly smile. He was tall, not as tall as Naithon and his men, but over average height. He wore the blue smocks and carried a clipboard in one hand.

Naithon moved his arm to block Kiri from shaking hands with the nurse. "I go with her," he stated.

Haziq finally looked to Naithon, his expression turned bland and polite. "I am sorry sir, hospital rules, only immediate family goes in the ICU."

"I am her brother," Naithon snapped.

Haziq's gaze lit on the possessive arm Naithon had around Kiri. "Nice try. We have names and pictures of the family members, and you are not one of them, and I'm pretty sure none of them have that accent," he said with a hint of insult.

Naithon's arm tightened around Kiri until she squirmed. "I go with her," he stated obdurately.

Haziq crossed his arms with the clipboard against his chest. His tone blithe, he said, "No. That door is to ICU and only an employee can open it. If you insist on being with her, then she can't go in. You might as well go home."

Kiri swung around to face Naithon. "I am not leaving, I am going in there alone. He's in the ICU, Naithon, nothing can happen to me in there."

194

Naithon's face hardened into fierce rock. "Kiri-"
"Naithon." They were at a standoff, and every person in the area was watching them like they were in a movie.

"Ahh," his lungs emptied angrily, he scrubbed a hand down his face. Why couldn't he have fallen for a compliant female instead of this stubborn chit? "You have ten minutes. Any longer and we come in, locked door or no."

Glaring at Haziq's smug face, Naithon cupped Kiri's chin, lifting it. Glowering at the beauty that had slivered under his skin from day one, he threatened harshly, "I mean it, Kiri. No fucking around. You're not back in 10 and everyone's safety in the place will be in jeopardy." He bent and swiped their lips, and he let her go.

Naithon glared at Haziq, his tethered fury was hanging on by a thread. "You fuck with her, you're a dead man. Feel me?"

The smug look gone, Haziq swallowed hard and nodded. His mouth suddenly too dry to speak. He went to take Kiri's arm to guide her.

"Don't fucking touch her," Naithon barked in a low, vicious voice. The bad feeling he had was digging into his gut. But like she said, ICU, what could happen in a locked area? Still…

Kiri started walking with Haziq, Naithon called out, "Ten minutes, there better be a clock on the wall." Kiri turned around with her sweet, shy smile and waved delicately at him as she disappeared through the whooshing doors.

Naithon stood like an angry, immovable mountain staring at the door. Vlad came to his side with an iPad in his hand. "She'll be okay, Nait, there's no way in or out of there except by that door according to the schematics of this area."

Naithon didn't respond. His itchy gut was never wrong. Right now it was swimming with snapping piranha.

Chapter Twenty-Two

Naithon paced furiously in front of the doors. All staff gave the tough looking blond man in a suit with shoulders that could span a football goalpost, a wide berth. His men hovered scattered around the area, alert and ceaselessly scanning the nurses' station, elevators, hallways, doors, the staff, roaming patients.

There was a clock on the wall behind the nurses' station; Naithon's head lifted every other second to look up at it, then down to the watch on his wrist.

She had gone in at 2:30, it was 2:41. A wave of fear suddenly blew like an icy wind through him. He started towards the door, one of his men tried to stop him.

"Boss, it's only been eleven minutes. You don't want the cops here for a disturbance, give it a few more minutes."

His glare of wrath could have shriveled the man until he was dust, but he paused.

Then a few more minutes passed, then a few more. His shoulders rigid as blocks of concrete, Naithon's teeth were grinding to the bone. Then, something struck him so wrong, *oh shit*- "Vlad," the capo looked to him with question.

"There are none of Delducci's family here, the sister, none of his soldiers, no one. How the fuck did the nurse know Kiri was coming? We didn't call ahead." He stomped quickly over to the station and barked, "Someone open that goddamn door."

Everyone froze, all eyes wide on him, no one moved. Naithon's men drew their weapons. Face growing red with fear and impatience, accent rugged, Naithon shouted, "Open that goddamned door or bullets will start flying!"

A nurse broke from the cowering herd and scurried over. Hands shaking, she swiped her ID card over the pad and the doors whooshed open.

Naithon stalked to the door, stood in the threshold so it couldn't close, he commanded, "Vlad, Georges, Frankie, you're with me. Tomas, Angelo, you keep this door open. The rest of you make sure no one leaves, or moves."

He paused again, turned and pointed to the nurse with red hair that had opened the door and demanded, "You, take me to ICU."

Mid-thirties, a parade of freckles popped across her pasty face, lashes flapped anxiously over hazel eyes, she placed a hand over her heart, and gulped. Taking a deep breath, she strode past him, spine erect and said firmly, "Come with me, sir."

They traipsed down a tan and gold tiled hallway with white walls, then down another, she reached a second nurses' station. People stopped what they were doing and gawked at the nurse with four huge bruisers at her heels.

She took them to another corridor then, her chest rose with a tense breath she informed him, "That is ICU," and pointed to a set of open double doors.

"Everyone stay here," Naithon ordered and he stalked into the room. There were a dozen beds, only one had a patient in it. He strode over and looked down. A frail, elderly woman lay with tubes stuck in her. He swung around and moved to a connecting restroom, a storage closet, he jerked the door open, mops, sheets, cleaning supplies. Spinning on his heels, he stormed back to the nurse, spitting nails.

He roared in her face, "Where the fuck is Mr. Delducci?"

The red hair about flew back from the breath of his fury, hazel eyes rounded with terror. She stammered, "The- there is no one by that name in this unit." Now her eyes bulged out of her head at the way Naithon seemed to grow bigger, an enraged bull about to charge and destroy.

"Find out where he is located."

She nodded like a puppet and rushed to the nurses' station. She hurried back and said, "He was moved this morning, he's on the second floor, room 236, bed A."

"Who was the nurse that came and retrieved Kiri Delducci from the front nurses' station? Why did he come and get her if her father wasn't here?"

Stuttering her fright, the nurse said, "I...don't know. He had come to the station a few minutes before you arrived and said for us to call him when she got there. That was it, we...didn't know why. I thought your woman was...uh, the nurse's girlfriend or something?"

Naithon tapped his earpiece. "Mazonn, have someone check room 236 for Ignacio Delducci, fast." His eyes speared the nurse, her already pale face whitened. He asked, "Where is Kiri Delducci?"

She blinked at him.

He lowered his upper body to an inch from her face, accent scathing, he snarled, "You saw her, pretty with reddish brown hair go in here with that nurse, Haziq something. Where are they?"

"Uh, I- I don't know."

"Why would he bring her in here if her father was moved to another floor?"

"I, uh, d- don't know. Like I said, I just assumed the nurse was her boyfriend and he was bringing her in for a visit. I don't know who he is, I thought he worked on another floor or...someplace. I've never seen him before." She wrung her hands in front of her chest as if they could shield her from his wrath.

Naithon snapped, "Where can I find him?"

Her legs shook so much it was a wonder she was still standing. "I- I- I don't k-know. Last I saw him he was bringing the woman in here. I wasn't really paying attention, I-"

Naithon tapped his ear, cursed in Romanian, said, "Lock down the fucking hospital." He asked the nurse, "Is there another way out of here other than the way we came in?"

She nodded, too frightened to speak.

"Show me," he directed with a bark.

She started towards a hallway, as Naithon followed her, he turned to his men and ordered, "Search every motherfucking room, under the beds, closets, behind the nurses' station."

The nurse brought him to a room. It contained an unoccupied desk and some chairs and a bookcase. "The- there-" she pointed a quivering finger to a door on one side of the room. A clipboard was lying on the floor near it.

Naithon hustled to the door and shoved it open. It only opened a few inches then stopped. He shoved it harder, something was blocking the door. Both hands on the door, his arms rigid, grunting with the effort, he pushed the door until it was wide enough he could get through.

When he stepped past the door he saw what was blocking it and his hair stood on end. It was the nurse, Haziq. There was a neat bullet hole between his eyes. "*Fuck*," Naithon spat.

Stepping over the body, he tapped his earpiece and told Mazonn what was going on. "I'm hitting the stairs, fan the men out, no one leaves the fucking hospital."

Mazonn said, "That office you're in isn't on the blueprints of the building, neither is the door or stairwell. Must have been added later and never recorded."

"Keep in tabs with everyone, Maz, I gotta find her."

Leaping two or more steps at a time, Naithon hurdled down the stairs, grabbing the railing when he veered from one set of steps to the next. He locked his brain into stone cold work mode, he couldn't think about who had taken Kiri and what they could be doing to her. If she was still alive.

At the next landing, in a corner lay the helmet Kiri had been wearing, as if it had bounced down the stairs and rolled, coming to a stop in the corner.

Heart beating like a jackhammer, sweat making his palms slick, he raced down floor after floor until he reached the last one. The staircase ended at an exit door. A red exit light was lit up over it, a fire alarm next to the door. Naithon slammed into the door shoving it open, he ran outside.

Quickly scanning the area, he was at the east side of the hospital in the back. He saw nothing but an expanse of grass with a border of woods, there was no parking lot. But there was a narrow road, and further down there was a truck parked on it. A white van, and some fucker was dragging, carrying Kiri to it.

The side panel door was open, he could hear Kiri screaming as she hit and kicked her abductor. The male wore all black including gloves and a mask that covered his hair and face. He was a big fucker.

Pulling his gun from his holster, Naithon tore across the grass, boots clomping the ground like a galloping horse, the asshole hadn't seen him yet. She was small, but carrying and fighting Kiri was still slowing him down. He had reached the van and threw her inside.

Aiming without slowing, Naithon pulled the trigger and shot out a tire. He couldn't shoot the bastard, he was too close to Kiri. The man halted abruptly at the gunshot. His head twisted and his body jolted when he saw Naithon bearing down on him. The tire was quickly deflating. The kidnapper had no choice, he turned and ran into the woods.

Still running, Naithon shot at the figure as it disappeared into the trees. Leaving the man to flee, Naithon ran straight to Kiri, feet stomping the tarred driveway. She was slumped in the open door to the side of the van. When he reached her, he touched her arm, she screamed and hit out at him.

"Baby, baby, lamb, it's me, Naithon, you are safe now, sweetheart, I've got you." He scooped her into his arms. She threw her arms around his neck and sobbed. He didn't have to look to know his men were tearing around the building running to them.

Holding her, Naithon shouted, "Man in black, ran into the woods," he motioned towards the direction the guy had fled. A dozen of his men spread out and disappeared into the dense copse of trees.

Naithon sat on the floor of the van in the doorway in the open doorway and set Kiri on his lap. Her face was stuffed into his shoulder as she wept and shuddered. His arms like an iron fence held her so tight it was a wonder she could breathe.

His face shoved in her hair, he murmured as much to convince himself as her, "Safe, baby, you're safe now." They sat for several minutes listening to his men shouting to each other in the woods.

Mazonn appeared from around the front of the hospital and ran over to them. "Hey," he huffed warily, not sure of Kiri's condition.

Naithon peered at him through her hair. Maz grimaced at the emotion packing his eyes. Maz nodded silently at Kiri, brows arched to Naithon.

"Ah, I don't know how she is." Naithon cradled the back of her head, lifting it so he could see her face. A man made of corrupted steel, his hand shook for the first time in his life. "Baby, are you hurt?"

The tears flowed, she hiccupped, a shiver rolled over her shoulders then up her body.

"Tell me, Kiri, did he hurt you?" The rage barely contained, his voice was rough and thick in his concerned accent.

She blurted through sobs, "He- he k- killed that nurse, Naithon."

"I know baby, did he say anything when he shot him?" He felt the shudder run through her body again.

Sniffing, she wiped at her eyes. "Y- yes. The nurse was- was in on it. The man in the mask said, 'Your task for today is over, Haziq, sorry, no bucks for you' and- and he shot him, oh God, it was horrible!" The tears filled and rolled out again. "Haziq collapsed to the floor, and- and the man threw me right over his shoulder and pounded down the stairs. I couldn't get away, Naithon!" she cried.

"*Ja, ja*, honey, did either of them hurt you?" He couldn't slaughter Haziq, but when he catches the guy that took her…

"No, I- I don't think so," she stammered, trying to quell the waterworks.

But she was hurt, Naithon gently held the side of her face, there was a cut near her eye, and her jaw was turning purple. The bastard had struck her.

"Baby," he whispered, "are you injured anywhere else on your body? Can you stand?" He moved off the van and stood with her, and gently set her on her feet. Her legs wobbled but they were okay.

Naithon examined her arms for any injuries. There was a tear on one leg in her jeans, he could see blood oozing from it. "Maz, bro, get the car."

Mazonn gave a wink of support to Kiri and stepped a few feet away, took his phone out and made several calls to all of the squad capos. Moving back to them, he said, "Car is coming around, we should get out of here before the uniforms come."

"Teo will handle them. The Chief is his uncle."

The Lincoln came speeding around the corner down the narrow curved drive, several of the other cars were behind it. Naithon hustled Kiri into the Lincoln and climbed in after her.

He said to Mazonn standing by the door, "Have Doc Maankov meet us at the house. She needs care and she's not going back inside that fucking hospital. I want that van brought in and scoured. Pull all the surveillance tapes. Set the men to questioning the people."

He held Kiri the entire drive back, neither speaking. Naithon had never been so scared or so enraged in his life. Each time his phone rang, he mumbled briefly into it. The perp had gotten away. Apparently he had a backup vehicle hidden in the woods.

The doctor was there when they arrived. Bursting through the front door, Naithon ignored people gawking at them and carried Kiri up the stairs to their room, the doctor followed.

Inside the suite in the bedroom, the doctor laid a medical bag on a table and went to Kiri when Naithon set her on the bed. Nodding to Naithon, he said to Kiri, "Hi, honey, I am Doctor Maankov," his accent was as thick as Naithon's. "Let's get you out of those clothes, *ja*?"

Naithon's angry face got between them. "What the hell, Doc? She's not undressing in front of you."

The doctor stood impassively in front of Naithon, said calmly, "You will leave the room or I will go and you can take her back to the hospital." While the men stared each other down, Kiri slipped into the bathroom and came out wearing a thick white robe.

"Naithon," she said softly, "I am not glass, I won't break, please do as the doctor says."

His angry gaze stroked over her body, frustration pinching his lips, defensive eyes narrowed at her. "That is not the point, Kiri, I won't have him looking at your naked body."

"Mr. Adranokov," the doctor sounded somewhat amused and also annoyed. "I have seen a lot of naked women in my career. I think I can keep myself from jumping your girl." He moved to the medic bag and grasped the handle. "You go or I do."

Naithon knew he was being unreasonably jealous and possessive, he couldn't help it. Stuffing the unfamiliar feelings down, he muttered sullenly, "Fine. I will be right outside the door."

He pointed a thick finger at the doctor, said ungraciously, "You do not take liberties with her, and you," he growled, ignoring the doctor's offended yet still amused expression. Gesturing to Kiri he said, "You keep that robe on, and you better have," he stalked to her and jerked one of the sides of the robe open.

"Naithon!" Kiri gasped, shocked at his behavior.

Seeing her bra, Naithon pulled the lower half apart and nodded when he saw her panties. "Nothing else comes off, you hear me?"

Her eyes shifting to the ceiling she said sarcastically, "Yes, Naithon, the Pentagon hears you in Washington."

His mouth twitched, then his gaze zeroed in on the bruise on her jaw. The irritation in his voice softened. "I almost lost you, baby, please indulge me." He lifted his hand and stroked her face with his palm.

A shudder rolled through her. With a sigh, she smiled. "I know. Please don't worry. Let the doctor do his job."

The doctor stood patiently to the side. Crazy as it seemed, Maankov was in his sixties, not much hair on top and the fringe around his lower head was grey. He had a paunch because he loved Romanian and Italian food, still, he ran across many men who were reluctant to leave their women alone with him.

Especially as he did most of his work with mobsters, and they tended to be old fashioned and macho, chauvinistic with their women, and outrageously possessive. They treated them like property, beloved perhaps, but still property, and no one fucked with their property.

Naithon's eyes flittered around Kiri's face going from the cut by her eye to the bruise on her jaw, his mouth compressed. He grunted, "Okay." Leaning in, he pressed his lips on hers, pushing until she opened her mouth to him. His hand cupping her face, the other on her back, he pulled her in and gobbled her up. He kissed her hard, long, the doctor coughed politely.

Naithon drew back, gave the doctor a warning glare, face softened at Kiri. "I will be right outside that door," he stepped out and pulled the door, almost closed, but left it a hair open.

After the examination, Naithon walked the doctor to the door. Maankov said, "She is okay, Mr. Adranokov. Shaken up of course. She has bruises and a few cuts, a bad gash on her knee I bandaged up. She may have a slight concussion, she's been trying to hide her dizziness and nausea from you. Apparently when the perpetrator threw her in the van her head got slammed into the side of the door."

"Motherfuc-"

"Please calm down," he told Naithon as he saw the rage burn again in his dark eyes. "She will be fine. If she becomes acutely nauseas, or disoriented, has trouble seeing or hearing or standing, call me right away. Naturally she needs to take it easy for a few days. I left pills on the table for her headache."

After seeing the doctor out, Naithon trudged up the stairs, he had to tell Kiri another of her brothers had been murdered before she saw it on the news. Duce in a wood chipper, and now Piero charbroiled to a crisp in Naithon's sugarcane field. What the hell will happen next?

Chapter Twenty-Three

A carbon copy of the hospital visit, Naithon had his men immersed in the crowd at Piero's funeral. His arm around her weeping form, Kiri was dressed all in black with a black veil covering her face red and swollen from days of crying. Surrounded by a human barricade, Kiri paid her respects to her deceased brother.

Ignacio was too ill to attend the funeral. Rueford Montoblanco tried his damnedest to get to Kiri, but her male wall wouldn't let him within twenty yards of her. He tried to get to Naithon to talk to him, but Naithon just tightened the wall keeping him away.

At Duce's funeral, much to his frustrated chagrin, it was Naithon who had been barred from getting to Kiri, but now he had her, and he had the power to control the situation. She was enclosed in his tight, secure bubble.

After the hospital fiasco he swore she would never leave his place until the danger was cleared. He should have known. There was no fighting his tiny dynamo when she was set on something, thus, he was standing beside her as she cried for her brother.

The second the first shovel of dirt hit the casket, Naithon steered Kiri to the limo. The car was surrounded by dozens of other vehicles; a soldier was running a detector around all of the cars searching for bombs.

Kiri was so distraught, Naithon had to half carry her to the limo. They drove home, she wept on his shoulder. There was to be a reception at the Delduccis' put on by business associates and friends. Naithon put his foot down, Kiri was going straight home.

The next day, Naithon's brother, Novikav, narrowly missed being blown to bits in his car. He was downtown visiting his mistress. When he got in the car, he realized he'd left his phone in her apartment and just as he exited the car it blew to smithereens. The forensic team had a devil of a time locating all of the driver's body parts.

Novikav had to have shrapnel from the car dug out of his back, he had a concussion, hearing loss, both legs were broken. But he survived. His wife and mistress met at his hospital bed. They attacked each other like wild screeching cats. Security had to be called to remove them from the hospital.

Naithon refused to let Kiri out of their suite for a week. Wouldn't even let her go to her studio on the second floor. Not much scared Naithon, but after her attempted abduction, and the attacks on the Delduccis and then his own people were enough to chill him to the bone for fear Kiri would be next.

He barely slept a wink, checked with his security team every hour, checked and re-checked the alarm system, examined the video surveillance of the house and perimeter. Backtracked all of his guards, and had all nonessential people removed from the house. They'd found nothing on the hospital tapes. It appeared the deal made with Haziq was done elsewhere.

Videos of the van used in Kiri's abduction revealed the license plate had been removed, and there were no viable shots of the abductor. All cameras leading in and out of the streets to the hospital were viewed with negative results.

In the mansion, all meals were brought to the bedroom where a soldier tasted and drank everything before Kiri touched a thing. Aware he also could be a target, Naithon was more careful than normal.

He had already hired the best private detectives money could buy to investigate what gang was behind the attacks on the Adranokovs and the Delduccis. So far they hadn't come up with a single clue, not a single suspect. He knew his people weren't guilty.

Ignacio may be retaliating for the hits on his family thinking Naithon was at fault, but Naithon doubted it. He was too afraid of Naithon. Someone was pitting them against one another, and no one had an iota of a theory as to why.

It wasn't long when the men had no release for their stress and they started scrapping. After vetting them, Naithon allowed a few of the females to return. Silver Dae was one of them. He hated to have her in the same house as Kiri, but she was a favorite among the men, so to keep the peace, he let her room with a few of the other girls. Trying to recall which strippers he'd slept with, they were banished.

Kiri was sitting on the settee by the window reading a book when Naithon came in. He paused in the doorway. Closing the book, she smiled. "Hi. You here to spend some time with me?"

"Baby, I can't. I have to stay on the security of the compound." He grinned at her mouth turning down in a pout. "But," as he entered the room he pulled something from inside his open jacket. When he reached her, he held it up.

"Oh my gosh! Naithon!" She jumped up, yelped ecstatically, "A puppy! Isn't he adorable." Eyes like green saucers of delight focused on the black and white husky with sky blue eyes. "Where did he come from? Can I pet him?"

Laughing, Naithon held the dog out. "He's for you, lamb, I got him for you." Then the cheer fled into sudden distress on her face. She stepped back and moved her hands behind her back, ducked her head.

"Baby, what's wrong? You love dogs, you had them when you were-" it dawned on him. Cuddling the puppy to his chest, he said gently, "Your brothers can't hurt this little guy, honey. No one is gonna hurt him, I promise." He didn't remind her that Duce and Piero were dead and couldn't get their ghostly hands on the pup, that would just reignite her grief.

He stood patiently, scratching the dog behind his ears. The puppy whimpered, and Kiri peeked up at him, then took a step towards it. A few minutes, and she reached a hand out to pet his head. The puppy licked her hand making her giggle. Naithon held him out to her. "What are you going to name him?"

Accepting the dog, Kiri cradled him to her chest and cooed at the pup. "Hmm, I think…Kako. He's an Alaskan husky, there's a lake in Alaska I read about called Kako Lake."

"I like it, good choice, baby." Naithon slipped his arm around her and he scratched under the dog's chin. "He's tiny now, but see those big paws? He'll be a big boy and he will be extra protection for you, *ja*?"

A dog bed was brought in and placed in the bedroom, food dish and water bowl in the kitchenette. Naithon or one of his men would walk Kako.

The next day, it was around 11:00 a.m. when Naithon received a call. Not recognizing the number, he answered warily, "*Ja*?"

"Mr. Adranokov, this is Wick with the Riveaux Knights."

"What can I do for you, Wick, we're pretty busy here."

Wick cleared his throat. "Sorry. Roar, you know, the president of the club asked me to call you. There is a situation at the clubhouse, I think it's something to do with the hits on you and the Delduccis."

His heart skipped a beat. "*Ja*, yeah? What about them?"

The heavy breath Wick took came through the phone. "Roar didn't tell me. Just said to make sure I told you how serious it was, dangerous, but there's info about the attacks on you guys."

"Why does he think I need to be there? He can tell me over the phone."

"Man, come on, I don't fucking know. Roar just said it was important, but you needed to be careful of the danger when you get here. Probably should bring your best men."

Thinking for a minute, Naithon couldn't surmise what on earth Roar had going on, but he had to check it out. "All right. Tell Roar I'm on my way." He called his capos, Mazonn, Yash, Vlad, Blok, and Teodor. When they arrived, he told them about the call.

He ordered, "Maz, Yash, Teo, you come with me, bring some of your boys. Vlad and Blok, you stay here, watch the house."

Blok said, "Nait, the dude said it was dangerous, we need to all go, watch your back."

"It could be a trick to get me out of the house to get at Kiri. The compound is impenetrable, still, I want you guys to stay here, keep an eye on everything, *ja*?"

After apprising Kiri that he would be gone for a bit, and admonishing her sternly to stay in their suite, Naithon and his men hurried out to their vehicles.

****

A knock at the suite's front door startled Kiri. She was playing with Kako. As she made her way to the door, the puppy bounced around her feet with little yaps. The door was unlocked from the inside. Since the aborted abduction, Piero's death, and the assault on her father, Naithon didn't have to convince Kiri she was safest right where she was. He no longer locked her in, but did keep everyone else locked out.

She opened the door and was surprised to see a woman standing there. Kiri looked up and down the hallway. "Where's the guard Naithon posted at my door?"

The woman shrugged, stiff blonde curls scraped over her shoulders. "He looked horny, I had a couple of girls take him down the hall to entertain him. I talked Simon who was to bring you your lunch into letting me do it." Carrying a box, she wormed inside the door and past a confused Kiri.

Setting the box down, she gave Kiri a great big smile. "I figured you have to be bored to tears. Nait won't let you out, and he won't let anyone in. I took this chance while he's gone to come and visit you."

Her hand on the doorknob, Kiri murmured, "Um, I don't know…"

"It'll be fine, a little girl talk, be good for you, right?" She lifted two covered plates from the box, set them on the table then she sat on a chair and took the lid off of one. The aroma of spaghetti filled the room. "Mmm, come on, hon, it smells great," she nodded to the other dish.

What harm could there be? "Okay, sure." Kiri closed the door and took a seat at the small table. She removed a fork from the box and tasted the pasta. "It's good." She smiled politely at the woman. "I'm sorry," she smiled and said, "I'm Kiri, I don't know your name."

Flipping a side of the motionless blonde hair, the woman replied, "I'm Silver. Silver Dae Foxx."

A frown wrinkling her forehead, Kiri twirled spaghetti on a fork. "Silver. Yes, I've heard your name before."

"Yeah, you would have heard about me and Naity. We are...you know...we're in love." Silver pretended she didn't see the shock on Kiri's face.

"In love?" Kiri parroted in a small voice.

"Oh yes, we've been together for years. Of course he's been in my bed all this week, you know?"

Her mouth open ready to take a bite of spaghetti, Kiri set her fork down. Studying the older woman, Kiri saw she was pretty but the prettiness was hard. Her hair was stiff, she wore a blouse that exposed much of her very large breasts. Kiri had been sheltered, but she heard about implants. Silver's heels were six inches, her skirt barely covered her wide butt.

At first, Silver's words caught in her heart, Naithon was sleeping with this woman while he was...courting Kiri? Kako set his maw on Kiri's foot and peered up at her through fluffy black and white fur. Naithon had given her a studio, covered her with an army of men when she went to the hospital, and brought her Kako. She smiled fondly at her puppy. His tail flopped back and forth.

Recalling how Naithon's eyes smoldered whenever he looked at her, touched her constantly, and he may have been patrolling all day and all night, but he always came back to her when he took a few hours rest.

No, this woman was lying. Before she could confront her, Silver said casually, "I'm so sorry about your dad. I hear he's dying."

"What?" Kiri squawked, her head flung towards the woman.

"Yeah," she said idly with a hint of sympathy. "The guys were talkin'. They said he had a day or so before he...you know...sorry hon." Silver opened her purse and pulled out a flask. Twisting the lid off, she poured a good portion of what was in it in her glass of soda.

Kiri leapt to her feet, repeated aghast, "What?"

"I'm sorry hon, it's sad when you lose your folks, huh?" She chugged her soda, wiped her mouth with the back of her hand.

"No, no, no," Kiri exclaimed. Gripping the sides of her hair, she wailed, "I have to see him, I have to see him!"

"Well, sweetie, just have Naity drive you over there when he comes home."

"He won't," Kiri cried, as tears gathered. "He won't let me leave the house. He'll restrain me if I try to leave." Pacing, she wrapped her arms around her waist, chest heaving with despair.

Finishing the rest of her soda, Silver bit the end of a nail, said nonchalantly, "Well, I can take you there, if you want."

Kiri clasped a hand over her mouth, Naithon would kill her if she left the compound. But, it was her dad. She implored Silver, "How would I get out? He has his men watching me."

Silver pondered, then snapped her fingers. "I got it. I'll get you downstairs. A couple of the girls can distract the guards at the kitchen door where there's only two, like they did with the ones up here. When they're turned away, I'll slip you out the kitchen door. It's the least guarded area in the building. You duck down when I drive out the gate. What do you say? You game?"

Pacing some more, Kiri thought, maybe she could see her father and get back before Naithon does, he'll never know she left. "Okay, but we have to hurry."

"Great, let's go. The guards outside your door will be occupied for a while."

Silver unlocked the steel door at the landing and led Kiri down a little used staircase. Then to the pantry off the kitchen. The guards weren't there, the two women slipped out and ran for Silver's car that she had parked close to the door.

Hopping in the car, Kiri didn't let out her held breath until they hit the road. She couldn't believe they pulled it off. Watching the woods and fields pass by as Silver hurtled down the highway, Kiri said, "Naithon would be so livid if he knew his guards had allowed themselves to be distracted."

Suddenly her bottom burned. Naithon catches her and he will tan her butt but good. She forced herself to relax, he'll never know.

Chapter Twenty-Four

When Naithon and his men arrived at the Riveaux Knight's clubhouse they were stopped at the gate. Two men wearing cuts held guns on Naithon. They recognized him.

One with both sleeves of tats said, "What is your business here, Adranokov?"

His eyes shifted from one to the other, Naithon replied coolly, "Roar sent for me. Tell him I'm here."

The two men shared a vexed look. "Roar ain't here. They're down in Stuben for the annual races. There's only a skeleton crew here, everyone is down in Stuben."

Naithon immediately pulled out his phone and dialed Roar's number. When he answered, his voice cool, level, Naithon said, "Roar, you have your man Wick call me to come meet with you?"

There was silence. Then Roar said carefully, "Ain't got no member named Wick. We're in Stuben at the races, have no reason to meet with you."

Clicking off, Naithon shoved the phone in his pocket and barked to Mazonn who was driving, "Take us home, stat."

Tires squealing, they raced back to the compound. His fist rolled tight, Naithon slammed it on the door handle with a block of Romanian curses. "I knew it was a motherfucking trick, goddammit, I should have called Roar. All this shit, it's too much to keep track of."

Yash and Teo in the back said nothing, there was nothing to say. While Maz drove, Naithon called Vlad. It took several rings before Vlad answered.

"Fuck, Nait," he blurted into the phone.

"Tell me, Vlad." Naithon put it on speaker.

His panted breaths loud, Vlad huffed, "We just found some guards passed out. Looks like they were drugged."

"Kiri?"

"Ah," Vlad's voice rough, "she's gone."

Naithon held the phone out in front of him and blinked at it. "How?"

"We gathered everyone, the women too. Apparently Silver got into your room and convinced Kiri to leave with her."

A few voices rumbled in the background. "*Ja*, Nait, Jazmine said Silver made them drug the guards. Said she'd knife them while they slept if they didn't do as she told them. There were some strange loud pops out front, and then out back, me an' Blok separated and checked them out. I guess Silver had fireworks set off to draw us away from her sneaking Kiri out."

Naithon crushed the phone in his hand, then growled, "They have any idea where Silver's taking her?" He heard Vlad talking, and then several people yakking at once.

Vlad said, "Martina says she thinks she's taking her to her da's house. Silver had confided in Martina that she was gonna get some big bucks to deliver Kiri to the Delducci home. We put the compound on lockdown."

"Okay. Put everyone that was involved in the basement. Pull the surveillance tapes and any on the main roads, see if you can find her car to verify it."

Vlad replied, "Blok's lookin' now." Naithon heard Blok's voice in the background. Vlad said, "Yeah, it was Silver. Parked by that little side door near the pantry area. Only the two girls got in the car. What?" he said something to Blok. "Uh, Blok says Kiri looked really upset. Silver didn't have a weapon or nothin' on her but your girl was crying."

"Check the other camera tapes and get back to me," Naithon hung up. "To the Delduccis', Maz," he sat back and glared at the front windshield. Mazonn was already heading the car in that direction.

****

Silver parked down the street from the Delducci mansion. Kiri's brow creased. "Why are you parking here? What's wrong with-" she saw Silver's eyes glance at something behind her. Swinging around, Kiri saw a white van rambling down the street coming towards them. The windows were tinted, she couldn't see inside.

Kiri turned to Silver. "Silver, what is going on?" She swung back to look at the van. It resembled the van that she had been shoved into at the hospital. Prickles tingled up her spine. She looked at Silver, the woman had a smug, satisfied smile as she gazed out the window past Kiri's head.

Kiri frantically grabbled at the door handle, it opened, she tumbled out. Silver screamed, "No! Wait!"

Kiri ran opposite from the van, towards her family's mansion. It wasn't a compound like Naithon's with fences and gates around it. As she ran across the grass, she glanced over her shoulder.

The van had stopped and a man jumped out. Silver was standing outside her car shouting something at him. He looked like the same man who grabbed Kiri before, dressed in black, gloves, mask. She ran as fast as she could.

Screaming at the top of her lungs, she raced for the front door. The door sprung open and two men leaped out with guns raised. Kiri ran to them screaming for help. The soldier guards let her run into the house then stood in the doorway. The masked man slowed, then made a sharp turn and he tore back up the street to the van. Silver hurried after him.

The men closed the door. Janero, hearing the screams rushed to the foyer and was stunned to see his sister, hysterical. "Kiri, what the hell, girl?"

"He- he's trying to get me, Janero!" She ran into his arms.

Embracing her, Janero asked, "Who? Who is chasing you, Kiri? Is it Adranokov? You escaped him?" He said over her head to one of the men, "Muster everyone you can, armed, get them here now!"

"No, no it's not Naithon! Naithon saved me from this man that was trying to capture me. That woman, she tricked me into coming here!"

"Woman? What woman?" Her brother patted her back trying to soothe her panic.

"One of the…I think she's one of the strip girls from the club."

"Kiri-"

"Janero," a man broke in, "there's an SUV rushing up the driveway. It looks like Adranokov. Should we start shooting?"

"No!" Kiri screamed. "Don't shoot him! He's here to help me." She clutched Janero's shirt, cried, "Don't hurt him, please!"

Janero smiled wryly down at his sister. "Okay, don't worry, if that's Naithon Adranokov, we're the ones who are in danger." He motioned to several men. "Open the door wide, leave it like that, and get out of the way." They did as he said.

In moments, Naithon stormed in the door, trench coat flapping at his heels, gun in his fist. Seeing Kiri with her brother's arm around her, he cursed and charged across the room.

Kiri moved to stand in front of Janero. "No, Naithon, it wasn't him, he didn't trick me here. It was that man, the one who grabbed me at the hospital. Silver was helping him, she brought me here."

When Naithon slowed, brows still daggered down he asked, "Why did she bring you here if your old man didn't order it?"

Kiri pushed from her brother's arms and ran into Naithon's. The gun in his hand, he wrapped his other arm around her and pressed his face into her hair.

Janero grinned at Mazonn as he appeared in the doorway. Everyone's eyes were on Naithon and Kiri. Janero said drily, "I think there's been a change in things between my sister and Adranokov."

A rancid snort came from across the room. Melonie stood under an arched doorway, her arms crossed and a nasty scowl on her plain face. "Right," she sneered, "the two-bit prodigal slut grabs both the mobster and her family's attention. Of course. Life is so fair."

A man stood at the end of the room, he called out, "Jan, your dad wants to know what's going on, what's all the noise."

Kiri said urgently to Naithon, "I have to see him. Silver said he was on his deathbed."

Janero's lower lip pushed out, he frowned quizzically. "Deathbed? He's doing so much better. That doesn't make any-"

Mazonn said calmly, "They wanted us to think it was Delducci that took her. The guy outside was going to grab her before she reached this house."

"Take me to him, Janero," Kiri said, moving from Naithon's embrace, but he held onto her hand. Naithon said to Janero, "It was a ruse to lure Kiri here. I don't want-"

"Nait," Teo called, moving in through door. Naithon motioned for him to come to him, he wasn't letting go of Kiri, and he didn't want her near the door until he had things sorted out.

"Silver's dead," Teo announced, glancing over at Kiri's gasp. "She was lying in the street, bullet in her chest. Yash saw the white van, he ran back and hopped in the car to run after it, but I think he's long gone."

Face white as a sheet, Kiri whispered, "Dead? She's dead?" Tipping her head up to Naithon, her face wreathed with compassion, she said, "Your girlfriend was murdered, Naithon, I'm so sorry."

Brows knit in vexation, Naithon grumbled crossly, "Kiri, she was not my girlfriend."

"But she said you're in love and have been together for a long time, and that you've been sleeping in her bed."

The only good thing to Naithon, was the wounded sound in Kiri's voice. She was jealous, he hoped. But, she should be fucking trusting him, believing his word by now.

217

"Baby, I fu- uh, slept with her a couple of times to relieve stress and she was handy, this was long before I brought you to my home. She meant less than zero to me, and I told her that. The second I put my plan to take you into fruition, I told her directly that I would not be doing anything with her or any of the other bitches at the house. That you were it for me. Nonetheless, she still hit on me and I blew her off. Everything she said is a lie."

He twined his fingers around her arms, bent so their faces were close. "Baby, when are you going to get it through that gorgeous little head of yours that I have no interest in any other bitc- ah, woman, but you."

"But when you tire-"

"Oh, fuck, stop, Kiri," exasperation in his voice, his forehead bunched in pique, he squeezed her arms. "I don't steal women every day and force them to stay with me. I will never, never tire of you. You're the one I worry about not letting me get close to you."

"I think that worry is history, bro," Janero quipped, the men chuckled.

"*Ja*," Naithon smiled down at Kiri, "it's a work in progress. All right," he kissed her, then said to Janero, "take us to Ignacio."

Everyone trooped to the main salon and up the stairs and down the corridor to Ignacio's room. Inside the huge, masculine chamber, Ignacio was in the big four-poster bed sitting up against several pillows. A nurse sat in a chair by his bed with needlepoint on her lap.

To the side of the bed were four broad windows covered by gold brocade drapes. A brown and gold loveseat and two large, matching cushioned chairs hunkered in front of the windows, the door to the attached bathroom was open. A bit of white and gold marbling was visible.

"Pa." Janero went in first. "Kiri's here to see you."

"Huh?" Ignacio's face held disbelief when he saw his daughter come into the room. He crowed with delight, "The gypsy bastard finally grew tired of you and kicked you out? Jan, call Rueford-"

"The gypsy bastard is with her, old man, and he hasn't and won't ever tire of her," Naithon growled entering the room. He held

Kiri's hand, she tugged it loose and trod gingerly to her father's side. Naithon stayed right behind her like a shadow.

Ignacio's brown eyes flit from Kiri to Naithon. "Tell me what the hell is going on, why are you here in my home?" He ignored his other daughter hovering in the doorway, and the men, his and Naithon's that materialized into the large room.

Naithon moved closer to the bed. He explained, "The day you were poisoned and in the hospital, Kiri had me bring her to see you. We were conned by a male nurse into letting Kiri go with him to ICU to see you. It was a ploy to snatch her. I thought it was you at first, or one of your men." Lids levered low over dark, dangerous eyes aimed at Ignacio. "But, knowing I would skin you and toss you alive on the barbeque grill if you tried that shit, I assumed it wasn't you."

Ignacio studied Naithon for a long moment. Then he asked, "Why would someone grab my daughter? Rueford wouldn't have the balls, so who?"

Naithon's eyes darkened. "That red-headed fuck would have the balls, old man." He shook his head. "But I don't think it was that asshole, he wouldn't have acted alone, he's too big a coward. Same solo guy came after her tonight.

"The guy paid off one of the whores at my compound to lure Kiri here with the bogus claim you were dying. Knowing Kiri would be in danger, both from the guy that's after her, and," he set his hand on her shoulder and squeezed, "my wrath for leaving my house, yet, Kiri still took the chance to come and see you before you croaked."

Ignacio's gaze bumped back to Kiri with surprise. "Really? After how I've treated you?"

Kiri leaned over and kissed her father on his forehead. "Yes. You aren't a nice guy, but you are my father, and I love you."

Ignacio blinked in amazement at her. "Wow." Grey bushy brows lowered over brown eyes not as sharp as usual without his glasses on. His voice heartened, he said hopefully, "So, you're ready now to marry Rueford? I put the wedding plans on hold, we can call the planner and she can-"

Naithon moved in front of Kiri, face like thunder. "She isn't marrying any fucker but me. I don't want to hear that red-haired bastard's name mentioned in conjunction with Kiri's again. You don't knock off the crap, you won't be invited to our wedding."

Stubby grey lashes flew up, Ignacio turned wide eyes to Kiri, then they narrowed in disbelief. "You're gonna marry this scumbag gypsy thug?" He said furiously to Naithon, "You took her as collateral that there would be no more killings. They didn't stop, so you lied to and cheated us, Adranokov. You get the hell out of here, she stays. She will marry Rue-"

"I'll be your bridesmaid!" Melonie chirped from the doorway. "Rueford's wanted you since you were practically a toddler, he'll be so thrilled!"

In a beat, Naithon had Ignacio's pajama collar wrapped in his fist and he was lifting him up off the bed. "You listen to me you old motherfucker, she goes where I go. You give me any trouble and I'll-"

"Naithon, please." Kiri grabbed his arm to pull him back. "He's ill, please don't hurt him."

Ignacio's men, and Janero made moves to go after Naithon, but Mazonn and Teo planted their boots akimbo, hands on the weapons at their hips. "Uh huh," Mazonn shook his head at the men.

Naithon let Ignacio drop back on the bed gasping for air. Kiri tugged at his arm. "Naithon, we should go, please."

Chest heaving with rage, Naithon glared furiously at Ignacio, clearly he wanted to pound the older man into the ground.

Ignacio tried for bravado, but his voice shook, "Kiri, girl, tell me you aren't gonna marry that bottom feeding, gypsy slug." Clutching the sheet to his chin, he pleaded with his daughter to deny it.

Aware Naithon was still glowering at her father, but was listening for her response, Kiri said, "Right now, Dad, I just want to be home." She felt Naithon stiffen beside her.

Ignacio brightened. "That's it then, you're staying here with your family, what's left of it," he ended glumly. "But you and Rueford will soon cough out the babies and build us back up again!"

Feeling Naithon's fingers wrap around her arm, Kiri clarified, "No, home with Naithon," and she heard his exhale, the tenseness in his fingers eased a bit.

"Kiri," Ignacio's tone carried a small whine.

Shaking her head, Kiri said firmly, "No, I'm leaving with Naithon. I'll check on you tomorrow."

"By phone," Naithon put in.

Kiri looked up at him, her eyes rolling, they stopped moving at his smirk of promised punishment. "Maybe I should stay after all..." she murmured. Naithon leaned over and whispered in her ear, "Not on your life, pigeon, I go, you go. On your own two feet or over my shoulder, however you want it, you go with me," and laughed at her affronted grunt.

Everyone except Ignacio and the nurse traipsed down the hall. When they reached the staircase, Kiri kept going down the hall when the others started down the stairs.

"Baby," Naithon called after her. He looked to Janero who shrugged, he didn't know what she was doing. Then Janero said, "Duce's and Piero's rooms are down that wing."

Naithon paused, Janero said, "Let her have her moment, Adranokov. There are no exit stairs down there, all the rooms in that wing are empty, she'll be safe." His mouth curled up in a persuasive grin, he said, "We've got some fantastic rum down in the den. I'd like some time to get to know my future brother-in-law."

"I'll stay with her," Teo offered.

Naithon hated to leave her, but Janero was right. He didn't want to intrude on her grief. "*Ja*, okay." He kissed her on the top of her head. Lowering his head so their eyes connected, he said quietly, "Just a few minutes. Stay away from the windows." Ignoring the annoyed look she shot him, he joined the others as they tromped down the stairs and to the den. Janero handed everyone a glass and filled them with rum.

Upstairs, Kiri went first into Piero's suite. It hadn't changed since he was a teen. Except the bed was made. Because they have servants. Posters of rap artists were taped crookedly on the walls, among them pictures of naked women, some appeared young enough for it to be child porn.

Then she realized the pictures of the *very* young girls were actual photographs blown up. They were bent over, tied up, gags over their mouths, tears in their eyes, and whips flying at their backs. Apparently oldest brother Duce wasn't the only perv creep in the family. Kiri cringed at the sights. Over Piero's bed hung flyers extolling the use of drugs. She said a silent prayer for her sick brother's soul, then left his room and went on to Duce's.

Like Piero's, it hadn't changed. His suite was as large as Piero's, huge bed, over-large furniture, there was nothing on his walls. A door led to a hall and a separate sitting room, a second door opened to the large en suite bathroom even bigger than the walk-in closet that was so big an entire football team could fit inside. On his dresser there were pictures of Duce and his friends playing football, accepting trophies.

A small smile wavered with her grief. Disregarding the one of Duce at a strip club, a woman on his lap, his hands clutching her bare breasts, lewd grin as big as life, Kiri picked up one of the other pictures and smoothed a fingertip over the photo.

It was of Duce, Piero and Janero together. There was vast blue water behind them, probably at the beach. They were grinning, raising beers to the camera.

Her attention was drawn to their rings. All three wore the rings with their family's crest on the top, initials on the side. Kiri and Melonie both had asked for rings like them, but as usual, they were told it was only a male thing.

Staring at Duce's ring, her stomach fell; it reminded her of the photos her father had shown her of the scene where Duce had died. Blood on the wood chipper, his belt buckle and ring had been recovered and identified. Chewed up but still recognizable.

Setting the picture down, she said a quiet prayer and left the room. She jumped when Teo pushed off from the wall.

"Sorry," he apologized coolly, "I was guarding, I didn't mean to startle you. I figured you'd know Nait would never leave you unprotected."

She smiled at him. "I'm getting that idea pretty good by now, Teo. Thanks though, for being unobtrusive."

They went downstairs together.

In the den, Melonie was trying to talk to, and touch Naithon. Following him like dirty footprints, "Mr. Adranokov," she cooed, chasing after him, ignoring Maz's snickers and Naithon avoiding her. "Babycakes, you know, you've never seen my bedroom." One of her pudgy shoulders pushed up coyly she invited, "I'd love to give you a tour, perhaps now?"

Hell, Naithon grit his teeth, wasn't she listening when he told her old man he was gonna marry Kiri? Her fucking sister for fuck's sake? What a sleaze. Like he had thought before, she was as bad as his own brother Misolav. Horndogs, liars and cheats, greedily, shamelessly poaching other people's property.

When Melonie started rubbing against him like a she-cat in heat, he shifted away, turning his back to her. Any other whore and he would have dealt harshly with her, but she was Kiri's sister and he wasn't about to do anything that would upset Kiri and have her hating on him again.

Then again, he would hope that Kiri would not appreciate her sister's clear invitation to fuck, or have her hands and body all over him. *Ja,* he would hope.

The menace vanished and his face lit up when Kiri entered the den. He went right to her, slung his arm around her waist and pulled her against his body. Melonie's face twisted in loathing; with an obnoxious snort she went to refill her cocktail glass.

Everyone hung for a bit, had a couple of drinks with Janero. They discussed as usual who could be responsible for the vendetta against their families. Who could gain from pitting them against each other? Soon, Naithon set his glass down. His arm around Kiri, he said, "Call it a night, boys. I won't relax until I get her home." He hugged her to him.

A sound of jealous disgust erupted from Melonie. No one paid her any attention. They were used to her foul mouth and behavior. Some men could look beyond plain and plump, but they wouldn't appreciate such vulgar conduct.

In the SUV, Kiri was asleep in minutes, her head on Naithon's shoulder. When they reached the compound, Naithon carried her inside as he has before and laid her on their bed. He thought of it as their bed now, not his.

He removed her shoes, tugged her jeans off her, left her in her shirt and underwear. He didn't want to stir her anger up thinking he stripped her while she was unaware. The puppy yawned with a tiny yip from his bed on the floor. Looking over at the dog, Naithon sighed with relief, "*Ja*, little fellow, we have her back home safe and sound."

Standing beside the bed and looking down, Naithon didn't blink as he watched Kiri sleep. This hell had to stop, end. He couldn't take it if he lost her again. He would burn the fucking town down if he could to bring an end to her stalker, and the assassinations that plagued both her and his families.

Chapter Twenty-Five

Naithon decided to stay by Kiri's side the next day, cancelling all his meetings for the week. He was scared to take his eyes off her. If the kidnapper had gotten his hands on her, he would surely kill her, after doing *Dio* knows what to her first. Everyone was dismayed at Silver's deceit, what she had done, and shocked at her murder.

He kicked the women out that had been complicit with her. They had been threatened and coerced into helping her, but they should have come to him. They should have known he would protect them, but they believed Silver's lies that Naithon was in love with her and would never toss her out on her betraying huge ass.

The women also had to find new employment, they wouldn't be dancing in any of his clubs. The soldiers that had been duped and drugged were rotated to different sites. He didn't want unwary men guarding his house. He didn't fire them, or do worse as he normally would, because they were unwilling participants in Silver's scheme.

The fool Simon who had allowed Silver to take Kiri's food from him and deliver it herself so he could go bang one of the girls was recuperating down in the basement.

Naithon had his own soldiers, and detectives hunting everywhere to find out who had paid Silver to trick Kiri into going to him. One of the dancers told him Silver thought she had sanded both sides of the double–edged sword. She'd make money by delivering Kiri to the man, and she would also get the girl out of

Naithon's life, believing he would turn back to Silver once Kiri was disposed of.

What she hadn't figured on was what Naithon would have done to her, if she'd survived, when he learned of her heinous scheme, delivering Kiri to her death, and that when the man who hired the disposable Silver, when she had completed her mission, he would assassinate her as well. Stupid, stupid whore.

After lunch, Naithon brought Kiri to her studio. He carried Kako and sat in a big recliner he'd had brought in. Kicking his feet up, the pup tucked at his side, he powered up his laptop and toiled with his own business while she worked on an order from a new restaurant that was having a grand opening in a month. The order was for her to create and design food off their menu with mouth-watering, tempting scenes, and photograph them for their ads.

The restaurant was Indian-Chilean fusion. Occasionally Naithon peered over to see her progress, and thought what odd shit the fusion thing was. Kiri had pinned up on a corkboard various photos of India, Chile, and their native dress and foods, and dishware, serving platters etc. She had found pictures of both countries of their people in their native dress.

Chile was bright, bold colors, food like humitas, dough wrapped in green corn husks, sopaipillas, a kind of quick bread, and pastel de choclo, corn cake with beef, black olives, hard boiled eggs.

India was colorful too but more spicy warm. Kiri had made giant pink lotus flowers to set the plates of food on, she had other ideas for scenery.

They both worked for hours, then she stood back and regarded her work with a frown. She complained to Naithon, "It's hard to make rice and lentils captivating." That brought a chuckle from him. She turned to where he was sitting. "That is so nice, Naithon."

He mumbled, "Hmm?" without looking up.

"Every time I'd ever seen you over the years, and when you brought me here, I would have sworn your lips couldn't curve up, and that you weren't born with a laugh button."

"Ha!" he barked out a humorous laugh to prove her wrong. "You are silly, my little pigeon, it is wholly you that has put the happy in me, the smile on my face." He grinned when she tried to scowl a reprimand at him for calling her pigeon. Then she smiled and sighed, some things will change with him with her influence, and some won't.

"Sure," she said with a pretend scold, "you can punish me for calling you Mr. Adranokov but I have no recourse when you call me those silly, sexist pet names."

"*Ja*, well, that's what happens when I am the boss and you are not."

When she opened her mouth to retort, Naithon set the computer aside then put the pup on the floor, and Kako bounced right over to Kiri, tail wagging a mile a minute.

Laughing, she picked him up, kissed the top of his furry head and hugged him. His blue eyes shone so bright and beautiful, she said, "I have plans to paint you, little guy. Maybe playing with a polar bear on snow. What do you think about that? Hmm?" She bunted noses with him and smiled when he tried to do it again.

Grinning at their antics, when he stood up, Naithon yawned. "You ready for dinner, baby?"

Holding the dog, Kiri's attention lit on the way Naithon's button-down shirt stretched across his broad shoulders. Her gaze traveled down, pausing at the thick chest, his muscled pecs were defined in the material, even his taut abs were outlined when he moved. Jeans covered lean hips, her gaze lowered still, remembering their night at the distillery, pink flushed her round cheeks.

His voice husky, Naithon murmured, "You keep looking at me like that and I'll have you for dinner, lamb."

Her eyes shot up with embarrassment. "Um, I think we should go eat."

Waiting a second, Naithon smiled at her, adjusted the boner growing in his pants and said, "You're almost ready, lamb, maybe today?"

Kiri didn't pretend to misunderstand. Every day they grew closer, enjoyed each other's company, Naithon's caresses were becoming more sexual. His palms would skim down her back to cup her bottom, and he would pull her against his erection and knead the rounded globes until she moved away.

When he could get away with it, he groped and fondled her when they were downstairs, when people were present but not in view. He didn't do it when they were upstairs alone because he knew he wouldn't be able to stop himself from taking things all the way.

Except for having to jack himself off to keep from banging her, it was kind of neat, like reliving his teen years properly. Like most young people started slow, got to know one another, made out before they went all the way. He and Kiri were doing that, progressing the right way, enjoying the slow burn, but they are adults, it was time now, to consummate their relationship.

He insisted when they were alone that she didn't wear a bra. Then he would make comments about her nipples until they pebbled from embarrassment, and arousal. He had a constant hard-on, but he could tell he was wearing her down. She allowed his caresses to become bolder, linger longer, and she touched him. His arm, his fingers, his chest.

And their kisses, fuck. At first he thought there was nothing better in the world than kissing Kiri, but, she was dynamite on legs as she became more relaxed, allowed herself to feel when he sucked on her tongue, bit down her neck, nipped at her cleavage, rooted for a nipple, of course that's when she usually pushed him away with a giggle.

They sat with his friends around them at dinner. In the beginning, whenever she was there and other people were present, she kept her eyes lowered, didn't make eye contact. She could feel the stares, conversations stalled whenever Naithon brought her in. Before they used to just gawk at her in curiosity, the females with envy, the men with lust.

It was worse now, resentment steamed from the other women. They blamed her for Silver's death. They gossiped that if like a vixen siren, she hadn't soaked Naithon blind and mindless with her wiles, he would be with Silver, and she would still be alive.

Feeling a bit more comfortable today, flanked by Naithon and his capos, his captains, she felt safe from the women's wrath, and the men's desires. Naithon would not allow any males within ten feet of her, except his friends that he trusted with his, and hers, lives. She let her gaze wander the room while the men talked business and sports, and guns.

The dining room was almost pretty with paintings of colorful landscapes hanging on the blush walls, dark rose carpet, white sheers at the sunlit windows. The long dining table stretching the length of the room shone with a daily polishing, but was covered with white tablecloths during meals. There were two full time cooks each had two assistants, and servants set up and served the food and cleaned up after.

A few men had a fork in one hand and their other arm around a woman, some had two. The women weren't shy about their attire, flashing parts of their bodies with ribald abandon. Raunchy jokes were shared, loud raucous laughter bounced off the walls. If they weren't criminals and hookers, Kiri would think they were just normal folks having fun and enjoying each other's company, although more on the bawdy side.

Lunch over, people drifted off. Naithon took Kiri's hand and they went into the den with Maz and Teo. Maz and Teo played cards and smoked, Naithon sat down in a big easy chair and pulled Kiri onto his lap. Giggling, she swatted at him and tried to get down. "Naithon," she whispered with a laugh, "we aren't alone."

"They'll leave in a minute. They have a job to do." Stringing an arm around her, he caught her chin, and licked her lips making her giggle again. Slanting his head, he kissed all over her lips, her cheek, jaw, then sealed their mouths and chased her tongue.

Maz chuckled, sounds of chairs moving, footsteps heading to the door, Teo called out, "We'd tell you teenagers to go get a room, but you can have this one." The two men snickered down the hall.

"Finally," Naithon said against her mouth, "they're gone. Now you can chill." Seizing her mouth again, he plundered it until they were both breathless and aroused. His lips sucking at hers, he reached down to the top button on her pale yellow blouse. It was one of her favorites, she wore it a lot. Naithon liked it too, it was a nice foil for her reddish-brown hair. He paid one of the maids to buy a wardrobe for Kiri, he was pleased with the choices she'd made.

Naithon plucked at each button until they were all undone, never moving his mouth from hers. He ate at her, bit at her lips and tongue, slowly he pushed the sides of her blouse apart, exposing her bare breasts. Breaking from her, he groaned, "Oh baby, I didn't know you weren't wearing a bra." His lips pressed together, "You know I don't want you down here without one."

Lids low over sultry eyes, she smiled and wriggled in his lap. Angling her head up for more kisses, throaty sounds heavy with sensual tones Naithon had never heard before from her fired blood racing through his body, and heading down, swelling the already hard bulge. Kiri arched her back like a cat stretching, purred, "It's your fault."

Turning more towards him, Kiri bussed his lips, caught his bottom one with her teeth and tugged on it. She whispered into his mouth, "You brought me down here so quickly, I didn't have a chance to put one on. You're the one that insists on me not wearing one when we're alone."

She flattened her palms over his chest, gripped at his muscles, then smoothed her hands slowly up to his shoulders, there she dug the tips of her fingers in and dragged them back down, slower over his nipples that she pinched. Giggling at the shiver that rolled through him, her voice growly soft she said, "You say you like watching my boobs bounce and my nipples harden. Yours harden sort of too."

"Damn," he croaked, lowered his head to gawk at her breasts. "I like my new sexy pigeon."

"Naithon," she scolded without anger, more of a sigh.

"*Ja*, baby, pigeon because of these," he put his palms on her ribs then stroked up her skin to clutch her bare breasts. They spilled over his big hands. Staring down at them groaning, he said, "Never gonna get used to looking at these, baby, so hot, so hot." Gripping her supple flesh, he squeezed and molded them, he was rough, kneading hard, but her arching back and the sounds she was making low in her throat told him she was loving his strong vigorous touch.

Kiri's hands pushed into his hair and she twisted locks in her fingers. Naithon felt the twisting all the way down to his groin. "Baby," he growled, pushing her blouse off her shoulders, exposing her entire top half. Pinching her nipples, he moaned when her reaction was to yank on his hair. He pinched one nipple harder, then lowered his head with grunts of arousal, and sucked the other nipple in his mouth. Chewing on it, he continued pinching and twisting, pulling the other one until Kiri was writhing all over his lap.

"Fuck, Kiri, you do me in," his groan rumbled a growl deep in his chest, he grabbed both breasts and roughly groped them. His chest heaved with sky high lust for his girl. Kiri cupped his face and peppered kisses all over his head, his ears. Her bottom squirmed on his lap, wiggling all over the hard ridge that stretched long and thick down Naithon's leg.

His hands went to the button on her jeans and flicked it apart. When he pulled her zipper down, she didn't protest, just kept kissing his head, his face, sucked his neck like he'd done to her. Naithon moved his hand inside her pants, under her panties, and skimmed down, his fingers stretching to the folds of her bare sex.

"Naithon," uncertainty had entered her rousing, husky voice, her legs stiffened.

"Let me," Naithon whispered. "I won't hurt you, you know that." His hand pushed down further, he gently stroked the plump flesh that covered her woman's bud, and her hips bucked to his hand, a small cry escaped her parted lips.

Naithon tugged one of her legs, widening the space between them and watched her as he stroked her folds, her slit with his hard fingers, Kiri's eyelashes fluttered over eyes that had turned to green glaze. Her tongue slipped around her lips, his eyes tracked its trail. Smiling when her silk wetted his hand, he gently touched her swelling little bud, and her entire body writhed, her cry spiraled out in a harsh gush of his name. *Dio*, but he was crazy about this girl!

His lips at her ear, he observed her face flush dark pink, lips parted, lids almost completely closed. He looked down at her lush plump breasts, tipped with nipples that tasted sweet, tasted of her. Then he watched his hand inside her pants, the material moving as he caressed his woman, showing her what pleasure he could bring her. She was soaking wet, he slipped one of his thick fingers just inside her slick channel and she jumped with a squeak, tried to hop off his lap.

"Shh, shh, baby, relax, just feel me, feel what I do to you," he rumbled in English then roamed into Romanian as his own lust was peaking. He slowly moved his finger up inside her, then carefully pulled it almost out, and did it again. Liking what he was doing, yet frightened too, Kiri squirmed so hard on his lap, he had to hold her tightly with an arm around her or she would writhe right off his legs.

Naithon felt a twinge of concern. Clearly a virgin, she was extremely tight, and so bloody tender, he wanted to hold her like fine china, and thrust like a raging bull into her juicy little pussy at the same time. It was going to drive him mad when he finally entered her, so tiny, he'd have to move painfully slowly. And, it was likely going to hurt her a bit, until she got used to him.

If he wasn't extremely careful, she was going to hate her first time so much she'd never let him near her again. Of course that wasn't going to happen regardless, but he wanted her to love his hands on her, his dick deep inside her. There was something to be said for the whores he normally fucked, they could take his size, his violent roughness, he could do as he pleased with them.

Capturing her lips again with greedy bites, Naithon smiled, he was a lucky man that Kiri was all his, he would teach her the delights of sex. All kinds of sex. He would ruin her for any other men, not that she would ever be with another man.

He'd take the kinky stuff slow, otherwise he would alarm her and she would shut him down. Distracting her by nipping her lip hard, he increased the pace of his finger, he needed to add another one, stretch her so she could accommodate him more comfortably, right now she was too damned tight.

Judging by the gurgling, whimpering sounds that were now roiling from her mouth, Kiri was starting to really enjoy it, her hips pressed against the rhythm he was setting. Naithon lifted her, turning her so her back was against his chest and her legs straddled his thighs, and pushed his finger in deeper.

Her neck arched with a gasp, the side of her face brushed his, her moan susurrating in his ear. Clutching a breast, kneading it hard, now he could maneuver his other hand better, after every few thrusts of his finger he massaged and pinched her tender button until her entire body was bucking and writhing all over his, and her moans rose, her breaths fast and shallow, chest puffing out, up.

"Oh Naithon," Kiri cried, her face rubbing harder against his now, mouth open with her gasping desire. Her hips bucked to his finger, he was moving rapidly inside her, and his hand webbing her breast crushed the firm globe, soft flesh pushing out through his punishing steely fingers. Her rapturous sounds, chest heaving heavily, body in frenzied motion, she was at her peak, and he was going to propel her over that zenith.

"Okay, baby, I have you, let it go," he murmured against her ear.

"Oh, oh, Naithon, it feels…" gasp, "pressure down there, zinging in my- my…" He swirled her clit enticing a loud long groan. "It…" she sucked in a breath and bucked at his hand, "feels like I'm climbing, I'm about to explode, I'm scared, Naithon," a whimper mingled with a voluble cry.

"It's good, baby, just go with it, let your body go," and he crunched her other breast with a fierce squeeze, pinched her nipple, twisted it and pinched her clit at the same time, and she went over with a silent scream.

Kiri knifed forward with a hoarse cry, her hips came off his lap. Still crushing her breast in his strong hand, he held her down and worked her orgasm. A shudder jerked through her, she arched back against him, and he plunged his finger while pressing her swollen nub with his thumb, and she sobbed his name as her body convulsed, her sex undulating around his finger.

When he wrung every sensation of Kiri's climax from her, Naithon wrapped both arms around her and bound her to his chest. Tremors still rippled and shook through her body, tiny mews from her parted lips, the wheezy, rapid breaths started to decline.

They were still for a few moments. Then Naithon whispered in her ear, "You okay, baby?"

233

She squirmed against his chest with a soft murmur, "Hmm."

His chuckle rumbled against her back. Holding her tight, he glanced down. Her blouse was more off than on, he moved his arms to wrap around her ribs, her bare breasts mounded over his hairy arms. Her legs splayed wide over his, her pants open exposing the tiny lacy panties his hand had just been rapaciously under. He died and went to heaven, he was never moving again.

Their breaths, hearts, beat in unison. The only thing better than this was when he would be inside her. His Kiri, Naithon sighed in contentment. Never thought a woman would bring him happiness. Never thought he would ever feel true happiness. Hugging her tightly, he said, "Baby-" voices were coming down the hall. Kiri jerked up as if slapped.

"Aw hell," Naithon muttered and tugged her blouse down the front of her so she could button it. He slipped her off his lap and moved to stand in front of her, blocking anyone's view while she fixed her pants. He should have locked the door, he'd been too caught up in her to think about it. That wasn't good, she distracted him to the point that he went brain dead when with her, he couldn't keep her safe if he didn't keep his wits about him.

Yashin and Vlad entered the room, both paused, eyes shifting to each other with knowing looks when they saw Naithon and Kiri, and that the couple had obviously just been doing something together. Their hair was mussed, Kiri's face was pink and glowing, eyes dazed, Naithon's eyes were deeply hooded, but he looked satiated even though he clearly sported a hard-on. Streaks of red slashed his sharp cheekbones.

"Uh," Yash mumbled, tugging at the collar of his shirt. "We, uh, interrupting anything?" Vlad snickered next to him, Yash jabbed his elbow in his side. "Nait, we have a meeting, remember?"

Naithon forked fingers through his hair in irritation, he'd forgotten. What if he hadn't heard them or the rest of the team coming and they'd seen Kiri exposed in that compromising position? Everyone getting a good gander at her bountiful, beautiful tits, her legs spread with his hand between them finger fucking her. Fuck, he needed to be more careful, have more restraint. But he didn't regret for one second what they'd both just shared. It was hot as hell, and he could not wait for more.

Maz, Teo and Blok came into the room. Their glances around at everyone expressed that they also realized they had walked in on something.

"Ah, *ja*, of course I remember." His voice husky, Naithon panted slightly. Turning to Kiri, her face was now beet red, she stared at the floor in mortification, he said, "Just, ah, give me a minute to walk Kiri upstairs."

As expected, all his friends broke out in grins.

He set his hand on Kiri's lower back to usher her out of the room, then threw his men the finger behind his back, rowdy laughter burst out after them.

Chapter Twenty-Six

The next day, Naithon went into Chaleur to do business in his office there. He was gone most of the day. Kiri worked in her studio, her project was coming to fulfillment. She stood back and took preliminary photos of her work, just a rough framework so far. She walked around the project, studying it from all angles, her finger tipped under chin.

There was a soft rap on the doorframe and Maz entered with his customary friendly grin and twinkling blue eyes. The door had stayed open while Kiri worked, she felt stifled always being behind closed doors. Even though she seemed to be staying with Naithon willingly now, he still insisted she remain under guard either in their suite or her studio.

Blok had been sitting outside her door all day, typing away at the notebook on his lap. Naithon owned a lot of businesses so his capos always had plenty of work to do on their computers when not in the field. Maz had taken her down for breakfast and lunch.

"Hey, how's it goin' little chickadee?" he asked, striding in carrying Kako and coming to examine her work. "Wow, that is cool. The food looks real, good enough to eat, but more than that, it's…like living, breathing art. It looks like the flowers the plates are sitting on are colorfully prismatic, like you're standing right in a mystical garden, weird but totally eye-catching. Girl, you are good."

She blushed at the praise. "Thanks. I think when someone really enjoys what they're doing it can't help but turn out lovely."

"Hmm, I suppose." He scratched Kako behind his tiny ear and removed the leash from his collar. Dropping the leash on a chair, he set the puppy on the floor. The tiny husky immediately rushed over to Kiri yipping his delight at seeing her. Yash had brought him down to Maz, and Maz had taken him for a walk.

It still chafed Kiri that Naithon refused to allow her outside the front door, but in light of all the dire circumstances that were occurring, she didn't argue with him about his over-protectiveness.

"You ready for dinner?" Maz asked, laughing at the puppy running in excited circles around the room with little yips and yaps.

"Sure, let me just close up the wet stuff." Kiri set the camera down and put lids on materials that could dry out.

After putting Kako in his cage, they joined Vlad and Yash at dinner. Blok and Teo were out with Naithon. It had been a week since Silver's death and the other occupants stared and glared less at Kiri, they went on with their lives and their own dramas. Dinner tonight was a delicious pot roast with mashed potatoes, corn, and thick bread to sop up the juices. Almost everyone had seconds.

When they were done eating, Maz said, "I'll take you back upstairs, Kiri." He smiled at her sad frown. "Sorry honey, the boss' orders."

"I know," she grumbled.

A soldier came up to them. "A package has arrived from Steinman Lab for the miss," he said.

"Oh, it must be the crystals for the filaments of the stamens for my flower display I ordered." She turned a hopeful smile to Maz. "Can I go get them? Please?"

It was hard for any male to say no to her. Maz sighed, his lip tugged in the corner, he ignored the smirk the soldier sent his way. "I suppose. Let's go get it." He was rewarded with a brilliant smile. Sighing in resignation, he felt for Naithon, no wonder the guy's boxers were always in a bunch with this gorgeous, sweet girl.

They travelled to the grand room then on to the foyer. The box was inside the door on a table. A soldier held a wide gun like thing over it.

"What are you doing?" Kiri asked. She tried to approach him but Maz caught her arm, holding her back.

The man explained, "It's a bomb detector, somewhat like what we use on the vehicles." They waited while he opened the box. After examining the contents, he nodded to Mazonn.

"Okay, chickadee, it's all yours. I'll carry it for you." Maz went and picked the box up, and they started back towards the grand room. As they passed through, they heard voices.

A woman said, "Naithon Adranokov, sweetheart, you are one hunky male, let me see if you are big all over."

Kiri stopped dead. They heard Naithon's deep rumble. Her face washed white, she turned towards the stairs in a panic to get away from there. She felt a dagger stab her heart, everything he said was a lie, he was sleeping with the women in the mansion.

She got two feet away and Maz grabbed her arm halting her. He shook his head, mouthed, "*Wait.*" She struggled to get loose but his grip was as iron clamping as Naithon's.

The woman's voice grew louder, strident. Naithon sounded pissed. Then they heard him snap, "I told you girls to fuck off. I want nothing to do with you whores. You all know the only bitch I want in my bed is Miss Delducci. What the hell is the matter with you? Get your fucking hands off me and don't ever fucking come near me again or you're out of here and the club. Spread the goddamned word."

In a half a second a woman came storming from a hallway. Seeing Kiri and Maz standing there, she glowered a killing look at Kiri, then turned and rushed out of the room. Behind her, a furious scowl on his face, Naithon stopped abruptly when he saw them. His gaze flit from Kiri to Maz. Maz looked amused, as usual. Kiri's expression was unreadable, but her face was pale.

Fearful that she might think he was screwing around with that woman, Naithon strode quickly over to Kiri. Stopping in front of her, brows inverted, sounding unsure, he said, "Uh, baby, I didn't know you were down here. I just got home." In fact he still wore his trench coat and carried a briefcase.

Her lips pressed, Kiri said nothing. Maz grinned like a fool. Frowning at him, Naithon turned a conciliatory weak smile to Kiri. "Baby, uh, you…you know there was nothing going on with that bitch and me, right?" He growled at Mazonn's snicker.

Naithon snapped at his friend, "Don't you have somewhere to be?" Mazonn's grin only broadened. "Asshole," Naithon grunted under his breath. He held a hand out to Kiri. "You, ah, okay, baby? You ready to go upstairs?"

"Have you had dinner?" she asked him coolly.

Scowling at Maz for getting him into this position, his job was to take her directly upstairs after they ate, not loiter around the front door. "I had something brought in at the office. Let's go upstairs," he caught her hand, wrapping his fingers around it when she would have pulled it away.

Maz smiled a tease. "I'll put this in your studio, chickadee." Naithon's frown deepened at the pet name. Maz snorted, "Get off it, bro. When we heard you and Carianne in there," he nodded to the hall, "I knew you would shut her down, but Kiri didn't. So I kept her here. Now she knows. You're welcome," he grinned and took off for the stairs.

Then, he turned back, "Just a head's up, I'm thinking your girl's not liking it so much being called a bitch."

"Kiri, ah," Naithon's voice still held uncertainty. He owned strip clubs, saloons, there were women all over the mansion tossing around easy sex, it had to be untenable for Kiri. She would be in her rights to doubt him.

"It's okay, Naithon," she said softly, her smile shy. "I trust you. Mostly. Let's go." She turned to the staircase. Holding her hand, he was tugged along with her. Treading up the cream colored stairs, he asked, "Mostly?"

After dropping his coat and briefcase off in their suite, they went to her studio. Naithon did business on his laptop while Kiri worked on her project. Kako traipsed back and forth between them until he tired then went and laid down on his doggy bed. When

Naithon saw Kiri yawn, he shut down his computer. "Okay, lamb, time for bed."

"Just a few more minutes," she said absently, shaping a piece of clay into a pear.

Naithon got up and went over, plucked the piece from her hands and set it in a plastic box and closed the lid. "Come on, you can hardly keep your eyes open."

Kiri blinked bleary eyes at him, he was right.

Naithon walked her to their suite, closing and locking the door after they moved inside. He followed her to the bedroom.

Inside, he pulled down one side of the sheet and blanket. "Take your shower, sweet, then hop in. Your shirt's right there," he pointed to one of his white button-downs on a hanger, hanging on a doorknob.

Her brows pulled together. "Naithon, you bought me pajamas and nightgowns yet you insist I wear your shirts to bed. Why?"

His gaze went from her cherry brown hair down to her little ankle boots. A slow smile curved one side of his face. "I like you in my shirt. It's sexy, and I feel like I'm always wrapped around you. Now," he made a shooing motion at her, "go on. I have to go back downstairs and finish up a few conference calls with Maz, and some other things."

That tugged the reddish brows down. She questioned, "Why am I going to bed and you are staying up working?"

Clasping his hands behind his back, otherwise he would grab at her, then he wouldn't leave, he said, "Because you are sleepy, and require more sleep than I do. I have business I've put aside that I need to complete."

She frowned ruefully. "My fault. You've spent your time chasing after me and seeing that I am safe when you should be doing your work."

Naithon had to grip his hands, he direly wanted to touch her, longed to kiss her. Take her completely. Soon. "Baby, my work means nothing to me if I don't have you. My work has always been my life, all I cared about except for my friends. Now, you are my life. Some day you will understand that, and I hope," his mouth curved at one end in a crooked smile, "that you will feel the same way about me. Now, get that pretty little ass cleaned up and in bed before I remember the punishments I owe you and find another use for my belt."

He pretended to make a grab for her, Kiri squealed and ran for the bathroom. Naithon's chuckles warmed his heart, she was so good for him. He hurried out of the suite, the sooner he got his work done, the sooner he could come back to her.

Kiri heard a noise, it woke her, she blinked drowsily. She looked over, Naithon had only come to bed a short time ago, his light snore woke her. Glancing at the clock on his side of the bed, it was close to dawn. Except for his bare feet, he was still dressed, lying on top of the blanket.

He must have just crashed, fell asleep before he hit the mattress. The hair at his temples was still damp. He must have washed his face before plopping down. He lay on his side facing away from her. One of his arms stretched out behind him, his hand clasped her thigh. Even in his sleep he had to be touching her.

Wanting a glass of water, Kiri climbed out of bed, careful to not wake him. Yawning, she traipsed into the bathroom. There was the glass she'd left in there earlier, she filled it, drank some, set it down. Couldn't remember if she'd brushed her teeth. She felt her toothbrush, then Naithon's. His was wet, she couldn't tell with hers, so she brushed to be sure. Plodding back to the bedroom she climbed back in bed and snuggled up to Naithon's big, warm body.

She wasn't long in a deep sleep when she felt a cool breeze on her legs. The lower part of her body felt…strange, good, tingles prickled in her breasts. Kiri was dreaming, she felt hands on her thighs, pulling them apart, wider, something soft-rough rubbed the inside of her thigh. Hard fingers dug into her thighs, holding them apart, then she felt a hint of warm air, below, between her legs, on her sex.

Something firm, wet, stroked her sex, ran up her slit, bit her clitoris, her eyes popped open. She went to sit up, but a strong hand

241

pushed her back down. "Don't move, pigeon," Naithon's deep baritone rumbled against her sex. It tickled, and titillated, making her legs automatically draw together. He gripped her thighs, holding them apart.

"No, wait, what are you doing? Naithon, stop, I don't think you're supposed to-"

He laughed against her skin, and that tickled and titillated too. "Not supposed to lick your lady lips, suck your pussy, bite your clit?" His laugh deepened as her face reddened from his language. "Baby, I've been dying to taste you for so damned long," he stroked his tongue up her slit and smiled at the quiver that surged through her body. Her hips twitched.

Kiri lay on her back, her hands up by her head on the bed, palms up. Her shirt was pushed up past her breasts, under her chin, except for her arms, her entire body was nude, spread wide open to him.

She realized that her body was down the end of the bed. Apparently Naithon had arranged her to his liking while she slept. He was kneeling on the floor with his torso between her legs, his mouth on her core, his tongue dancing over, licking her lady parts. He kept one hand gripping a thigh to hold her still.

"Naithon, I'm not sure..." Her childhood spent running from Duce and his threats of assault had inured her to ever thinking about or desiring sex. She couldn't understand why other girls at her school had been so absorbed with it. For her it elicited only fear and dread. If it wasn't for her father's desire to marry her off to Rueford she would have assumed she'd die a spinster, a virgin. And she was quite content with that idea. But now...

He raised his head to smile at her, reached up and palmed a breast. It swelled and pulsed in his hand, just like his throbbing dick. "It is a natural act between a man and a woman, Kiri. Lie there and let me make love to your body, to you. It's time to trust me, to give me, you. You're ready." His thumb pushed on her clit, then rubbed it in circles, then he pressed, then more circles. Kiri's hips rolled, responding to his ministrations.

Obviously turned on, her silk poured into Naithon's hand, but Kiri was scared, he could feel the tremble in her legs, her belly. She didn't move, her legs were stiff. Naithon fondled her tit, massaged, kneaded it, then lowered his mouth back on her pussy. He opened his mouth wide and chomped her entire mound, she yelped, goose bumps sprung on her arms, she groaned out loud.

"Tell me if I hurt you, baby, I have to prepare you to take me."

Her voice trembled, "Prepare me? Aren't you going to just...shove it...in?"

He shook his head, his scruff rasping her tender thighs, he rubbed his stubbly chin on her mound, she shivered again. Nipping her clit, he stroked his finger up and down her slit, squeezing her folds together. "You're a virgin, baby, my dick is pretty big, and you are tiny, I need to get you ready, so it doesn't hurt. Besides," he bit her bud and she yelped, hips bucking up. "This is called foreplay, it gets us both hot and ready."

A ladylike snort. "You are always hot and ready."

His lips grinned on her tender flesh, and he carefully inserted his finger into her wet sheath. Her legs stiffened again, she tried to close them. "No, Kiri, keep your body relaxed, accept me inside you."

She was so sweet, his little pigeon. Naithon couldn't believe he'd had her for months in his bed, mostly naked, his hands all over her, and he hadn't fucked her yet. Any other bitch and it would been fuck and go, half the time he didn't know their names, or care. He was thrilled he was the one to teach Kiri, the only man to ever touch her beautiful tits, have his fingers inside her, his dick inside her.

Removing his finger, he sucked the inside of her thigh, sifted his palms up and down the soft skin of her thighs and belly but without touching her sex. Licking the slender flesh of her thighs, he sucked harder, here, there, stroked his fingertips everywhere but on her pussy. It wasn't long until Kiri was whimpering, her hips shifting, wanting, seeking more. He looked up and saw her breasts wobbling as her breaths sped up, she clutched the sheet under her with both hands.

"Ask me, baby," he murmured, moving both hands up her thighs, his thumbs dragging the insides, barely brushing the creases of her folds, but he didn't touch her sexually.

Her swallow loud, Kiri groaned, trying to move her hips so he would touch her where she now desperately wanted him to. "W-what, Naithon? Ask you what?" she cried with a breathy wail.

"Ask me to touch you, with my hands, my mouth, make you come. Ask me or I'll stop." He continued stroking, circling, squeezing, but nothing sexual. If she could see how intensely he was staring at her pussy she'd cringe with mortification. "So pretty," he murmured, drawing the pad of his fingertip across her lower body, chuckling when her skin quivered.

"P- pretty?"

"Ask me, sweet, say the words." He petted and stroked until her body writhed all over the bed trying to get his hands on the right places, and he had to hold her tightly to keep her still. He wanted her to state out loud that she wanted him. They were in this together, no going back afterwards and saying he forced her. Seduced her yes, but not forced.

"Naithon, *uhh*," the groan ripped from her throat, "please…"

"Please what, lamb?" His chuckle pressed against her thigh made her leg jerk. "I'm gonna stop, baby. Ask me."

She had to feel him touch her. "Naithon, please, ah," she moaned as he pressed his thumbs into the fleshy part of her thighs, in the crease where they attached to her body.

"Say it," he ordered, his lips sucking her belly.

With a rasping cry, she yielded, "Touch me, Naithon, with- with your hands, your…uh, mouth, touch- *oh!*" He gripped both thighs hard, holding them apart, and attacked her sex.

Biting her clit on the precipitous edge of painful, he plunged a wide finger inside her, and a gasping scream scraped from her chest catching in her throat.

"That what you want, baby? Is it?" He growled against her flesh, licked her slit and carefully pushed in a second finger. Her hips thrashed against the bed, his mouth, to him, away from him. He worked his fingers fast, hard, plunging them deeper, curling them inside searching for her woman's apex of fire. Her sharp gasp and jolting hips told him he found it. Stroking his fingers over it again and again, he growled, "Is it? Kiri, is this what you want?"

"Yes!" she screamed. "Yes, Naithon, yes!" her cries gushed in ecstasy.

He reached up to squeeze a breast, tweak a nipple, and when he shoved his fingers in and viciously ate at her female nub, Kiri's shrieks etched ringing grooves in the room. Her flat stomach sucked in, spine arched, body shuddered and bucked against him, and she cried his name again and again as she shattered. Music to his ears.

Naithon licked and petted her until her body stopped its violent spasms, breaths gasped and gushed and panted, her bosom rising and falling sharply, belly quivering in and out. And he watched and loved every bit, inch, every second of it. 'Oh *ja*,' he thought joyously, 'that's what I want to see for the rest of my life, my little lamb climaxing.'

When she settled, her breathing less rapid, Naithon climbed onto the bed and between her legs on his knees, set his palms beside her shoulders, and smiled down at her. Her eyes twitched and fluttered, lashes flapping on apple red cheeks. He felt his heart being sucked right out of his ribs.

Kiri slowly opened her eyes and saw him watching her, she felt too good to be embarrassed that she lay beneath him, naked, legs spread and loose as spaghetti, and he had had his mouth on her most private of parts, and she had *loved* it. "*Naithon*," it was a husky whisper.

"Hey, you okay?" His smile teasing. This was what Maz had described. Her lying nude on his bed, relaxed, sexy eyes raised up to him, smiling, and her arms reaching for him in welcome. He would give his fortune to have this sight for life.

"Uh huh," Kiri whispered, she tugged at the top button of his shirt until it opened. Then she opened the next one, the next. "You are still dressed, Naithon, it makes me feel, uncomfortable that I am naked, and you are dressed."

"You aren't completely naked, lamb," he gripped the shirt she still wore and tugged it off her. "Now you are."

"Your turn," she insisted, her smile shy, soft green eyes beguiling.

Chapter Twenty-Seven

Grinning, intensely happy, Naithon sat back on his heels, reached behind his back, grasped his shirt, yanked it over his head and tossed it to the floor. "Better?"

Kiri nodded, her gaze drinking in his physique. "You have a lot of muscles, Naithon." She studied them with earnest interest.

He leaned over her, she put her hands on his chest, slid her fingers into the dark hair that matted it. His bulging biceps drew her attention, she tried to squeeze them and giggled when she couldn't.

"Too strong, Naithon," she admired, her fingers couldn't even halfway encircle the huge arms.

Kiri touched a tattoo that scribbled across a collarbone, and felt the hard muscles of his pecs. She pushed up on her elbows and licked then bit one of his flat nipples.

"Hey!" he squawked sitting back with a shiver, his hand over his nipple. She laughed at him, he grinned. "You little minx, now, it's time." He sat back on his heels again and tugged at his belt, his expression turned serious. "Okay?"

"I, uh, yes," she said softly. The daze left her green eyes as they widened in fear even as her skin flushed in desire. "I'm...ready, Naithon."

His held breath blew out, and he grinned broadly. Unbuttoning, unzipping his pants, he shifted off the bed, stood up, and shoved his trousers down, kicked them off. His feet were bare, he wore only his briefs, then they were gone. His erection was thick and heavy, he wrapped a fist around it, pumped once. Kiri's smile fell.

Climbing back on the bed between her legs, he pushed her slender thighs wider as he moved closer to her. "I'm not going to hurt you, well, maybe a little, but it'll get better, I promise. Don't be afraid of me, Kiri, I can't stand it."

Lying on her back looking up at him, she blinked wordlessly, worried her lower lip with her teeth.

Naithon lowered to her, his hand holding his dick near her opening, he said quietly, "You want me to stop, you tell me, I will." He braced on one palm and touched his penis to her opening, and she said, "Stop."

"Stop?" he froze, disappointment curled up his chest.

"Condom."

"Condom?" he repeated, confused. "I haven't been with a woman the second I planned to take you, baby, that's been a long while and I always wore latex. I've recently seen Doc Maankov for insurance purposes, I have no diseases." He hadn't told her he'd opened a huge insurance policy making her his beneficiary.

"I could get pregnant."

That brought a big grin. "*Ja*, you could." He nudged at her opening, she pushed at his chest.

"No. I can't get pregnant."

"Yes, you can. I can't wait to fill your belly with my babes. I've wanted that since I first saw you. I mean, not when you were little, but every time I saw you later over the years. I told you, I want a family with you. I want miniature Kiris dashing all around the house."

"But you don't care what I want. You never did." Her frown said she was back to believing he would use her and toss her aside. He was like that gorilla ready to escape his cage, looming in front of her, waiting to pounce. The big, brawny, huge chest matted with dark hair over slabs of muscle hovered over her. His virile heat pushing around her, his masculine scent sifting inside her nostrils.

Shifting to kneel, he sat back on his heels. He pronged thick fingers through his wavy blond hair then set his tough hands on his muscular thighs. "That was true, in the beginning. I never lied about who I am, what I am. *Ja,* I took you for me, didn't care about your fears, concerns, desires. I just had a…burning hunger for you that I knew deep down inside was permanent. But, baby, I'm a gangster; we don't give a shit about anyone or anything else except our own goals. We're bred to be self-centered sociopaths."

"Yes, you see-"

He kept talking, "I knew if I took you it would be forever, whether you wanted it or not. In our mobster world we can do that. Take and keep women, willing or not. Just like your da selling you to Rueford against your will. But, Kiri, I didn't know you then. Now I do. Slowly, surely, gently, you are changing me."

"You don't care about my happiness." Her lips pouted in a sad purse.

He shook his head, palmed thick hair out of his eyes. "I do want you to be happy. That's why I gave you that studio, letting you do work, design the tasting room, got you Kako. Everything I can think of that you could want that would make you happy, content.

"Even took you to see your da in the hospital when every atom in my body screamed to keep you safe behind my locked doors. But I did take you to the hospital and Piero's funeral, to make you happy." *And because you threatened to withhold yourself from me.*

"Make your prisoner content so she won't try to run away from you."

A slice of guilt flicked in his eyes, he shrugged. "That was part of it in the beginning. But, Kiri, I swear to you, I really want you to be happy, to stay with me because you want to. Baby," his shoulders tensed, "those two times when I thought you had been taken, I was mindless with terror. Sure, because I didn't want you to leave me, but, the idea that you were being hurt, or worse," a shiver slid up his spine at the memory of seeing that man shoving her in that van.

"I…I think I wouldn't survive it if you were ever…badly hurt." He couldn't push the word *killed* past his lips.

For once in his life, Naithon Adranokov felt joy waking up in the morning, because his day would begin with Kiri, continue with her in his mind knowing she was in his house even if he wasn't home, and end in bed at night with her. She brought lightness, and light, soft music and color to his world. He would wither like a flower without sunlight and die if she disappeared from his life. He had become more now, almost human, he'd said it before, she was saving him.

"Kiri, I'm a selfish bastard, I want it all. I want you, you are the very air I need to breathe to live, and I want you to be happy, to want to stay with me, build a family with me."

"But, tell me, Naithon, if I didn't want to stay, would you let me leave?"

Lines around his eyes constricted, his mouth tightened, their eyes were connected, hers wide and pure, he lowered his without answering her.

"That's what I thought. The mobster mentality."

Naithon looked off to the side, he moved to leave the bed.

Her voice soft, she asked quietly, "Where are you going?"

He glanced back at her, tried to hide his disappointment, and guilt. "Gonna put my clothes on."

"Why?"

"I, uh, have work to do."

"Naithon," she said gently.

He didn't look at her, said gruffly, "*Ja?*"

"I want to stay, for now anyway. And," she sat up a little, drew her fingers down his arm, tracing a tattoo, said softly, "I want to make love with you."

Naithon blinked, his shoulders contracted, he looked over his shoulder at her. A tress of mahogany hair sexily covered one eye, more waved over her bare shoulder, one lock curled around her breast. "You do? You want to stay with me?" He experienced the sultriest look he'd ever seen on a female, it zipped down and ignited his dick. Sumptuous lips smiled at him, her eyes inviting him to be with her.

A small laugh trickled from her gorgeous lips. "Yes, for now. We need to see how we work out."

"Oh." He turned fully around, his gaze hot and hungry ran over her naked body. He watched her fingers trail down his arm. One brow arched and wriggled, he asked, "You really still want to fu- uh, make love with me?"

Her head bowed, she peered up at him shyly though her long lashes. "Yeah."

His voice thick, he whispered, "Lamb," and moved to face her, to crawl back between her legs.

She held a hand up. "Wait."

He halted, but his heated eyes never stopped moving over her body. "What?" The erection that had ignited hung like a wooden bat between his legs.

"Condom."

"*Ja*," he sighed. Stretching, he reached to the end table, opened the drawer, took out a condom.

"You said you never have brought a woman in here before, yet you have condoms right by the bed?"

His grin unabashed, he admitted, "Bought them the day I decided to take you. I knew we would be banging eventually, I was prepared." Moving back to her, he smiled as she lay back down. "Baby?" he said in question, a hand coiling over her breast.

"Yes?" Her arms raised to receive him.

"Do you want children?"

"Someday. Not today. I'm too young, I want a career, and I want to know that the man *I chose* to have them with, is the right one."

He paused. "What does that mean? Are you saying you can't want me, because I'm a hoodlum and I abducted you and am holding you against your will?"

"I shouldn't want you because you took me yeah, but," her smile lifted, she stroked her palm over his forearm, she said, "you are growing on me. Go figure, last thing I would want would be to fall for a mobster, like my family."

Naithon's jaw worked. "I know. You are way too good for me. I am corrupt and my hands are dirty and filled with blood. It's well known I'm a bad man. You are way too sweet, and pure, kind and brave, so gorgeous you could have any man you wanted. I knew you would never have given an outlaw, a crude thug like me a shot. That's why I just took you."

"Well, let's see how things go, okay? For now."

He shifted down and spread his body over hers. His brow down low, he said with displeasure, "I don't like that you keep saying, 'for now.' I want forever. I want to know you're mine, that you will never leave me." A shoulder bumped. "I guess I'll have to work really hard to make that *for now* of yours, turn into forever. *Ja*?"

"Yeah," she agreed with a grin. Stroking her hands up his chest then around his neck she pulled his head down.

Naithon suckled her lips then her breasts, he moved to the side of her and stroked her feminine parts until her hips squirmed against his hand and she moaned his name. He pushed two fingers inside her and caressed her hot spot and she started begging.

"Naithon, Naithon, please, it's too- too-" her head rocked back and forth.

Staring at her lovely face, Naithon watched her eyes rolling back, her chest billowing, and he removed his hand from her body smiling at her groan.

"Naithon, please…"

"Patience, lamb, I'm doing what you asked." He tore the package open and slid the condom down his length, then moved to his knees and stroked his shaft up and down her wet folds until she was crying nonsensical words.

Pushing her legs wide, he nestled his hips between them and prodded at her opening. "Okay my beautiful baby, I'll try not to hurt you," the strain of holding himself back wracked roughly in his throat. He pushed a bit hard to get the head of his manhood inside her, and she gasped, he felt her tighten around him.

"All right, baby, just relax, like when my mouth is on you, my fingers inside, let me in."

With short shallow breaths, Kiri strove to relax her legs, ease the tightness in her sheath to allow him to press further inside. Naithon pushed a little, then paused for her to adapt to him, then he pushed slowly, carefully. Her body opened to his heavy length inch by inch, him grunting, her gasping through the slight pain of his filling her, stretching her. He had gotten her so wet it made his shaft slide in easier.

When she accepted every inch of his aching erection, their bodies knit together like lovers of the millennia have done since the dawn of time, and they sighed in blessed joy. Naithon let out his held breath, he had feared this day, this moment would never come. Finally, she was his.

Reaching the end of her, Naithon stopped, let her adjust. He smiled as she squirmed a little to get more comfortable, wedging him in more deeply, he asked, "You okay, lamb?"

A short huff, her vagina clamped on him and he croaked, and she laughed. A purr ruffled out, she murmured, "I'm good, Naithon, real good." Her small fingers curled over his shoulders.

"*Ja?*" He braced on his elbows, and grinned. "Finally, right where I've always wanted you. Pinned beneath me naked, staked on my dick."

He sobered, said quietly, "I love you, Kiri Rose," and he bent and kissed her. He sucked her lips then drew his head back and said, "Okay, lamb, hold on tight, we're goin' for a wild ride," and he pulled back slowly then thrust in, did it again, and thrust harder.

Naithon was fairly gentle at first, as he studied her, judging how she was taking him. Her breasts bobbled, he bent and nipped at one and smiled at the smile that relieved the tension from her face. Seeing that he wasn't hurting her, he went to town. Reaching under her, he gripped her bottom, squeezed, and lifted her off the bed so he could drive deeper into her soft body.

Kiri squealed, and he laughed, and drove deeper, hastening his rhythm, until neither was smiling. Soaring in their own orbit, they were carried away together, blasting off in a spiraling wildfire of sensation.

Kiri dug her nails into his shoulders, and did the only thing she could do, hold on. Naithon thrust in her so hard, so fast, he shoved her deep into the mattress. He lifted one of her knees, wrapped her leg around his hips, she did the same with her other leg, and he pummeled faster until both were unraveling in rapture, gasping and grunting. He reached between them and roughly thumbed her clit.

"Ready, baby?" he grunted. He wanted this to last, stay as they were right now forever, but the strain of holding back was killing him. Brain hurtling toward absolute inebriation, tweaking her clit hard, he urged, "Now, Kiri, let go now," and he pounded her over the mountain.

Kiri went flying ablaze with color, the blood rushed in her head deafening her, yet she could feel vibrations of Naithon's grunting rumbles as he thrust her off the cliff. She shrieked, flying through the air and then cried his name tumbling all the way down.

Feeling her channel wringing his dick, her body convulsing around him, his balls pulled in tight as a fist, Naithon released his control, and he followed her over the moon.

White heat sizzled through his brain, he'd never felt so high, his balls clamped and then let loose. He gave one enormous push then held taut, his seeds burst from his shaft. As it pulsed he thrust in hard jerks again and again, roaring Kiri's name, his seeds undulating out of his body, jerking him spastically as they expelled.

Spasms rippling through him, Naithon thought he was going to black out, never before had he felt this extraordinary sensation, exquisite pain and ecstasy so entwined he couldn't tell one from the other. He held his shuddering body over Kiri, until he was spent, and he flopped down beside her, gasping into her neck, with only part of his body covering hers.

All they could manage was to lie there, their breathing loud and heavy, rapid, pleasantly dizzy and dazed, as their pulses slowed.

After a few minutes of blissful afterglow, Naithon stirred. Grumbling, he rolled off the bed, stumbled into the bathroom to dispose of the condom.

He cleaned up then brought a warm damp cloth to take care of Kiri. Little pleased mews purred from her as he cleaned her. Dropping the cloth on the floor, he crawled back on the bed and pulled her into his arms.

She snuggled, smiling in weary contented happiness, humming her joy as her lids fell over drowsy eyes.

"Baby?" Naithon murmured in her ear.

"Yeah?" she sighed already half asleep.

"Let me know when you're ready to go again."
She giggled against his chest, yawned a dreamy, "Okay."

Chapter Twenty-Eight

After breakfast the next day, Kiri working in her studio, looked up to Naithon standing in the open doorway.

The man had a completely inscrutable expression, a perfect poker face. To most people he was blankly unreadable, nothing but cold eyes and hard features, it was like something nonhuman resided in his body. It made him bone- chilling when he set his sights on a person.

His friends could read him, and Kiri was beginning to, and when she saw his expression, her stomach sunk like a ship. Something was wrong. She set down the piece she was working on and stood up. Wiping her hands on a towel, with a small catch in her voice, she said warily, "What is it, Naithon?"

He took a step inside, and she saw whatever it was flicker across his face and it was gone. "Naithon?" Clearly, whatever it was he didn't want to tell her. Her hand at her throat, she asked, "Who?"

Three long strides and he was to her. He grasped her arms to steady her, said brusquely, "It's Janero."

Her breath sucked in sharp with her desperate cry, "No, oh no, God, no, please," she fell against him.

Naithon rolled his arms around her, supporting her as her legs suddenly had no strength. He said quickly, "He's not dead, Kiri, he's…in bad shape, but he's still alive."

She jerked back from him but he held her. "I have to-"

"I know. I will take you to him. He's not in the hospital, he is at an Urgent Care that we...control. Get your jacket, the car is already out front."

They took the elevator as her wooden legs refused to carry her. Naithon held her up with his arm around her. All the way to the Urgent Care, they held hands.

In the car, her palm pressed against her heart, she asked, "How...what happened, Naithon?" It took everything she had to keep the tremor out of her devastated voice.

He squeezed her hand and told her, "A bomb. Same kind that was used on my brother."

She shifted from staring out the side window to him, the line between her brows showing her consternation. "But, if your brother, and my brother were attacked by the same...are you sure that different people didn't make the bombs?"

Shaking his head, he turned to look down at her. "Same everything down to the way the pieces were put together. *Ja*," he absently squeezed her hand again. "We can't figure it out. It just makes it seem even clearer that it isn't the Delduccis hitting the Adranokovs, and the Adranokovs aren't hitting the Delduccis. Appears to be a third party trying to instigate war between us. But then," he sighed.

"But then," she filled in, "that could be the devious person's plan so they aren't perceived."

"Devious like Zhilov, my da."

"Do you think it's him?"

He considered the question. "It could be. Maybe he fled to make us think he was scared, so he could stay on the sidelines and pull the strings."

"For what conceivable reason? He almost killed two of your brothers, is he that cold-blooded?"

Naithon grunted a sarcastic laugh. "*Ja*. He'd take out anyone even his own mother to get all the power in the world."

The car parked in the back to attract as little attention as possible. Naithon suited Kiri up in the vest and hat again. He tapped the bill of the helmet and ordered, "This stays on this time. The entire time we are here. This time you do not leave my side, my sight. You do not want to anger me, lamb. I am already tense as shit just bringing you out of the house."

He had his own vest on under his black leather jacket. Dressed in black; jacket, jeans and heavy boots, the helmet made him look like he belonged on a Harley with his wallet chained to his back pocket.

Aware Naithon's men were in just as much danger, he had snipers scattered around the area protecting everyone present. Before the driver opened the door for them to exit the limo, the vehicle was swarmed by Naithon's men. They cocooned the pair until they were safely inside.

As they moved into the one-story sprawling establishment, more of Naithon's soldiers surrounded them. Others were tasked to patrol the perimeter and all roads leading into the property.

Like a hospital, it had a waiting area and an emergency entrance. They passed the lobby, the reception desk was empty. Naithon's crew stood at attention around the room. As they walked down the tiled corridor, Kiri felt like she had a dozen shadows keeping in step with her.

Naithon held her hand, no one said a word. It was then she noticed they didn't pass another person except for Naithon's men. No doctors, nurses, no patients, no anxious families waiting.

"Naithon?" She tipped her head up.

They kept moving, Naithon didn't look at her, he relentlessly scanned the hallways and doorways just like his soldiers did. He bowed his head to her. "What, baby?"

"There aren't any people...I mean like civilians here. Are there any patients?"

Giving her hand a little squeeze, keeping his head forward, he smiled. "You are my observant little lamb aren't you? *Ja*, you are correct. Before we brought Janero in we cleared everyone out except for staff we vetted. Ignacio is here as well."

Her head snapped to him. "My father is here? Is he worse?"

"I will explain everything when we get to Janero's room, no he is not worse. Also, so you don't worry, Ignacio had Melonie taken to a safe house."

They moved down a corridor that had doors every ten feet or so, the patients' rooms, Kiri supposed. Naithon's men stepped into one then waved Naithon in.

They spread out in the room. Blinds closed most of the light from the window, as well as the view of possible non-friendly snipers.

A few cupboards, small door in the back likely the restroom. There was only one occupied bed. As in a hospital, there were machines making quiet beeps and whirs. A figure lay on the bed. Her heart in her throat, Kiri tugged her hand from Naithon's and hurried over.

"Oh, my gosh," her anguished cry a choked whisper.

Janero was one big bandage. There wasn't a speck of skin not covered. Including his face. Tubes attached to his hand, more in his nose, and one in his mouth. Kiri could see angry, red blistered skin around the tubes.

She went to touch his arm but a man said, "Best not touch him, miss, it could harm him." She jerked her hand back. Looked at the man who appeared to be a doctor. Her head lowered to her brother, a tear splatted on his chest.

"Oh, Janero," her wail soft, filled with pain for her so seriously injured brother. Blinking back the tears, she said a prayer for him, then asked the doctor, "Is he going to…"

Above average height, the fortyish doctor fit in with Naithon's big men. Handsome with neat, wavy brown hair and blue eyes that smiled in warm sympathy at her. He filled out the white lab court with wide shoulders. He moved closer to Kiri, a wry smile tipped the side of his mouth up when Naithon moved between them.

He introduced himself, "I am Doctor Douglas Whitten." He had a sexy smile which he endowed on Kiri, he said, "Call me Doug," and reached to shake her hand. His brows lifted and a smirk tugged his mouth when Naithon blocked his arm.

"Ah," he murmured, glanced at Naithon then turned his attention back to Kiri. "I spoke with Mr. Adranokov earlier. Your brother is in critical condition. Parts of his body were burned. Right now he is in an induced coma so his body can heal itself without having to deal with the pain."

"But- but is he going to be all right?" Clutching her fingers together, Kiri held them up by her chest and took a step towards him, and felt Naithon's heavy hand come down on her shoulder holding her in place. He trusted no one, not even doctors. Especially handsome gregarious doctors.

Tucking his hands in his big lab pockets, the doctor had a charismatic smile that made most women swoon and he directed it straight at Kiri. Naithon's hand tightened on her shoulder.

Spreading his legs to plant his brown oxfords on the white tile, Whitten inclined his head to her. "He looks worse than he is. He was luckier than the others. Fortunately there were people nearby when the explosion happened and pushed him to the ground to put out the flames."

"Flames?" She gulped with a quiver of horror.

Naithon set his other hand on her shoulder to anchor her. He told her quietly, "Janero and some of his soldiers were going into a small tavern they frequent. When one of them opened the door, the bomb went off. The men in front of Janero, ah, didn't make it. Normally your brother is first in, this time he stopped to speak to a woman strolling down the street. Apparently she had a very short skirt and very enticing sashaying ass. That ass saved his life. If he hadn't been trying to hit on her he would..." he trailed off. Kiri was distraught enough.

"Okay, well," the doctor held his arms out directing them, he said, "you have been here long enough, none of you really should be in here at all. The man doesn't need your germs in his fragile condition. So, everyone, out."

The soldiers poured out to the hallway. Whitten shifted to stand at the foot of Janero's bed. A nurse they hadn't seen behind the crowd of men moved to the other side of the bed to adjust the drip thing. Kiri bent over her brother and gently smoothed the hair on his forehead. Naithon waited, letting her have her moment.

Wiping at the tears that were falling, sniffing, she snuffled out, "Thanks doctor, please keep in touch with me." She didn't see the doctor look over her head to exchange a glance with Naithon. He would be calling Naithon, and Naithon would pass on any messages.

"Okay, lamb, let's go, we have things to talk about. As soon as there's any changes the doc will call." Naithon put his hand on her lower back.

They reached the door and the nurse called out, "Oh, wait," she trod over to them and held out a plastic bag to Kiri. "We had to remove his jewelry."

Kiri looked at the clear bag and saw the thick gold chain Janero always wore, his Rolex, and his ring. The one that all the Delducci men wore and she felt a horrible pang in her chest recalling the ring was the only thing left of Duce. She clutched the bag to her chest with a nod of thanks, and Naithon ushered her out.

Kiri thought they were going to see her father next but Naithon led her into another room. A waiting room, some of his men stood, others were sitting. Naithon brought her to a chair and nudged her to sit.

Confused, she asked, "Naithon, what's going on? Aren't we going to see my dad?"

Maz, Vlad and Teo waited outside the room.

Naithon moved a chair to face her and sat down. "Not right now. Right now I want to tell you what we're going to do about them."

Holding the bag in her lap, Kiri took out the ring and fiddled with it. Her face lifted to his in question. "I don't understand."

"*Ja*, baby. What we want to do is let the report go out that both your da and Janero passed. Your da is better but we let it out that he's failing." He held a hand up at the startled gasp she made.

"Listen to me. If it is known they are still alive, the killer will come after them again and maybe succeed the next time. That's why we brought them here instead of the hospital where you were fucking ambushed." Enraged red flared up his face at the image of that bastard shoving her into the van.

Kiri set a hand on his thigh and said, "I'm okay, Naithon, please calm down." It stymied her that he was so obsessed with her. In the beginning she thought it was faked, that what he really wanted was to get at her father, humiliate him.

But in all this time Naithon had never shown anything but his unrelenting desire for her and he really did do everything in his power to try to make her happy. His despair whenever she was in danger certainly wasn't feigned.

Naithon sat back and raked his hand from the top of his head and down the back with frustration. His lungs expelled a torrent of exasperated air, he patted her hand. "*Ja*, sorry. The thing is, we need to convince the assassin that they are...dead. Then we need a strategy to flush this fucker out somehow-"

"Naithon," she cut him off, a strange look crossed her face. Naithon saw it.

"What is it, lamb?"

She was studying the ring, turning it this way and that, then, cocking her head to the side with a wrinkled brow, she said, "There is something...wrong, here."

He waited, she stared hard at the ring. Shaking her head, then, "I don't think that ring they found at the wood chipper is Duce's."

A confused beat passed before he said, "Huh? How can that be?"

Fingering the bag thoughtfully, she explained, "All of their rings had the family crest on top, but they also had their initials on the side. I saw photos of Duce's ring they found, there were no initials, it wasn't his ring. It was a Delducci ring, but it wasn't his."

"Who else has that kind of ring? Other male relatives?"

"No. Only my father and brothers."

Naithon stared at her as if she was being hopefully delusional. "Maybe you only saw the side of the ring that didn't have the initials."

"No, Naithon, there were several shots of it. I'm 1000% positive it wasn't Duce's ring."

They stared blankly at each other. Mazonn came up to them. "Nait, I don't think you guys should linger."

Naithon nodded, deep in thought. He said, "On the way home, we need to stop at the Delduccis' house and check something out."

Inside Ignacio's office they found where Ignacio had put Duce's ring when the CSI's were done with it. Kiri held it in the center of her palm, eyes crossed on it. "This is not his ring."

Maz pronounced with bewilderment, "How can it not be? What the hell does that mean?"

Eyes bedeviled with confusion as she studied the ring, Kiri replied, "I don't know, this was Duce's pride and joy. Dad gave them to the boys when they graduated high school. Duce never took it off, never. He got a kick out of getting in fights and joked how the crest left imprints on their faces."

Naithon blinked, rubbed the back of his neck. "*Ja*, the beating he gave me when I was a young teen, took a week for the fucking imprints to go away."

Mazonn commented as if thinking out loud, "If he would never take it off, why wasn't his ring found at the scene? Why the fake one?"

Naithon stood up. He paced several steps pondering his question. Then he stopped, his eyes narrowed in contemplation, he said, "There was a shitload of shredded clothes, chips of teeth and bone fragments that layered inches on the ground like sawdust from all the men killed there. Everything was saturated in blood." Everyone looked mildly nauseous as they pictured the grisly scene at the wood chipper.

"The forensics tested some of the dust for DNA and matched one other body but couldn't make a determination of any others, everything was too mixed together like soup. Once they concluded the blood smear was Duce's, as well as Ignacio identifying the ring, the authorities reported him as one of the deceased and the others as 'unknown'. They had to identify the other victims by the witness who claimed he saw them there when they had arrived." Naithon paused and his face grit as thoughts raced through his mind.

Then, he took a harsh breath, exhaled hard with his words, he announced his theory, "Your sonofabitch brother faked his own death."

The men frowned as they considered his words. Kiri's face scrunched trying to comprehend the truth of what he was implying. Her voice small and uncertain, she asked, "But, why? Why on earth would he make us believe he was dead? Why make a phony ring?"

Naithon believed Duce was fully capable of such a wretched plot, but Duce's bereaved sister would be harder to convince. He told her, "Because he needed to leave concrete evidence of his death. But, he couldn't bear to lose his ring, so he had one fabricated, and left a smear of blood as evidence that he died in that chipper. Apparently he was either not paying complete attention to the details, or the jeweler forgot to add the initials. As far as why he faked his death…"

His gaze connected with Kiri's stunned eyes. "Maz," he said, "go find the fucker that said he saw Duce being put into the chipper. I want him in the basement. Call me when you have him."

Kiri opened her mouth, but Naithon grasped her hand and pulled her to her feet. He ushered her quickly out of the building and to the waiting car.

Chapter Twenty-Nine

A day later, Naithon had to forcefully stuff Kiri in their suite and lock the door in her face. Maz had called to tell him they found the witness to the wood chipper murders and he was currently under suspension in the basement.

Unfortunately, Kiri overheard them talking, he thought she was still on the balcony finishing her coffee, but the little sneak snuck in and eavesdropped.

Being the stubborn young woman that she was, she insisted on going with him while he interrogated the man. Like he would ever let her observe the torture, and assured death of the guy. Especially at his hands. She would never let him touch her again if she saw how brutal and ruthless he really could be, he didn't need her to literally see the blood of the witness on his hands.

When Naithon hit the first floor, Maz came up beside him looking grim.

Naithon said, "Tell me what's happened so far. Who is the poor bastard?" They fell in step on the way to the cellar.

Maz told him, "His name is Patrick O'Malley, they call him Patty. He's a fucking uniform, Nait."

"The wit's a cop?" They reached the door to the basement. Two soldiers stood on either side of it, they both lifted their chins to him, "Boss." Naithon and Maz headed down the cement steps.

264

"*Ja*, that was unexpected. He's as dirty as a mud wrestler. Corrupt as hell, been stealing drugs from dealers he busts and resells the dope, he keeps the dough he takes off offenders he arrests, and he runs some girls," Maz made a face.

He went on speaking through twisted lips, "Real young ones, some not even into puberty yet. The word I got was, he snatches them from parents that are going for long prison terms and forces the children to work in a couple of seedy brothels. He posts videos of the children on the dark web porn sites, people view them for a fee. We were told the little girls are chained and needled with drugs to keep them...cooperative." His voice lowered, "Nait, find out where he stashes 'em, we need to get them out."

Already straining to control his rage at the man's involvement with Duce Delducci's duplicity, he had to be in on the fake murder, the info Maz was feeding him only tossed more deadly fuel on the fire. "What's his condition?"

Maz slipped him a side grin. "We tenderized him for you. Once we heard about the children, well," he shrugged, "it was tough holding some of the men back. I had to kick everyone out except Vlad, Yash and Teo or there wouldn't have been enough left of him for you to question." Shaking his head with a humorless grin, he said gravely, "We all wanted to shred the fucker into pieces tinier than his little victims' pinkies."

At the end of the stairs, the two friends paused at the bottom. The cellar was used for interrogations, and things along that line. A typical basement, it was dank and musty and cold, there were chains bolted to the concrete walls. A few small dusty windows let in only a blur of light, making the whole place appear macabre, like a torture chamber. Which it was.

A series of plain light bulbs laced the ceiling casting ugly shadows, adding to the frightening creepiness, along with the dried blood on the old, more grey than white walls and floor.

A wooden table held a variety of cutting tools: knives, scalpels, an ax. Also, electrodes and Tasers, whips, pliers for pulling teeth, vice grips, burning implements, and more. The floor slanted slightly to a drain so the place could be hosed down.

There was a steel gurney and several chairs bolted to the floor. In one of them in the center of the room sat a bloody mess of a male.

Wearing only a pair of blue plaid boxers, a black hood covered his head, his arms were strapped down, his forearms tied immovable on the chair arms. A strap crossed his ribs, his ankles were bound to the chair legs.

Naithon's boots tromped across the gritty cement. He halted a few feet in front of the man.

Next to him, Maz said with pretend rebuke, "You wore white, Nait? You'll never get his blood and brain matter out of it, even with bleach." Patty O'Malley's body revved up into high shaking gear at his words.

Naithon cocked his head with reproach at his friend's humor. He jutted his jaw at Vlad who was standing on one side of the chair, Teo the other. Yash stood behind the prisoner. The man couldn't see them, but their movements and terse comments apprised him of their continued presence, and threat.

Vlad grasped an end of the hood and whipped it off O'Malley's head. Sandy hair tufted up and stayed wisped from the static of the hood. Tears ran with sweat and blood down his damaged face, his head drooped, his bare shoulders shuddered with sobs.

Naithon moved to stand directly in front of him. "Look at me, Patty O'Malley," he ordered.

Entire body quivering with terror, O'Malley slowly lifted his quaking head and squinted at Naithon through two bruised and swollen eyes. His body shuddered harder when he recognized Naithon. He stammered quickly, "Adranokov, listen, I'm a cop." Sucking in snot and blood, he spat off to the side, Vlad had to jump back to miss it.

Scowling, Vlad bashed his fist into the side of O'Malley's jaw. With a grunted cry, Patty's head bounced then wobbled back to face Naithon.

"I know you're heat, Patty, don't give a fuck. I have some questions for you." The chill in Naithon's voice could make the dead shiver in fright.

Trying to focus his swollen, bleary eyes on Naithon, O'Malley tried again. "But- but I can do shit for you, Adranokov. I can make sure your men are never arrested, I can get goods to your crew that are in jail. I can pay you, a lot, you name it."

Naithon silently rolled one sleeve to his elbow, then the other. O'Malley stiffened, knowing what that meant. Naithon said coolly, "You have nothing I can't do, or get for myself."

His eyes wide at Naithon's big hand turning his sleeves up exposing brawny arms tainted with prison and gang tats. It was no secret in Louisiana that Naithon Adranokov had earned every one of his tattoos, and not in an easy way. Each inked picture or Romanian word or symbol proclaimed his butchering lethality. "But- but-" Patty sputtered. "Girls, I can get you girls, Adranokov, the cream of the crop."

"I can get all the pussy I want, Patty."

A slight smirk sneered up Patty's face, due to the damage, only one side of his face lifted. "Ah, but I can get you young ones," he tried to lean forward as if he was offering him a huge secret, a magnificent treasure. "I mean, *really* young, I got some at five, six, younger, tender babies-"

Blam-

Naithon's fist pounded into O'Malley's temple. Patty's neck whipped to the side with the sheer ferocity and strength of it. Blood and sweat flew off with the blow spattering everyone close to him.

When his head snapped back forward, Naithon bent over and set his hands on top of O'Malley's tied arms, and leaned his weight on his wrist bones, until cracks echoed off the walls.

His prisoner wailed, "Please! Please! I can get you childr-"

Whack-

This time Maz struck him, hard enough O'Malley almost blacked out.

"Don't want him unconscious, boys," Naithon muttered, and leaned back over, crushing O'Malley's wrists more, more bones splintered under his weight, O'Malley shrieked in agony.

"Look at me, Patty, and keep your filthy mouth shut until I ask you my questions. I know you can guess what I will do to you, very,

very slowly if you stonewall me." He paused, O'Malley nodded, crying.

"First, give me the addresses where you're keeping the females, all of the addresses, right now. Spit it out or I cut off your dick first before moving on to other parts. And, Patty," Naithon leaned in close, making sure his prisoner heard and believed him. "You are one sick motherfucker that doesn't belong walking this earth. So after your dick, I'll chop off your legs. We'll cauterize your flesh to staunch the bleeding, keep you alive for as long as I want."

"Ah! Ah!" O'Malley wailed as Naithon crushed his wrists, his hands, he shouted, "Okay!" He rattled off a half dozen addresses. Yash was recording on his phone, and Vlad took out a notebook and handwrote the addresses.

When Patty was done spilling, Naithon punched him in the gut, and then hit him again. O'Malley heaved but didn't puke. Naithon commanded, "Now, step by step, you tell me what happened that day at the wood chipper with Duce Delducci."

O'Malley peered up at him through swollen eyes and a sweat soaked jumble of slimy hair. Sniffing hard then swallowing loudly, his eyes turned down, then back up to Naithon.

"Don't try to fuck with me, Patty," Naithon warned with another gut punch, "I already know Duce is still alive." He sidestepped a slug of vomit that spewed out, Patty coughed, hacked. Naithon raised his fist, waiting for Patty to recoup.

O'Malley's puffed eyes rounded. "How did you-" and gagged when Naithon hit him again.

"Just talk, Patty, all of it. Start at the beginning." Naithon stood back, flexing his fingers. Yash retrieved a mop and bucket of water and efficiently cleaned up the mess Patty was making.

Sniffing noisily, swallowing blood and snot, O'Malley wiped his nose on his shoulder, leaving a smear of snotty blood on his skin. "Okay," sucking in a raggedy breath, he stared at his knees while he spoke. "Me and Duce been workin' a lot of shit together over the years. One day he told me his idea, this crazy scheme." He swallowed some more, spat again but was careful to avoid hitting the men. The goop slapped on the floor to the side of his chair.

"Tell me the scheme," Naithon barked raising his fist when the man stopped talking.

O'Malley jerked at his menacing voice, turned his head to deflect the blow. His face twisted to the side, his words blathered quickly, "Yeah, okay. So, he was snooping through his old man's desk, well, broke in and rifled through his papers. Ignacio had been crying the money blues that they were in dire straits, but Duce found a couple of secret accounts loaded with dough."

Excitement lifted his crusty voice. "I mean, millions, maybe hundreds of millions. Ignacio had told everyone the businesses were going into the red so he would have to pay his crew less, and he could siphon more." He drew a wheezing breath then fell into a coughing jag.

Naithon waited for him to continue. He was giving him two seconds to speak then he was going to stab a knife into his leg and pin it to the chair, make him squeal like a pig.

With Naithon radiating such rage and disgust, O'Malley could feel the threat of his malevolency looming around him, searing his skin with his fury.

He cleared his throat, swallowed more gunk and spoke fast, "So, Duce wanted all of the dough for himself. He had this plan," Patty wheezed in, sounded like a few broken ribs and maybe a collapsed lung. "He decided to kill all of his family members," he glanced up at the other men's muttered responses.

"Yeah, I told you, crazy. He figured he'd kill them all, then inherit everything."

Naithon asked, "How could he inherit if he was dead?"

A grotesque grin showed broken teeth and a blood-filled mouth. "That's the best part. He always had a thing for his baby sister. Like, you think I'm sick, he wanted to do his sister when she was like four or five or something, incest crap, and has never gotten over that he couldn't get to her."

"Which sister?"

O'Malley's snort said *are you kidding*? "The older one is fat and plain as a stick, mean as a rattler, and from what I hear, the skankiest slut from hell. Was always climbing all over Duce, he hated it. Apparently incest lust runs in the family, buncha twisted motherfuckers. No, he wanted the youngest one, Kibly or something. He tried to get at her but Ignacio caught on. He had other plans for that daughter," if his eye wasn't so swollen it would be giving a leering wink.

After a drawn wheeze he went on, "The old man planned to sell her in marriage as soon as she was legal age. In the meantime he had shipped her off to some godforsaken, lockdown boarding school out in the middle of the Italian mountains. Out of Duce's reach, and out of any other males' reach too. Her virginity would bring him a higher price. The word is, the bitch is cock-stopping gorgeous."

Naithon's fists itched to pound the fucker sitting there beaten to gross pulp yet still cocky, and he couldn't wait to get his claws on Duce. The things Naithon would do to him would make Jack the Ripper look like Barney the singing dinosaur. "What does his hots for his sister have to do with the scheme? Get to it."

Patty's sigh ended in a choking coughing fit. The men stood back out of reach of his hurling blood.

When Patty got a grip, he wheezed, "He killed your men, Adranokov, as well as his own to divert suspicion from him. If he only murdered his family, the cops might start looking more closely into his death. His plan was that he would kill everyone except his little sister. She would inherit everything, then Duce would grab her, force her to sign it all over to him. Then he would transfer it to off-shore accounts under a false name."

"And then kill his baby sister?" Naithon asked.

O'Malley shook his head, nasty sweaty hair slapped his face. "Naw. I told ya, the dude has it bad for Kirby or whatever her name is. After he got the money, he planned on keeping her. He didn't need to kill her because he'd have the dough. He couldn't let her go because she'd tell on him. As it turns out, he really wants to keep her. You know, like chained to his bed, so he could plow her whenever he felt like it."

Blinking eyes that were almost completely shut, he tried to grin, but with torn up lips and missing teeth, the drool rolled out making his speech and expressions a sloppy mess.

He slurred, "See? Great plan, huh? Fuck, I never thought it would work, yet, he's almost there. His brothers and father are dead, the older sister I guess is next, then he takes his little sister and flees to places unknown. Anywhere but America for sure. Smart dude, eh?" He grinned at Naithon like a bloody jack-o-lantern.

Suppressing the overwhelming urge to rip his head off his neck, Naithon said, "Tell me about the wood chipper. How did that go down?"

Rolling his head to stay alert, O'Malley stretched his neck that ached from the blows he'd taken, yet he seemed delighted and proud to tell him the story. "Yeah, dude is sharp as a tack, ya know? There were some men he did business with that he wanted out of the way. He set up a meeting, said he had info to give them that would bring them in tons of dough. The meeting was actually set at one of the dude's places. He owned a wood mill.

"It made it appear more on the up and up that way. If it had been one of Duce's places, they would think Duce could double-cross them. So, he looked innocent when he suggested the wood mill. Thinking he wasn't setting them up then, they came willingly, and the stupid gullible fools didn't bring their posses with them. Dollar signs made them blind to the dangerous duplicity. Plus, they all frisked each other to ensure no one was carrying, including Duce.

"When Duce got them all there, he pulled out a faked blueprint and set it on a barrel for them to all study. I was already hiding in the rafters before they even knew they were going there. Jako Martelli had his mill searched before they arrived, but the jerks didn't think to look above them," he scoffed with a raspy gurgled laugh.

"When they were all focused on the blueprint and unaware, I tossed a gun to Duce, and between us, Duce and me took 'em all out. When they were dead, we fed 'em to the chipper. Duce left his ring and belt buckle and cut his arm to leave some blood so they could identify him as one of the vic's, and with my eyewitness testimony, it worked like a charm.

"My story was that as an officer, I had informants pointing the finger at Duce involving arms dealing, and I followed him to the meet. I told my chief that I had been hiding out down the road, waiting for them to get settled and involved in their meeting, and then I was gonna sneak up on 'em, eavesdrop and bug 'em. Record their meeting; see what could be used against them for a warrant.

"I claimed that when I heard gunfire, I raced to the scene, but when I got there, they were all in the chipper, and whoever put them down it was gone."

The grin bloody, he drooled. Sucking back the blood, he said, "My chief bought my story, and would you believe they never caught the fucker who did the killing? My boy Duce is a cunning dude, eh?"

Naithon had to hang on just a little more. He pushed back hair out of his eyes with the back of his hand then propped his hands on his hips, his boots planted on the cement, he asked, "Where can I find Duce?"

O'Malley tried to shrug but with broken ribs and the strap around his lower chest it was more of a twitch than a shrug. Wincing in pain, he wheezed, "Have no idea. After the chipper shit, he paid me and disappeared. Heard he had a boat he might be living on. But it's stolen, the owners…well, I guess they're in watery graves. There's no way to trace it.

"He mentioned once that he has a false passport and open tickets to Portugal. He's in the wind, a ghost, fell off the face of the earth, and I have no way to contact him. Not that I'd want to. I hid out myself for quite a while figuring knowing Duce, he planned on eliminating any loose ends. I don't understand how your people found me."

Patty's bleeding lips pushed up into a smug toothless smile, like he was also a clever man. He squinted through the blood, then frowned. "Listen, Adranokov, you may be tough shit, but I ain't testifying against Duce if he's ever found and caught, he'd have me killed in a New York minute. Besides," he huffed a weak breath, "so many lies, no one would believe any of us anyway, eh?"

Naithon hauled his fist back and slammed it into O'Malley's nose. Patty's hoarse screams railed off the walls.

Picking up one of the towels stacked on the wooden table, Naithon dipped it in a bowl of water then wiped his hands and tossed the towel on the table. Turning his back to Patty, he said to his men, "Get the girls and children out of the brothels. After you verify that's all of them, do what you want to him, then take him to the acid pit."

He decided he wanted to have cleaner hands, in more ways than one, when he saw Kiri. She would be sick and repulsed if she thought he'd tortured and killed the man. Of course that was what was going to happen, but not with Naithon's hands. His conscience was almost clear as he strode up the stairs, O'Malley's screams ripping after him.

When he entered their suite, Naithon was prepared to find either a spitting mad Kiri, or be frozen out for not allowing her to go with him downstairs. Surprisingly, she was sitting in the living room with a sketchpad on her knees. Leaning over it, she was drawing, and writing, furiously. On the coffee table in front of her sat her laptop, he could see the glow from the monitor.

Closing the door softly, he kicked off his boots and padded over to her. He thought she would ignore him, but, she rendered a vague half-smile, and blinked as if to clear her head and bring him into focus. Setting the pencil on the pad, she asked, "Did you get what you wanted?"

"*Ja*," he answered, heading for the hall to the bedroom. "I need to…clean up, I'll be right back and tell you." Naithon had crossed his arms over his chest to hide the worst of Patty's blood, and cover the marks and blood on his knuckles.

After a quick shower and change of clothes, he returned to the living room combing his wet hair back with his fingers. Tugging the knees of his jeans up, he sat down beside her on the sofa and told her what Patty O'Malley had confessed.

After Naithon had left the basement, as they separated to go their own ways, Mazonn had his phone to his ear and was barking out orders to begin raids on the addresses O'Malley had given of the brothels. He also reluctantly called the police, the victims would need medical care when rescued, and families located.

When Naithon told her that after Duce killed everyone, her brother's plan was that he would take Kiri and force her to turn the inheritance over to him, her mouth dropped open, long lashes fanned straight up.

She put a palm to her forehead and sat with her back against the couch. "Oh, Naithon, how could he? Trafficking in children?" Up until she'd seen Naithon's ominous expression when he came in, she had held out hope that what they suspected wasn't true.

"Baby, you know what a truly bad man your brother was. He cared about nothing but making bucks, fucking broads and living large." He didn't tell her Duce's plan to keep her chained to his bed and violate her body as he pleased. It was bad enough she knew he wanted all the Delduccis dead.

Naithon himself wasn't a nice guy either, but he never preyed on the innocents, especially women and children. His gut still felt raw at the shit O'Malley had spilled about Duce, and about Patty's own despicable exploits with the children they had forced into prostitution and turned into junkies.

A shade of guilt sifted in, he had taken an innocent woman, Kiri, and originally had thought nothing of planning to force her to have sex with him. Abducting her was bad enough, at least he hadn't raped her. It gave him the sick chills now to even think about assaulting her. Maybe her goodness was rubbing off on him. That wouldn't be good for business, but it might save his soul.

Settling his back against the sofa cushions, he said, "I need to brainstorm with my guys about how to convince Duce that your da and Janero are dead, and, figure out a way to flush him out before he kills again." He nodded to her sketchpad. "You getting some work done?"

Kiri gripped the edges of the pad with tense fingers. "Sort of. I have an idea on how to resolve both of your problems."

Dark blond brows moved up in curiosity. "Oh yeah, tell me, lamb."

The edge of her pretty lips kicked up in a tight smile. "You aren't going to like the second part. So, I'll tell you the first part."

His brows dipped down into a frown, then leveled out as Kiri held up her pad to show him what she had been working on. She had drawn figures, and there was a numbered list of products. "You know what I do with my craft, creating fake food and photographing it for ads and stuff, some even to be displayed in bakery windows."

He smiled with pride. "*Ja*. You are very talented."

With her, "Thanks," her smile brightened somewhat. "But I also have done scenes that included landscapes, animals and people. I can make...fake people. I think I can make effigies of my dad and Janero. You know, like in a wax museum?"

"Uh huh." Naithon nodded, his eyes narrowed as he tried to follow her tract.

"So, I create the renditions, but instead of making them exact copies, I make them look like," her lip curled with a grimace of grief, "like they're dead. You know, dad would be grey and gaunt from the poisoning, and Janero," she took a shattering breath, "would be burnt and...horribly damaged."

Another long drawn breath, she went on, "Then I can photograph them, and you can get the pictures released to the media."

Naithon nodded as he imagined what she was describing. "*Ja*, Duce would see them and believe they were dead. Then he'd go after your sister and," his lips bunched with anger and a tinge of fear. "You. He will come for you, Kiri."

She decided it wasn't the best time to tell him about the second half of her plan. "Yes. I'd like to get started right away, can you take me to my studio? I've already ordered the materials I'll need. And, I'd like to get the clothes Janero was wearing when," she broke off at the memory of her brother lying in a coma swathed in bandages.

"Hmm, *ja*, okay. But first," Naithon took the pad and pencil from her and set them on the coffee table. Then he grasped the bottom of her t-shirt and pulled it up so fast her arms went up with it and he popped it off her head and tossed it aside.

"Naithon! What are you-"

"The entire time I was downstairs I had this in the back of my mind," he grinned seductively at Kiri. He palmed her breasts over the bra, fondled them, roughly squeezing the soft globes in his hard hands, then he reached behind her and flicked the clasp of her bra. While she was still talking, he swooped the bra off, dropped it.

Pushing her on her back, as he covered her body with his, he yanked the button open on her jeans, by the time he had them and her panties removed, she was no longer talking.

Chapter Thirty

With the enlistment of several soldiers assisting her, Kiri was able to create the effigies fairly quickly. She had photographed the bodies from several angles. When everything was done, Naithon leaked the pictures to tabloid mags, and the sleazier news stations that took candid, and lurid pics of celebrities doing bad or foolish things.

Several days after the pictures were smeared all over the media, Kiri and Naithon were in a yelling, knockdown, drag out fight. She had told him the second part of her plan.

Naithon was shouting at her, hovering his big body over her petite figure to intimidate her, and she wasn't having it. He bellowed, "You are not going to be the fucking bait, Kiri Delducci! You are not leaving this house!"

She opened her mouth to retort with a shout of her own, but then spoke more softly. Her hand on his arm, she said, "Naithon, there is no other way. Melonie is tucked away in a safe house, he can't get at her right now. If I put myself out there, it will draw him out and maybe he'll think that after he kills me, the money will go to Melonie and he can force her to sign over-"

"No fucking way!" Naithon roared, shrugging her hand off his arm. Bending down to yell in her face, he shouted, "You are not leaving this fucking house and that's it!" He sliced a hand down declaring, "No further discussion."

She glared at him, he glared back. "Naithon, listen-"

"I said no. Now," his voice calmed a little, his mouth curved up in an enticing smile. "I have other ideas of what we can do with our time," he threw his hand out grabbing for her blouse, but she danced out of his reach.

"No, Naithon, listen-" The landline rang drawing their attention. He hadn't gotten her a cell phone because she wasn't leaving the house so he felt there was no need for her to have one. So when anyone called for her, they dialed the landline. Their heads turned in unison to the ringing phone. Kiri went over and picked it up.

"Hello?" she said, her voice curious. She had few calls, only customers discussing orders. Her father had called when Naithon had specifically ordered him to keep a low profile. If the phone was tapped their ploy would fail. Rueford called almost daily. Even under threats of dismemberment and death from Naithon, he persevered. Naithon wanted to marry Kiri as quickly as he could talk her into it, that would get the prick off their backs.

"Kiri?" Melonie's voice came through without its normal sneer of venom.

"Hi...Melonie," Kiri answered a bit hesitant. Her sister barely ever said two words to her that weren't nasty and hateful. "Everything okay?"

"Sure, sure," Melonie replied. Then paused. She said, "Um, thing is, they got me stashed away and I am bored out of my mind! I mean, I don't think I'm in any danger, no one has taken a potshot at me or tried to blow me up," she gave a little giggle like they weren't all rigid with trepidation of when the killer would strike again. Naithon had warned Kiri not to tell anyone, not even Melonie that Ignacio and Janero were still alive.

"Yes, I can see how you would be going stir crazy. I at least have my work and," she glanced at Naithon who was staring fiercely at her. "Uh, well, I have things to occupy myself," and almost swallowed her tongue when Naithon cupped his balls and stroked his hand over his penis. The fierce stare turned to a lewd soliciting grin.

"Sure," the bitterness crept into Melonie's voice. She said with undisguised resentment, "You've got that super stud Naithon Adranokov at your beck and call. I hear you finally let him between your legs."

Kiri gulped and lowered her head as flames of embarrassment flooded her cheeks. "Melonie," she cleared the discomfiture from her throat, "it's-"

Her sister spoke over her, "Yeah, you got the prize bull all right. I've got slim pickings here at the safe house. Small dicks and pansy-assed sex, these soldiers here are boring, I'm tired of screwing the same- same. You know what I mean?"

The phone to her ear, Kiri shook her head, her face grew redder. Feeling Naithon moving closer, if he thought Melonie was disrespecting or upsetting her he'd snatch the phone out of her hand. She turned away so he couldn't see her aghast expression. "Listen, Melonie, I'm kind of busy, I'm working on a project-"

"I know," the sneer resumed in Melonie's voice. "You're a big shot artist or some shit now." A slight feel sorry for herself whine entered her nasally voice, "You have no time for your sister. I'm all alone and lonely and no one cares. Don't worry about me, I'll just," her tone grew desolate, "oh, stare at the walls some more I guess."

The guilt struck Kiri just as Melonie knew it would. "Oh, now, please Melonie, what can I do to help? I'll do whatever you like if it helps you feel better," feeling Naithon's scowl heat her back, she turned further from him.

"Really?" the cheer blasted right back into her voice. "You mean it? Because, I'd hate to get my hopes all up, my heart couldn't take a rejection right now."

"Yes, yes, of course I mean it. What can I do, Melonie?" Naithon's growl stirred the hairs at the back of her neck. Melonie had asked a few times, well, maybe a million, if she could come and stay at the compound.

Naithon refused to even hear her plea, and shut Kiri down every time she tried to bring it up. He did not want that vindictive nasty shrew within a hundred miles of Kiri. Forget the fact that she was always falling all over him, who knew what kind of plot the bitch could hatch to get Kiri to sneak out again, and fall into Duce's hands.

"Wow, great, you are a wonderful sister, Kirs," Melonie gushed. "I am so claustrophobic cooped up here in this boring place. I thought maybe you and I could do lunch."

"Lunch?" Kiri echoed. She murmured quietly, "Mel, you know Naithon won't allow you to come here."

"No, no, I know, he's such an asshole. Even if he'd let me I don't want to go there now. No, I was thinking we could go to a restaurant. Naithon could have his silly soldiers guarding us. It would be broad daylight, in plain sight, crowds of people around us, no one would ever take the chance on trying to pop either of us there."

Kiri grew silent, Naithon reached for the phone, she turned away from him again.

He growled, "What, Kiri, what is she saying?"

"Kirs?" The nasally sound slunk through the wires. "Please, please make him let you go. I," she sighed dramatically, "I don't know if I can go on living like this...you know what I mean?"

"Mel, come on, you know he won't let me-"

Naithon broke in, "Let you do what, Kiri? What the hell is she asking you to do?" He slid his arm around her shoulder to hold her from moving away from him. He knew Melonie was a snake if there ever was one, and he wished Kiri would just write her off, banish her from her life. But his lamb was too soft hearted to do that. Instead, she allowed her sister's sick venomous mouth to continue slinging poison at Kiri's sweet heart.

"Please, Kiri, I'm begging you. I swear, if I don't get out of here, I'll...I'll slit my wrists. I swear."

"So, why don't you just go out yourself? The guards will take you if you insist."

A heavy sigh ground through the receiver. "Kirs," she pleaded, "they won't protect me to the nth degree like Naithon would if you were with me. Do you want me to die of suicide? Or getting shot because my detail was too lax? I'm your blood, Kirs, your sister, we're all we have left of the family, can't you do this one little thing for me? Going out alone is just as bad as staying here alone. I need company."

"Besides," she said with a loud sniff, "we need to plan Dad's and Janero's funerals. As soon as the pathologist releases their bodies, well," she sighed sadly, "we have to bury them, Kirs. Don't make me do it alone. Please?"

Kiri's sigh matched her sister's, the guilt forced her to give in. "Okay, I'll meet you. When and where do you want to-" she scrunched her eyes at Naithon's roar.

"Kiri, fuck, you are not leaving this fucking house! How many times do I have to fucking tell you!"

Melonie giggled. "I hear the master's bellow. He has a violent streak, they say his temper is monumental. But," her voice lowered in sisterly collusion, "the word is that you have the big man by the balls. You close your legs to him and he will do anything you say to get back in your cunt."

"Melonie!" Kiri burst with mortification and shock at her sister's vulgarity.

"Kiri," Naithon warned that he was reaching his limits. He couldn't hear Melonie's side of the conversation, but by the red in her face, and the distress in Kiri's voice, she wasn't talking roses and kittens.

"Okay, okay," Melonie sighed with irritation. "I forget what a little goody two shoes you are. Anyway, tomorrow at 12, how about we meet at the Sailor's Fork? It's on the water, we couldn't be in a more secure location."

"All right." Resigned to going and therefore getting into another big fight with Naithon, Kiri said, "I'll meet you there, gotta go now, bye," she hung the phone up quickly because she knew Naithon was going to explode.

"Meet her? You think you're going to meet that bitch somewhere?" Naithon rounded on her as Kiri tried to put some distance between them. "You think I'm letting you out of this house, and especially to go see that piece of shit, sorry excuse for a sister of yours? Fuck, Kiri," he shook his head. "I thought you had better

281

sense, more pride than to subject yourself to her relentless rancorous abuse."

"Naithon, please," she said soothingly, trying to calm him. Wasn't happening.

"Please nothing," he spat, "forget it. Don't even fucking ask. No." Kako whimpered off down the hallway to the bedroom to hide from their yelling.

Now her ire was rising. Crossing her arms over her chest, one foot stuck out in a tap, brows firm in an angry frown, she claimed, "I am not asking. I am telling you. Tomorrow at noon, I'm meeting Melonie at the Sailor's Fork." She kept talking as his mouth opened, "If you don't take me, I will find a way to get out of here-"

"I will fucking chain you to the bed," his words rebounded back at him, that's what Duce had planned. But Naithon would be doing it to protect her. "Just- just, fine, have the bitch come here, just this once."

Shaking her head, she said, "No. She knows you hate her and she said she doesn't want to come here, she really wants to go out, be out somewhere where there are people and activity."

"Goddammit," he roared, "the chains then-"

This time Kiri got up in his face. Her lips firm, she squinted at him. "Naithon Adranokov, you may command an army, but you do not command me. I swear to God, if you don't take me, I will at some point, maybe not tomorrow, but I will find a way to get out of here. I've done it before, I'll do it again. And I won't come back. You will never find me. And in the meantime, there will be no…intimacy between us."

"Huh," he grunted. Hands on his hips he glowered at her. "You threatening me, little pigeon? You know quite well that I can fuck you any damned time I want. You split from here, I will always find your ass and haul you right back. Your threats are meaningless."

The red had faded from her cheeks and now it blew right back with anger. "Yes, you can, uh, take me, you're bigger and stronger, you can force me. But you can't make me want you, or touch you, or," her voice taunted softly, "kiss you."

282

He had forced his kisses on her before so she corrected, "Kiss you willingly, with passion. There are other things you said you would teach me. You know," her lids lowered in sensuous promise, "that thing you described with me on my knees and something of yours in my mouth?"

Naithon's mouth snapped shut, he blinked at her.

"I'm thinking you would want me to *want* to do that to you? Put my all into it?"

Picturing her naked on her knees with her plush lips wrapped around his manhood and looking up at him with those shining, gorgeous, sweet green eyes, he nodded dumbly.

Gripping the bottom of her shirt, she pulled it up and off and tossed it at him. It hit him in the chest, his eyes on her tits, he was oblivious of the shirt hitting him and dropping to the floor.

"Well then, make the lunch happen," she said, and sauntered away, heading for the bedroom.

Naithon stared at her for a few stunned seconds, then followed her like Kako after his favorite doggy treat.

Chapter Thirty-One

Naithon was so on edge he had paced, barked orders, punched one of his men that questioned one of his orders, knocking him out cold. His usual entourage of soldiers, and caravan of cars flanked them as they drove to the restaurant.

Teeth clenched, jaw gnashing, scowl that could fell a grizzly, he was livid that she could lead him around by his dick, he refused to say a word to Kiri. Just tugged at his suit coat and shirt sleeves in aggravation.

She'd gotten her way, and he was terrified. Idiot that he was, wanting her willingly in his bed, he had given in. Again. And now that she was out of the protection of the compound, he was insane with fear.

As they parked, his eyes, skilled at seeking out treachery, darted everywhere, searching for hidden danger. She refused to wear the vest or helmet, said she would only look more of a target, the manager may even deny her to come to his restaurant thinking she was drawing danger to his customers and staff.

Tony opened the back door and stepped aside for them to alight.

Hearing the damned catch in his voice, Naithon covered it with blunt gruffness, "Kiri, please, let's go back home. I don't have a good feeling about this."

She swiveled in her seat to face him. "I know. I'm not stupid. Melonie would never call me to have anything to do with me.

Something is up. But it might be a way to lure Duce out with both of us here. Two stones at once," she smiled.

His face darkened. "That's not funny, Kiri." She moved to get out, he grabbed her arm, stilling her. "You're setting yourself up as bait, if I had known that, I-"

"You would never have let me come here. Naithon." She patted his chest, "We have to end this before he kills anyone else. You know that. There's no other way."

"*Ja*, there is. We will find him, I have people looking for him"

Cocking her head she smiled at the big guy that had grown so important to her. "But before someone else is harmed? Before he finds out dad and Janero still live and he comes after them again? No. We're here, we'll follow through with this. At least we can see this coming."

His sigh laborious, he set his hand on her thigh. "Kiri," his face stayed hard but his voice softened. "If I see, hear, think, feel there is anything wrong, we're out of here. You can close your legs all you want to me, but I'd rather fuck a cold angry live Kiri, than throw dirt on your bloody casket. We clear on that?"

Kiri tenderly caressed his face with her palm, green eyes alight with her smile. "Yes, Naithon, I hear you." Stroking his skin, rough with early stubble, she moved her lips to near his, almost touching. Her breath warm and sweet on his mouth, she whispered, "I love it that you care so much for me that you want to protect me at all costs."

Her mouth joined to his, and their kiss gentle at first, quickly grew heated. He spread his hand on her back pulling and lifting her up, his other hand gripped her hair and he slanted his head with a harsh moan, grinding their mouths, in seconds they were dizzy with hunger for each other.

"Geez, Nait, my man, you guys can't do that shit at home?" Mazonn's amused voice rudely intruded on their passion. He grinned at Naithon's scowl, and the way Naithon was tugging at his pants to give his erection some room. "Need a minute?" he teased.

"Asshole, just get everyone in line," Naithon growled. He did need a minute, he couldn't get out of the car with a boner bulging out of the front of his pants, and his breathing fierce like he'd run a marathon.

Maz stepped away to give them privacy while Naithon cooled his ardor. He cupped Kiri's face. "*Dio*, I wish this was over and we were home in bed." His features lost their lust and sharpened in ire, he swore, "Never again. I am not going through this ever again. You wanna try to entertain your threat to shut that pussy down from me, then so fucking be it. You ready?" he snapped.

Kiri knew he was on edge so she didn't take offense, she smiled tenderly at him, "Yes, I'm ready."

Huffing out a harsh breath, Naithon got out first and made her wait while he conferred with his men and scanned the area. He had to place his men discretely in and around the restaurant or they would get thrown out, and then he'd have to do this all over again somewhere else.

He could kick himself, he should have just allowed the sister from hell to come to the compound in the beginning. It was just that she was so fucking nasty he didn't want her vile vibe in his house. He didn't trust her to not plant bugs or bombs or something they couldn't see hidden on her body. Or sneak someone inside, or trick Kiri into leaving.

He was never going to be ready to put his girl out there, but when he was as satisfied as he could be with the security, he buttoned his suit coat, leaned in and held his hand for Kiri to take. He guided her out and immediately tucked her under his arm, using his body to shield her. He wasn't even going to be able to be at her side during the lunch.

Melonie had complained to Kiri when they spoke again earlier on the phone that she wouldn't feel comfortable with him lurking at their table, giving her the stink eye, and listening to their conversation.

Against his better judgment, he gave in once again. Damn, he was turning into the world's biggest pussy. He kept this up he'd lose the respect of his men. The type of business he was in, they required a tough, cold-blooded leader, not a pussy-whipped wimp. They get back home, and he will let that little girl know who is in charge.

Tucking a thick digit under his collar, he tugged to loosen the knot of his tie that was pressing into his Adam's apple. *Ja*, he knew who was in charge, a tiny, delicate female who had him wrapped up in silken ropes. All she had to do was lift her shirt and he would go running, tripping over his tongue to get at her, promising her anything she wanted. Hell.

But then again, a slight grin nicked, he was learning the things that turned Kiri into a sultry, sex goddess, he knew how to make her plead to him to give it to her. He could make her want him even when she didn't. She could say no, but he knew how to have that hot little body scream yes.

Ja, this was the last time he let her out into danger, he was the boss, and he would fuck her into obeying him. He felt slightly better. Plus, he had a promised blowjob as thanks when they returned home. Now *that's* gonna be fun lesson.

Half of the restaurant extended over the rippling sapphire water. The back half on stilts, allowed a 180 view of the ocean. A wide deck surrounded the entire building for outside seating. Patrons could watch the shrimp boats coming in with gulls dive-bombing them for discarded bait.

The sun warm at high noon, the restaurant jammed packed inside and out with yammering customers and bustling staff. Melonie had made reservations. They would be sitting out on the back deck overlooking the restless ocean.

They followed a wooden ramp to the restaurant. Over the door a red and black hand painted sign said, 'Sailor's Fork.' The outside of the A-framed building was painted rust colored with dark wood accents. The long planked walk led from the parking area over the water to the restaurant.

Naithon's keen eyes observed his men blending in with customers, and around the perimeter acting as patrons coming and going.

A rustic marina busy with boats loading up for a day of fishing an acre to the left, was lively with activity, sporadic shouts bounced across the water that separated them from the restaurant.

Naithon would be damned if he wasn't going to deliver his girl safely to her table. He told the maître de they had a reservation, and the tall man in a white button-down and black slacks led them around one side of the building to the back. Their footsteps clunking on the wooden deck barely heard over the robust customers. A horn from a large boat tooted in the background, urging a smaller vessel to get out of its way.

Scattered around the deck, dozens of patrons chatted while eating lunch and enjoying the view. A double-beamed varnished wooden railing roped around the deck to prevent people from falling overboard. Boats tied to pillars bobbed in the back.

The cloudless sky was bold blue, the sun beamed saffron, tipping cresting waves and boats in the distance with glistening white, and glaring bright off the tiled roof. Colorful umbrellas shone like tossed jewels on the brown-planked flooring.

Melonie was already seated at the table. She gave a jaunty wave when she spotted Kiri. Her welcoming smile dimmed at Naithon holding onto Kiri as they threaded their way to the table. She had deliberately told the busboy to remove the extra chairs leaving only two.

When the couple arrived, Melonie gave Naithon a dirty look. "Kiri," her pout snarky, "you promised it would be just you and me. No one else," she glared at Naithon.

The maître de pulled out a chair for Kiri. Kiri said, "It's okay, Mel, he's not staying. Right, Naithon?" She smiled up at him. Her smile tugged his mouth down and also pulled at his heartstrings.

He never graced Melonie with a glance. Naithon drew Kiri closer and kissed her lightly then let her go. "*Ja*, no worries," he muttered. Bumping the maître de to the side, he helped Kiri to sit.

Leaning down, he placed his hands on her shoulders and murmured in her ear, "Remember what I said. Just a whisper of a threat, and I will haul you the fuck outta here, over my shoulder if I have to."

Kiri gave him another quick kiss and said softly, "I know, Naithon. I'll call you when we're done." He had finally given her a phone. It was tucked in the small purse she set on the table. The diamond earrings twinkled in her ears, and the gold watch he gave her glinted delicately on her wrist. Although she wore jeans and a blouse, he had insisted she wear the jewelry he bought her. Since she never went out, it was an opportunity to enjoy them.

"All right." Clearly reluctant to leave her, Naithon said squeezing her shoulders, "Call me. Soon." He stepped away and strode back to the restaurant where he'd sit at the bar by the window watching her and everything else.

"Geez, girl, the man is so overbearing. What the books call a dominant alpha male." Melonie swooned, waved at her heated face. "You are so lucky. What'd I do to have a shot at that. Anytime he wants something different, you gotta let me know, yeah?"

"Uh huh," Kiri murmured uncomfortably. Melonie never bothered to hide her lust for Naithon, she could care less he and her sister were involved. Kiri had seen her fawn over him, touching him every time she had ever been near him. Even as he had stood there, Melonie's crude gaze was blatantly trained at his crotch.

They ordered lemonade and lunch, and people-watched until their food arrived. The server brought salad with blackened shrimp, olives and roasted tomatoes for Kiri, and lobster ravioli for Melonie. Melonie turned her nose up at the side salad that came with the lobster ravioli and ordered a side of french fries, and onion rings, and a tub of coleslaw instead.

"So," Melonie murmured, taking a bite of ravioli. "I hear he's quite endowed and extremely rough and kinky in the sack. Is that true? What's it like living with the violent gypsy thug?"

"Mel," Kiri scolded, "please don't do that."

With a shrug, Melonie set an elbow on the table and waved her fork as she spoke. "Okay, whatever." She narrowed her eyes in skepticism at her sister. "I can't believe you've fallen for the brute."

Taking a sip of lemonade then adding more sugar, stirring the spoon, Melonie said, "I mean, heck, it's all kinda romantic the way he stole you out from under Dad and Rueford's noses, literally swept you up and carried you off to lock you away in his castle. I mean, being the refined lady and all, I would think you would be kicking and screaming over being kidnapped and ravaged." She sounded horrorstruck, but looked excited and envious.

Pouring dressing on her salad from a small pitcher, Kiri said, "I'd really rather not talk about it." She couldn't explain her attraction for her abductor, how every day she grew closer and closer to Naithon. Even now she missed the big lug looming over her giving her orders. She stifled her giggle, Melonie didn't need to know anything about her life with Naithon, she would only somehow use the information against her.

"Fine," Melonie grunted and stabbed a fat ravioli. Thrusting the whole thing in her mouth at once, some sauce dribbled out as she spoke with her mouth full, "So, I suppose we can chat about what's been going on with us, our family?"

Kiri paused with her fork in the salad, sighed sadly. "I guess."

Eagerly, Melonie asked, "Do you think it's Adranokov behind all the murders? Or one of the other gangs trying to weed us down and then take over everyone's territory? Maybe it's Reece Walford who's running the Delducci enterprises at the moment and he knocked everyone off to become number one."

Crunching on a blackened pink shrimp, Kiri mumbled noncommittally, "I have no idea." Then she quickly said, "I mean, I'm sure Naithon is not involved in any way."

"It's all very strange. Remember, we need to plan the funerals, Dad and Janero's, we can discuss that."

They spent the rest of their lunch planning the dual funeral. Then Melonie regaled her sister with lascivious stories of her sexploits with her guards at the safe house.

When she got to her evening with four guards taking her on the rug in the living room, her description of how they filled every hole at the same time and then some, red-faced Kiri spouted, "Okay, Mel, enough. Please, TMI."

One brow rose over a sneering eye. "Oh, are you judging me, little sister? You're living with the biggest, baddest mobster in the state and further. He's killed more men and fucked more women then you'll ever meet in a lifetime." Her eyes tapered at Kiri. "If you think he's fucking only you, you are a fool."

Kiri tried to get a word in but her sister rolled right over her. "That man has a reputation, girl, he owns strip joints. You don't think he's not fucking a different slut every day while he keeps you locked in your ivory tower? Ha!" she snorted crassly.

When Kiri shook her head, Melonie went on, "He probably does way more than my measly four soldiers, he can fuck as many women as he wants at one time, all the time. He'll soon tire of your staid little ass and out on the street you will go. He's only keeping you because he wants a piece of the Delducci's business."

Biting back her angry rejoinder, with her insecurities being fired up anew, Kiri already believed half of what Melonie was spewing. She set her napkin on the table. "I think it's time for me to go. I believe Naithon has taken care of the bill up front." She reached for her purse and pushed her chair back.

Melonie scrambled for her own purse and jumped to her feet. "Wait, Kirs, I'm sorry. I know you like the gypsy thug, I won't say anything else about him, okay? Please don't leave me."

Knowing Naithon would be on pins and needles the entire time she was out there, Kiri said gently, "Really, Mel, I need to go. You can stay if you want, I saw your security detail conferring with Naithon. They'll watch over you." She got to her feet, slipping her purse strap over her arm.

"All right," Melonie snipped rudely. Then she inserted some cajoling in her tone, "But at least hit the ladies room with me before we go. I have a longer drive back than you do."

Kiri gave in again with a sigh and a mild smile. "Sure. Where is it?"

A cheerful grin split Melonie's plain face lifting her pudgy cheeks. "Great. It's this way, follow me," she took off almost at a jog. Kiri had to hurry to catch up with her. She thought she heard Naithon yell out her name, but, geesh, she should be able to go to the ladies room for crying out loud. Ignoring him, she hastened after her sister.

Melonie was rushing to the far back of the deck and around a station where the servers typed in orders on a computer screen, and housed stocks of cutlery, glasses, water pitchers, cups and saucers, coffee pots steamed on stacked burners.

"Mel," Kiri called out, "I don't think it's that way, there's only the water passed there."

Melonie kept racing so Kiri ran after her. Running around the station, Kiri suddenly found herself right at the edge of the railing. "Mel?" she called in confusion.

Suddenly, Melonie jumped out at her from behind the station and gave her a hard shove. So hard she was shoved off her feet. While Kiri stumbled, Melonie lifted her clumsily and pushed her over the railing.

Chapter Thirty-Two

Kiri screamed, expecting to plunge into the cold water, instead, a pair of strong arms caught her and dropped her on her feet. Before she could get her bearings, Melonie jumped down behind her onto the boat deck, snatched the rope loosely wound around a pier, and Duce hit a few steps going up a level then he ran into a glass-enclosed bridge.

Kiri could hear the engine rumbling, Duce had left it idling. He rapidly punched buttons on the control panel, clicked a lever, and slammed the gear to the hilt.

The vessel revved, and flew away from the restaurant so fast Kiri was knocked off her feet and she fell smacking hard landing on her butt. Glancing around, she realized she was on a boat.

A big boat, a yacht, and it was racing over the tossing waves, the engine roaring. In seconds the restaurant was a dot in the distance.

Bouncing on the wood flooring, she sat catching her breath, her brain spinning, what the heck just happened? Gaping in stunned shock through hair tossing over her eyes, inside the open door to the bridge she could see Melonie standing beside Duce, gazing up at him in awe.

The boat rocketed, thrusting through high waves spewing a wild foaming crest of surf behind it. The movement of the boat made it difficult for Kiri to struggle to her feet, and stand steady. She made her way to a steel railing to hold on. Gripping the cold rail, her hair whipped in the wind, tears pulled from her eyes.

Last thing she wanted was to be anywhere near Duce, so grasping the rail tightly, she followed it with hand over hand pulling herself to the stern. As soon as the boat stopped, she was jumping off, whether they were on land or water. She put a foot on a seat ready to climb up and jump.

"Oh no you don't, babydoll," Duce's rough voice abraded her ear. He grabbed her arm pulling her off the seat. "We're going inside the cabin." He tugged her, she held onto the rail, he jerked her harder breaking her grip. Kiri fought him, punching in a frantic frenzy, he only laughed, picked her up and carried her across the deck to a short set of stairs, and stomped down them.

The first opening was to a huge, lavish living room. Luxurious creams and blush, gold bedazzling everything. Plush sofas and chairs, huge glass windows exposed the open ocean around and beyond.

Duce hauled his sister inside and plunked her on an ivory sofa. Blue accent pillows squished as she fell into them. She popped up to run, he shoved her back down and growled, "Don't make me hurt you, Kiri, I will, you know that, but I don't want to. Not yet, anyway."

Her brother was a big, well-muscled man. He would be good looking if the aura of sadistic creep didn't flow around him, and the violent lust of harming someone to get his rocks off etched on his face. Dark hair on the edge of being shaggy, pure cruelty marked his chilling eyes and flattened his callous lips.

She scooted back out of his reach, pulling her knees up protectively. "Duce, what is this all about? I don't understand. How could you kill your own brothers, our father?"

His head fell back with a rabid laugh. "I'd kill the president, honey, to get what I want." Then those chilled dark eyes narrowed at her. "How did you know it was me that did the hits?"

"I just reasoned it seeing you alive." She whispered fearfully, "What is it that you want, Duce?" The boat continued hurling over the buoyant sea, water sprayed at the windows, Melonie must be driving.

A sheen of lascivious desire misted his handsome face, lids levered low over insidious dark eyes that traced her figure. Greedy tongue slicking his hungry lips he replied, "Since you ask, baby sister, I'll tell you. I want it all. I want Dad's fortune and I don't want to share it with anyone else."

Her lips pulled in. "Duce-" the boat shifted sharply making Duce stumble and Kiri sprawl on the couch.

"Goddamned useless bitch," Duce cussed tersely, "can't even drive a boat right. I only kept her around so I could get my hands on you, baby button. That fuck Adranokov had you too sealed up, I couldn't get to you again." His leer so sick and grotesque Kiri's stomach heaved.

Correcting his balance, he started towards her and the boat lurched again tossing him sideways. "Goddammit!" he thundered, changed direction and stomped to the doorway. He turned to Kiri and said, "We'll get reacquainted baby sister when I get back." He closed the door and she heard the lock engage.

As soon as he was gone Kiri leaped to her feet and ran to the door. Grabbing the handle she yanked and wrenched and twisted it, to no avail. The door was solid, there was no way she could break it open. She looked up at the hinges, she'd need a tool to get them apart. Turning on her heel, she raced to the windows.

Frantically, she scanned the room searching for something to break the glass, a vase, a statue, something. A lamp. She hurried and grabbed at the lamp, it was bolted down. Quickly she found out everything was bolted down, even the ashtrays and decorations probably so they wouldn't topple with the fitful swaying and rolling of the boat over high waves.

There was not a tool, or anything she could find to use as a weapon. She pounded on the glass windows until her hands bruised. They were hurricane resistant, she wasn't breaking them. Finally, she had to give in, she wasn't getting out until Duce let her out. Her heart thumped, was he even planning to let her out, alive?

He was probably going to throw her over the side, gleefully watch her drown, let the sharks feast on her remains. If they were far enough out over the rough waters she wouldn't be able to swim to any land. Swimming wasn't something she excelled at. Doggy paddling was the best she could do to keep her head above water.

Staring out the window, she saw nothing but blue. Blue sky, endless blue water, there wasn't any visible land or another boat in sight.

Panicking fear strangled the breath in her lungs, exterminating rational thought. Kiri struggled to fight down the terror that was rapidly overwhelming her. She dropped down on a chair by the window and watched the infinite sea range far and wide, white foamed waves rolled and slapped into each other.

After what seemed like hours, the rocking motion lolled her. Her head twitched, she was falling asleep. Kiri sat up straight. She wasn't letting Duce sneak up on her. Rubbing an eye, she peered out the window.

She and Melonie had finished lunch around two. It was late autumn and the sun was settling along the horizon. The orange orb spread into the water, painting a vertical, orange streak wavering down the endless, deep dark aqua. Naithon had taken her towards the beginning of fall, and now it was almost winter. The past few days had been temperate, like an Indian-summer.

Climbing to her numb feet, Kiri stared out the glass smeared with saltwater drops and a crusty film. It had to be around four or five o'clock judging by the sun's descent. Her pounding heart squeezed in fright, there was no way Naithon could ever find her. Ever. As soon as he got his money Duce was going to kill her. Panic gripped her heart, started rising in her throat it was smothering her in dread.

The boat slowed for a bit before she heard the engines ratcheting down, then it came to a rocking stop. A long grinding sound scraped down the side of the yacht, Kiri wondered if Duce had lowered the anchor.

She looked out the window at the shrouding darkness, sky and sea slowly becoming indistinguishable. Still, it would be near an hour though before the sun fully set. There was nothing in sight, not land, another boat, a plane, nothing.

They had stopped out in the middle of nowhere, what could he anchor to? Was this to be her final resting place? Shivers of terror sprinted up Kiri's spine, chilling the hairs on the back of her neck.

A noise at the door made her swing around in a start. Eyes wide, her hand at her throat, she watched the slow, wicked grin roll up Duce's fiendish face as he entered the cabin. He was Satan, evil incarnate. A man so morally bankrupt he would murder his entire family for money.

Kiri instinctually stepped back, although there was nowhere for her to go. At well over six feet, shoulders like an ox, she wasn't getting past that wall of perdition.

He moved into the room, his smile almost friendly, exhibited a shade of confusion at the sheer terror whitening her face. "Baby button, why are you so afraid? It's me, Duce, your brother." He held a computer in his hand.

As afraid as she was, she still snorted. "Huh, my murdering, money-grubbing brother." She sucked in a deep breath. "Have you come to kill me now? I'll fight you, Duce, to the end. I won't go easy like a kitten drowned in a sack."

Dark brows hopped up in surprise. "Kill you? Never, my little button. I plan to force you to transfer all the funds you received from Dad's estate to me. I hacked into our attorney's files and saw that the money is already under your name. They did it quickly to keep the businesses running. Dad hadn't dared to put it under our idiot sister's name. She'd squander every dime and let the business go under."

Kiri knew this. Naithon had his IT guy put the false information in the lawyer's computer files and left it slackly protected so Duce could hack in and access it. Once he thought the funds were in her account, he'd make his move. And he did.

Of course Kiri had always thought when Duce came for her, that Naithon would be there and miraculously save her. Boy was she wrong. No one thought of an ocean attack. The men had all been guarding inside, and outside the front area of the restaurant.

Duce set the laptop on a table, lifted the monitor up and wrapped his hand around Kiri's neck. He pushed her head down towards the computer. "Now, use your password and transfer all of the funds from your account to the one there," he motioned to a paper taped to the keyboard.

"But, what if I-"

His fingers pushed bruising into her throat digging into her windpipe, cutting off her air supply. "Not playin' here, Button, no prevaricating, just fucking do it. You got two seconds. One, two-"

Her fingers typed over the keyboard even as she gasped, choking for breath. They both watched the screen as the money flowed from her account to his. When it was done, he released her; she stumbled back with both hands at her neck.

He closed the lid with a huge rapturous grin, manic euphoria glowing sickly in his brown eyes.

Stalling for time, time for what? To get away? Did she have wings? Anyway, Kiri asked, "Now that the money has gone through, you'll kill me? Throw me overboard? Let the sharks do their thing?"

He looked genuinely surprised. "No, sweet button," he shook his head, moving towards her, "I'm keeping you."

The hair on her head stung in fright. "Keeping me? For what?" Was the world filled with Naithons? In the gangster world she was purely a possession.

He laughed. "Seriously, Kiri? You are still that naïve?" Another step closer, his voice lowered, darkness inked into it, "Honey, you know I've always wanted you. A child, a teen, an adult," he shrugged negligently, "don't matter, I just have to have you."

"Have me?"

With a perfidious chuckle, he said, "Come on, Button, I want to fuck you. I always have. Don't care if you're young or old, I admit I am obsessed. I will bind you in our bedroom. You were juicy as a child, now," he appreciated her figure with a leer, "you are even juicier with all those sexy as shit curves. There's more to play with now."

Stumbling back from him, she asked, "You- you're going to keep me? For how long?"

His mouth hooked in a raunchy smile, in his eyes erotic degeneracy flared. "I'm thinking like forever, babe. I always understood Adranokov's taking you, his desire to lock you away somewhere with the intent of marrying you so you could never leave him."

Large hands curled over his jean-clad hips, head cocked, his indecent gape roamed every scintilla of her body, pupils dilating when they traced over her curves. The salacious smirk bunched into a frown, he said, "I would have married you if it had been legal, alas," he shrugged blocky shoulders, "I can't. So, I'll just have to do as that gangster has, keep you hidden away and secured."

He took a few steps towards her. "But right now, I have'ta fuck you, baby sister, I've waited a long damned time to get you under me."

Kiri held her hands up. "No, Duce, stop. You're sick, you're my brother for heaven's sake! It's- it's monstrous! You can't do this-"

"I'm a male, you're a female, it's quite normal, so yeah, I *can* do this. Yeah, we're siblings, but our parts will fit together just like anyone else's."

"You fucking bastard," Melonie's furious snarl drew Kiri's attention.

Duce didn't bother to turn around, he ordered, "Get the fuck out, Mel, this is between me and the baby."

Melonie stomped into the room. "You son of a bitch, Duce. You said you were going to kill her after you got the money." Her voice wound into a petulant whine, "You said it would be you and me, just us together, without her," she spat at Kiri with a twisted face, throwing her an antagonistic gesture. "She won't take care of you in bed like you know I can!"

Flabbergasted, Kiri's anguished eyes widened in bewilderment. "You too, Mel? For heaven's sake, you guys keep talking about incest like you're making out a grocery list. It's- sick, against human and God's law." Shaking her head with stunned incredulity, looking from one to the other, she cried, "My siblings. Lord almighty, murder, rape, incest, what foul seeds did you come from?"

Duce regarded her calmly with a jaded smile. "I had to have someone satisfying my needs while I stayed in hiding. It's not all that unnatural, Button, plenty of isolated clans fucked each other when there was no one else around, they had to keep the population going, right?"

Melonie was beside herself, whitecaps of homicidal rage rattled spasms all over her body. Uttering a wild shriek, Melonie ran towards Kiri with her arms out, fingers deadly talons. "I'll kill you myself you man-stealing whore!" Kiri shrank back, but Duce snaked out an arm, snagged Melonie's plump waist, bringing her to an abrupt stop.

Melonie pounded at his arm, screaming, "You let me go, I'm gonna get rid of that skank once and for all!"

Fisting her hair until she cried out, Duce snarled into her face, spittle smacking her skin, "You aren't gonna do fucking shit, Mel. I give the orders here, you do as I say. Sit down and shut up while I show the baby who owns her now." Gripping her hair and her arm, he hurled her hard, Melonie flew across the room crashing into a chair. She slumped to the floor with a grunt.

"Now, where was I, baby button-" he swung around, and cursed. "Where the fuck did she go?"

While her siblings were fighting, Kiri bolted out of the cabin, slamming the door, she locked it and tore up the stairs to the upper deck. The yacht was big but the sea was rough making the hull bob and roll over large waves. Saltwater slapped the sides and spewed over spraying the deck.

With only the thought to get away, Kiri ran to the railing and grasped it. Her lips parted in dismay, still, all she could see were miles and miles of open water. A faint thunderous roar rumbled somewhere. "Great, a lightning storm, can things get any worse?" Her purse, she suddenly thought, "My phone!"

She ran to the part of the deck where she had tumbled aboard. When Melonie pushed her and she dropped, her purse had flown off. Maybe Naithon could follow the GPS in her phone. There was no question in her mind that he would come after her.

300

They were so far out it was unlikely she could call on the cell. She spotted her purse, her phone was on the deck a few feet from it. Hope withered, the phone was smashed to smithereens, probably by Duce's boot. There were only pieces of the shell, he must have thrown the guts overboard.

"What to do now?" She tried to think. Hurrying to the bridge, maybe she could drive the boat. Sure. It was worth a try.

The yacht had three decks, the bridge was on the top level. As Kiri slipped into the bridge, she could hear Duce bellowing and beating at the door downstairs. She went to the control panel, and her stomach fell. She hadn't a clue what to do. "Well," she told herself with determination, "I have to try something, anything. First, the anchor." Glancing around, she scrutinized buttons and switches but saw nothing that said anchor.

The rumbling grew louder, only a few cotton clouds shuffled across the darkening blue sky. The sun was melting into the sea, but it was still light. She couldn't see the dark clouds of the storm, but she could hear it, it sounded closer every second. Growing more frantic, "There has to be a lever," she muttered, "somewhere." Kiri bent and read every label on every piece of equipment, button, switch, then-

"Oh yes!" she crowed, spying a small lever, under it read 'anchor.' She reached for it, her fingers pushed, and a hard hand dropped on hers and crushed her hand in his palm. She cried out with the pain.

"Don't think so, baby sister," Duce grated, anger mixed with a speck of amusement. Squeezing her hand to stop her action, he snapped it off the lever. Still holding her hand, he swung her around and jerked her against his body and grinned down at her.

"Now, baby girl, we're done fooling around, actually, we're about to begin fooling around," his voice went from hardened with wrath, to husked with lust. "You aren't getting away from me again. Not ever again. Finally, there'll be no father or two-bit gypsy gangster to get between us."

Curving his arm like an iron brace around her back, he grabbed fistfuls of her blouse. Growling into her hair, "I wanted our first time

to be special, downstairs on the bed, candlelight, music, wine. But," he sighed with annoyance, "Mel ran into the bedroom and locked the fucking door where she's having a fit. As soon as we're safely away, I gotta dump her ass in the ocean. She ever gets anywhere near you she'll gouge your pretty eyes out."

"Duce, don't do this," she begged, but like a mountain he didn't budge when she shoved at him.

"No, I can't wait, I won't wait any longer to have you," he exclaimed and wrenched her blouse, buttons flew pattering against the bridge, seats, the floor.

Kiri screamed, pushed him, he laughed and jerked her right back against his chest. Duce dug his fingertips into the side of her face and dragged them down her skin leaving red trails in their wake.

Smiling at her wince of pain, he told her, "I was gonna make our first time nice, gentle, slow, now," his hand moved to grip the front of her throat, he tightened his fingers. "You've pissed me off. I had to break the damned door downstairs and chase you up here. You're gonna be sorry because I'm gonna beat you bad and fuck you raw, baby sister, right into the ground."

Adding his other hand to wrap around her neck, shaking her roughly, he snarled, "Every time you try to run from me, you'll pay. And it won't be a tiny playful smack on your little ass like Adranokov would give you. I'm not like those Romanian mobsters that think spanking their disobedient women is punishment, keeping them in line."

Grinning in her face, he said, "Don't worry, I won't scar up that beautiful face, but I'm not averse to breaking a few bones. You can't run away on broken legs. Dig me?"

"Duce," Kiri croaked through her squashed trachea, scrabbling at his hands. "Don't do this, you don't want to do this-"

"Oh yes I do," he said and bent his head and smashed his mouth over hers. Clamping his teeth on her lower lip he bit, hard enough a split of blood rose. Duce licked it, then shoved his tongue inside, and like the gluttonous beast he was, brutally raped her mouth, the foreshadowing violence of what he planned to do to the rest of her. She cried into his mouth, and he laughed.

He held her thrashing body so tightly she couldn't breathe. Gasping for air, she struggled to thrust away from him, her actions only brought more hilarity to her depraved brother. "Keep struggling, my babydoll, your fear and pain excites me. I hung with your fiancé Rueford, learned a lot about S&M, not the normal fun stuff but all the real sick, violent stuff. Can't wait to explore shit with you."

An arm wrapped around Kiri, Duce kicked her legs out from under her and dropped her to the floor. He scrambled down on top of her, forcing her legs spread wide to accommodate his. Grasping both sides of her torn blouse, he pulled them apart, eyes gleaming, his tongue rolled out. Lowering his head, he sank his teeth savagely into her breast and she screamed.

Chapter Thirty-Three

Outside, the thunder grew into loud rumbling engines, and the thwat-thwat of helicopter propellers twirling nearby. Duce's head popped up. "What the fuck?"

Dragging Kiri to her feet by her neck, Duce suddenly had a gun in his hand. Hauling her out of the bridge, he squinted up to the darkening cobalt sky. A helicopter hovered, slowly moving in on the yacht. Several boats bee-lined over the waves, streams of surf trailing them like white bushy tails.

"That fucking Adranokov, it has to be him, how the hell did he find us?" His hand still on her neck, he held her a few inches away and perused her body. His gaze hit her diamond earrings, then lowered to the watch glinting gold on her delicate wrist. Lips quirked in a wry smile, he nodded with admiration. "The guy loaded you up with tracers, my girl. You captivated yourself a clever one indeed."

Snapping her around, he slammed an arm under her breasts, over her arms, cuffing her tight against his broad chest. He jammed his gun into her temple ignoring her whimper of pain. "But not clever enough. Melonie!" he roared. "Get the fuck up here!"

The boats and chopper moving closer, Melonie's footsteps hit the steps and slapped the tile as she ran across the deck. Her eyes bugged in startled fright at the boats, then rose to the chopper, she turned to Duce, shouted, "You just had to take her, you idiot! You got the money, you have me, why didn't you just kill her and toss her body into the sea? What are we going to do now?"

Smirking at his sister like she was a moron, he told her, "Get the anchor up, start up the engine. We're getting out of here. As long as I have this gun trained on his sweetheart, Adranokov will do as I tell him."

Towing Kiri with him, Duce stayed in the shelter of the doorway to the bridge, out of sight of snipers. His cell rang. With a grin, keeping the gun pressed hard against Kiri's temple, he fished it out and swiped it on. Naithon's name came up.

Putting the phone on speaker, he set it on the ledge and wrapped his arm back around Kiri. "Adranokov?" he said smugly into the phone. "I'm a hacker and even I can't figure out how you got this number."

Naithon's heavily accented, deep voice rumbled out, "You give her up right now, Delducci, and I might let you live. Draw this out or hurt her, and you won't make it back to shore alive."

It sounded like Naithon; Kiri frowned in confusion, but not quite.

Duce chuckled, "I'm the one holding the prize, you filthy gypsy jailbird." His voice shifted to anger. "Now, it's you that has five minutes to back away, and do not follow us. I'm removing the watch and earrings and tossing them into the drink. You come after us and I swear, I'll cut tiny pieces off my sister until you back off."

Sounds of the anchor scraping up the side of the boat and the engine revving could just barely be heard over the rumbling of the other boats and hovering chopper.

Naithon growled from the phone, "Delducci-"

"Three minutes," Duce threatened with slight amusement. The boats inched closer, the helio hovered. "Melonie," Duce called out, "come here." To the phone he said, "Time's up, hero." He pushed Kiri to her knees, snapped a wire out of the counsel and tied her hands behind her back.

Melonie stepped from the controls and went to him. Worry wrinkled her brow. Her thin lips turned down in an impatient sneer, she asked him, "What are you doing? I need to drive the boat."

Duce ordered, "Hold your hand out." When she just stared at him in confusion, he barked, "Now!" She raised her arm, one brow arched in question. He grabbed her wrist, slammed her palm on the counsel and yanked a small emergency ax off the wall.

"D- Duce?" Melonie tried to pull her hand away, he held her fast. "Wha-" Duce whipped the ax down and chopped off half her pinky. It rolled, she screamed, Duce grabbed it, muttered, "I didn't say which sister."

Jerking Kiri to her feet, using her as a shield, he dragged her to the side of the boat and set the finger on the broad edge. With her hands behind her back no one could see that it wasn't her finger he'd chopped off. He traipsed back to the phone, his arm around Kiri, gun to her head.

Smiling at the phone, he said, "Okay, gypsy boy, get your scope out and see what I put on the ledge. Your precious girl's finger. I have nine more to go, then I start on the toes." Inside the bridge, Melonie rolled on the floor screaming, holding a towel around her bloody hand. It was all Kiri could do to not lose her lunch.

"Stop caterwauling Mel, and get us the fuck out of here," Duce demanded. When she just scrunched up wailing, he warned her, "You want to go to prison, just lay there like a wallowing sow."

Her face white as a sheet, Kiri cried, "Duce, please, oh my God, what is wrong with you? Stop this madness!"

"Delducci!" Naithon's voice shouted from the phone.

Duce moved back to it, staying ducked just inside the bridge. "Yeah? I don't see anybody moving away out there, thug, do I need to go for another finger?"

"I'll leave as soon as I see that Kiri is all right. Bring her out!"

Melonie curled into herself, writhing and wailing on the floor. Making an impatient sound, Duce pushed Kiri back to her knees, trod to Melonie. Bending, he grabbed her arm and wrenched her to her feet then roughly hauled her to the wheel and shoved her violently at it. "Get this bucket of bolts going, Mel, before I think I'm better off without your useless ass."

She fell onto the counsel, her face banging on the counter. She had to grab at the wheel to keep from falling. Sobbing, she wrapped the towel back around her hand and put her shaking fingers to the key.

Pulling Kiri up on trembling legs, curling his hand around the front of her throat and the gun to her head, Duce pushed her to the door. He threatened, "You run, girl and I'll shoot you in the back. Now, don't fight me." Nudging her through the narrow doorway first, he had to move the gun to the side so he could still hold onto her and step sideways out the door.

Just as he fully cleared the doorway, Kiri was suddenly torn from his hand and thrust aside. Her hands bound behind her back, she eeked a tiny squeal as she stumbled against the side of the bridge then fell to the deck.

Stunned momentarily into a statue, Duce gripped the edge of the doorway to quickly pull himself back inside.

Too late. Naithon drove his fist smashing upwards into Duce's nose. Bones cracked, blood gorged, Duce howled. One hand on his broken nose, Duce swung the gun around to shoot him, Naithon caught Duce's arm and slammed it down on his knee. The loud crack sounded as his arm broke in half.

Duce dropped to his knees with a wail, and folded over clutching his injured arm, blood gushed from his nose.

Wet blond hair sticking to his forehead, Naithon clamped his fists together and brought them down on the back of Duce's neck, another crack, Duce face planted, legs sprawled, and stopped moving. Naithon gave him a brutal stomp on his back, more cracking, then stepped from the door.

Kiri had fallen, landing sideways when Naithon had grabbed her and threw her out of the way. She balanced on her elbow, legs curled, hands still bound. Naithon rushed to her, crouched down, pulled her into his arms.

"Baby, baby," he groaned against her neck, hugging her fiercely. He sat down and moved her between his crossed legs.

"Naithon," Kiri sobbed into his shoulder, "you came for me," she gasped, "you came for me."

Hugging her tightly, he murmured in her hair, "Did you ever doubt I would?"

She shook her head, sniffed, whispered, "No, never."

"It's always you, you fucking bitch," Melonie snarled from the arch of the bridge. She held a gun aimed at them. "For the last time," face twisted in an outraged grimace she ranted, "the last time you come between me and my men!" Her finger moved on the trigger-Naithon curled his body over Kiri.

"Good riddance you bitch!" Melonie shrieked, then she gasped, uttered a cry of pain, dropped the gun and crumpled to the floor. A knife stuck out of her shoulder. She lay writhing on the deck, screeching for help.

Naithon looked over and saw Mazonn grinning cheerfully at him, he smiled back, "Always the good timing, Maz."

Maz nodded happily, then strode to where Melonie lay screaming. Kicking the gun out of her reach, he crouched on his haunches, yanked his knife out, wiped the blood on his jeans and shoved it in the sheath in his boot. He clutched Melonie's arms and rolled her over on her belly then cuffed her wrists.

"Oww," she wailed, "my finger, my shoulder- you stabbed me you fucking asshole, get these things off me!"

Maz clamped the cuffs tight. "Shut up, honey, or I'll gag your filthy mouth."

"You stabbed me! You're a murderer!" she shrieked, kicking her feet.

"Ah, just a tiny prick. The hole in your arm I mean, not you," he joked. "You're lucky I have excellent aim, coulda missed your shoulder and gashed your black heart. Now, quit whining, you'll thank me later. I got your finger on ice. They may be able to reattach it, eh? Be a wicked scar, but a great reminder of your fabulous vaca here on the yacht."

He grinned at Naithon, shaking his head, he tut-tutted at his friend. "You allowed yourself to get distracted again by the chickadee, let the bad guys get near."

Lines from boats tossed on board, men swarmed the yacht. They trolled over the entire boat searching for anyone else that might be hiding. Vlad and Teo cuffed Duce, who was conscious, but lay unmoving, too much in agony to do more than whimper weakly.

"Here, baby." Naithon moved Kiri so he could untie the cord around her wrists. Tossing it aside, he cupped her face, and frowned miserably. His thumb brushed above the cut on her lip. His gaze lowered to the bite mark that was bruising on her breast. "Kiri, *meu Dio*, what did that animal to you?" He set a palm over the bite. Then his head turned towards Duce lying groaning in mind boggling pain.

Naithon made to get up, finish the bastard off. Kiri caught his arm. "No, leave him. Brutality in self-defense is okay, cold-blooded, no," she shook her head. Her eyes filled with tears.

"It's called vengeance," he responded fiercely, but he allowed her to hold him back. Gently cupping the back of her neck, he turned her to search for more injuries. "Baby, are you hurt anywhere else?"

Her head shook. "No, I'm okay, now. Just...relieved that it's over. And happy to be with you," her soft smile cooled the rage burning in his chest. He gathered her back in his arms. She leaned back a smidge. "Um, Naithon, what are you wearing? You're wet."

His chuckle rumbled as he pressed her head against his shoulder. "It's a wet suit. Or more accurately, a dry suit for the cold water. I knew we could only get the boats so close to this yacht before Duce would retaliate. I distracted him with the phone call," he wriggled his eyebrows at Maz, who grinned back at him.

Melonie cursed, Maz pressed her face into the floor on the cold tile that was roughly abraded to avoid sliding, and she quieted.

"I don't understand," Kiri said, nestling in Naithon's arms as his men scoured the ship and paramedics hopped aboard to work on Duce and Melonie.

Cradling her jaw, he tilted her head up and kissed her softly, avoiding her cut lip. "I brought the boats as close as I could, then donned the dry suit, flippers, snorkel, and slid into the ocean. Maz impersonated me on the phone keeping Duce distracted while I swam here. We have the same accents, deep voices, close enough to fool Delducci."

Her head angled back, his hand still holding her gently, her lids fell half-mast, her smile curved sweetly. "I knew it wasn't you, but I didn't know what you were up to."

"While Duce spoke with Maz, and butchered his sister, Maz talked him into bringing you out on the deck. If you stayed inside the bridge with him, he could have hurt you before I could get to him. I had already climbed aboard the yacht and was waiting behind metal casings," he nodded to the side of the bridge. "You know the rest."

She raised her wrist, the gold watch glinted in the diminished sunlight. "Duce said you put tracers in my watch and earrings. But we were pretty far away for something like that to work, weren't we?"

Naithon agreed, "*Ja*, that's true. What Duce hadn't figured on was that since I knew he had a boat, and you were dining on the water, that it was likely he would be using the sea to his advantage."

"Okay, so?"

"So, I had boats at that nearby marina ready to fence him in if he tried to do anything on the water. Problem was, some idiot tourists came in from boating all day and fully blocked the channel, thereby obstructing my boats. By the time they got out and Teo swung by the restaurant to pick me up, you were already fucking gone."

The fear and frustration of that moment, standing helplessly on the deck watching Duce's yacht grow tinier than an ant disappearing into an anthill while he waited for his own boats to get into action, gouged lines of anguish around his eyes that would stay for days.

Heaving a settling breath, he said, "But, because we were on the boats and heading in the direction Duce fled, even if we couldn't see you, we eventually got close enough to pick up the trace. I also had a handful of choppers searching the entire radius from the restaurant and out. There was nowhere he could hide from me."

Kiri smiled meekly, ducking her head. "I guess you get to say I told you so, that you warned me I could be putting myself in grave danger. You were right."

His mouth flattened into a grim line. "Honey, I'd rather not ever have to say that to you. I could have lost you forever today, it's not something I want to joke about." He climbed to his feet and gently drew her up, his arm still around her. "Let's go home, baby. Okay?"

Her head nodded wearily against his shoulder. "Yes, Naithon, I'm ready to go home, to our home," her head dipped back, she smiled up at him, "with you."

"Good." He pulled her in tight against his strong body. "When we get home you can show me how sorry you are for not listening to me."

"Naithon," she was going to rebuke him, then she shrugged. "Okay, you can tell me what I can do to show my repentance."

He grinned down at Kiri, hugged her and said, "Now that's a plan. I have many ideas. By the way…" he trailed off.

"Yes?"

"I told you so."

Epilogue

Naithon lay on his side, his hand curled over Kiri's breast. Fondling the soft, firm flesh, he bent and nipped her nipple, goose bumps rose on her ivory skin and the nipple hardened into a tiny pink bud.

Kiri giggled as he played with her body. "Naithon, we've spent all day in bed, aren't you ever sated?"

"Never." He licked her breast, squeezing it, he chewed on her nipple. "I will never have enough of you, baby, I've told you that."

She sighed and relaxed into the mattress and let him play.

An hour later, Naithon rolled off the bed with a grunt, traipsed into the bathroom, cleaned himself then came out with a warm wet towel and cleaned Kiri while she giggled.

Chuckling at her, he dropped the cloth and sat on the edge of the bed. Brushing her hair off her face, he asked, "Are you happy, my lamb?"

Smiling easily, she responded, "Yes, Naithon, I am very happy."

"Will you stay with me?"

312

Her brow furrowed. "I'm pretty sure you've always said I have no choice."

"What if I gave you that choice?"

"You mean you would let me go? Set me free?"

Sadness palled his rugged face, he replied, "I love you, Kiri, more than life itself. I would die inside if you left me, but," he sighed sadly, "yes. If that's what you really, truly wanted, like the caged bird that sings songs of lost freedom, I would...let...you go."

Kiri sat up. "Do you mean it?"

His shoulders slumped, he nodded glumly. He slipped his hand around the side of her face, thumb caressing her satiny cheek. "I love you, Kiri. That means I want what makes you happy. If that's what you want, we'll find you a house, you choose it, I'll pay for it. I insist on buying you a car, you take your wardrobe, jewelry, I'll buy you a studio.

"I would...like it if you can, finish the mural...with me, at the distillery and the decorating of the tasting room. It'll never turn out right if you don't do it."

She nodded slowly. "Yes, sure, if that's what you want."

Naithon looked so sad, dejected, miserable, Kiri thought he was going to cry. He moved off the bed and pulled his jeans on. Looking away from her, he murmured, "Okay. When do you want to...go?"

"Naithon," she said softly. He stood with his head turned. "Naithon, please, look at me." He did, his lips pressed firmly together, jaw working. One brow lifted over a sad eye.

Kiri asked, "Do you want me to leave?"

His mouth fell open. "Of course not. Are you insane? Have you not heard me repeatedly tell you I want us to stay together, forever? Do my words just bounce off your skull?"

Her smile twitched. "Uh, yeah, kind of hard not hear your declarations. But, that's lust, Naithon," she turned serious. "That's not strong enough of a thread to hold a couple together. We'll grow old, I'll grow old. You'll be surrounded by young, gorgeous strippers that will throw themselves in your lap until you die. You will not want me then."

His face crunched in pain. "Baby," he picked her hand up and kissed her fingers. "Sometimes you can be a dense as a rock."

At her frown, he said, "Listen to me, I. Love. You. I don't want, will never want another woman. I can't wait to grow old with you. Together. Raising our children. Even when we die and move on to the forever realm, whatever that is, we'll still be together however it works. Our energy will stay entwined, baby."

Dropping her hand, rifling his fingers through his thick hair, he sighed. "But, I told you, if you want to go, I won't stand in your way. Don't expect me to do fucking cartwheels over it." Mouth turned down desolately, he stared at her like he wanted to imprint her in his brain. Her lovely naked body, gorgeous, soft face, glowing green eyes.

Rubbing his palm over a muscled pec, he muttered, "How, ah," his voice hoarse with loss, he asked, "when do you want to go?"

Kiri climbed to her knees, Naithon drank in her hot naked body like rain on parched earth. "Ah, pigeon," his grin twisted bleakly, "you kneel there like that with those gorgeous chubby tits," his gaze slid down, "tiny waist, tight tender sex," the gaze could heat fire on a stark winter day.

Air tore from lungs constricted in despair, he said, "I, ah, need to go. If I look at you for one more second, I won't be able to let you go." He pivoted to walk out of the room.

"Naithon," her voice a lilting purr, he stopped dead in his tracks. "Come here, Naithon."

Murmuring, "Babe," he shook his head without turning around. "I can't. I can't watch you leave me."

He started walking, her voice a sexy hush, she spoke, "I said, come here, Naithon."

His bare feet stopped, toes dug into the plush carpet. "Kiri, please…"

"You get your fine ass over here right now, Mr. Adranokov."

His shoulders rippled with a chuckle, he said, "Hmm, sounds like someone is itching to feel my big hand smacking her round little bottom, *ja*?"

"I'm sorry, Mr. Adranokov, I can't hear what you're saying."

314

Slowly he turned, a half-cocked smile on his rocky face. She was still on her knees with a sultry little grin; hands clasped behind her back, displaying her perfect, naked body.

"Pigeon." He started moving back to the bed. "I get there, and you're still sitting like that, I'm gonna grab those tits you're shoving at me, and crush them, grind them in my hands and bite those nipples until you scream. Then I'm gonna slam you on your back, dig my face between your thighs, use my fingers and my mouth to make you scream some more."

A few steps away, she didn't move, her grin grew sultrier.

Still approaching, he told her, "Then, baby, I'm gonna climb up your body, plunge inside that tight silky channel of yours until you're shouting my name, and I'm yelling yours. Then I'm gonna flip you on your hands and knees and do it again. Harder. You hear me? You have half a second to tell me to back away."

Her head tilted to the side, beguiling him, Kiri cupped her breasts, provocatively squeezing them. Her bare hips swiveled, she licked her lips- and he was on her.

Naithon flattened her with his body, she squealed and squirmed under him giggling. She bit then licked his flat nipple.

A shudder whorled like a corkscrew of fire through his body, making his already hard erection thick and heavy. "Hey, quit it," he groaned, "I want to be inside you when I come."

He moved up on his elbows and smiled down at her. "You are the sexiest vixen I've ever seen," his expression stiffened. "What's going on, Kiri, you can't tease me then walk away. What is this, one more fuck before you go? One for the road?"

Raising her head she licked his chin. "I never said I wanted to go, Naithon, I only asked if you loved me enough to let me go. You do. Baby," she stroked his face, her caress loving.

Lowering his head, he kissed her, long, slow, seductive. Drawing his head back, he said, "Are you saying you want to stay, with me? For...how long?"

Both her hands stroked his face. "Like you keep saying, Naithon, forever. You see," she lifted her head to kiss him then laid back down. "I love you too. Heaven knows why. You're a dominating bully, over-protective, sexist, chauvinistic, hotheaded, bossy as all heck-" He seized her mouth, kissed her until she was drunk with passion and quiet.

Grinning at her, he said, "Had to do something to shut you up." Kissing the tip of her nose, his tone more serious, he said, "Do you mean it? You want to spend the rest of your life with me? Have children, raise a family? Kiri? Tell me, do you?"

Nodding suddenly shy, she said softly, "Yes, Naithon, I do."

"Great! I plan to hear those words again, in front of a priest and an audience." He rolled off her and hopped off the bed.

"N- Naithon, what are you-"

He tugged something out of his jacket pocket, then dropped to his knees on the floor beside the bed.

"Naithon?"

A small black box was sitting on his palm. He lifted the lid, and pulled the diamond ring from the box, and tossed the box on the nightstand. "Give me your hand, baby," he said holding his hand out.

Eyes huge green moons, mouth falling wide open, she covered her mouth with her hand, and gasped.

Smiling, he reached out and grasped her left hand. He said solemnly, "Kiritina Rose Delducci, will you do me the grandest honor and agree to be my wife?"

She blinked reflexively at him, her hand still at her mouth, she watched him slide the ring on her finger. "You- you- you want me- really-" she stammered foolishly. "You really do want us to get married?"

Rolling his eyes, he grinned at her. "Lamb, I've told you every second since I took you that that was what I wanted. I never stopped telling you. I've always known I wanted you to be mine til the end of time, I had to wait for you to catch up. Now that you have, I mean," brows slanted down, he asked, "you do love me, right?"

Still blinking inanely, she nodded mutely.

Laughing, Naithon said, "Can you say it? Out loud? It'd be really nice if you did." He waited, then shook her hand to break her stupor.

"Oh, oh," she smiled dearly at him, "I do, Naithon, I love you. When I knew for sure you'd find a way to rescue me, I knew then. I trusted you, couldn't imagine not being with you. That was my biggest fear with Duce abducting me, I was afraid I'd never see you again." Her lashes fluttered, she said shyly, "I love you, Naithon."

Big broad grin, he said, "Good, so now, you say yes. You say, 'Yes Naithon, my love, I will marry you.'"

Laughter bubbled out, she cried, "Yes! Yes, my beloved Naithon, I will marry you!" She hurled her body into his arms.

An *oof* punched out of him when he caught her. Naithon wrapped his arms around her and they kissed. He got up briefly to tear off his jeans then lay back down, pulled her back into his embrace.

Bare torsos pressing together, Naithon ran his hands down her back and cupped her bottom, pulled her hips to rub over his erection hard as concrete, starving for her.

A while later, after a nap, they lay in bed, Kiri held her hand up admiring her ring.

Naithon lay on his side, his palm stroking her thigh. He said, "As soon as Duce's and Melonie's trials are over, and Ignacio and Janero are well enough, lamb, we can start planning the wedding. Can't wait to see you in flouncy white, carrying posies coming down the aisle, ready to become my bride."

"Um, Naithon." She twirled the ring watching it catch the light and sparkle rainbows.

"Hmm?"

"I…I'm not sure about living at the…mansion. Those men are dangerous, and the women, well…I just…it's not…"

He caught her hand and kissed the back of it. "I've given it a lot of thought, pigeon," he chuckled at her grunt at the nickname. "I think I'll turn most of the businesses, the clubs and stuff over to my boys to manage.

Mazonn will be in charge with Teo, Vlad, Yash and Blok to assist him. They can still stay in the mansion. I'd like to put all my time and effort into the distillery, that's all I ever wanted anyway. We'll build a house on the land near it, just for us."

"Oh, Naithon, the countryside around the distillery is beautiful. Soft rolling hills, forests of freshly scented trees, I can picture rose gardens surrounding the distillery, and," she said shyly, "our house."

She kissed his chin, and said, "Thank you, baby, thank you for giving me this. You, and a perfect life together. I love you so much."

He rolled over on top of her, his hand netting her breast, his mouth seeking hers, he whispered against her lips, "I love you, my beautiful lamb."

The End

www.ingramcontent.com/pod-product-compliance
Lightning Source LLC
Chambersburg PA
CBHW020247200626
46816CB00001BA/178